MAVERICK

PIPER STONE

Copyright © 2023 by Stormy Night Publications and Piper Stone

All rights reserved. No part of this book may be reproduced or transmitted in any form or by any means, electronic or mechanical, including photocopying, recording, or by any information storage and retrieval system, without permission in writing from the publisher.

Published by Stormy Night Publications and Design, LLC.
www.StormyNightPublications.com

Stone, Piper
Maverick

Cover Design by Korey Mae Johnson

This book is intended for *adults only*. Spanking and other sexual activities represented in this book are fantasies only, intended for adults.

PROLOGUE

Brothers in arms.

Bad boys, cowboys, soldiers, sailors, airmen, and Marines.

We'd been labeled delinquents, incapable of redemption.

And we'd gone our separate ways.

Heroes. Monsters. Sinners and saints.

Above all we were men honoring our country even while a terrible secret loomed just below the surface.

There were those who would never forget, praying we'd never return.

Others would stop at nothing to prevent us from doing so.

We were intent on finding salvation by protecting those we loved.

But demons from a single act would never allow us to forget.

Six men determined to right the wrongs from our past.

Six men prepared to do what it took.

No matter the cost.

Together in life.

Together in death.

CHAPTER 1

melie

My bad day just turned into a nightmare.

I'd found my piece of shit ex in my bed with my now ex-best friend.

I'd had a flat tire.

I'd lost my waitressing job.

Now this.

Being summoned to my father's house was never for a happy reason.

And it wasn't about giving me a Christmas gift.

We didn't live a Hallmark card kind of life complete with festive celebrations and heartfelt emotions. There was nothing but animosity between us, which had been the only thing I'd felt for as long as I could remember. He'd made it perfectly clear from an early age that I was nothing but a nuisance in his life and that he was doing me a favor in allowing me to grow up near him.

While most children would crumble from his harsh words and prison-like rules, I'd grown strong and wise, capable of ignoring his rants and demands. Once I'd turned eighteen, he'd ignored me altogether other than the required twice a year dinners where nothing but business was handled. Checks written for tuition. Doling out an allowance like I was a five-year-old asking for money for candy. And the same lecture on how I was wasting my life giving a shit about animals.

But today was entirely different.

I sensed it in my bones.

The meeting had to do with the release of my trust fund, money he hadn't been able to get his grubby hands on. My mother had done her best to protect me, even while falling under his spell. The executor was an attorney, a friend of my mother's family. I was certain the man who'd professed to love my mother had conned her into marrying him, funding his unprofitable company. I'd been too young to remember anything but arguments. How many times had I heard their harsh words, screaming battles that had lasted for hours? My mother had taken me on a special trip to get away.

I'd returned alone, my mother killed in a crash. But I'd never believed the reports. My gut told me he had something to do with her death. As hard as I'd tried, I hadn't been able to pin her murder on him. But one day I would. So help me God. I was still alive for a reason, and I was determined to find out what that was.

He'd rarely talked about her, finally acting as if she'd never existed. One day I would learn the truth.

I doubted that would happen today. This was a turning point. I was certain of it.

Something was very wrong.

Carmine Rathbone didn't have a decent bone in his body as far as I was concerned. He was a con man, someone not to be trusted. Today, he wore a smile as if he'd just won the Mega-millions lottery, only he'd consider that chump change given his worth was well over two hundred million dollars. But he'd been antsy, his stock dropping. I was no business major, but it was obvious he'd lost millions.

I'd continued to dig and would do so until I found justice for my mother.

He needed my cash. I was certain of it. Without interference, it would be in my hands in three months. By the look on his face alone, I could tell he was worried.

I was leery, on edge, which hopefully I'd find the opportunity to take out on my father.

Be smart about this.

"Come. Have a seat," he told me the moment he ushered me into his office.

As I usually did when I arrived at the house I'd grown up in, I wrapped my fingers around my locket, sliding it back and forth on the gold chain. Almost instantly, my father noticed my actions, scowling as he did every time I toyed with my only piece of jewelry that had ever mattered.

He hissed in disgust, and I was surprised I didn't get my usual sermon about my nervous tic. Little did he know I'd been doing it on purpose for years because it reminded him of what we'd lost. No, what he'd tossed aside like garbage.

Who he'd murdered.

That was something I could never forgive him for. After I'd gotten older, I'd searched for years for evidence, finding nothing useful. At least until recently. A trip to the mountains would be my present after graduation, to find the source of a gift I received a few years before. The postmark had been from Missoula, Montana with no return address. The answers were there.

Even if it meant derailing my career for a little while, I wouldn't find peace until I knew exactly what happened and why I'd been sent her picture and a locket.

"Sit down, Amelie. I don't want to tell you again." My, how his slightly pleasant tone had crashed into darkness, and in record time.

I hadn't changed before racing over. I was painfully aware he was annoyed with my attire, holey jeans and a worn tee shirt. If he had his way, I'd be living the glamorous life of the vice president of his company, a single suit costing more than what I'd paid for my economy car. That would allow him to have full control over me, which would never happen.

My friends asked why I continued to endure his stranglehold over me. The answer was as screwed up as my life had become. The money he handed over was barely enough to get by, the soaring costs of surviving in Chicago getting outrageous. He held the key to a fortune that he'd dangled over my head since I understood the meaning of the words 'trust fund.' Did that make me greedy? Maybe so, but in my mind, I was owed the millions of dollars for having to put up with his bullshit.

And because technically, it belonged to my mother.

"What is it, Daddy dearest?"

He gritted his teeth, another sign my ugliness was already wearing on him.

I eased into a seat opposite his Herman Miller desk, offering a sweet smile, but I had more butterflies than usual.

My father had something up his sleeve. I was certain of it.

It was barely two o'clock in the afternoon yet he took the time to pour a single finger of scotch, of course not bothering to ask me if I'd care to join him. Then again, this wasn't a social call.

When he finally sat down, his actions were more formal than usual. He took a sip, swirling the liquor in his glass as he studied me, amusement replacing aggravation.

His stall tactic put me further on the edge. In response I crossed my legs, placing my ankle on my knee, a gesture that always got on his nerves. I was twenty-five, a semester shy of graduating with honors from the University of Illinois, becoming a doctor of veterinary medicine and I was acting like an impetuous ten-year-old.

However, it was the only way I could tolerate his holier than thou attitude.

"Amelie. I've tolerated your childish desires for as long as possible."

"My childish desires?" Other than working my butt off between classes and waiting on drunks, the only hobby I had was my photography. I'd won a few awards, which had driven another wedge between us. He believed the hobby to be frivolous, a detriment to the Rathbone name.

He drummed his fingers on the wooden surface, never blinking as he stared at me. While he always made me uncomfortable, today my skin itched from head to toe. Why did I have a feeling two of his security guards were planning on carting me off to some unknown location, forcing me to disappear just like my mother had so long ago?

A lump formed in my throat when he leaned forward, a smirk crawling across his face. "I thought I should be the one to tell you that you won't be returning to college this spring."

I glared at him for a few seconds then started to laugh. "What the hell are you talking about?" In my mind, I started doing the calculations regarding the remaining fees. At minimum without money for my apartment and food, I'd need at least eighteen thousand dollars. He never paid more than a semester at a time, and it hadn't dawned on me why until now.

He'd planned on using it as a bargaining chip.

The fucking son of a bitch.

I bit back a combination of anger and tears, hiding behind the same mask I'd learned to portray so well.

"What the hell am I talking about," he repeated then rubbed his jaw. "I must admit, I lost track of how many years you've spent wasting your life. I'm grateful to my accountant for bringing it to my attention." He continued to drum his fingers on the desk, every sound echoing in my ears. "Your particular skills are needed elsewhere."

He glanced down at my attire for a second time and I was ready to jump out of my skin.

"What do you want, Carmine?" We'd never been close, which is why I'd chosen to call him by his first name after I'd turned eighteen. He wasn't fond of me either. But since he'd been responsible for me after my mother had… disappeared, he hadn't been able to toss me aside.

But that didn't mean he couldn't use me for something else altogether. I was no fool. He was the kind of man who did nothing without getting something in return.

"Your cooperation, of course. In truth, you have no choice. Your apartment is being cleaned out as we speak."

Shock tore through me, my throat immediately starting to close. Whoa. He must have found out I was investigating him. "What did you say?"

"Yes, I took the liberty of contacting the cheap college you've been going to, explaining that you won't be returning."

I jerked to a standing position, backing away as the horror of what he'd done began to settle. "I *am* returning to school. I'll find a way even if you don't pay for it."

"I happen to know exactly how much money you have in your bank account, Amelie. Does eight hundred ten dollars sound about right?"

He'd gotten into my bank account. I was sick inside, my skin clammy.

My God. He couldn't have picked a worse time to toss me out on the street. With asshole Tommy out of my life, my options were limited, but I knew I could stay with Monica until I figured this out. She'd been a good friend over the years. I hadn't realized I was pressing my fingers across the bulge in my jeans pocket where I'd placed my keys until he laughed.

"If you'd like to take a look out that window, you'll see your car is being impounded."

I flew toward the window, smashing my hand on the glass as I peered outside. Oh, my God. A moment of fear swept through me, becoming crippling within seconds.

Get your shit together. He can't steal from you.

Knowing the great Carmine Rathbone, he could do anything he wanted. With a multibillion-dollar corporation under his control, and his cunning and power in controlling his influential friends, I had no doubt he had certain members of Chicago's finest under his thumb. He'd positioned himself extremely well over the years, gathering a circle of friends who would do his bidding without question.

I folded my arms and walked closer to his desk. If he thought he could intimidate me, he was wrong. "What do you want, Carmine? That is the truth, isn't it? You need something from me so you're going to punish me in the only way you know will matter." I had to find out every detail about what he was trying to do in order to nail his ass to the wall. I'd stop at nothing to do so.

"I'm still your father, Amelie. I deserve your respect if nothing else."

"You haven't been my father. You couldn't care less about me. What. Do. You. Want? Depending on what it is, I'll see if it's acceptable or not. One way or the other, I will have my life back."

The smug look on his face remained. Seeing the twinkle in his eyes created a level of rage that I hadn't known existed.

"That won't be up to me, Amelie." As he pushed a file across his desk, I did what I could to keep from shivering visibly.

I glanced at the plain manila folder and a wash of anxiety settled into my system.

"Open it. Time is running short."

My glare remained as I pulled it into my fingers. The moment I flipped it open, I sensed he was ready to laugh.

Then I realized why.

* * *

Three months later

Maverick

"Yo. Wolfman. What's shakin'?"

I bristled, hearing the moniker that I couldn't shake. I'd been called that after preventing an ambush on a secure compound during my stint in the Marines. The asshole who'd coined the phrase hadn't intended it as a compliment. I had a feeling it would be on my tombstone.

Sooner versus later.

Hissing, I didn't bother turning my head toward Gage Beckham, a local sheriff in Missoula. We'd known each other for two decades, running with the same crowd of bad boys who'd once terrorized Missoula. When my buddy tracked me down, usually inside a bar, that meant he needed something. "Whatever you're selling, I ain't buyin'."

"Who said I needed anything?"

"Cause I know you. Remember?"

He slid next to me, immediately reaching for the bowl of peanuts I had in front of me. I concentrated on my bottle of Bud, taking another swig. I'd had a rough few days, tracking down a family of tourists who had no business being on the mountain. The fuckers had almost gotten me killed.

Twice.

"Come on. Why can't I say hello to a friend?"

Exhaling, I shifted toward him, lifting an eyebrow. "Because you're coming to me on official duty, which means you need my expertise."

"I just need your brawn."

"Fine. Go ahead and tell me. You're not going to leave me in peace until you do. And stop eating all my freaking nuts." I yanked the bowl away, only to have him tug it again, grinning like he'd just won a victory.

"Okay. I received a rather frantic call from old man Washington over at the Yellowstone hotel."

"You mean motel. That's a rat trap."

"Yeah, maybe," he admitted, "but he still draws in the tourists since he can pontificate with the best of them."

The aging former firefighter had somehow managed to get his crappy motel registered as a historical location, thereby making it virtually impossible for any developer to snag the property out from under him. And he had dozens breathing down his neck. "So what does he want?"

"He says a girl took off hours ago up the mountain and hasn't returned."

"That's my issue why?"

"He thinks she's lost. She took off using one of his maps."

"Then she could be hopelessly lost," I grumbled. Mr. Washington had a knack for sending people in the wrong direction, map or no map.

"Yeah, but you are the best tracker in the business. Hell, in the country."

I finished off the beer in one swig, twirling the bottle after doing so. My reputation for being able to locate anything in the wilderness had allowed me to pad my bank account, but I was getting too old for the shit. Especially when tourists didn't pay any attention to the weather.

"Nice try, buddy. I couldn't give a shit about compliments. Besides, it's going to snow," I told him.

"Not in the forecast."

"The forecast is wrong."

"Then you better get going."

"Are you asking me all official like?" I asked through clenched teeth, giving him a hard, cold stare.

He shrugged, keeping the same grin on his face. "You owe me."

"Bullshit."

"She's young and pretty."

"Very funny. You're not fixing me up. How much do I have to go on?" The last thing I needed was some caustic connection with a tourist no matter how beautiful. I was off women forever.

"Her license plate." I could swear Gage's eyes were twinkling. "You can find a needle in a haystack, buddy. But maybe you should get going if you're going to make it back before dark and before this mysterious snowstorm sets in."

I stood to my full height, yanking out my wallet. "Now, you owe me big."

"And I'm certain you'll collect."

After tossing the two twenties, I grabbed my keys, expecting him to follow. I was right.

As I usually was.

"Did you hear Houston got on with the Zullies and he's moving back?" he asked, trailing behind me as I walked toward the truck.

"Why come back? I thought he liked Washington State." The man was a wildland firefighter, now coming home to work with the smokejumpers in Missoula. He'd been the one out of the six Missoula Bad Boys who'd stated dozens of times that he would never return. It was funny how the group of us who'd been considered rebels in high school were slowly coming home.

"Yeah, I don't know. Maybe he was homesick. Anyway, Phoenix is having a big party for him in a few days. You could drop by. You've been a freaking hermit for months."

"Saving all those pretty tourists from being eaten by bears. Text me the information. I'll stop by and see Mr. Washington on the way. This had better be quick and it will be at my going rate."

"Yeah. Yeah. I heard you."

I glanced at the sky before jumping in my truck. While it was still partially sunny, my bones told me the storm was going to be a doozy. I'd wanted a beer, to grab a few groceries, some dog food and to head to the cabin, where I'd had plans to hole up for a solid week. Looked like that wasn't going to happen.

At least I had the dog food or Sam might chew my arm off. If I'd known I was going to be waylaid, I'd have brought him with me. He'd become my tracking buddy the last few months, one big galoot that went with me almost everywhere. At least I always carried a gear bag or the little lady on the mountain would need to wait.

I hauled ass toward the motel, ignoring speed limits like I always did. When I pulled up in front, it was only thirty minutes later, but the second I stepped out, I hissed. I had a knack for telling the weather, and not just from my aching joints given all the abuse over the years. I could smell a storm brewing two days before.

A whopper was headed toward the mountains.

As I headed inside the small lobby, the various neon signs and colorful banners he'd installed in the tiny space assaulted my senses. He was nowhere to be seen, which prompted me to slam my hand on the old-fashioned ringer more than once.

"Hold your fuckin' horses," he said gruffly as he sauntered out from the back, grinning when he saw me. "Ain't you that famous tracker?"

"You know who I am, Bubba. Just tell me about the girl."

"She's a real looker. You know the kind with hair the color of a freshly minted penny and when the sun shines across it, every strand sparkles in the light?"

I glared at him, doing everything I could not to punch him in the mouth.

"Oh, yeah. You want to know which trail she took. Right?"

"That would be helpful. And her name as well."

"Lily Sanborn and she sure reminds me of a flower, but I don't think that's her real name." He scratched his head.

Now he was playing detective. "Why do you say that?"

"You know, you get a feeling. Plus, she paid in cash. I tried to tell her that a storm is brewing but she didn't seem to care. She had a purpose. You know? Taking a camera with her and all. Those nature lovers."

That was interesting but we got all kinds in Missoula, including nature lovers who made Montana a destination. Tourists kept me in business, even though I'd been trained for something else altogether. "The hike?"

"Getting there." As he gave me the information, I quickly realized she wasn't a typical hiker. She'd left with a camera and light clothing. Time was of the essence. "Thanks, Bubba."

"She was asking about some woman too," he said in passing.

"Some woman?"

"Yeah, didn't know her name but showed me an old photograph." He scratched his jaw, looking at the ceiling.

"I need to know this why?"

Shrugging, he shuffled behind the counter. "Just seemed odd. You know?"

"Sure." I started to turn away when he coughed.

"Wait. Do you want a picture of her?" he asked, his grin almost repulsive.

"You took a picture?"

He looked sheepish then reached into a box, shifting through at least four dozen photographs, finally tossing me one. A freaking Polaroid picture. I didn't even know they made the instant processing cameras any longer. It had been my father's favorite. He never left home without it.

"I'm not going to ask why you took it but it's mine now." I slipped it into my jacket pocket, shaking my head. There were weirdos everywhere.

"Hey, bring it back if you find her."

If.

That didn't bode well for my reputation.

Or my mood.

CHAPTER 2

A few hours earlier...
Lily

A historical treasure, huh?

The lobby looked like a treasure box from the nineteen eighties had exploded in the middle of the teensy-tiny room, splatter-fucking the walls with vibrant neon and provocative posters from God knows what. Did the old dude who owned the place really think he was attracting tourists?

Exhaling, I tried not to overhear his conversation but the way he was depicting the motel from hell to an unknown party almost made me laugh.

Or throw up a little in my mouth.

"I'll be happy to pencil you in for a reservation. Six nights? Fantastic!" He was like a kid in a candy store, scratching down information on a notepad instead of using what appeared to be a computer positioned right in front of him. Then again, it had seen better days, likely at least ten plus years old.

I grabbed one of the maps in the cracked acrylic magazine racks, studying the artwork used on the cover. Whoever had designed it had thought using cartoon characters was the way to go. Whatever. As long as it got me to a gorgeous destination for a few photographs of the mountains, I couldn't care less.

"I'll see you then." He snorted as he ended the call, fingering the sheet he'd written on before bothering to look in my direction. "Can I help you with something?"

"I'm in room six? Remember me, Lily Sanborn?"

Amelie Rathbone was dead, Lily Sanborn taking her place. I liked the name. It was softer, like a brush with velvet or a whispered kiss on a spring day. I'd known some people, getting a fake ID before leaving Chicago but under close scrutiny, I knew it wouldn't pass the fake test. Still, it made it real, something I could stand behind.

I'd spent four days in Missoula, venturing out several times in my search for answers. It had been worse than looking for a needle in a haystack. No one had heard of Elizabeth Rathbone or her maiden name of Robinson. It was as if she hadn't existed and with how little I remembered, my search was becoming abysmal.

I was stressed, fearful of being found and determined to bring my father to his knees. I needed a break, to pretend my life hadn't been destroyed. Maybe a hike in the mountains, taking a few pictures would ease the tension.

"How could I forget a pretty face? What do you need, little lady?"

The guy was creepy, but at least the crappy room had a decent lock. "Is this the best trail to see wildlife?"

He lifted his sunglasses, peering at the map. "Yup. It's right behind the motel too. I'd hiked it many a time but if you want to go further up the mountain, I'd take your truck part of the way."

At least I wouldn't have to walk up the steep incline. And if the man had been hiking recently, I'd been transformed into Cinderella.

"Perfect. What do I owe you for the map?"

"Just a picture will do."

I narrowed my eyes then opened them wide in horror when he pulled out some contraption. Oh, shit. It was an old Polaroid camera. I hadn't seen one of those in years. I doubted they made the cartridges for it any longer. Before I could object, he snapped a shot. The dude wasn't just creepy. He'd shifted into the stalker category. Ordinarily, I would have ripped it from his hand then punched him in the nose, but I sensed he meant no harm. It was just some crazy trinket to add to a collection.

Still, that gave me the shivers. I didn't want anyone owning a photograph of me. If it got into the wrong hands, I'd be hunted down like a dog.

The outcome wouldn't be pretty.

"Thank you."

"Sure thing but be careful. There's a storm brewing."

I glanced out the window and smirked. The sun was waning but high in the sky. "I'll be careful." I was at the door, my hand on the glass when I took a chance, tugging the single photograph I had with me into my hand. "By any chance, do you know this woman?"

He was spending far too much time leering at me until I gave him a harsh glare, shoving the photograph in his face. After scrunching his brow, he shook his head. "Kinda looks familiar but my memory ain't too good. Sorry."

"Thanks anyway."

Grousing, I headed to my truck, yanking off my jacket and shoving the picture into my back pocket before climbing inside. At least it wasn't freezing cold. I'd yet to purchase a heavy jacket. Someone in this town had to know who she was. If my mother was still alive, I was determined to find her. I had little to go on besides the memories I'd held dear as a young girl, and the clues that had festered inside since then.

As I started along the trail, I was struck by just how beautiful everything was. The forest was pristine, untouched by man. I could see why people flocked to God's country. Maybe it was a place I could find my center. Maybe I could eventually feel at peace. I fingered the locket I always wore, wondering if there was a possibility that she was still alive. Somehow, I'd find out.

Fifteen minutes later, the trail started to narrow. There'd been several turnoffs, small parking areas designed with picnicking in mind. I wanted to find an area where most tourists didn't go.

So I continued on.

Another twenty or so minutes and the trees were thick, their canopy darkening the sky. Snow covered the ground, but it wasn't too deep, the truck easily maneuvering the few inches, the tires crunching on the frozen substance. Finally, I noticed a small clearing and decided this was the spot. As I eased the truck through the clump of trees, I was offered an incredible surprise. There was a picturesque view of the snowcapped mountains, the limited sun providing a halo that was majestic.

I found a spot to park, still taking in the view behind the wheel for a few seconds before climbing out. As I grabbed my camera, I noticed the temperature difference, cursing myself that I hadn't worn thick layers. I wouldn't be up here long, but maybe I could grab a few perfect shots.

I'd always taken photographs, capturing moments of happiness during celebrations as well as the heartache of existing. Grabbing the perfect shot of life and love had provided a respite from my studies, a hobby that had allowed me to experience love and adventures vicariously. I'd been able to pretend I had a wonderful family during the worst times of my life. Even after three months, I still found it impossible to believe my father had tossed everything that had belonged to me into the trash, including the items I'd left from my childhood inside his home.

It was as if I hadn't existed, sold to a monster. At least I'd gotten away before being forced into marriage.

But the ugliness of my experience, the terror of escape, and the consequences if found were never far from my mind. I'd thought of going to the police, but I was one woman against what felt like an army. Even with what I'd managed to photograph, I'd doubted it would be enough. However, if I found out what happened to my mother, maybe, just maybe someone in law enforcement would listen to me.

Stop thinking about it. Just stop.

Taking a few pictures might provide some peace, if only for a little while. I couldn't stand to sit inside a cheap motel room by myself any longer or combing the town in search of clues I wasn't certain existed.

The camera had been a gift to myself, a treat I'd hidden away from the bastard who'd purchased me. If Giovanni had any clue what I'd captured during my stay with him, he'd put a bullet in my brain.

I'd endured three months, earning the man's trust in order to escape. At some point, I'd need to talk to an attorney, but I needed distance more than getting my hands on my trust fund.

Truth would set me free.

Maybe.

With what little money I'd managed to squirrel away, including stealing some from Giovanni, I'd purchased a truck while on the run, although I was beginning to wonder how long the rust bucket would last in Montana's harsher conditions.

One step at a time, baby. This is your new life.

I'd yet to work out all the details of maintaining my new life, but no one was going to stop me from achieving my goals. I shoved the keys into my pocket, taking a deep breath and forging forward. There was nothing like fresh mountain air, the crispness yet to find its way to my bones. I took several photographs, venturing across the rocky terrain, careful where I stepped.

The ugliness continued festering in the back of my mind. I'd been so blindsided that when two of his security guards had appeared from the shadows, driving me to my new home, I hadn't resisted. What I'd yet to figure out was why the deal had been made in the first place.

One thing had been perfectly clear. I'd become a possession to be used and nothing more.

Now I wondered if I could resurrect my dream of being a veterinarian. At this point, it would take a miracle. I wouldn't be able to finish school while keeping my earned credits unless I used my real name. That would be a red flag flashing on my father's screen within seconds.

I shook it off, taking another deep breath. Montana was a world away from Chicago.

As I trudged through the snow, my breathing more labored than I was used to, I felt exhilarated for the first time in months. Years. This was what pure freedom was all about and I planned on taking full advantage of it.

There were so many splendid aspects of nature that I'd never seen before, this part of the country dazzling in color even in the cold early spring months. I took a chance, moving further up the mountainside, resting only a few times. I hadn't bothered to pay attention to what time I'd started, but at least an hour had passed, maybe more. When I headed into another clearing, I realized there was no sun in the sky, the clouds thickening.

I couldn't stop, fascinated by everything around me, the sounds of nature echoing in my ears. From somewhere, I heard the flow of water. When I found the source, a gorgeous river tumbling over rocks, my breath was taken away.

I'd taken at least sixty photographs and I was eager to see how they'd turned out. When I rested against a massive oak, I was finally able to smile. Maybe my life had taken a turn for the better.

Seconds later, I heard a noise, a crackling sound. Instantly, hairs raised on the back of my neck, terror racing through, chilling me to the core. Oh, God. What if I'd already been found? With the kind of people who worked for Giovanni, I knew they could track almost anyone down.

Stop it. Breathe. Think of the chances of anything finding you.

At least my rational side was making some sense.

Gasping, I closed my eyes, trying to control my breathing. There was no way possible that I'd been found. Neither Giovanni nor Carmine would have any idea where to look. I'd been very careful not to tell anyone about what I'd suspected over the years, learning early on that my father was a slug. He'd put listening devices in my room, which I'd found prior to leaving for undergraduate school.

The source of the noise had to be from something else, a natural occurrence. Crouching lower, I moved through the trees, trying to keep from making any noise. When I found the reason, I held my breath. There were six deer, all of them attempting to find nourishment through the fallen snow. I hunkered down, taking several photographs, leaving them undisturbed. They were incredible animals, the buck watching carefully over his family, the two fawns so tiny that I wondered when they'd been born.

When the buck finally noticed me, there was no reaction at first, more curiosity than anything. Sadly, only seconds later he shooed his family away from harm, the creatures bounding deeper into the woods. Perhaps against my better judgment, I followed, able to capture a few more pictures before they faded into the distance.

That's when I realized I had no idea where I was. Disorientation flooded my mind, my throat threatening to close. What was wrong with me? I knew better than to get off track. I moved in a full circle, another rush of adrenaline prickling my skin. I was shivering, but only partially from the cold. Even worse, snow had started to fall.

As I tried to figure out which direction I'd come from, I shut down the emotions, concentrating on the area around me.

Then I started walking. Nothing seemed familiar and I couldn't see any footsteps in the snow. This was bad, so very bad.

I walked another hundred yards, shifting directions as panic rushed to the surface. Terrible visions of what could happen filtered into my mind. This had been a ridiculous idea. I had no business hiking let alone in the middle of a storm. Trudging through the mean streets of Chicago in the middle of a snowstorm was entirely different.

As the snowfall picked up in intensity, I yanked my coat around me, unable to stop shivering. Then I heard another noise, louder this time. As I turned slowly, I could swear there was someone only yards away, a man. Was it possible? I almost screamed for help, but my instinct told me otherwise. I moved closer, cautious in my steps. Then my first fears came to realization.

There was a man carrying a gun, acting as if he was searching for something or someone in the woods. Oh, God. Oh, God. No. By instinct, I took several photographs of him, zooming in to get as close up of a photograph as I could. Then I thought about how much danger I could be in. This couldn't happen. I turned and raced in the opposite direction, jumping over fallen limbs, sidestepping debris while praying I could get away. If I could just make it back to the truck everything would be okay.

How could it be alright? I had no weapon, no way of defending myself. This was crazy. I was going to die. Die. Die!

Breathe. Don't panic. Don't you dare panic.

Something broke inside of me, my survival instinct kicking in and I kept going, fueled by anger and petrified at the thought of losing my life to not one monster but two. I'd found a way out. I'd risked everything to escape.

And I'd done it.

Now I was going to be captured in the mountains? No one would hear me scream. No one would come to my rescue.

I threw a look over my shoulder, unable to see anything in the haze of snow as it blanketed the area. When I jerked back toward where I was going, my foot caught something. As I was pitched into the air, all I could think about was the bastard was right behind me. I began to fall and my entire life flashed in front of my eyes. I'd never believed the theory, all those people on the verge of death reliving every moment of their past, but they'd been right.

Yet sadly, the vivid images floating through my mind were all filled with violence and bloodshed.

"No!" I screamed as he wrapped his hand around my throat, slamming me against the wall. As he lowered his head, baring his teeth, he dug his fingers into my neck.

"You belong to me, my beautiful bride. Don't you dare forget that. I bought you. Remember?"

When I didn't say anything, just continued to stare at him with defiant eyes, he backhanded me with his other hand. The sting was harsh, but I refused to allow the bastard to see me cry. I was finished with accepting his rage, cowering as if I had no self-worth. He'd made me this way, but I'd grown stronger.

"Fuck you. One day I'll escape but I'll return so I can cut out your heart," I hissed, ignoring the anguish as he tightened his grip.

A flash of fury sparked in his eyes, and he tightened his hold until I could no longer breathe. "Go ahead and try but know this. I will hunt you down. Then the fun will really begin."

The memory of his words echoed, adding another layer of terror.

As Giovanni's face rushed into the forefront of my mind, I tumbled again. Going down. Down. Down. Then I hit a hard surface with a thud, stars floating in front of my eyes and...

CHAPTER 3

M averick

"Goddamn snow," I grumbled as I peered out the windshield then twisted the knob on the defroster onto high. If the girl was still out here, she was in a bad place. I grabbed the photograph, cursing under my breath. She had a freaking light jacket on. What the hell was she thinking coming up here wearing a single sweater and a coat meant for fifty-degree days?

I pulled to a stop, trying to think where she'd go. I hadn't seen a single sign of her. After slamming the gear into park, I climbed out, moving around the truck and searching the area. The snow had already picked up in intensity, the covering deep enough I doubted I'd find any trace of her tire tracks. I walked a few paces then hunkered down, brushing away the freshly fallen snow.

Shit. I got lucky, the clear marks from worn tires providing an indication that I was on the right track. I jogged back to the Cherokee, jumping inside. The old vehicle was a tank, what I used for tracking, equipped with everything I needed for hunting. I pushed the old girl forward, passing two turnoffs. Had she ventured further or turned around and I hadn't seen her? I allowed my gut to take over, continuing on the same path.

The sky was darkening, and my cabin was miles away. While the old girl could likely make it, I wasn't in the mood to push my luck. If I didn't find Ms. Sanborn's vehicle in a few minutes, I was bagging it.

Even if the ugly voice inside my head told me otherwise. I'd never left anyone on the mountain. Not one. I'd risked my life countless times, a broken leg and cracked skull to prove it. Fuck me.

A sick feeling slammed into my gut, the ugliness of my past never far from the dark edges of my damaged soul. Lying to myself all these years hadn't made anything easier nor had it erased the truth.

There'd been one person I'd left on the mountain. Her death continued to haunt me. I'd spent years doing everything I could to drive the agony and near madness from my mind. Meditation. Pain meds. Hell, I'd almost choked the therapist my commanding officer had sent me to while serving in the Marines. Alcohol had done nothing but give rocket fuel to the nightmares that had plagued me for years, but I'd continued to drink heavily until my doctor told me my liver couldn't take much more.

Even sex hadn't dulled the ache behind my eyes. The only thing that had dampened the agony had been hunting down insurgents while serving in the Marines. My unit had taken to calling me the Killing Machine, the Wolf, both monikers I'd grown accustomed to. Then the ability to kill indiscriminately had been stripped away and I'd been forced back into the land of the living.

At least my career choice allowed me to stay the fuck away from people, almost all of whom I found repulsive.

Huffing, I leaned forward, noticing something just up ahead. There it was. A broken-down vehicle. Upon initial inspection, it was easy to see the truck had seen better days. I pulled to a stop, grabbing my gear and weapon then headed toward it. I had to brush the snow off the window to peer inside, but that offered nothing in the way of information.

If she was some photographer, she'd find the mountains a perfect backdrop, heading across the ridge. It was a longshot but the only one I had. I hoisted my bag and followed my gut, stopping every so often to brush snow away, trying to find any footprints.

I got lucky a couple of times, the prints a clear indication by the size a woman was alone in the woods. Damn girl. She was a fool to be out here, and I planned on giving her a piece of my mind.

Just as soon as I had her stuck behind the blasting heater in my truck. There was no way her truck could make it back, not with the slickened tires she had on it.

I forged on, scanning the perimeter for any signs. With every sound, I stopped and listened. Soon, I'd start calling her name.

After going even deeper, I realized I could be heading in the wrong direction, but my instinct was working overtime, the same little bird I used to help me in my endeavors telling me the woman was in danger. Experts said I had a gift, the ability to sense dangerous situations, feeling the terror that always built inside a person when they realized they were lost. There was a distinct stench to terror, and I could smell it from hundreds of yards away.

And even with the fresh falling snow, the odor was distinct.

Something had happened to her.

I picked up my pace, taking long strides over fallen logs. There was a lot of debris, more so than normal given the rough few seasons of weather. There were also dozens of drop-off points that could easily be missed if someone didn't know the territory like I did. I knew almost every square inch of the mountain range, my photographic mind holding pictures of the most dangerous areas.

If I was right, and I was never wrong, Lily Sanborn was headed to one perilous area, some of the drop-offs a hundred feet or more. If she'd fallen over one of those, she was likely dead. Shit. I couldn't think that way. I'd lost one person in my tumultuous life. I wasn't going to lose another.

"Lily!" I called, knowing the deep bellow of my voice wouldn't go very far in the snow. I heard nothing, not a peep. I continued on, stopping every so often to listen. "Come on, girl. Cry out. Fucking cry." I muttered the words, shifting my path slightly. When I bent down, I found one precious footprint. "Lily!"

The silence was annoying.

I was about to head to the right when I could swear I heard a rustle. "Lily."

The slight moan was all I needed. I bolted forward to the edge of a ravine, dropping to my knees and peering over. Fuck. She'd fallen over, clinging to the side and I had a feeling she was hurt. As I tossed my bag to the ground, unzipping and reaching for the rope I carried with me, I assessed the situation. "Lily. Can you hear me?"

When she slowly lifted her head, the distance couldn't hide the fear in her eyes or the stunning vision of her beauty. I was momentarily taken aback, something that never happened to me. Shit. I had to get my act together. "Listen to me. Stay where you are. I'm coming to get you. Can you hear me?"

"Yyyeeesss…"

"Are you hurt?"

"I don't… think… so."

Her voice was little more than a whisper. She could be going into shock. I found the perfect tree, tying it off then yanking the climbing harness into my hand. The snow continued to fall, the rate increasing. I needed to get this done quickly. When I was ready, I peered over again, calculating the distance. While the decline wasn't particularly sharp, the snow and packed ice would make the return climb somewhat treacherous, especially carrying her on my back. But it had to be done.

I rappelled down with no issue, dropping to within inches of her. As I bent down, she recoiled, acting as if I was going to hurt her. "It's okay. I'm a tracker sent by Mr. Washington. He was concerned."

Relief flooded her face but as soon as she tried to move, she winced.

"O-kay." Her lips were already blue, her body shaking. That meant she hadn't gone into hypothermia yet, but it would happen soon.

"I'm going to put this harness on you, attaching it to mine. Then I'm getting you up this ravine. Do you understand?"

"Uh-huh."

"Don't try and fight me or you'll get hurt. Can you stand?" As soon as she tried, she almost slipped. With another drop-off feet away, I had to watch her every move. I grabbed her arm and she almost jerked it back. "Do not do that. I'm not here to hurt you. I promise you that. Stay still or you could die."

Her eyes opened wide and for a few seconds, I was mesmerized by them. They were hazel but the iridescent flecks of gold around her irises were shimmering. *Get a fucking grip. Do your job.* Blinking, I went to work attaching a harness around her waist, clipping ours together. Thank God she didn't try to fight me again.

"Alright. We're going to do this. Just hold onto me however you can."

Lily swallowed hard and I could tell she was searching my eyes, ripping right into my soul in an effort to figure out if I was a good guy or not.

Little did she know I was a very bad man.

I positioned her behind me, wrapping my hand around the rope and waited until she grabbed my shoulders, digging her fingers into my jacket. Her actions were tentative, the fear she had crippling.

I'd been through something like this countless times, several more treacherous than this, but I sensed at any moment she could freak, which could prove fatal to one if not both of us. There was nothing more perilous than for a victim to flail, fighting to free themselves. I wasn't much of a talker, but I also sensed she was close to the edge of losing part of herself to the fear. I had little to offer to try to calm her down.

"New to Montana?" I asked, snarling at the fact the wind had picked up. Even with our combined weight, we were swinging back and forth.

"Uh-huh."

"Staying a while?"

"Maybe."

I sucked in my breath, lifting us a couple of additional feet. The snow was now blinding, the frigid air cutting straight through my down parka. I could only imagine how much she was suffering.

"It's a good place." What the hell was I doing? I had no idea what to say to the girl.

"Oh, yeah?" Her teeth were chattering, her hold slipping.

I glanced up at the precipice. There was at least ten feet to go. Even though she was clipped onto my harness, her dead weight would make things precarious. "Yep. Some nice people here. Hang on, Lily. We're almost there."

After grabbing the rope a few inches over my head, there was a sudden crack, a limb crashing to the ground. That's the moment she decided to freak, flailing so hard that she managed to pull us away from the cliff, but inertia slammed us against the rocks four times. Her hand managed to find its way under my hair, sharp nails digging into the back of my neck.

Gritting my teeth, I almost lost hold on the rope because she was flailing so wildly.

"Fuck! Stop moving."

"You don't get it. I need to get away!" she yelped, clawing my neck.

"You ain't going anywhere unless I can get us to safety. Stop. Moving." The anger I felt was evident, but I wasn't sorry if I created additional anxiety. She needed to follow my orders or else.

"I can't. I can't. I can't." She said the words like a mantra, unable to hide the terror she was experiencing. Maybe old man Washington was right in that she was pretending to be someone else.

Didn't matter. I wasn't here to fixate on a sob story or care about some chick who'd left her husband. I just needed to drop her off at the motel and go on with my life.

Too bad Mother Nature wasn't cooperating.

"You can and you will. Suck it up and hold on or else."

Lily issued another ragged moan but did as she was told. I grabbed the rope again and this time, I was getting us off the damn cliff.

In less than two minutes, I pulled her to safety, yanking her away from the edge. As I rolled over on my back, the falling snow did nothing but piss me off.

Nothing shocked me any longer in life or with people but when she suddenly jerked to her feet, bolting away from me, I took a deep breath. Then I cursed Mother Nature all over again before lumbering to my feet, forced to go after her.

She was taller than I'd originally thought but no match for the ordeal she'd been through, slowly falling face down on the snowy ground.

"Shit." I rolled her over, checking her pulse. It was thready but she was alive. After quickly grabbing my things, I cradled her against my chest, doing what I could to use my body heat to keep her warm.

Then I began the long trudge through the forest to my Cherokee. As I peered down at her ashen face, I was struck for a second time by how beautiful she was, her features strong yet delicate with her long eyelashes and plump rosy lips. The attraction was significant, enough so my cock was pressing hard against my cargo pants. What the hell was wrong with me that I was attracted to a victim?

I guess there was a first time for everything.

She also felt good in my arms, something I hadn't experienced in one hell of a long time. I hadn't been with a woman in so long, I couldn't remember the time of year, let alone a date. Sure, I'd been tempted, but I wasn't into one-night stands any longer. They were unfulfilling, leaving me with an ache deep inside.

No one could fill her shoes, the only girl I'd ever given a damn about.

As Lily uttered a single moan, I yanked the scarf from around my neck, covering her face. I had to get her warm. "Just hold on," I said absently, not expecting her to respond. When I noticed she was staring at me intently, I took a deep breath. At least old man Washington had had the good sense to contact Gage.

By the time I made it through the dense trees, the snowfall had accumulated by several inches. So what if I'd been right about the storm? Being right all the time did nothing but add another layer of shit to my life.

I struggled to open the passenger door, finally able to ease her onto the seat. She remained dead weight as I buckled her seatbelt, yanking a blanket I kept in the back over her then closing the door. I was worried I hadn't gotten to her quickly enough. By the time I made it to the other side, she suddenly made a miraculous recovery, not only jerking off the seatbelt and opening the door, but also sprinting several yards away.

What the hell was wrong with this girl?

"Get back here," I bellowed, immediately dropping my bag and chasing after her. It didn't take more than a few seconds, but as she collapsed in my arms, I sensed another wave of terror paralyzing her system. She pressed her palm against my face, struggling to breathe.

"You're gonna need to trust me, Lily. I ain't no hero, but you're not dying out here."

"I… Can't…"

"Yes, you can. I'm taking you to a safe place."

"There is no safety. Not for me." Her eyelids closed and her arm fell away.

Jesus Christ. There had to be an easier way to make money. What in God's name did she mean by that? Once I had her settled into the Cherokee again, I searched her pockets, finding the keys to her truck. I'd seen a bag inside. After grabbing it, I resisted searching the contents. I didn't have time to find out anything else about her. It would have to wait until we were safe inside my cabin.

I wasted no time slipping into the driver's seat, tossing her bag onto the floor behind me.

As I headed off, I glanced out the windshield at the mountain range, the same one I'd sworn I'd never return to again. There were too many ugly memories, the kind that could break even a man like me.

Maybe it already had, my return a required atonement. Perhaps that's why so many people had been lost on

Sapphire Ridge. A memory shifted into the back of my mind, images becoming clear and vibrant.

And I was forced to suck in my breath.

"What the fuck is wrong with you?" I snapped, realizing the sound was lost in the explosion of fire erupting in the forest.

"We're surrounded on all sides!" Gage yelled from behind.

This was ridiculous. How could we allow this to happen?

Riggs continued to stare at the fire as wind carried embers high over the thick canopy of trees. What the hell was wrong with him? Why wasn't he moving?

"Riggs. We have to get the hell out of here," Houston snapped as he rushed toward the paralyzed man, holding his arm over his face. Thick smoke billowed high in the sky, blanketing out every star. When Riggs remained silent, Houston grabbed his arm, doing what he could to yank the man into action.

I ventured closer, raking my hand through my hair, my chest so tight I couldn't breathe. I wanted to call out her name, to do something, but the fire had already consumed several acres. How in the fuck could this happen?

"No fucking way," he yelled, jerking from our buddy's hold. "No one will be left on this mountain. Do you fucking hear me?" Riggs threw himself into the wall of flames, another blast of heat singeing my skin.

"This can't happen!" I snapped, trying to go after him. I made it through the furnace blast of heat, struggling to be able to see anything. Jesus Christ. I turned in a full circle, unable to make

out anything but huge balls of orange. I could hear Riggs calling her name, yelling it over and over again.

I barreled through another section of forest, my lungs on fire from the lack of air.

"Jesus. We're can't get through this," Colt yelled from somewhere close. Everything was disorienting, the hissing sounds drowning out everything else. As I heard a massive cracking sound, I banked to the right, barely avoiding the falling limb. It crashed to the ground with a thunderous boom, igniting another fire.

"Fuck," I yelped, wiping my eyes as I tried to focus.

"I can't... I tried... No. Use." Ricardo's voice was filled with agony.

"We have to. I can't. I won't." There was nothing like the agonizing sound of Riggs' voice, the sadness and anger exactly the way I felt.

I couldn't allow this to happen. No, I wouldn't. I rushed forward, locating Riggs and Colt, refusing to allow her to die. No one was going to die on my watch.

"Fuck, no. Get out of here. I'm not coming back until Belle is found. Do you fucking hear me?" I snapped out the words then headed into the thickest part of the forest.

And directly into another explosion of flames.

"No! We're not losing you too. We're getting the fuck out of here," Riggs called after me.

"No. No..."

. . .

Six boys had trudged up the mountain acting like kings of the hill. When they'd come back down, they'd been forced to turn into men because of a horrible tragedy.

Phoenix refused to use his given name of Riggs Wentworth, preferring the moniker earned while in the Marines. Ricardo Garcia had left a broken man, now using the name of Snake, returning after being held a prisoner of war then lost in the system. Houston Sowers refused to use the earned nickname of Jaguar, acting as if he didn't deserve the title. Colt Rivers had been a damn good helicopter pilot, earning the label of Falcon, but he'd gone from the Marines to Nashville without looking back. Only Gage Beckham had remained in Missoula, facing the ugly criticism for the horrible event, almost landing himself in prison while spiraling out of control.

Then there was the Wolfman, a guy so riddled with guilt that he hadn't been able to have a normal relationship with anyone. I wasn't proud of it, but it was something I thought about from time to time. I'd been told it was time to exorcise the demons. I didn't have the skills to do that.

But the stir of need in my system was undeniable, even if it terrified the hell out of me.

As the wretched vision faded, I slowly turned my head in Lily's direction. There was no way of knowing who this girl was or why she was here, but I refused to allow anything to happen to her.

Fuck anyone who tried.

CHAPTER 4

*L*ily

Warmth.

Comfort.

Licks.

What? I shifted, feeling as if my body was floating on a sea of pillows, a warm breeze floating across my skin. I sensed I was smiling, basking in the moment. Then I heard something, a slight sound that seemed so far away.

Suddenly, my skin tingled from another series of wet... wet? Hold on. As a rush of heat blasted across my face, I struggled to comprehend what was happening to me. My eyes couldn't focus, my mind fuzzy.

Woof!

A dog?

"Sam. Come here. Now."

The voice was gruff, dark, and foreboding, yet sensual all at the same time. When I felt another slice of wetness, I finally let off a moan, the sound startling and unrecognizable. I jerked up, finally able to open my eyes. And I was staring into the face of a huge… beast. "No!" Every muscle ached, my head pounding. I struggled to take a deep breath, rolling over, still unable to focus enough to figure out where I was.

"Leave her alone, Sam."

Woof. Woof!

Squinting, I turned my head toward the sound of the man's voice, the flicker of firelight highlighting a huge, brawny man sitting in a massive chair. Did he have a drink in his hand? When I felt hot breath skipping across my skin a second time, I turned my head in the other direction, fighting the dull ache coursing through me.

As a massive dog's features came further into focus, I managed to smile. "Hi, big fella." My hand was shaking as I reached out by instinct, ceasing my reflex actions and curling my fingers. What was I doing? What was I thinking? The dog could eat me alive, he was so huge. A strange series of sensations and fears crept through me, and I was suddenly stricken with a near panic attack. As I started to take deep breaths, they quickened until I was panting then gasping.

"Jesus Christ, Lily," the stranger said as he jumped to his feet, thudding the drink he had in his hand on the table in front of him then heading toward me.

I managed to throw my arm out, fighting to sit up as my throat closed off entirely. Fear turned to sheer terror, and I tried to cry out, only able to make gurgling sounds. Then I found my voice. "Get away from me." My instincts kicked in, fear consuming every cell in my body. Who was he? Had he been hired by the monster? I couldn't think clearly.

"I'm just trying to help you, Lily." He kept his distance, his expression conciliatory. It could be fake.

Oh, God. He knew my name. I tried to get up but immediately fell back on the couch, shaking like a leaf.

"Sam. Assist," he commanded, and the dog placed his paw on my leg, nuzzling his huge head against me. "He's not going to hurt you. Touch him. Pet him. He's a licensed therapy dog, or he was until I picked him up."

What was he saying?

Mountains.

Snow.

Very little memory surfaced, but my entire body ached.

Where was I? I didn't know this man. He could be an accomplice, prepared to take me back. Or cut me into little pieces.

"Lily. Do what I say. Just pet him."

Tipping my head, I stared at the mysterious hulking mass of a man I didn't know but did what he said, sliding my fingers across the top of the dog's head.

Sam nuzzled into my hand, his tail thumping. He was a beautiful dog, his fur soft. As a few images floated into my mind, short memories surfacing, another wave of fear became nearly crippling. The mystery man had saved me from certain death. That much I did remember. Why?

Within seconds, I felt better, my breathing less labored. As I continued to calm down, I spent quality time studying him, my memory of the events from minutes, hours before slip-sliding into my mind.

He was huge, my mind not playing any tricks on me. I was forced to lift my head to look him in the eyes. If my ability to size up a man was still intact, I'd say he was at least six foot five, his muscles so large his arms and legs pushed against the bulky clothes he wore. He wore a thick beard and mustache, but neither were able to cover over his chiseled jaw and carved cheekbones. While there was only one other light on in the room, the firelight captured the essence of the man, including full lips and a head of thick curly hair.

But his eyes were the most striking feature, a rich deep blue that kept me staring into them long enough to capture a sense of sadness.

As well as rage.

Whoever he was, he was without a doubt the sexiest mountain man I'd ever seen. A strange ache formed around my nipples, their sudden plumpness pushing against the fabric of my... wait a fucking minute. Where were my clothes?

Had the bastard removed them? I jerked back, taking another strangled breath.

"Your clothes were wet. I had to get 'em off you. Don't worry, I didn't touch you."

He was not only a mountain man savior but a mind reader too?

I had no idea what to say to him, so I concentrated on Sam, whose thumping tail required my attention. My breathing easier, I rubbed his muzzle, finally feeling comfortable enough to bend down and kiss his head. "He's beautiful."

"Guy dogs ain't beautiful." The husky quality of his tone dragged me back to the event in the ravine. He'd risked his life to save mine, dragging me to safety.

"Well, I think he is. Aren't you, Sam?" He was so warm and fuzzy that all I wanted to do was wrap my arms around him.

Woof!

"See? He appreciates my praise. All dogs do. You need to compliment them every day." I was babbling to a stranger. What next?

The mystery man was still staring at me, never blinking. Then he lifted his head, moving away with more agility than a man of his size should have. What was I saying? My mind was still too jumbled, nothing making any sense. I shifted from under a throw he'd tossed over me, planting my feet on the thick rug.

Sam refused to leave my side, nuzzling so close his body heat became oppressive. But he was comforting, which is exactly what I needed. It wasn't usual that monsters with intentions on killing you coaxed their dogs to provide anxiety relief. A laugh bubbled to the surface. I was in a strange house somewhere in the middle of a snowstorm? I had to guess that's where we were. As I looked around, I was expecting something rustic befitting a man of his stature, but nothing inside the man's house was as I'd expected it to be.

The furnishings were colorful in their ruggedness, the leather sofa and chair huge and soft. The stone fireplace went all the way to the A-line roof, the thick stone in shades of charcoal and light gray. And there were beautiful pieces of art on the walls. I was no art critic, but they seemed original or at least very expensive.

And there were books, hundreds of them in the most gorgeous bookcases I'd ever seen. Hold on. He'd likely broken into someone's cabin to take us to safety. That had to be it. Did that make me feel any better or worse? For all I knew, he could be an escaped convict. It was best to keep to myself, hoping that he would ultimately let me go. The tightness in my throat swept into suffocation when a drink magically appeared over my shoulder. I let out a yelp, which started Sam howling.

"Jesus F. Christ," the stranger muttered. "It's a goddamn whiskey, which I think you need. It'll warm you up. Just do what I say."

"How do I know you didn't spike the drink?"

When he said nothing, I tipped my head, catching his icy stare. But at that very second, a hard slam of current jetted into my system, every nerve ending standing on end, my skin a blaze with the strongest desire I'd ever felt. I was breathless, my throat completely dry, forced to blink several times and I wasn't entirely certain why.

He wasn't my type, the rough around the edges, messy-sexy look not my thing. But on him it looked damn good.

Oh, God. I had to be worse off than I originally sensed given the ridiculous, juicy thoughts racing through my mind. This wasn't the time or the place. Besides, I'd sworn off men completely. I needed time to heal and think, finding a way to have my own life.

"Lady, if I was the kind of man who wanted to hurt a woman, I'd just have left you on that rock, watching how long it took for exhaustion and icy conditions to do you in. Take the damn drink."

He was bossy as hell, more so than any man I'd ever met, including the asshole I'd been stuck with for years. But I took the drink, hoping the alcohol would help with my nerves. When our fingers touched, I sucked in my breath, fearful he'd heard me.

"How did you know my name?" I tossed another look at him and while he continued to stare at me, I didn't think he'd caught my wave of lust.

"I told ya. The dude at the motel and I go way back." He moved around the couch, easing back into the chair. As he reached for his drink, I noticed the tattoos covering his forearms, black ink crawling onto his large fingers. "Although he can be a pain in the ass if you ask me. You shouldn't have believed his line of crap about an easy hike."

"It was a beautiful day."

"Yeah, but he knew a storm was coming."

"He is creepy."

"Yeah, he can be." He chuckled for a few seconds before another hard, cold look crossed his face.

"Motel Hell," I said absently. When he was silent, I threw a glance into his eyes. He was grinning, which I didn't think he could do.

"You pegged it right. Then why the hell were you staying there?" Now he was barking at me?

"None of your concern." Asshole.

He gave me a hard stare then shrugged. "Fine by me."

A few seconds of additional tension settled in.

"Would you believe me if I told you because it was listed as a historical site?" I asked almost timidly.

He snorted his answer. "The place is a shithole."

"I know. I just…" I hated admitting anything about me. It was dangerous to do so.

"Then what?"

"It's none of your business."

He laughed, taking a noisy swig of his drink. "Whatever."

I was terrified that while I was here, someone would steal the money I'd hidden cleverly inside the room. Or so I thought. It had to last. Maybe I could get a job. But with what, fake ID? Sure. Other people had done it before. Right?

"What about my camera!" I snapped, almost jerking up. "My things!"

"Your camera is safe. I put it on the kitchen table for ya. Your bag's beside it. But there ain't no pictures worth your life."

He had no idea just how wrong he was. The pictures on that camera could possibly save my life, even though using them would leave a trail for the monster to follow. I'd weigh the risks later but not now. I just needed peace for a little while.

"Did you break into this place?" I blurted out the question and he glared at me, his jaw clenched, his eyes narrowing. "I mean if you did that's admirable. I appreciate you finding some place."

"Do I look like a fucking thief to you?"

"I don't know what they look like." But that wasn't the truth. I knew every ugly detail about men who took whatever they wanted no matter the cost. They believed in their power, as if they were gods. Another shudder coursed through me. Sam instinctively sensed something was wrong with me and issued a slight growl of warning to his master.

"It's okay, Sam. I have a feeling the lady can take care of herself. And this is my place. I had nowhere else to take you."

"What about back to the motel?"

Sighing, he placed his feet on the table and leaned back. "I might live in the mountains, but I ain't no fool. I'll get you back tomorrow. As long as the snow is still coming down, we're not going anywhere."

A lump formed in my throat. "I need to get back now."

"You ain't going nowhere. Your truck is a piece of shit, the tires ready to blow."

"I demand you take me back. Thank you for rescuing me but I have things I must do." Right. I had nothing concrete on my agenda, but the thought of spending the night in a cabin with a stranger was too much to take.

"Lily. I'm going to say it one more time, so you hear me clearly. We're not going anywhere. The snow is still falling and it's getting dark outside. Ain't no one gonna hurt you up here. Least of all me. I might be a bad dude, but not that way. Just relax. Make yourself at home. But I'd be careful moving around too much if I were you. You were pretty bad off and I suspect you came close to hypothermia. Just take it easy."

I was suddenly clammy all over, uncertain what to do. "Will you tell me your name at least?"

Five seconds passed.

Ten.

"Maverick," he said reluctantly.

A first name, not a last. That wasn't usually a good sign. However, he was a man of few words, which meant he wasn't going to start up a conversation. Could I trust him?

He did save your life. My stomach started to revolt from nerves, my heart racing. "Where's your bathroom?"

"One door down the hall."

I stood, likely too quickly, my body swaying. When he immediately started to get up, I threw out my hand. "I'm fine. I can do this. Okay?"

There was something enigmatic about the way he looked at me, as if he was capable of protecting me from all the challenges I'd yet to face, the horrors I already had. As if he'd accepted the title of hero, planning on staying around for a while. I didn't know a thing about the man other than he had good taste in dogs and artwork.

And that there was a searing electric connection between us that was difficult to deny.

I started to ease around the couch and within seconds, he was right there, ignoring my request. When I tried to push him away physically, the foot I'd caught on the fallen log didn't want to work right and I was tossed into his waiting arms, falling against his chest.

The man was rock hard, his thick cock pressing into my stomach and every butterfly that existed west of the Mississippi swept into my stomach, fighting for dominance.

He pressed his hand against my back, holding me tightly against him. As I slowly lifted my head, I could swear the look in his eyes was carnal, his hunger entirely inappropriate. We were lost in a time capsule for a few seconds. He lowered his head, his lips impossibly close to mine. All I had to do was tilt my chin and I could taste his mouth.

No. I was thinking crazy.

But I couldn't help dragging my tongue across my lips. His ragged breathing registered desire. That allowed me to push away from him, crowding the wall. "I'll be okay now. Promise."

"Yeah? Don't make promises you can't keep. Do you want some food?"

"No. My stomach is in knots. I think I just want to rest a little while."

He eyed me carefully then nodded. "I got an extra bedroom down that hall. There's plenty of blankets. Or you can just stay by the fire. I'm headed up to bed. It's been a long day."

"I understand. Thank you."

"Sure." He eyed me carefully before motioning for Sam, the oversized dog trailing behind him as he walked up a set of wooden stairs. I folded my arms, watching him until he'd disappeared. Then I moved toward the fire, standing in front of it.

I'd almost died today for what? A good reason? Not really. I'd left with a crazy thought in my head, a longing to erase the immediate past, finding someone who likely didn't exist and certainly didn't want me.

My legs still wobbly, I headed to the bathroom, shocked at the way I looked. But seeing Maverick had placed my clothes over the top rail of the shower to dry gave me an additional level of comfort. After using the bathroom, I washed my face, hating the look of the girl in the mirror. I wasn't a sight for sore eyes, disheveled, scratches on my face. But I had to keep reminding myself that at least I was alive.

Steadying myself, I headed for the kitchen for water or something else to drink, stopping short when I noticed a set of keys on the table. I swung my head over my shoulder, half expecting him to be standing there. Everything was quiet, too much so.

You can't steal his truck.

No, my inner voice was right. That would be a terrible thing to do. What if I left my keys in replacement? No. No. That was crazy. I didn't know my way down the mountain. After staring at them for a few seconds, I grabbed a bottle of water from the fridge, laughing off the ridiculous thought. I was no mountain girl.

A couple of minutes later, I headed for the bedroom, flicking on the light. The room was small but tidy, the furniture simple and elegant. I wanted to relax, but I knew that in doing so, I ran the risk of losing the money. If the asshole on the mountain had been sent, he'd check in town at crappy motels first. The creeper wouldn't have any issue describing me, even showing off the picture he'd taken. Oh, God. This was a nightmare that I wasn't certain I'd ever wake up from.

I took a swig of water, placing it on the nightstand, determined to get some sleep.

As soon as I sat down, I managed to take a deep breath. Then I fretted, trying to relax, even lying down and allowing several minutes to pass. Then I knew what I had to do. I'd find a way to apologize to Maverick. Maybe. I'd definitely leave his truck. Or maybe I wouldn't. Things were muddled, but I knew something for certain.

I had to get the hell out of here.

As I walked into the hallway, I listened for any signs that he was still awake. A solid twenty minutes must have passed. After taking a deep breath, I headed for the kitchen, grabbing my things, replacing my keys with his. Then I returned to the bathroom, struggling into the still damp shirt and jerking on my stiff jeans, thankful I had brought a dry pair of socks with me. After dressing, I padded into the living room, glancing at the stairs one more time. He was likely snoring away.

I fumbled to slide my feet into the boots, waiting a few seconds before I pulled my coat off the rack, easing into it as quietly as possible. Slinging the bag over my shoulder, I took my time opening the door, praying there were no creaking sounds. Once outside, I was disoriented immediately from the darkness, but shuffled my feet, almost tumbling down the set of stairs. The truck had to be around here somewhere. I hadn't gone two yards when a bright light permeated my retinas, the harsh flash making me wince.

Shit. Shit. Shit.

I let out a shrill yelp, immediately turning and trying to run away from the source. But a couple of seconds later, a hand was wrapped around my arm, yanking me back. I yelled and fought like a warrior, kicking the assailant in the shin, breaking free then tumbling face first into the snow.

The light was suddenly over me, the person straddling my legs.

"Where the fuck did you think you were going, princess?"

Maverick. I'd recognize his gruff voice anywhere. That's when Sam barked, jumping back and forth in front of me, another deterrent to keep me where I was. A moan escaped my throat from the icy chill as well as the rush of adrenaline that had kickstarted my nervous system.

He wasted no time yanking me to my feet, whipping me around to face him then pulling me closer. Close enough I could feel the extreme heat resonating through my body.

"Well?" he demanded.

"I was… I was just…"

The growl he emitted was one of frustration, his cold eyes staring back at me a clear indication I wasn't going to get off easy.

"Let me finish that for you. I was just going to steal your truck and try and make it off this mountain, crashing less than a hundred yards away since I don't know the area. Then I'll come crawling for more help from the man I stole the truck from. Is that about right?"

The dark edge to his voice penetrated my eardrums, adding to the heightened terror. When I didn't say anything, he shook his head, cursing under his breath.

"I guess you're going to need to learn a hard lesson."

That prompted me. "What the hell does that mean?" I tried to jerk away, almost successful until he used one muscular arm, pitching me over his shoulder, turning and trudging back inside. After Sam trotted by, he kicked the door shut, still carrying me further into the room.

"Let me go this instant!" My demand was met with a laugh.

"Oh, I will, princess. At some point. But not until I'm good and ready." He tugged my bag away, tossing it onto the couch then proceeded to walk down the hallway, returning to the bedroom he'd assigned me. Once inside, he dumped me on the bed.

I refused to take his wrath, scrambling to the end and jumping off. He was right there, easily pushing me down again. He pointed his finger, narrowing his eyes as he glared at me. "Stay right there or else."

"Or else what?"

"Or else your punishment is going to be much worse."

"You are not going to punish me."

He leered at me in such a way I wanted to punch his face. "You really want to challenge me?"

"You're an asshole."

"Yeah? You're a woman with a bad attitude, a desire to get herself killed and caustic mouth. Maybe I should grab a bar of soap to clean it out with."

By the look on his face, I could tell he wasn't kidding. I'd met my match with this… brute.

"Stay. Right. There," he said again.

I remained on my knees, thrown by his command, momentarily paralyzed as he came closer. Grumbling, he had to fight to get my coat off, tossing it to the side seconds later.

The second I tried to jump off again, he body-slammed me to the mattress, pointing his index finger at me. "That's it. I'm using my belt."

"What are you talking about?"

"I suggest you remove those jeans yourself, cause if I do, I'll rip them off. Then you won't have anything to wear when I take your ass back to the motel."

Was this man out of his mind?

"Uh, no."

"I was starting with twenty-five. Do you want to make it thirty?" He reached for his belt and I couldn't take my eyes off what he was doing, sucking in my breath as a combination of fear and a crazy sense of arousal tore through me.

What? Was I completely nuts?

"Wha... Why?"

"Cause you're getting one hell of a spanking. That's why," he snorted, his jaw clenching. There was a different kind of fire in his eyes, his expression like that of a primal beast. I was flabbergasted, more so than I'd been in a long time.

Then I found my voice.

"Hell, no."

He cocked his head, raking his heated gaze down the length of me and before I knew it, he'd overpowered me, tossing me onto my stomach and shoving his hands underneath, fighting with me every step of the way as he unfastened my jeans.

"Stop it!" My squeal was unrecognizable, my mind buzzing from the thought of what he was going to do to me.

"Nope. You earned a hard spanking, princess, and that's exactly what you're going to get."

I don't know how he managed since I continued struggling, flailing my arms and making contact to a part of his body with my fists, but within seconds he'd wrangled my jeans down to my knees. I was stuck, no longer able to get up or get away.

I couldn't believe he was going to do this to me. How dare he!

"I'll get you for this." I almost laughed at my words. Right. How was I going to do anything to the rugged, dominating, overtly gorgeous man? Another wave of heat and burning desire rumbled in my system, heating up my core. My panties were even damp, and it had nothing to do with the weather conditions. A flood of embarrassment swept through me like a tidal wave.

"I'd love to see you try, sugar."

"Don't call me that!"

His snort angered me even more. "I'll call you anything I want. This is my house and you're under my rules." He finally got the stiff material past my boots, but he didn't stop there, tugging on my panties.

"No! You're crazy!"

"Spankings are meant to be given on a bare ass."

I could have sworn I heard him laugh. He was enjoying this entirely too much.

The adrenaline rush was slowly fading, leaving me with the feeling of utter exhaustion. By the time he tore off my panties, I was panting but barely moving. This was uncalled for. This was ridiculous.

Even if a small part of me knew that I deserved it.

I was no thief. I was a good girl, just one who'd been turned into a survivor.

When he pressed his hand down on the small of my back, I took a deep breath. His touch alone was enough to light a dozen forest fires and the first scent of my longing wafted straight to my nostrils. This was horrible. Oh, my God. He'd get the wrong impression. He'd think I was enjoying this.

No way.

I hated dominating men.

Like he cared. "Now, if you're a good girl and stay in position, maybe I'll cut it back to twenty-five. If you're not, then I might add on."

"No. No. Please. I'll be good. I promise." I never begged, not even when the monster was hurting me.

"You should have thought about that before. I can't believe a goddamn word you're saying. Stealing my fucking truck.

You would've gotten yourself killed. Jesus!" He dared to rub his hand from one side of my bottom to the other.

When he took a step back, I gathered enough energy to try to crawl to the other side.

With one massive hand wrapped around my ankle, he yanked me back to the edge of the bed. "Do I need to tie you down, cause I have some thick rope and I'm happy to do it."

I wasn't getting out of this. "No. I'll be good. I promise."

"Uh-huh. I'll be the judge of that."

The second I heard a snapping sound, I gritted my teeth. Thank God I did because when he cracked the thick leather across my bottom, an explosion of pain occurred in my butt and down my legs.

"Ouch!" My scream was high-pitched, and I could swear I'd amused him.

"We're just getting started."

He brought it down twice more, the sound almost as bad as the sharp sting coursing through me. I buried my face in the comforter, squeezing my fists around the material. This was one of the worst things I'd ever been through.

Maverick didn't waste any time, issuing four in rapid succession, the hard thudding sound echoing in the entire room. And I was still aroused, electrified by the experience. How was that possible?

"That's better," he mumbled, taking a few seconds to rub the rough pads of his fingers in lazy circles across my heated skin. I'd never known a spanking could hurt this much.

I squeezed my eyes shut, fearing tears were about to form. I refused to allow him to see me cry. Another volley of harsh strikes came within seconds, so many that I lost count.

Unable to stop my body's reaction, I kicked out, pushing up on my hands at the same time. He shoved me down immediately, his growls deeper than before.

"Didn't I tell you to stay in position?"

"Didn't I tell you that I'd be good from now on?" I countered.

His laugh was deep, husky, and sent another thread of shivers into every muscle. "Yes, you will."

My pleas didn't work, the spanking continuing. I couldn't stop wiggling, moaning, and clawing the bed. All the while I was moaning from both anguish and arousal, my nipples so sensitive that every touch of the bedding material made them more electrified.

I had no sense of time, the round of discipline setting me on fire, my bottom aching and would for some time. When he finally stopped a second time, caressing my aching skin, I took gulping breaths.

"There. That should be an excellent deterrent for you. It's called stealing, not something you want to aspire to." The intense rumble of his voice skimming over me set off a series of firecrackers, only some of them about the longing that left the insides of my thighs slickened, my mouth watering from the thought of taking his big, thick cock.

Appalled at my thoughts, when I heard his boots taking a few steps, my natural survival kicked in along with pent-up rage that had been brewing for two years.

I jumped off the bed, flying toward him with my fists clenched. I could tell I'd surprised the hell out of him when he turned sharply toward me, forced to attempt deflecting my blows.

"You think you're a big, bad wolf, don't you? You think you can take what you want?" The words just flew out of my mouth and as much as I wanted to be annoyed with him, his actions had enticed me to the point every inch of skin was over-sensitized, my heart fluttering. He had the most incredible effect on me and it was confusing.

But I hungered for more.

"Yeah, I am and I do." Even the way his upper lip curled make me want to pull it between my teeth, sucking and biting.

How had this man made me lose all my inhibitions so quickly? However he managed, I wasn't finished with trying to get the upper hand.

I got in several hard jabs, half expecting him to hit me back. Instead, a grin crossed his face. Then he wrapped his long fingers around my wrists, taking two long strides then smacking me against the wall.

"Careful, cowboy. I don't play fair," I whispered.

"I noticed. But in case you haven't figured it out, I don't take no for an answer."

"Oh, yeah?" My tone was completely challenging.

"Oh… yeah." His was full of arousal.

All time stopped as we glared at each other, our eyes boring into each person's soul. Then something even more terrifying happened, something I wondered if I could recover from.

He captured my mouth with his.

CHAPTER 5

averick

The sweetest strawberry fresh off the vine.

That's exactly what her lips tasted like.

Lily wiggled in my arms and the ache in my cock intensified tenfold. Goddamn, the woman was a firecracker.

Why the hell was I attracted to a woman who had a mouth full of rocks and shards of glass, ready to spew them on me at a moment's notice?

Because it's an act. Yeah, well, maybe.

Her moans were like sweet music, the feel of having her in my arms so unexpected that my balls were tight as drums. I wanted to taste every inch of her.

The moment Lily had attacked me again, pummeling her fists against my chest, shock had kept me from reacting. Then I'd witnessed hatred in her eyes, but not for me or for the situation.

For whoever the asshole was who'd hurt her before.

And the beast inside of me instantly roared to the surface, the lion who'd tear apart anyone who tried to hurt any creature belonging to him. The thought was ridiculous, out of character for me, but strong as a piece of steel. I hadn't experienced such intense desire in a long time because I hadn't allowed it. I couldn't remember the last time I'd been on a date, let alone had a half-naked woman inside my house.

And on top of everything, I'd spanked her. What the hell was wrong with me?

I couldn't resist and in truth, I could tell neither one of us could stop the roar of passion that threatened to consume us both.

Her lips were soft, plump, and delicious and the moment I'd captured one look at her huge doe eyes and long lashes, I'd wanted to drive my cock deep inside her pussy. Then she'd fought me like a lioness, refusing to allow the stronger male to overtake her. I almost laughed at the thought that we were two beasts in the wild mating.

But my cock agreed, my balls so tight the pain was increasing every second. I'd sensed her arousal, the scent so sweet that it had taken everything I had to control myself, refusing to drive my fingers past her swollen folds. But enough was enough, our attraction too strong. I'd heard crazy things about chemistry, but with the sparks of electricity skittering through every muscle and bone, I knew there was something to it.

So, I pinned her against the wall, pressing the full weight of my body against hers. Even though she opened her lips, allowing me access, I wasn't gentle in my actions. That wasn't the kind of man I'd turned into. I was a brute and always would be.

She fought the round of passion like I knew she would, moaning into the kiss, her body undulating against mine. That only created wave after wave of friction, building my desire to a point I wouldn't be able to back down. I couldn't believe she tasted so sweet, like cherries in the springtime. What the hell? I wasn't a romantic dude by any sense of the word. I wouldn't know where to take her out on a date and forget about acting like a gentleman. I wasn't set up that way.

But every scent was more explosive around her, filling my system with a drug that had already turned me into an addict.

I dominated her tongue, sweeping it back and forth, tasting every centimeter. The feel of her lush body against mine could make any man turn into a predator. And that's exactly what I'd become. With her. Because of her. Filthy thoughts were fueling me, the need to taste every inch of her skin tops on the list. But I wanted more.

To drive my tongue into her sweet pussy.

To thrust my cock into her tight channel.

To have her lips wrapped around my aching cock.

And to claim her tight little asshole, every inch of her becoming mine.

Did she know she'd walked into the lair of a beast?

As the moment of intimacy continued, she slowly rolled her arms around my shoulders, tangling her fingers of one hand in my hair, clawing me with the other. Our actions became a mirror of need, both unrelenting in wanting control. But she'd soon learn that I would always be the one in charge.

We'd both crossed a line and there was no going back.

Her moans of fury turned into whimpers of longing, as she tore at my clothes. When I broke the kiss, she took several deep breaths. Then she managed to shove me away, acting as if she was going to run. Laughing, I grabbed her arm, yanking her close. "You're not going anywhere, princess."

"We'll see about that." Her eyes were dancing with amusement, the fire in them tearing into me. Goddamn, the woman turned me on.

I wasn't expecting her to twist then kick, the force just enough to drive me backwards by a full foot. But she took too long enjoying her slight win. That allowed me to grab her around the waist, tossing her onto the bed. When she rolled, almost tumbling off, all I could do was laugh. She was making me work hard for this.

And I loved it.

At first, she was still. Then she jumped onto all fours, lunging toward me. The girl was like a cat, springing off the bed, wrapping her long legs around me. As the momentum drove me us against the wall, the way she was riding my jean-covered cock was at the point of driving me insane. Even with her tight hold, I managed to jerk her sweater up and over her shoulders, freeing her from the tight confines.

Lily's eyes were glassy and the way she dragged her tongue across her lips was far too seductive.

There was no need to say another thing, our hunger far too great. I shoved one arm over her head then the other, wrapping the fingers of one hand around her small wrists. Then I kept my eyes pinned on her as I unfastened my jeans, freeing my aching cock.

This wasn't about pretense or spending any additional time getting to know each other. My cockhead slipped past her slickened folds easily. Then I drove the entire length inside, immediately throwing my head back and roaring like a beast.

She panted, laughing softly as she struggled in my hold, arching her back. The look in her eyes was wild, her needs as great as mine. The way her muscles were clenching around my cock and her extreme wetness made me uncontrollable. I pulled out, driving into her again, knocking the wind out of her.

As I started plunging into her like a wild man, she tried to meet every brutal thrust, moaning and squirming, the friction adding another layer of electricity. My balls were aching so badly lights flashed in front of my eyes. If I wasn't careful, I'd come within seconds, and I wanted this to last.

"Uh. Uh. Uh. Uh. Uh." Her sounds were like rocket fuel and while taking her this way was primal, damn hot as it could get, I wanted to feel her naked skin against mine. I drove hard and fast for a few more seconds, then yanked her away from the wall, freeing her hands. Her smile was wry as she clawed my neck, instantly sucking on my lip.

When I dumped her on the bed again, I leaned over, pointing my finger. "Stay."

"Or what? You've already spanked me."

"There are worse forms of punishment." I dragged my sweatshirt over my head from the back, dropping it like a rock. She pursed her lips as she'd done before, crawling onto all fours but instead of running, she tossed her hair back and forth.

Jesus. The woman was trying to set my entire body on fire. As I kicked off my shoes, I allowed my eyes to roam over every inch of her. With her hourglass figure and rounded hips, she was created with me in mind. I didn't like skinny woman, preferring them to look just like Lily. Soft. Feminine. Beautiful. But she was a little fighter, refusing to give in.

I couldn't get my jeans and underwear off fast enough, immediately joining her on the bed. But instead of finishing what I'd started, I pushed her down, immediately lifting her legs, bending her knees and shoving them wide open for my perusal.

In preparation of a feast.

Lily seemed flustered as well as embarrassed, as if this was far too exposed and vulnerable. But I wasn't the kind of man to take no for an answer. I dropped down, running the tip of my tongue around her bellybutton, my gaze pinned on her shimmering face. Now she seemed tentative, pressing the back of her hand across her mouth as she blinked several times. Every muscle was tense, and it drove me crazy that I had an ugly thought in the back of my mind.

Her actions made me think she was waiting for me to hurt her in some ungodly way. If I found out some asshole had done something horrific to her, I'd go hunting. And I was a damn good hunter, always catching my prey.

But for now, I'd take what I needed, giving her the kind of pleasure she deserved.

She mewed several times, her breathing ragged and her eyelids fluttering. While she wiggled a little, as soon as I blew across her pussy, she issued a series of whimpers. She was so wet, her sweet folds shimmering in the dim lighting. I could do nothing but eat her for hours, savoring every drop of her sweet nectar.

When I swirled the tip of my tongue around her clit, she smacked her hands on the comforter.

"Oh, my," she murmured, still tossing her head back and forth. "You're so bad."

"Mmm... yup." I continued teasing her, finally pulling the tender tissue between my lips. There was nothing like sucking a woman this way, gauging their reactions, making their little nub swollen. I opened her even wider, lifting her pelvis slightly off the bed. Then I settled in, burying my face into her wetness.

The way she flailed, half laughing and half murmuring under her breath was adorable. She was embarrassed, her face almost as red as her bottom. That kept me going, bringing her to the very edge of a climax then pulling back. I tormented her for several minutes until her entire body was shaking. As I drove several fingers inside, flexing them open, she gasped and jerked up again.

"Oh, yes. Oh, sweet Jesus."

As her juice trickled down the back of my throat, I pushed a little further until I knew she was at the point of no return. I used my fingers and tongue in perfect unison and within seconds, she was pummeled into a strong orgasm, her body spasming.

This time she opened her mouth in a silent scream, her eyes open wide as she pushed up from the bed. I refused to stop, driving her to a second wave, growling at the sight of goosebumps appearing across her skin. I held her tightly, digging my fingertips into her thighs as she bounced up and down.

Only when she finally stopped moving, allowing her arms to slowly ease to the sides did I back off. I pressed my lips against one inner thigh then the other, moving so I was hovering over her.

She bit her lower lip, laughing softly when she tried to look me in the eye.

"Tell me, princess. What do you want?"

The little vixen was trying to regain control, sliding her finger all the way around her mouth.

I pinched her nipple, allowing the slice of pain to awaken her senses some more.

"Tell me," I roared.

"Fuck me," she whispered far too softly for my tastes.

"Say it again. Louder. Tell me what you want me to do to you."

Just as I would expect from her, she slammed her palm against my chest, her voice deepening. "Fuck me."

* * *

Lily

Oh. My. God. I'd just told a complete stranger, a man who'd dared to treat me like a child to fuck me. How far down the rabbit hole of insanity had I gone?

Well, in all fairness, he had just given me two of the most powerful orgasms of my life. But still. That shouldn't mean I'd just beg the savage bastard, the sexy savior to use me at his will.

Right?

I could tell by the carnal look in his eyes that there was no going back. I'd opened Pandora's Box. I'd wanted the sense of freedom, a man who obviously desired me. I hungered for a touch that had nothing to do with anger. Maverick was everything a man should be and nothing I should get involved with.

He was a mystery man.

Dangerous.

Angry.

Closed off.

But I couldn't help myself.

I'd been crippled by fear too long and he felt safe, my hero. But was it all a mirage? Would I wake up, realizing I was back in my cage?

Stop it. You're alive. You're okay. Maverick saved you.

As he eased between my legs, I finally had the chance to wrap my fingers around the thickest, longest cock I'd ever seen. My muscles still ached from the way he'd plunged into me earlier and I couldn't wait for more.

I pressed my palms against his chest, tingling from the feel of his rippled muscles. He was even more muscular than his bulky clothes had shown, his rugged arms and the carved V in his abdomen something I could stare at for hours. Every touch was electric, the way his beard tickled my skin when he kissed me creating dazzling sensations. It took my breath away how quickly he'd learned my body, every desire fulfilled.

He'd tormented me earlier. Now I was returning the favor, twisting my hand as I rolled it up and down, never taking my eyes off his. I'd never had a single man who'd looked at me the way he was, including the monster. Maverick's gaze was dark with intense need, a burning desire that he'd kept to himself for a long time. I felt special, wanted, and being able to touch him freely was as exciting as everything else about the man.

Even if he was infuriating, pigheaded, and required my full obedience. He had another think coming. I wasn't going to be forced to follow any man's rules.

I slid my fingernail down his shaft, teasing him relentlessly before slipping my hand between his legs, cupping and squeezing his balls. He simply lowered his head ever so slowly, issuing a series of low and husky growls, his beard tickling my skin. He knew how to keep me fully aroused, my mind foggy from all the lurid thoughts racing through it.

He exhaled, his hot breath cascading across my breasts, his muscles tensing. Every sound he made kept me on edge. The way he cocked his head, studying me intently heated my core to an explosive level. I'd never expected I could tolerate this man, let alone crave him. When he rolled his finger around first one nipple then the other, a single moan slipped past my lips.

His eyes twinkled, his forehead crinkling. Then he pulled my hands away, dragging one of my legs up and to the side, pressing his hand against the bed as his cock found its way back to my aching pussy.

"My tight little princess," he said gruffly, taking his time to return it to my tight channel.

Moaning, I gripped his arm, digging my fingers in as he slowly seated himself inside. A wry smile crossed his face as he pulled out, teasing me relentlessly.

"That's not fair," I told him as defiantly as I'd said anything before.

"You'll learn that I'm not a fair man, at least with regard to fulfilling my needs." His grin widened and he drove the remaining inches inside, both of us gasping for air. I was shocked my muscles clamped and released several times, almost pushing me into another wild orgasm. He slipped out again, leaving just the tip inside. His thrusts became even more powerful.

I rolled my fingers along his arm, drinking in the tattoos covering both. They added to his dangerous persona, every one of them artistic and beautiful, but I knew better than to ask him about them. As he developed a rhythm, I wrapped my other leg around his thigh, trying to pull him even closer.

"Perfect." The single word almost made me cry. How could a stranger make me feel so beautiful, taking away an entire layer of ugliness that I'd forced around myself with such ease? He lowered his head until our foreheads were almost touching, stretching my muscles even more.

He was so deep inside, filling me so completely that I remained breathless. I'd never wanted a man as much as I did with him, my needs continuing to build. I kept my eyes open, longing to watch everything, shocked the way every single touch seared my skin. How could anything be so hot? Because it was wicked? Because we didn't know each other?

I shushed my little voice, trying to meet every hard thrust.

Maverick was so powerful, so controlling, and I finally allowed myself to close my eyes, floating away into a moment of pure bliss. He rose onto his arms, shifting the angle. Vibrations rushed through me, a burst of light crisscrossing my field of vision.

"Oh, God. Oh. Oh. Oh…"

"That's it, baby. Come for me. Come."

His words added fuel to a fire I'd snuffed out ages ago. He'd awakened the woman inside and I never wanted to return to the darkness. As another incredible orgasm swept through me, I fell into a sweet abyss. There was no worry, no fear. Only pleasure. I lolled my head, trying to control my breathing, half laughing as the vibrating sensations trampled every nerve. "You are… Oh, my gosh."

The rugged man refused to allow me to rest, rolling me over in a split second, forcing me to straddle him. He was obviously enjoying himself, even bending one arm, placing it behind his head. "Ride me, princess."

Every time his voice dropped into the deep baritone, my skin prickled from heat clawing at the surface. I squeezed my knees against his sides, leaning over and planting my hands on either side of his head. As I lowered mine, tossing my hair into his face, he did nothing but lower his eyes. Using a single finger, I rolled it down his forehead between his eyes, taking my time shifting it around his mouth.

His cock continued to throb, swelling even more, and my body was begging me to do what he asked, the rapture too intense.

But there was something oddly special as well as strange about this moment, the time I was taking to explore his ruggedness better than asking him questions about himself. At this point I couldn't care less if we were compatible in any other way but what we were sharing. But I would never break the promise I'd made to myself never to fall for another man again.

And my convictions had nothing to do with the bastard I'd been sold to like cattle.

When Maverick started fiddling with my hair, I could tell he was losing patience. I bucked my hips forward, giving him a mischievous look. He responded by wrapping his hand around my long strands, jerking me forward so our lips were almost touching.

"You don't want to keep teasing me, Lily."

"Why?" I whispered, bucking against him a few more times then stopping.

"Do you really want to find out?" He tugged me harder until our lips were touching. He was daring me to kiss him, but I refused, doing nothing more than opening and closing my mouth several times.

"Uh-huh." Unable to resist, I slipped my tongue inside, enjoying the intimate taste.

There was such ease about everything he did, the man so strong that his grace surprised me. Using the strength of his legs, he rolled me over with ease, then pulled away, lifting and turning me over and onto all fours within seconds. I was shocked, but not nearly as much as when he thrust his cock in with such force that I was shoved down onto the comforter. He still had his hand around my hair, using it as the reins as he rode me instead.

"My beautiful baby."

He would never know what the three little words meant to me. As I bucked against him, his rough playfulness returned, our fiery passion the most scintillating thing I'd ever felt. I could lose myself in him for hours, days. The thought kept my breathing ragged. Maybe a rugged he-man was exactly what I'd needed.

His actions were even more savage than before, every sound he made like a primal beast. I palmed the comforter, but he was relentless in his actions, taking exactly what he wanted, his stamina unlike anything I'd experienced before.

I was kept out of breath, stars floating in front of my eyes. Finally managing to arch my back, I closed my eyes, allowing the evocative sounds he was emitting to add to the rush of excitement.

My pussy ached, my mind a blur but when I sensed he was finally close to releasing, I squeezed my muscles around him. He gripped my hip with his other hand, thrusting in four long drives before his entire body began to shake.

There was a sense of peace reborn inside of me as he released, filling me with his seed. While I'd opened Pandora's Box, he'd found a key I thought lost, one allowing me to feel again.

I could never see Maverick again, let alone having him in my shaky little world, but he'd given me a beautiful gift and not just in saving my life.

He'd returned a portion of my lost soul.

CHAPTER 6

Maverick

Damn, the woman turned me on.

Lily also infuriated the heck out of me. She'd managed to get under my skin with her beguiling smile and her incredible scent. Then there were her plump lips made for kissing.

As soon as I walked out of the bathroom, Lily was opening the door to the bedroom where she'd stayed. Her eyes opened wide. Sam bounded out of her room as well, his tail wagging.

"I'm sorry…" she started, looking away immediately, her face flushing. She must have come out after I'd left, grabbing her jeans since she stood in the same clothes I'd found her in.

"I should have warned you. I need to get some parts to fix the shower upstairs." I was only wearing a towel wrapped loosely around my hips, but she'd seen every inch of me only hours before. I'd noticed a several yellowed bruises, which had yanked out the protector in me.

The second I'd seen the fading marks, I'd almost grilled her until she admitted who'd been responsible. But I knew she wouldn't tell me. Why should she? I'd just been a man who'd spanked and fucked her like she belonged to me. Even with saving her life, there was no way she could trust me. My guess was she couldn't trust another man, period.

That's why I'd left her room minutes after our heated round of sex. Not that I was the kind of guy to sit around and have small talk. What did the women call it, pillow talk? That wasn't my thing, but I'd left her alone because I hadn't known what to say to her.

She was a tourist, likely heading home in a couple of days anyway.

"We can't save her!" Riggs' voice powered into my eardrums, drowning out the hissing of the roaring fire.

"We are. I'm not leaving here without her!" I snapped, ready to rush through the flames.

"We'll all die up here," Houston said from behind me.

The memory flashed through my mind so fast I was left breathless. Why the fuck now? Because I'd managed to save

Lily? That had to be the reason. I shifted the towel and her eyes slowly crawled down my chest. The way she chewed on her bottom lip was just about the sexiest thing I'd ever seen. The beast inside of me wanted to drag her into the shower, staying until we used every drop of hot water.

"It's your house. You don't need to apologize," she said, the fire that I'd seen in her so many times all but disappeared. Why? Because I'd seen the bruises? Maybe I should ask about them. Hell, no. She was so damn reserved that she'd clam up even worse.

"Still shoulda told you. There's plenty of hot water and fresh towels if you want to take a shower."

"I'll wait."

"I don't know how long it'll be before I can get you out of here. I'll grab you a shirt of mine to wear."

Lily threw out her hand. "No. I don't want to owe you. I'm not that kind of girl." She half laughed after making the statement, but it was further affirmation she was putting a stop to our lurid interaction.

"Owe me? For wearing a damn shirt?"

"I'll never see you again so I won't know how to get it to you."

I gritted my teeth. At least I knew the answer if I'd wanted to ask her out again. A big, solid no. That was just fine. I didn't need any complications in my life. I liked being alone. "If you're so inclined, you can leave it with Mr. Washington. How about that?"

She chewed on her lower lip, looking everywhere but at me. When I inched closer, lifting her chin with a single finger, the same desire I'd had roaring to the surface like some freight train. Then she shivered from my touch.

And not in a good way.

She placed her hand against my chest, immediately retracting it as if her fingers were burned from the touch. "Don't, Maverick. Last night was…"

"Pretty damn amazing." I pulled my hand away, fisting it. The scent of her had remained covering my skin long all night long.

"Yes, but… a mistake," she finished.

I couldn't help but growl. This wasn't a relationship in the making but a mistake? "Okay then."

"It's not you. Okay? I just can't right now." The pain in her eyes as she looked at the floor just put another stake in my gut, one I might use later if I had the chance.

"Sure."

"I mean it." She lifted her eyes, finally allowing me to see that she'd been crying. "I'm just too damaged."

Fuck. Who was this freak?

"Who hurt you, Lily?"

I knew immediately I'd pushed her too far. "Nobody. Well, I found a guy I'd dated for a couple years going down on my best friend in my bed." She laughed and while I believed her, that had nothing to do with the pain I'd seen in her eyes.

"Ouch."

"Yeah. I'm not saying you were a rebound but before I get involved with anyone, I need to figure out my life."

"Understandable."

"Good." She gazed at me sheepishly, her cheeks burning from slight embarrassment. I wasn't going to break through the wall she had surrounding her. The truth was it was none of my business in the first place.

I adjusted the towel so it wouldn't fall off then started to walk away. "I'll make some coffee and breakfast."

"Thank you for everything and I'll take that shirt."

As I turned toward her once again, she allowed me to catch the fact her expression was one of longing.

Who was I to act as if I wanted to get in the middle of some shit? As I'd told her before, I was no hero.

* * *

Lily

Damn it. He was without a doubt one of the hottest men I'd ever laid eyes on.

"Whew," I whispered, my nipples aching. I wanted him all over again, but it was a terrible idea. The worst I'd had.

Losing control was stupid.

I had a sense he was suspicious about what I was doing in Montana. What was I supposed to tell him?

Oh, my father sold me to this notorious kingpin for unknown reasons? My future husband was a horrible man who kept me under lock and key? At least he hadn't touched me intimately. That was the only saving grace but still.

That would go over well.

A horrid lump formed in my throat. I'd almost forgotten about the bruises because of the way Maverick had made me feel.

Wanted.

Needed.

I moved to the bathroom door quickly, but couldn't take my eyes off him, feeling the same stirring of desire crashing into me. He was trying to be nice, and I'd shut him down. It was better this way. He didn't need my crazy world dropped in his lap and I had no clue how to be normal.

Exhaling, a cold shiver sliced down my spine and when I tried to close the bathroom door, Sam almost slipped in. "No, baby. Go be with your daddy. Okay?"

The dog whined, which allowed me a smile, but I didn't want to get attached to him either, even if his company the night before had allowed me to sleep.

After the nightmare.

One horrible, vicious nightmare.

Then a tree limb had slammed against this side of the house so many times I'd remained on edge.

Sam hadn't given me away when I'd been so ridiculously terrified that I'd searched for a weapon, taking a butcher knife from the kitchen. Then I'd found a small cabinet of weapons in the closet of the bedroom where I'd been staying. I'd been tempted to try to pick the lock but had talked myself out of it. Sam's company had taken away the feeling of panic.

Now I felt guilty closing the door in the pup's face, but I needed time to get my shit together after what Maverick and I had shared together. If I could.

The room was still warm from his shower and after grabbing a set of towels, I started the water, allowing my thoughts to return to how sexy he looked wearing a towel and nothing else. I really didn't know what I was doing any longer.

I dropped my clothes, hating that my hands were shaking. Then I made certain the locket was still in place, squeezing it for a few seconds. Maybe I was kidding myself that I'd ever find her. When I moved into the shower, I leaned against the corner, fighting the same darkness that threatened to take away the joy from the night before.

"You're nothing but a whore, Amelie. Don't you forget that."

Amelie. My real name. I'd selected a name from a book in a hurry. I only hoped it was enough of a cover.

As I closed my eyes, I envisioned Maverick.

But only seconds later, the beautiful vision was crushed, my father's face when he'd shoved the contract in my hands returning. The chance that I'd already been found was slim to nil, but that didn't make the memories any easier.

I moved under the water, allowing it to splash against my face.

And for the first time since I'd escaped into the darkness, I allowed myself to cry for one reason.

I felt safe.

* * *

Maverick

Lily had been quiet since our accidental meeting in the hallway, doing nothing more than staring at the front window at the snow and my truck. At least she'd accepted the Henley shirt and sweatpants I'd provided. I found myself staring at her far too often. She looked adorable in my clothes and I almost told her as much.

Like that was going to get me anywhere.

I didn't claim to be a good cook, but she refused to eat any scrambled eggs or toast. At least Sam had a good breakfast.

With my coffee cup in hand, I headed for the living room, studying her from behind. "I can probably take you to your truck now. But I'm going to warn you that your tires are very worn, and the roads are slicker in the snow. While the sun helped pack down the snow, there's still a chance you'll get stuck. If that happens, I'll dig you out."

"Really?" She glanced over her shoulder, giving me a onceover.

"Yeah. I'll follow you back to the motel to make sure you don't have any issues."

"You don't need to do that."

"I know what you said before. You can handle yourself, Lily. You're one tough girl. However, this is Montana and your truck is shit. We'll leave in a few minutes. You're gonna need to put up with Sam in the Cherokee. He's coming with me today."

That brought a smile to her face and without any hesitation, she dropped to her knees, Sam reacting immediately. "That's no problem," she said, using ooey-gooey words with him. "He's such a baby."

"He's a tracking dog." There was no reason for me to tell her. Maybe I was trying to find a way to open up a line of communication. Shit, I sounded like the psychiatrist I'd been forced to see for a couple of months after returning from overseas.

"That doesn't mean he's not a cuddle-wuddle bug. Right, baby boy?" When he whined, pressing his entire head in her lap, I threw him a harsh look.

"Traitor."

At least she laughed. "Your daddy is a mean man, Sam."

"Don't you forget it," I teased, although I was still grousing as I walked into the bedroom.

By the time I grabbed a jacket, finding my keys and Sam's leash, she was standing by the door with her coat on, her duffle in her hand.

Even worse, she'd changed back into her clothes, which meant she'd cut the last tie between us. I wasn't into picking up lost puppy dogs anyway. I'd done that with Sam and that was my limit.

She started to help me with clearing snow off the vehicle, darting only one look in my direction.

"That'll do it," I told her, immediately opening the back door, giving Sam a look.

My buddy hopped in the back, which I thought was going to annoy him since he usually rode shotgun, but he'd lost a part of his heart to the feisty redhead. I hated to break the news to him that we'd likely never see her again.

As I climbed in, I couldn't help but notice her intention was to look out the passenger window and nothing else. Christ. I roared the engine to life, throwing it into gear.

"You might want to wait until tomorrow to head out, I mean if you're going back home," I told her.

"How do you know Missoula isn't my home?"

"Cause you wouldn't be staying in a fleabag motel if it was."

"Oh," she said. "You're right."

She didn't tell me where home was, and I didn't ask. All I knew was that she had pennies to her name, which was the reason she'd picked the Yellowstone. There was no other logical reason for it.

"Look, it's none of my business, but if you're looking for a job to earn some quick cash, there's a place in Missoula called Raunchy Ride. It's owned by a guy I know."

"I don't want any handouts."

I had to laugh. "I assure you that you'd be working your ass off." As I threw a glance in her direction, I could tell she was contemplating it.

"What kind of place is it?"

I wanted to say, 'The kind that could eat you alive, but you can handle it,' but scaring her any more than she seemed wasn't the best idea. "Think *Roadhouse* mixed with even more cowboys, top notch bands, and some damn good barbeque food and that's Raunchy Ride. Plus, my buddy is a stand-up man who won't allow his employees to take a second's worth of shit from anyone."

"Sounds like you."

"Yeah, well, Scorpion is a decent man."

"Scorpion? That's really his name?"

"It is now. It's a military thing."

"Oh, and you're not a decent guy?" she asked genuinely.

I shrugged, still hating the fact I had no idea what to say to her. "I wouldn't let anything happen to you, Lily. If that's what you mean. You're scared of something and that bothers me. Call me old-fashioned. Call me some asshole getting in your business, but of all the bad things I've done in my life, I followed one of my mama's rules."

"Which is?" Now she was looking at me.

"Never to treat a woman, a kid, or an animal badly."

I was rewarded with a smile. "Your mother sounds like an amazing woman."

"She was."

"I'm sorry."

"Don't be. She's out of pain."

"Pain is debilitating."

She said the words quietly, but I heard them. "Yeah, cancer ate her up. At least I have Sam." Maybe I was purposely being vague hoping she'd continued talking. I'd never wanted to get this personal with anyone before. Why her?

"He's a beautiful dog." She leaned her head against the window of the glass.

"I rescued him from a high kill shelter."

"Really? You're an amazing person. How can people do that? Dogs are precious little creatures who deserve to have a wonderful family with dogs and treats."

"He came from a puppy mill. One day he could be blind so the jerks who owned him couldn't get top dollar. That's why he's a damn good tracking dog, his other senses heightened."

The look on her face was different. "Do you know what's wrong with his eyes?"

"Glaucoma."

"That's treatable although he'll have it for the rest of his life. That doesn't mean he'll go blind as long as you keep the intraocular pressure low. I hope to God your vet told you that."

As I slowly turned my head, she blushed several shades. "That's exactly what he said. How would you know?"

Her laugh was cold and haunted. "I read a lot."

Uh-huh. She was keeping all kinds of secrets.

"You're really good with Sam. You've had pets before."

Sighing, she shook her head. "No. Never. One day when I settle down."

That wasn't a lie, just an expression of regret for a past that ate her alive.

"I hope you can. To answer your question, people don't think of animals as anything but a possession they can discard. They're selfish assholes who buy dogs they can't handle and bring 'em back, trading them in. He was a couple hours away from getting the goddamn shot. If a buddy of mine hadn't brought him to my attention, he wouldn't be here today."

"He's a great little boy for you. He loves you very much." Sam knew he was being talked about, sticking his head in between the seats. "Yes, you are."

"He's more than just a good tracker. He's my family now." I was getting close to the area. The storm wasn't as bad as I'd thought, but I'd been right to have her stay with me.

"You track a lot of lost souls? Your job sounds fascinating. You get to be outside, combing the beautiful mountains. You don't have to kowtow to anyone."

At least I could chuckle. "The job isn't glamorous if that's what you're thinking. Tourists are notoriously bad about getting lost and ignoring maps, so I'll get hired by the forest rangers or smokejumpers to hunt them down. And I assure you every government operation has rules that infringe on how I handle business. Fortunately, they're usually quick jobs, decent enough pay. It's tracking criminals that makes the most money, which means I travel wherever they are in order to hunt them down like dogs."

"So you're a bounty hunter?" she asked more nervously.

Snorting, I threw her a look. "Bounty hunters are untrained in this state. They think they're going to make big money from idiots who skip bail, thinking they can get lost in the mountains and people will forget about them. A small percentage are successful. Plus, they're assholes."

"Ouch. I didn't mean to compare the two. What's the difference? Educate me."

"I'm hired by the US Marshal's service most of the time to track down more dangerous criminals than a few assholes who skip trace on a few thousand dollars' bail. Sometimes, I get those who escaped prison. They're the most dangerous people to track."

Her body language changed, her face turning pale. Then she chewed on her lip again, her nervous little tic that told me far too many things I didn't want to know.

She was running from something or more likely someone.

"I thought I saw a bad man in these mountains. That's why I tripped and fell over the edge."

A bad man. "Somebody you know? Tell me who it is." My tone had changed, the forceful savage peeking his head from his lair.

Laughing softly, she tried to pass it off. "No, but he seemed odd, and he was walking around with a big gun in his hands."

"A big gun. Was he hunting? We are known for wildlife."

"No. It was an assault rifle."

How the fuck would she know what an assault rifle looked like? I didn't have a chance to ask her before I pulled up next to her truck. Within a split second of me stopping, she jumped out. When Sam tried to go with her, I had to pull on his collar. "No, buddy. Stay right here."

I grabbed her bag, surprised when she acted like she was going to leave it. I managed to grab her arm before she climbed inside. "Whoa. What the hell is really going on here, Lily? You think you saw a man in the woods with an assault rifle and you're just telling me this?"

She jerked her arm free, trying to do the same with the bag. "I knew you could take care of us. You're big and strong. You have weapons you could have used."

"You searched my house?"

Lily closed her eyes. "I was scared. I heard noises."

"Why didn't you come find me?" When she didn't answer, I shook her. "Why?"

"Because it's my life. Okay?"

I let her go, holding out her bag.

"Something for you to keep in mind in the future. If that person really is an escaped convict, then they aren't discriminating about who they rob or kill, including whether or not they're a strong guy. You should have mentioned it to me. That's part of my job, Lily. I'll follow you to the motel." I turned and headed toward the Cherokee, anger and frustration fueling me.

"Thank you, Maverick. For everything."

After jumping in, I glanced out the window at her before backing the vehicle out of her way so she could turn around.

Whatever the hell was going on with her, the fact she was keeping it a secret meant it was either very personal or she was a part of it.

And I certainly didn't need to get involved with anything illegal. I'd see her to the motel and that would be it.

Period.

That's exactly what I did, waiting until she found her way into the room. I don't know why I expected her to come say a goodbye or tell me to fuck off and die. She did neither. Sam whined from behind me, and I glanced into the rearview mirror, inviting him up front seconds later. "I know, buddy. I'm sorry she didn't say anything to you. She's got some issues she needs to deal with."

Woof!

"That's what I say." I waited another few seconds before heading out, tapping my fingers on the steering wheel. I wasn't comfortable at all leaving her there, but I couldn't hogtie her down, forcing her to stay with me.

For now.

What I could do is find out if there was any truth to what she was saying. It was painfully obvious that she believed what she'd seen and being that specific meant she'd either watched far too much television or one had been shoved in her face before.

I yanked out the phone, first dialing Gage. Maybe he had some clue about whether or not there was some escaped criminal running around. After three rings, I got his voicemail. "Hey, buddy. Just checking on if you've got any reports of a convict roaming our mountains. There might have been a sighting of someone with an assault weapon. Might mean nothing but I thought I'd check." I was about to hang up when I thought of something else. "There's one more thing. Run the name Lily Sanborn through your database and see if you come up with anything. Yeah, don't say it. I found her, kept her safe all night long but there's something weird about her. I think she's some kind of victim. Call me when you can."

After ending the call, I looked over at Sam. "What do you think, buddy? Is she gonna skip town?"

He whined and lay down on the seat, stretching his head over the console to my lap.

"Yeah, I think she's skipping town too. Oh, well." Oh, well, my ass. I liked the girl, more so than I wanted to admit, but I reminded myself I had no room in my life for wayward girls with dubious pasts.

Or any women for that matter.

Still, I could do her a favor. That wouldn't be so bad. What the hell? I found Scorpion's number, realizing I hadn't talked to him in months, maybe close to a year. I'd been to Raunchy Ride once. Not my thing. I just needed a cold beer, a stiff drink, and a few minutes watching some sports game. The bar scene didn't agree with me.

"Hey. My God. Is that really Maverick or an impersonator?" Cooper 'Scorpion' McKenzie snarked as soon as he answered. I'd known him from the ill begotten days of my youth, a good guy who'd gone into the Marines almost the same time I had. He ran with a crowd as tight as the ones I used to, men who'd served their country in one way or another, all broken and jaded. But he was a good guy.

"Uh-huh. And how's the entertainment man?"

"Busy as usual. Now, I know you're not calling about our hot band at the club."

"Hell, no. I saw a posting online that you need some help at the bar. Is that true?"

"You looking for a job?" he asked, already laughing his ass off.

"You couldn't handle me. I got a friend that I might have mentioned to that you're looking for some folks."

Scorpion chuckled again. He'd always been able to read through me. "A girl, huh? She must be something pretty special for you to be sending her my way. What's her name?"

"Lily Sanborn."

"Has she ever waited tables before? Or does she have a license to kill?"

"That rowdy, huh?" A part of me wanted to go back to the motel, demanding she tell me what the hell was going on. "I have no idea about most of her skills, but she's feisty and a looker."

"Depends on the night as far as the assholes who pop in. If she can handle you, then I guess she'd do just fine working here. When's she coming in?"

"I don't know if she is. I mentioned it, but she's a free spirit."

"Do you want me to let me know if she pops in?"

I thought about his question. What right did I have to check up on her? Why should I give a damn about anyone who wanted nothing to do with me? "Yeah, let me know."

"Will do. It's good to know you might be settling down."

"Very funny. Keep that to yourself."

He laughed. "Not a chance, partner."

I tossed the phone after ending the call, fighting to get her out of my mind.

She had her life.

I had mine.

I'd done what I could do. But if she stayed, all bets were off. I wanted the girl more than I should.

As I headed further away from the motel, something told me we'd meet again. Only I was worried that it would be under entirely different circumstances. I had no doubt the person she was terrified of was a man.

And he was out to get her. If my gut was right, he was the kind of asshole who wouldn't stop until he'd taken back what he believed belonged to him.

If he tried, he'd learn that in my world, those who attempted to hurt or destroy anyone I cared about faced an entirely different kind of punishment.

Then I'd drag him straight to hell myself.

CHAPTER 7

ily

"What do you think you're doing?"

The harsh barking sound was more brutal than usual. I tried not to jump, but Giovanni's voice instilled fear every time he got this way. "Just walking in the gardens." 'Gardens' was stretching what I'd called the strip of land surrounding his estate. His estate. It was my home too. While I'd seen a grounds company through the window of my prison, they never tended to the flower garden. Now the flowers were gangly, weeds taking over most of the area, but the vibrant colors were still beautiful. I'd only recently been given permission to go outside, although always under the watchful eye of his men.

"You know better than to stretch your boundaries, my stupid pet. Maybe I'll need to shorten your leash." He came closer, the evil grin on his face one I knew far too well.

I usually cowered, trying to prepare myself for his anger. When he touched me lovingly, rubbing the back of his knuckles across my cheek, I shivered, hating myself for once finding him attractive. He was a true monster in every way, the devil incarnate. He was simply missing the horns. To everyone else he was a respectable businessman, feared by many but loved by other women. I knew what he was made of, the ugliness that filled his soul.

I also knew what he was capable of. How my father had become involved with him I'd likely never know. Nor did it matter.

Shuddering, I closed my eyes, trying not to react any more than I already had.

When he suddenly wrapped his hand around my throat, I instantly couldn't breathe. He pulled me onto my toes, twisting my neck to an uncomfortable angle. Then he dropped his head so our lips were a few inches apart. "Listen up, stupid pet. You might think I don't know what you're planning but you're wrong. If you ever try and escape, you know what will happen. The hunt will be delicious."

I closed my eyes, doing everything I could to shove out the wretched memory. Giovanni always liked to threaten me with the hunt, even taking me to the woods flanking his house, the several acres of natural woodlands as terrifying as the rest of my surroundings. He'd filled my head with stories of the boobytraps he'd placed throughout the acreage: bear traps and hidden pits full of sharp spears and venomous snakes; trip wires that brought down machetes and fired off weapons. Then he'd share with me the previous hunts he and his men had indulged in, tracking down whatever enemy or person who'd betrayed them.

And he'd explain in vivid detail what he'd do when they were captured, the methods he'd use to maim then kill them.

The man was twisted.

But he wasn't here.

That's the day I'd decided to make him trust me. It had taken three weeks but as soon as I'd started attending functions with him, acting the part of his dutiful fiancée, he'd become less interested in keeping me locked down. While his goons normally followed me, the leash Giovanni had mentioned had been lengthened.

I remained in my truck, staring at the bar Maverick had suggested I try to get a job at. Since I wasn't new to waiting tables, it wouldn't be a stretch to make a career out of it for a little while. I just wasn't certain I should stay in Montana at all.

Don't let the bastards push you away. You're here for a reason.

How many times had I reminded myself of this very thing? Enough I shouldn't be hesitating at all. Well, at least if I made some money over a couple of weeks, that would help with wherever I decided to go if and when I found no evidence of my mother's existence. I'd called ahead, making an appointment with Scorpion. The least I could do was meet with him since he'd been nice enough to ask me to come in and talk.

Exhaling, I shoved aside my fears, climbing out of the truck. While it was early in the evening, the place was already hopping, the music blaring out the doors making me smile. As I walked closer, I wasn't certain if I was under- or overdressed. I'd found a thrift store, thrilled that I'd snatched up a hot little denim skirt and sexy blouse in emerald green. They'd even had a few pairs of softly used cowboy boots in my size. Did I look the part of a cowgirl waitress? How the hell would I know.

At least it gave me a laugh as I walked inside. Holy crap. The place was huge, the exterior of the building deceptive. I felt out of place, not only because I was the only chick in the bar but also because of my attire. Within seconds, there were at least eight hungry men sizing me up like filet mignon. I did my best to ignore them as I walked further in, wondering if I could even do this.

When Maverick had mentioned *Roadhouse*, one of my favorite movies, I'd expected to see a barbed wire fence enclosing where the band performed and half broken tables from unruly customers. I was shocked that the place reminded me of something I'd seen on the Grand Ole Opry. There were gorgeous light fixtures everywhere, and wooden tables that had been carved out of some expensive woods. There were two bars, both massive in design. And the location where the band played was huge with an intricate lighting system.

This was no cowboy joint but a country bar that would do Nashville proud. I headed for the closest bar, still feeling all eyes on me. While they should make me feel creepy, they had the opposite effect. I had a feeling that if I got hired and somebody messed with me, I'd have a few burly men coming to my rescue.

I waited to catch the bartender's eye, noticing an electric bull on the other side of the room. I could imagine Maverick on it right now, spinning around. No, that wasn't true. I was certain he'd make fun of it, calling people pussies who dared go on the ride. If he were here, maybe I'd try it out just to piss him off.

My thoughts drifted back and forth from the passionate night we'd shared to the ugliness that constituted my life. I'd enjoyed being with him, even if he was a gruff son of a gun who thought his shit didn't stink.

"Can I help you?" The voice was female.

I spun around, forced to accept that I look ridiculous in comparison to the girl behind the bar. She wore a tight pair of black jeans and a snug red tee shirt that left nothing to the imagination, Raunchy Ride's logo smack in the middle. "I have an appointment with Scorpion."

She gave me a hard onceover then nodded toward a neon sign over to the left. "He's in his office."

"Thanks." I was more nervous than I'd been when interviewing for my first job as a vet tech what seemed like a lifetime ago. As I headed toward the hallway, I took another look around. The restaurant and bar were lively. I could only imagine when it was filled with people. Before I had a chance to knock on the door, it was thrown open, a huge man barreling into me.

"Oh, shit," he growled, immediately backing away. "Are you okay? I didn't see you there."

"I'm fine. Just a little startled."

"You must be Lily. Right on time. I like you already. Go ahead and sit down."

"Aren't your employees on time?" I did so, now wishing the skirt wasn't so short.

He laughed as he invited me inside. "You'd be surprised around here. The waitress whose position I'm filling ran off with the guitar player from the last band. I doubt I'll hire them again cause you're pretty enough the damn bass player will try claiming you."

I must have had my eyes opened wide because he held up his left hand, wiggling his fingers to show off his wedding band.

"I'm sorry. I'm just… a little skittish being in a new place."

"You don't need to worry about me. Not only is my wife the promoter for the club but Maverick would fucking kick my ass."

I reacted badly and immediately, jerking up. "I'm sorry. I was very blunt and clear to him that I won't take handouts from anyone. *Ever.*" I realized I'd put a little too much emphasis on the last word, but I was serious about it. Why couldn't Maverick just mind his own business? If I saw him again, I planned on giving him a piece of my mind.

"Whoa, little filly. Hold on here. I assure you that I'm not into giving a job just cause you're a pretty face or because

Maverick and I go way back. That's not me. Plus, while the man was looking out for you, one of the nicer things he's done in his life, trust me in that, you don't want to get involved with him."

I wasn't certain if he was tossing out bait, but I took it anyway. "Why is that?"

"He's not good with women." He was straight and to the point and I liked that about him. "Now, tell me about your skills."

After easing back into the chair, I gave him a limited rundown, even tossing out I'd been in college during the time I'd waited tables. After I stopped talking, he gave me a pointed look.

"Can you handle rowdy cowboys? I have a staff of bouncers, one assigned to the employees, but I can't stop all the tourists and country star wannabes from coming in and creating a ruckus. You gotta stand up for yourself. You're a tiny little thing. That's why I ask."

I stood up, cocking my hip and giving him a hard glare. "Trust me, cowboy. If any of the rowdy customers get in my face, I'll make certain they realize that respecting women is in their best interest. And I'll do that using my three years of martial arts training."

He grinned, his eyes lighting up. Then he moved to a locked cabinet, spinning the combination lock. After opening it, he grabbed something, tossing two tee shirts in my direction. "I love your chutzpa and I can see why Maverick adores you. When can you start?"

"Anytime. Now, if I had on jeans." I managed to laugh easily, thankful that at least I'd be making some money, maybe able to get out of the hole in the wall motel sooner versus later.

"I tell you what. Why don't you shadow the bartender and some of the waitstaff for a couple hours. Then I'll buy you dinner and a couple drinks of your choice on the house. You need to taste the food as well."

It was an offer I couldn't refuse. Besides, I didn't want to go back to the motel to spend another night alone. "It's a deal."

"Why don't you go ahead and change shirts," he offered, grinning afterward. "That way you'll fit right in. We'll deal with all the paperwork later."

When I swallowed hard, he seemed to notice my discomfort.

"Is there something you need to tell me, Lily?" When I hesitated, he came closer, easing onto the edge of his desk. "Look, I've been in tough spots before. Okay? I know all about trying to find a new life. But it's best if you tell me what's going on so I can help you if possible."

Could I trust this man? I wasn't certain but if I didn't, I'd be out of a job before I started. "No one can know I'm here or who I am."

He lifted a single eyebrow, waiting for a few seconds to see if I'd continue. "Okay. I'm not in the habit of giving out personal information anyway. You're not an escaped criminal, are you?"

At least I could laugh. If only it were that easy. "Not by a long shot. I haven't even had a parking ticket."

Scorpion nodded several times. "Alright then. Your business is your business. Just don't make it mine and we'll get along just fine."

Relief flooded my mind, even if I remained anxious. "Don't worry. I'm a private person."

"Then get to work and welcome aboard. Oh, and I'll pay you for tonight, but in cash. At least until we get everything set up. That okay with you?"

The man was a godsend.

I don't know what I was expecting, but it certainly wasn't to feel comfortable in the environment after only thirty minutes. As soon as the female bartender knew I was a new employee, she changed her tune, becoming helpful, including pointing out which regular customers would give me heartburn. While not all of the waitresses welcomed me with open arms, I was able to hold my own against their sneering glares.

This wasn't what I'd expected out of my life, but I had a job and from what I could tell, one where I'd earn decent money. For now, it was good enough. The band was about ready to start and I was shocked at who was playing in the place. They were a hot commodity, winning a Grammy a couple of years back. Everyone in the crowd of now hundreds seemed excited.

Then time started to fly, some of the waitresses allowing me to run food orders out to the tables. Within three hours, I was exhausted, more so than I'd expected. But I felt good about myself for the first time in as long as I could remember.

I noticed Scorpion out of the corner of my eye, his grin as wide as before. As he approached, he was interrupted by several customers, two of them shaking his hand. When he finally made it to where I was standing, he took a few seconds to watch the band. "What do you think?"

"It's nothing like I expected."

"I get that a lot. It's a work in progress," he told me.

"You should be happy. It's amazing." I was genuinely excited, the tone of my voice entirely different.

"Why don't you take a load off and grab a drink. Order anything you want and as I said, it's on the house."

"You don't know how much I appreciate it."

"Here's your earnings for the night."

When he handed me a wad of cash, I was floored. I'd never even asked how much I'd be making, although I assumed most would be in tips, and I hadn't made any. There had to be two hundred dollars in twenty-dollar bills. "Wait a minute. I didn't earn this."

"You'd be surprised how much money folks earn around here. That is if they hustle. You helped a few gals do that and they offered up a portion of their tips in return. Plus, I do pay a pretty decent hourly wage."

I wasn't the kind of girl to cry over everything, including sappy movies, but a mist formed over my eyes, and it was the second time in a couple of days I was terribly embarrassed. "Thank you."

"Don't mention it. There's more where that came from."

Whether he was trying to help out a waif who landed on his doorstep or telling me the truth, I wasn't going to shove it back in his face. But from now on, I'd earn my place in this world.

If only for a little while.

He winked, as if knowing that I was somewhat desperate then moved back into the crowd. I took a deep breath, finding the only open barstool nestled all the way up against the wall near the restrooms. It gave me a perfect perch to view the crowd while allowing me to feel anonymous. After ordering a glass of wine, I closed my eyes and said a small prayer of thanks. I wasn't religious, but it seemed like the appropriate thing to do. The band was taking a break, the noise level high. I heard laughter coming from everywhere, people having a good time.

I longed to find that one day, just being able to enjoy a night out without fear of being seen.

Or caught.

"Bourbon. Neat."

The deep voice resonated through me like a tidal wave of heated water cascading across my naked skin. I'd recognize it anywhere. Every inch of my body responded as well, my skin prickling and my nipples swelling. My reaction was ridiculous, but it left my mouth dry and my heart racing.

When I opened my eyes, I tried not to react openly. Maverick had crowded in next to me. For some reason, it was like I was noticing for the first time just how insanely gorgeous he was.

And how huge.

I'd been correct in my earlier assessment. He had to be six foot five, his arm muscles accentuated by the leather jacket he was wearing. He'd trimmed his beard and for some reason, I thought it made his jaw more pronounced, adding to his sex appeal.

What are you doing?

The little voice could nag me all she wanted but I was allowed to enjoy delicious eye candy. As long as that's all I succumbed to. I was befuddled as to what to say to him.

I didn't have an immediate chance, another guy appearing from the shadows. "Hey, sugar. Would you like to dance?"

Maverick bristled instantly but remained quiet.

I spun around on the barstool, trying to be polite. "No, but thank you."

"Oh, come on. One dance. A lady as beautiful as you shouldn't be alone," the guy continued.

I was about ready to say I wasn't alone then felt awkward. "I said no."

The poor asshole made the mistake of putting his hand on my arm, almost pulling me off the barstool.

That's when Maverick jerked into action. He had his hand wrapped around the guy's throat, shoving him against the wall so fast I blinked and missed it. Then he slammed the dude twice more, inching closer.

"The lady doesn't want to dance with you, asshole. Get it through your thick, fucking head."

"Maverick," I said as I moved behind him. "I can do this."

Maverick snarled with the mystery man gurgled, clawing at my savior's arms. A few people had gathered around, and I was certain they were going to start cheering.

"Shitholes like this need a reminder in how to treat a lady." Maverick growled in a low, husky voice and the poor guy looked like he was going to piss in his pants.

"Maverick. Come on," I admonished, but secretly inside I was thrilled he'd come to my defense.

Dear God, I didn't need more light to know the poor guy was being choked to death.

"Say you won't do it again." Maverick was enjoying every second of squeezing the life out of the man.

The guy sputtered, flailing his arms as he tried to speak. "Na... I... won't."

"Let him go, Maverick." Scorpion appeared out of nowhere, leaning against the bar with a grin on his face. "He's harmless, albeit without manners. Frank. Just go home and sleep it off."

Maverick refused to let go. I finally got in his face, planting my hands on my hips. "Hey, tracker boy. Let. Him. Go."

That seemed to do the trick and Maverick finally released his hold, cursing under his breath. "Do it again and you and me are going to have a problem. Frank. Now, say you're sorry."

"I'm sa... sorry. I'm sorry." Frank coughed and wheezed, keeping his eyes pinned on Maverick. I had to admit I was amused at the whole thing.

"Not to me, asshole. To the lady."

Frank spun on his heels, his body swaying. "I'm sorry. Never again. I promise."

"Go on, Frank," Scorpion chided.

Frank stumbled away and I heard at least four people clapping. A wave of heat rushed to my face. No man had ever taken up for me, let alone been prepared to start a fight.

Scorpion clapped Maverick on the back. "Lily is a tough girl, buddy. I think she can handle herself."

"Yeah? Well, she shouldn't need to."

Scorpion threw me a grin. "I'll leave you two lovebirds alone."

"We're not lovebirds!" I called after him before giving Maverick an evil eye. "You can't go after every man who looks at me."

"Yeah? I'll do what I want, princess."

The big lugging mass of a man was stubborn as all get-out. Huffing, I flopped down on the stool, pretending to ignore him.

He grabbed the drink that had been delivered while he was being the big he-man, sucking back a huge gulp.

Neither one of us said anything, but I could tell he was still seething. I realized I'd been holding my breath, trying to look cool when I felt like mush inside.

"I really can handle myself," I said to him, unable to look in his direction.

"It ain't you I'm worried about."

"You didn't sign off as my protector. And I didn't ask you to become one."

Exhaling, he swirled the glass, shaking his head slowly. "You're right."

"Then why don't you just go?"

"Is that what you want?"

I wasn't entirely certain what I wanted at this point. As I rolled my index finger around the rim of the wineglass, I sensed he was watching me intently. He deserved an honest answer. "No. I don't want you to leave."

"Good answer."

"Can we just talk? You know, like friends?" Friends. Who was I kidding? He wasn't the kind of man to have a single friend. He'd always be a brooding loner, a man who hated all social activities.

He slowly turned his head, the same sly smile I'd seen a half dozen times sliding across his chiseled face. "Fine. Then how's this? How's work?"

The man was infuriating, pushing every button. A part of me wanted to berate him, another wanted to wrap my arms around his neck, kissing him for hours. I was a complete, utter mess.

"I'm not really working. I mean I was for a couple hours. But good."

"Glad to hear it." His words were clipped, his usual grumpy self shining through.

"You told him to hire me." The rebellious girl wanted to chastise him, but I couldn't seem to find the right words. If he was going to act like a bear, then I could counter him.

Shrugging, he took another gulp. "I just said if he didn't hire you that he'd be missing out on a true gem. Nothing more. The rest was up to you. Seems like you landed on your feet."

While every syllable out of his mouth was gruff, I sensed he was being genuine. "Thank you, Maverick."

"Yup."

We remained quiet and I'd never felt so nervous around anyone before. "Are you tracking anyone?"

"Not right now. Do you plan on getting lost again?" He threw me another look, his eyes floating to the way the tight tee shirt fit around my breasts.

I was trembling from his expression of desire, my mind shifting to all the filthy things we'd done. And all the ones I wanted to happen again. "If I did, would you save me again?"

He seemed to contemplate the answer then turned toward me, crowding my space. "In a heartbeat, but I might remind you that taking chances isn't in your best interest."

"Some of them are. Without taking chances, you might not find what you're looking for."

"Is that right?"

I nodded slowly, a lump forming in my throat. "Yes."

He polished off his drink, placing the glass onto the bar with a thud. "You still on the clock?"

"No. Just getting ready to go back home." Home. What a ridiculous word for the place I was staying, but it kept me with a roof over my head.

"If you're staying in town, you need a better place."

"I doubt there are options for what I can afford."

"I know a guy. Can't promise anything but he rents out some decent little places. They ain't much but they're better than the fucking Yellowstone Motel."

"I won't take handouts."

Snorting, he managed to inch even closer, the scent of his aftershave permeating every inch of me, igniting another round of dirty thoughts. "And I don't give them. You can take it or leave it. I'll just make a phone call."

"Okay."

When he backed away, yanking off his jacket and shoving it across the bar, I couldn't seem to take my eyes off him.

Then without hesitation or asking me a question, he slid his arm around me then pulled the wineglass from my hand, placing it next to his empty glass. "Come with me."

"Where are we going?"

"I ain't gonna tie you up if that's what you're thinking. Yet, anyway. But the night is young and it depends on your bad attitude." He wasn't going to take no for an answer, wrapping his fingers around mine and pulling me into the middle of the crowd. As the band started to play, I couldn't have been more shocked when he led me to the dancefloor. A man like him danced? I had to be in an alternative universe.

"Bad attitude? Look who's talking."

I could tell he was having fun with this. Damn him. When I tried to pull out of his hold, his grip tightened. "You should know by now, sugar, that you aren't going anywhere until I say so."

My God. The man had been born in another century. But his aggressive words kept my pussy quivering, my panties damp.

When he swung me around to face him, I pressed my palm against his chest. "I'm not good at this." I'd loved dancing in my younger days, going out with friends often. I wasn't certain I could ever feel the same way again.

"Do I look like I'm the kind of man who does this on a regular basis?" He pulled me close, so much so his thick bulge pressed against my stomach.

"No. I guess not."

"Then we'll just sway a bit. I figured this wouldn't spook you."

"Should it? Should I be scared of you?"

His grin was mischievous. "Yeah, you should, but I think you like that about me."

"Who said I liked you at all?" I slid my arm around his neck, running my fingers through his thick hair. It was easy to be playful with him, which continued to surprise me. I'd tried to push him away but the gravitational pull existing between us refused to allow that to happen.

"Good point. I guess I'll need to try harder." He kept his head lowered, enough so if I rose onto my tiptoes, our lips would mesh together.

It had been rare I'd danced with a man, and his absolute domination of me, his control in everything he did should be a complete turnoff, but it wasn't. Within seconds, I felt the rhythm as I used to, enjoying the closeness. Maybe too much. He and I weren't destined to be anything together, certainly not for the long haul. If I was a smart girl, I'd push him away permanently. When he found out what I'd been through and the danger I placed him in by being near him, he'd shut the door between us.

But it was impossible to resist his animal magnetism, the feel of just being in his arms. I was vaguely aware the music had changed, but it didn't matter. I managed to block out almost everything else but the moment we were sharing.

Then I felt a horrible tightness in my chest as the monster's words reverberated in the back of my mind.

"Once a whore, always a whore."

A rush of anxiety jetted through me, the sensations so suffocating that I quickly shoved him away, breaking the hold. The moment I tried to rush off the dancefloor, Maverick grabbed my arm, jerking me against him, sliding his hand down my back, cupping my buttocks.

"You're not going anywhere. You're safe with me, Lily. I ain't gonna let anyone hurt you." There was such defiance as well as assurance in his words that I almost broke out into sobs. But as his eyes pierced mine, his hold even tighter, I melted into him, hungering for the same passion we'd shared before.

"I'm damaged," I whispered, uncertain he'd heard me.

"So am I." The three little words were exactly what I needed to hear. The second he captured my mouth, holding our lips in place, I felt all the fears slipping away. I wasn't a fool. This was still just a moment in time, but one so beautiful that fighting what had furrowed inside since I'd met him would be useless.

He took his time, his tender actions igniting more than just a heightened layer of passion. There was no one else in the room, no sounds permeating the ragged beating of my heart. There was just the two of us. As he slipped his tongue inside, dominating mine, I arched my back. The kiss became a wildfire within seconds, and I felt as if I was spinning out of control. He held me so close that I could feel his scattered heartbeats, could sense his desire increasing with every passing second.

When he finally broke the kiss, he pressed his forehead against mine, his chest rising and falling. Then he grabbed my hand, his eyes narrowing. "Baby. You're comin' with me."

CHAPTER 8

*M*averick

I'd told myself at least ten times to stay the hell away from her. I wasn't good for anyone, especially someone as vulnerable as Lily. All I'd done was think about her in the last twenty-four hours. Her lush body. Her voluptuous lips.

The way my cock felt being inside of her.

The moment the asshole drunk had pawed her, all bets were off. She was mine. No other man was ever going to touch her again.

I knew my attitude and my actions were as close to being Neanderthal as humanly possible, but she obviously needed someone to watch out for her.

There was a mystery surrounding her and I continued to sense danger, but I didn't give a shit at this point. Maybe I was thinking with my dick, but the increased need when I was within a few feet of her was like a ticking time bomb ready to explode. Devouring her was the only possible option. Just seeing her in the tight miniskirt was enough to keep my blood pumping, tightening my balls.

"I can't," Lily insisted.

"Yeah, you can. I'm not taking no for an answer." The fire in her eyes made me want to drag her into the bathroom of the bar, fucking her like a wild animal, but she deserved better.

She shook her head, dragging her tongue across her lips. Then she nodded once.

As if the woman had a choice in the matter.

Chuckling, I tossed a couple of bills on the bar, grabbing my coat and waiting as she'd gone to get her things. Then I'd ignored her cries that she needed to get her truck, planting her inside my Dodge Ram instead. I half expected her defiant streak would come alive, the woman doing her best to get away from me, but she remained in the seat as I climbed in.

Sam immediately tried to jump over the console into her lap. To hear her laughing brought a smile to my face.

"You do take him everywhere," she said as he continuously licked her face.

"If a place doesn't take dogs, I won't go there." I started the engine, unable to keep a grin off my face. It had been a long time since I'd smiled. She was the reason.

I sensed her heated gaze. "I like that about you."

"At least you like something."

"This isn't a good idea." Her voice suddenly seemed so small. I preferred the rebellious woman who fought me every step of the way.

"Do I look like I care?"

"I'm bad news."

"Damaged and bad news. Are you trying to keep me away, Lily? It ain't gonna work if you are. I already told you once, but I'll say it again. I take what I want and no one and nothing can stop me." Whoever had abused her in the past had stripped away her ability to trust, mostly in herself. Maybe I was a fool to think I could heal even a small part of her, but the protective side of me wanted to try.

"Just take me to my motel." There was no conviction in her tone.

I laughed and swung out of the parking lot. "That's not happening, sweetheart."

"You're an incorrigible man."

"I've been called a lot worse." I laughed again as I rolled down the road, heading to my second house.

"I bet you have. So, where are you taking me, cowboy?"

"You'll see."

I was able to keep the grin as I drove. I hadn't expected her to take the job. I'd almost convinced myself it was better if she'd left. Then Scorpion had called, letting me know she'd made an appointment with him, and I'd headed to my parents' old place, making plans I knew I shouldn't. But she'd crawled under my skin far enough I wasn't finished with my exploration. The thought pushed my cock against my jeans.

Damn, I had it bad for the girl.

She remained quiet, enjoying Sam's heavy head on her shoulder. The two of them had bonded and I would hate to see what happened to him if she disappeared suddenly. I'd tried looking her up myself, but with almost no information, short of getting her fingerprints or if she confided in me, I doubted I'd learn the source of her terror.

At least for tonight, I was shoving all the garbage out of my mind.

When I pulled into my parents' old neighborhood, she leaned forward. "The houses are really huge."

"Yup."

"You own one?"

"Yup."

"Wow. You're a man of mystery and intrigue," she said, her tone teasing.

As I pulled down a long driveway, she stiffened. "What's wrong?"

"It just reminds of something."

"What?" I glanced over at her.

She half laughed but when she pressed her fingers through her hair, I noticed her hand was shaking. "Just an old acquaintance I couldn't stand. His driveway was similar."

His. At least I'd received confirmation that the person who was derailing her life was a man. "I assure you that the house isn't like anything you've seen before." My parents had eclectic tastes and I hadn't gotten around to redecorating it yet.

When I pulled in front of the massive front door, she stiffened. The second clue was whoever had forced her to run was wealthy.

"This belonged to my parents."

"Belonged to. I'm very sorry about your mother dying of cancer. You didn't say anything about your dad."

I cut the engine. "That's not what she died of, although the disease would have killed her eventually. My Pops was determined to check off everything on her bucket list before that happened. They'd been to dozens of countries, but never Switzerland. They were on a skiing trip and perished in an avalanche."

"Whoa. Are you kidding?"

"I wish I were. But they lived and died the way they wanted. Free spirits. I'm surprised they owned a house at all. I haven't figured out what to do with it."

"I'm so sorry."

As soon as I opened the door, Sam jumped over the seats, shoving her into the dashboard in his effort to scramble out from my side. She started laughing again and the sound was like sweet music. "No reason to be sorry." The dome light from the truck created an aura around her and my hunger was off the charts. I wouldn't be able to wait for any additional conversation or romantic interludes. I was far too aroused.

As I grabbed her things from the backseat, she slowly climbed out, walking around the front of the truck. Her face was pensive.

"I still am." She moved closer, pressing her hand against my chest. "You won't let anybody get close to you. Will you?"

"Will you?"

"I didn't realize we were keeping score."

"Maybe we are, but not in the way you're thinking. Come on." I watched her reaction as she walked inside, immediately pressing her hand over her mouth and laughing. "As I said, my parents were different creatures." Between the red leather sofa and chair, the garish rugs on the floor, and the vivid accent walls all throughout the house, you'd never know both my parents grew up on massive ranches.

Everything to me was ridiculously outlandish from the bizarre lamps that likely cost a fortune to the artwork they'd found in various countries. I'd wanted to gut it and start all over again because there wasn't a soul in Montana who'd buy the place. Somehow, I couldn't force myself to lose what was left of my parents.

As strange as they were.

"I love it. It's so... you," she cooed, amusement in her tone.

I dropped her bag, lifting an eyebrow then sending Sam out of the room. "Uh-huh. Oh, yeah?" The woman had no idea what she was doing by teasing me.

She turned around to face me, a mischievous look on her face. As she nodded, she allowed her gaze to fall. "Oh. Yeah."

Every section of my body—muscles, tendons, and every red blood cell—was ignited, the flames searing my skin. The need to claim her, make her mine burrowed deep into my bones, the ache I felt increasing every second I didn't have my cock buried deep inside.

I took two long strides in her direction, gripping her wrist and yanking her toward me. The feel of her snuggled next to me poked the bear inside, but her perfume was intoxicating, the scent sweeter than the smell of ripe peaches on a warm spring day. She tried to fight me as she'd done before but there was no conviction behind her actions. Yet she playfully slapped me, using the momentum to jerk herself free, charging away from me as if she owned the place.

All I could do was grin. When I fisted her hair, she acted as if I was the enemy all over again.

"What do you think you're doing, cowboy?" she purred, daring to tease me by sliding her hand down my chest, toying with my aching cock.

"First, I'm gonna kiss you. Then I'm gonna fuck you. And after that, I'm gonna drive my cock into that tight asshole of yours." I crushed my mouth over hers, my mind foggy as she wiggled against me. She continued to struggle, which tossed gasoline onto the already raging fire. I held her tightly against me, fisting her long strands. It was impossible not to savor every second of kissing her lush lips.

The way she wiggled against me, the mere essence of her made me long to devour every inch of her. I swept my tongue back and forth, sucking on hers after a few seconds. Every moan that escaped her mouth, every shift of her body against mine made it impossible to think clearly.

Lily knew exactly what she was doing to me, taking every opportunity to try to maintain control. We'd need to make certain after tonight she knew that wasn't going to happen.

When I broke the kiss, I nipped her bottom lip, but she slammed her hands against my chest, pushing me away. Then she lunged at me, ripping at my jacket, fighting the leather to get it off. I couldn't help but laugh, the sound bordering on evil. "Be careful, sweetheart. You don't know what you're doing."

"Oh, I know exactly what I'm doing." As soon as the coat started to fall to the floor, she ripped at my shirt, tugging it over my chest and head, tossing it halfway across the room.

"You're not in charge, princess." When I grabbed her tee shirt with both hands, acting as if I was going to tear it off her, she gasped.

"No! Scorpion will kill me."

"You should have thought of that before teasing me." While a part of me wanted to follow through with my evil thoughts, I ripped at the hem, spinning her around and easily maneuvering it over her head. When I wrapped one arm around her shoulders, keeping her from going anywhere, she had the nerve to kick me in the shin with her cheap cowboy boot. "You'll need to do better than that."

"Don't push me." To see her this playful shocked the hell out of me. I unsnapped her bra with a single finger, surprising her enough she gasped. She didn't move as I slowly slid one strap down her arm then the other. But as I held her close, her breathing became more rapid than before. I couldn't help myself, lowering my head, nuzzling against her neck. When I nipped her earlobe, she tugged off the lacy bra, holding it out to the side for several seconds before allowing the material to drop from her fingers.

I cupped her shoulders, digging my fingers into her skin as I dragged my tongue up and down the nape of her neck. She shuddered in my hold, keeping her head to the side. I noticed a few goosebumps popping along her naked skin, and the sight of her taut nipples made my mouth water.

I slowly rolled my arms to her chest, flicking my fingers back and forth across her hardened buds. She lolled her head against my chest, her mouth pursed. Every sound she made was breathless, her entire body trembling. I could do this for hours, but I doubted either one of us would last that long, our hunger too intense.

The second I pinched her nipples, she moaned, her body swaying. "That… hurts."

"Imagine what else I'll do to you," I answered before raking my teeth all the way down her neck.

"Oh, you are so bad."

"I'm just getting started." I nipped her earlobe, twisting her nipples painfully. I was addicted to her scent as well as every scattered sound she made.

"Mmm... We'll see about that."

She kicked me again with enough force this time it broke the connection. Truth be told, I let her have the advantage. I wanted to see what she'd do. I didn't have long to wait.

She dropped to her knees in front of me, immediately reaching for my belt. This time, she didn't fumble with the buckle, staring up at me as she unfastened it, licking her lips the entire time.

When she unzipped my jeans, freeing my cock, I placed my hand on her head. "And what exactly do you think you're going to do?"

She gave me a wicked grin then wrapped her hand around the base. "This."

* * *

Lily

As I pulled his delicious cock into my mouth, swirling my tongue back and forth, Maverick threw his head back.

"Jesus Christ," he muttered, panting like a dog after a few seconds.

He had his hand on the top of my head, massaging my scalp aimlessly. I had a feeling he was already floating in a moment of rapture, barely able to concentrate. Good. I wanted him on edge, salivating for all of me.

I took my time, rolling my fingers around the base of his cock, creating enough friction his body was already shaking. I was still surprised that being with him allowed me to feel free, as if I didn't have a care in the world. While it couldn't be any further from the truth, tonight it just didn't matter.

As I jerked his jeans down even further, he stared down at me with lust in his eyes. They managed to twinkle in the unusual lighting, illuminating his entire gorgeous physique as if he were a god. I opened my mouth wider, trying to relax my throat as I sucked on his shaft, immediately pressing my hand between his legs. The moment I wrapped my fingers around his swollen balls, he fisted my hair, his chest heaving.

"Be careful teasing me."

I adored the way he was trying to take possession, his entire body tense from the pleasure I was providing. I'd wanted to do this since he'd dragged me around the dancefloor. Then again, we'd both had carnal activities on our minds.

As soon I took him down another two inches, struggling to breathe, he took over, pushing down my head until my bottom lip rested against my hand. I squeezed his testicles with enough force he issued several growls.

"Damn it, woman. So hot." His words were almost slurred, and it had nothing to do with alcohol.

As he started to fuck my mouth in earnest, rolling onto the balls of his boots, I closed my eyes. The tip was shoved against the back of my throat, pre-cum already trickling. The taste of him was sweet yet tangy and I continued to sweep my tongue back and forth. I knew he wouldn't allow himself to come in my mouth, his other needs far too potent.

Seconds later, he proved me right, yanking me to my feet. Then he pointed his index finger at my face, shaking his head. "Do not move."

I folded my arms, giving him a heated look as he struggled to remove his boots and jeans. Before he had a chance to toss them aside, I backed away, teasing him even more by unbuttoning my jean skirt, peeling away the two sides and allowing him to see a hint of my crimson thong. Then I grabbed at my boots, not nearly as graceful as I'd hoped in fighting to get them off. When I tossed them aside, I heard Sam whimper from somewhere behind us.

Maverick let off a heady growl, the sound savage and delicious. The man now completely naked, I swallowed hard as he slowly lowered his head. "Take it off," he commanded.

"Nope."

"Then I'll rip it off."

"Not if you can't catch me." I took off running through the house, trying to find a place to hide. When I threw my head over my shoulder a few seconds later, I was surprised I didn't see him on my heels. I bit back a laugh, still shocked that I was enjoying being around him as much as I was.

Maybe he'd become my respite, allowing me the ability to pretend I was someone else.

I raced into a room, trying to figure out which way to go. When I thought I heard him, I bolted through another door into the kitchen. I backed up by a few inches. Then a delicious fragrance wafted into my system.

That was a split second before he tossed me over his shoulder, immediately yanking at the tough denim.

"You're so mean." I pummeled my fists against his back as he easily tugged the skirt down my legs. No amount of my kicking stopped him from being able to rip it off. When he started walking through the house, I could swear he was whistling. What? I lifted my head, trying to figure out where he was going. The house was huge, designed almost as if a maze.

I continued smacking my fists into his back, fighting hard enough I almost managed to slip out of his hold.

"Eh. Bad girl." He cracked his hand on my bottom several times, the sound just as startling as his action.

"Stop it."

"Nope. You need to learn."

"Oh, you. I'll get you for this." As he brought his hand down several more times, I was suddenly breathless, crazy numbers of stars floating in front of my eyes.

"We'll see," he growled, resuming whistling some tune. There was no doubt he was enjoying himself tremendously.

I jerked up, gasping for air as real pain tore through me. He wasn't kidding with what he was doing, trying to remind me that he was the big man. When he stopped short, I struggled to find out what he was doing. Then I heard a sound and felt the cold night air wafting in.

The second he walked outside, I was floored, shuddering immediately.

"What are you doing?" I asked, pushing against his back to try to see anything.

"You'll see." He kept walking. He kept whistling. "Oh, you better close your eyes and hold your nose."

"What? Why?" Then I realized why and shrieked just as he leapt into the air and almost as if in slow motion, he dropped us both into the still, turquoise waters of a massive pool. I'd never been a fan of the water, mostly because I hadn't been around it, never taken on vacations to the beach.

Everything shifted to slow motion as my feet hit first. I expected an icy realm but as we tumbled down, down, down I was shocked that the water was warm, almost soothing.

Maverick never let me go as we were plunged into darkness. As soon as the momentum stopped, I struggled to free myself. He let me go and I followed my instinct, raking my arms through the water as I tried to head to the surface. When I burst through, I gasped for air. I was going to give him a piece of my mind. I spun around, expecting him to be right behind me, grinning like the wicked, teasing man he was.

But he wasn't there. He wasn't anywhere.

While the water was crystal clear, festive lights shimmering from the bottom, I still couldn't see him. "Maverick. Maverick!" What if he'd hit his head? I turned all the way around again, finally fighting my way through the water toward the other side. There was a waterfall and fake rocks. Oh, dear God. He'd killed himself. "Maverick!"

I could swim, my skills were rusty, but I wasn't going to allow him to die. I dove under the water, trying to find him, holding my breath until my chest ached. When I was forced to come to the surface, I was near panic mode. No. No. The pool was huge. He could be anywhere. Why didn't the reflective lights show me where he was? Maybe he was trapped. There were bridges over the pool, another lagoon-style area at the end. And a damn waterfall. Who had these people been? The richest folks in Montana, that was for certain.

The waterfall. I swam closer, trying to keep the panic from settling in. When I was a few feet away, I held my breath and dived under.

Seconds later, I could feel a pair of hands gripping my arms and by instinct I struggled, fighting whoever was holding me. When I was pulled to the surface, spun around one hundred eighty degrees, my reaction wasn't what I'd expected it to be. Relief rushed through me seeing Maverick's face. Then anger rolled in beside it and I started punching his chest. "You asshole. You son of a bitch."

"Whoa. Whoa," Maverick said, laughing as he fought to grab my hands, spinning me around close to the waterfall. We were behind it, a series of shimmering lights highlighting the cascading water. "I'm right here. I was teasing you."

"That's not fair. I thought you were hurt. I thought you might be dead. I thought..." As my chest rose and fell, the adrenaline rush kicking my butt, I cupped his face, shaking my head. "Don't you ever do that to me again."

He slowly lowered his gaze. "I won't leave you."

I pressed my lips to his, digging my fingers into his skin. I'd never felt so horrid or so afraid for another human being. It didn't make any sense. I didn't know him. I certainly couldn't care about him, but I did. My heart racing, I wrapped one arm around him, clinging to him as I tangled my fingers in his hair.

The kiss was more powerful than any before, my emotions all over the place as he thrust his tongue inside. He continued to spin us around, pushing us closer to the waterfall. As the spray trickled over me, I shivered in his arms. Then I felt his hand ripping at my thong, managing to tug it off in seconds. As he pressed his cock against my stomach, I realized I'd never wanted a man as much as I did this brawny rogue who'd captured a part of me I'd long since thought dead.

Within seconds, we were both frantic, our hunger knowing no bounds. I managed to wrap my hand around his cock, shifting far enough away from his heated body to place the tip against my pussy. He slid his arm under my bottom, jerking me against him, filling me completely. My muscles stretched, clamping around the thick invasion. I was electrified by the moment, more so than I'd been before.

He was all male, proving that he was very much in control of me. When he broke the kiss, we both panted, trying to catch our breath. I laughed then immediately bit down on his lower lip, growling as I shifted my head back and forth. He pulled out, leaving only the tip inside, driving into me again. I was surprised how the water made the sensations entirely different, my mind a blur as he repeated the action.

There was no way for him to be rough, the water forbidding it, but as he thrust in and out, I was immediately thrown into a powerful moment of bliss.

Maverick wrapped his hand around the back of my neck, holding me in place as soon as I leaned back enough to gaze into his eyes. "This is beautiful."

"Mmm… Yes, you are."

"I can't really swim."

"Baby, you won't need to. I'm right here."

I pressed my fist against his chest all over again, closing my eyes. "Who are you? Who are you really?"

"I already told you. A man who doesn't like to take no for an answer."

"Mmm… I'll keep that in mind."

As I lifted my hand to his face, spreading my fingers open as I lightly touched him, he narrowed his eyes. "Who's chasing you, Lily?"

The question surprised me and I immediately tried to pull away. "Nobody. You're making too much out of it."

"You don't need to lie to me. I can and will protect you."

"No, you can't. No one can." Just admitting the few words, showing the anguish I felt inside was terrifying and I knew he was going to press me for more information. But he took a deep breath, his eyes darkening as he continued fucking me.

"I will find out and when I do, they'll die by my hands." His words were gruff, full of rage, and I believed him.

There was no more talking, no more grilling me for answers as he filled me, pushing me closer and closer to nirvana. I entwined my feet, raking my fingers through his wet hair. I couldn't remember the last time I'd felt so much joy, freed from the chains that had held me down for so long.

"You're so handsome." I tickled his chin through his beard, laughing as his eyes lit up. "I wonder what you'd look like without all that fur."

"Ugly. *Uglier*." For a rugged, dangerous man, when he smiled, he could light up a room. I was swooning from his touch, every cell on fire.

"Not possible. Fuck me, Maverick. Just fuck me. Don't stop."

"I don't intend to."

He held me as if he cared, not just hungering for my body. His eyes pierced mine, his touch lighting me on fire. In the next few seconds, the most intense wave rushed through me. I threw my head back, staring up at the bright stars, the climax so powerful that I couldn't hold back a scream. My entire body was shaking, my mind a blur as bottle rockets slammed into my brain.

"So fucking beautiful," he muttered, pressing kisses against my neck, dragging his tongue from one side of my jaw to the other.

I felt beautiful for the first time in so long. As another orgasm roared into my system, I could swear there were now shooting stars crisscrossing the horizon. When he moved us under the waterfall completely, I threw my arms into the air, laughing from the freedom I felt.

He never took his eyes off me, his clenched jaw adding to his dangerous appeal. As he walked all the way through the water, I slumped over his shoulder, dropping my arms.

"I told you I'm taking all of you," he whispered. "And I keep my promises." His cock continued to throb and when I squeezed my muscles, he issued a series of growls. "Not yet, baby girl. Not yet."

He eased me against the steps of the pool then turned me around, planting me on all fours. As he pressed my legs apart, I threw a look over my shoulder. There was nothing quite as wicked as what we were doing. His grin was laced with evil as he raked his fingers down my spine, taking his time to roll them down the crack of my ass.

When I jerked forward, acting as if I was going to try to get away, he smacked me on the bottom. "Ouch!"

"Remember what I said. You're not going anywhere." Maverick rubbed the tip of his cock from one side of my bottom to the other then slid the tip against my dark hole.

Tensing, I sucked in my breath, closing my eyes as the anticipation of blinding pain tore through me. The man wasn't gentle by any means but as he pushed just his cockhead inside, another wave of explosive sensations rushed down my arms to my legs. The light breeze tickling my skin made me shiver, but as he drove another couple of inches into my asshole, I could feel a blast of heat rushing to the surface.

The discomfort was immediate, the slice of pain expanding as soon as he pushed past the tight ring of muscle. But my pussy was quivering, my breasts aching from being taken this way. I wiggled in his hold, water splashing over us.

"Oh, God. Oh…" As the pain began to subside, he thrust the remainder of his cock inside. I threw my head back but there was no sound erupting from my throat. "Oh… Yes…"

He caressed my back for what seemed like an eternity before folding his body over mine, rolling his hips forward until he was fully seated inside. "You're so tight."

"Uh-huh." I slapped at the water again, shocked how good it felt.

As he developed a rhythm, I bucked against him, meeting every hard thrust. There was something safe and warm about having the full weight of his body pressed against mine. We were as one, which seemed as strange as the fact I was letting go, enjoying every second of what he was doing to me.

And I wanted more.

"I could do this all night long," he muttered.

"Then do it."

He laughed softly, his heated breath sending another shower of vibrations along every inch of my naked back. I felt so small in his hold, his massive body easily dwarfing mine. He tangled his fingers in my hair, pulling it aside and as he licked the shell of my ear, I melted against him.

Maybe this was a sin. Maybe I'd burn in hell for being a… no, I refused to think something so ridiculous. I wanted this to last all night long.

His breathing became irregular, but he refused to stop, thrusting more brutally, the force driving me into the water. The sounds of the waterfall almost drowned out our throes of passion but when I squeezed my muscles again, I was rewarded with a strangled growl seconds before he erupted deep inside.

I closed my eyes, allowing a smile to cross my face.

That was the moment I tried to convince myself to leave town. If I didn't, I knew what would happen.

I'd lose the one man I actually cared about, the only person who'd allowed me to be me.

And I refused to allow the monster to kill him.

CHAPTER 9

Maverick

As I pulled into the parking lot of the sheriff's office, I noticed a US Marshal's vehicle. Gage had called me early in the morning, interrupting the best sleep I'd had in a long time. Maybe it had been because I'd had Lily by my side, something that hadn't occurred in a long time. Maybe I could be called the love 'em and leave 'em type, but I had my reasons. With her, it felt natural, even if she'd been reserved after being awakened by the call.

I parked my truck and sighed. I had a bad feeling I was going to be working some overtime. When a marshal showed up, it usually meant they'd lost a fugitive. While I usually enjoyed the hunt, I was more interested in finding out about the monster who was obviously stalking Lily. I'd hoped she'd come clean with me after our night together, but she'd acted as if we were just friends, and not even close ones when I'd dropped her off at her truck. Granted, I hadn't asked for her phone number but I knew how to get in touch with her.

"What do you think, Sam? Are you ready for another adventure?" I turned my head, half laughing at the sight of my sidekick. He'd wanted to go with Lily. The two certainly had created a bond. He'd even managed to slip between us on the bed, acting as if we were just one big family.

Before I walked in, I grabbed my phone, dialing Jeff Jones' number. He was a shyster, but he owed me a favor after I'd found his lost little girl. "Jeff. It's Maverick."

"What's shakin', buddy?" he asked. I detected he knew I was calling to even the score.

"Payback time."

"What do you need?"

It was funny that he was none too happy. Maybe that's because he'd rightly surmised I knew that he was selling drugs in addition to pretending to be a real estate mogul. The fact I hadn't turned him in allowed me to keep a hold on him. He had certain friends that I knew could be useful in certain situations. "I need a little house to rent. Nothing too fancy but clean and in a good part of town."

"You lookin' to move?"

"Not for me. For someone who needs a break."

"Well," he said, muttering under his breath. "I got a couple but they're a pretty big chunk of change. A couple thousand."

I rolled my eyes. I knew damn good and well the shit he usually rented wasn't worth that. "You're going to cut it to fifteen hundred, of which I'll pay a thousand. But you will not tell the woman who'll be calling you that I'm funding a portion. If I find out you do, I'll cut your nuts off myself. You hear me?"

"Jesus. You don't have to go to that extreme," Jeff sputtered.

"With you, I do. Do we have a deal?"

"I'll need four k as a security deposit."

"Not gonna happen. Remember, you owe me big time. And make sure it's furnished too with some good shit. I'll know if you don't."

"Do you want me to throw in a vacation in Tahiti as well?" His laugh pissed me off.

"Just. Do. It."

"God, somebody pissed in your Wheaties this morning. Fine. How long is this woman staying?"

I cringed hearing the question. She'd been so skittish after getting up that I had a bad feeling she already wanted to run. "I don't know. Hopefully a few months. Don't give me any shit about it. I'll pay the extra in cash."

"You drive a hard bargain but fine. What's her name and when can I expect her?"

I'd left Jeff's number on a small card, placing it in her hand. The feisty chick needed to do the rest.

And goddamn, I hope she did. I'd grown far too fond of her already. If she ran, I might have to track her down. She wouldn't like me when I did. Grinning, I noticed Sam was watching me intently. He could tell I was talking about her. "Lily Sanborn. Hopefully in a couple days. You just remember what I said. After this, my name isn't to be mentioned."

"Don't worry. I like my family jewels."

"I bet you do." Ending the call, I shoved the phone into my jacket, yanking the keys from the ignition. "Stay here, buddy. I'll be right back."

As I climbed out, I glanced at the mountains and had a slight flashback, one I hated remembering. It had been a beautiful day, a bunch of kids acting like they owned the world. Then tragedy had struck, a fire consuming a couple thousand acres.

And we'd started it.

Fuck. Why did it hit me hard today?

There was something about Lily's entire past that haunted me, reminding me of a girl who'd captured the hearts of six rugged boys hellbent on claiming her. Even if none of us wanted to admit it.

When I heard Sam whine, I was brought back to reality, but not without a gut-pinching pain remaining. "Yeah, I know. I miss her too." Lily had brought the life back to me when I thought I was dead inside. I closed the door and headed inside the station.

"Well, if it isn't the Wildman tracker," one of the deputies said.

I gave him a hard look. "Somebody needs to take up the slack around here."

"Very funny. Looks like you might be a busy man."

"Yeah? How so?" I studied Bart, the kid still wet behind the ears. My buddy Gage had gone through several deputies over the last year. Once the rookies found out the life wasn't as glamorous as the glossy brochures claimed, they almost always migrated to something else.

Bart glanced over his shoulder. "Better let the sheriff tell you. You know how he is."

Gage was a hard-ass when he wanted to be, his less than illustrious past giving him reason to toe the line between right and wrong. I took long strides down the corridor, hearing male voices before I rapped on the door, not bothering to wait for an invitation before walking inside.

There were two marshals in the visitor chairs, both standing when I walked in.

"You're late," Gage told me, lifting a single eyebrow.

"I had stuff to do. What's so urgent?" I glanced from one marshal to the other. They weren't in a shitting mood.

"This is Marshal Tyson Walker and Chance Sheffield. They just happen to be in the need of your services. Maverick Dane is hands down the best damn tracker I've ever worked with. You have a copy of his resume so you can see how many fugitives he's apprehended over the years. I think he qualifies for the job you have."

What was this, some freaking audition? I wasn't into dog and pony shows and if they didn't handle it right, I'd walk out the door and not look back. "As I asked before. What the hell is so urgent?"

Marshal Walker glanced down at the paperwork in his hand then tossed it on Gage's desk. "While you've brought several criminals to justice, none are quite as heinous as the man we've been after for almost ten days."

The fuckers had lost a fugitive for ten days? No wonder their tighty-whities were in a bind. "That means what to me?"

The two marshals glanced between themselves, and I glared at Gage. He knew better than to offer me up on a silver platter if the parties weren't up front from the get-go.

Marshal Sheffield cleared his throat, still fingering a file he had in his hand. Then he extended his arm. "We have a situation, a man who escaped federal custody while being transferred. In the process of doing so, he gunned down two police officers."

"What crime did he commit before?" I grabbed the file, opening the flap and staring at the man's picture. The accompanying notes indicated he'd fled Chicago. No wonder they needed a tracker. Even if they used scent dogs, the trail was ice cold on day two.

"Bruno Escavetti is an enforcer for the Butelli crime syndicate. He's been on the Feds' radar for years, but no charges against him stuck until he made a single mistake. I have no doubt the family helped orchestrate his escape."

"Let me guess, he's a brutal killer." If the crime syndicate had helped him, which was likely, they'd do so with a purpose in mind. I snorted and flipped through several pages. The notes were pretty good, the man supposedly killing at least fifteen people in his illustrious career, including several women.

"The worst. He'd been called Dr. Evil," Walker said dryly.

"Nice. What makes you think he's in Montana?" I closed the file. At this point, I wasn't certain I wanted to take the case.

"An informant who works for the organization. Supposedly, Bruno was ordered to head this way. But none of it has been confirmed, just a possibility."

I laughed, tossing the file on Gage's desk. "Uh-huh. That means you don't know shit. He could be enjoying a vacation with his family."

Sheffield bristled. "Don't you think we already checked that? His family is in Boca Raton where he put them. There are a dozen reasons he could have headed this way. They're all detailed in that file if you'd bothered to look all the way through it."

I didn't like the man's attitude. "You need a tracker. I need details. It's a normal course of business to be given all the facts. It appears you have jack shit. I'm not interested." I turned toward the door and sensed Gage was up in arms.

"For the love of God, Maverick. Listen to what they're saying. Bruno is a dangerous psychotic who doesn't mind killing anyone who gets in his way. And if you read those notes, you're going to see that he's extremely creative in the methods he uses. He enjoys torture, including of women. He even killed a kid, or so I heard."

My chest tightened when I heard that. I took a deep breath, still uncertain this was a good idea. Then I turned around, glaring at all three men. "How long do you think he's been in the mountains?"

Sheffield shrugged. "A couple of days."

A couple of days. My thoughts drifted to the man Lily had insisted she'd seen. The one with an assault rifle. "Have there been any sightings to corroborate your claim he's already here?"

"Two sightings, the last just outside the Montana border." Walker rubbed his eyes. "Maybe you're never gone to a crime scene after a victim has been tortured, their intestines hanging out, but I have. Bruno needs to be caught."

I could tell those sightings hadn't been confirmed. They were going on hunches, not facts. This was nothing but a wild goose chase in my opinion, which obviously didn't count.

Yeah, he certainly did, but whether or not I was the man to bring him to justice was beyond me at this point. "I'll glance over the information and let you know."

"Mr. Dane. I don't think you seem to realize how important it is we find him quickly," Sheffield said, trying to block me from leaving.

I was about to shove his ass against the wall but figured it wasn't in my best interest. "I get it. You need to save face with your superiors and with the public. And you know I'm the only man who can do it. If I take this case, it's going to cost you."

"Name your price." Walker grinned, already thinking he'd won this round. Why not shoot the moon at this point?

"Two hundred k in cold, hard cash."

I was surprised when they didn't blink or give each other a gloomy-eyed stare. Sheffield walked closer, holding out his hand. "You have yourself a deal, Mr. Dane. As long as you can start immediately."

I thought about it again and sighed. Tracking someone of this caliber wasn't going to be easy. And if I had to guess I'd say it would be time consuming. I wanted to spend time with Lily, getting to know every inch of her. After debating the issue, I made my decision. "Fine. I'll do it. But there will be other conditions."

Gage cocked his head, giving me that same look I'd seen since I'd met him. He had no doubt I'd get into some trouble, and someone would wind up dead.

"That's fine," Sheffield said, although I noticed he'd clenched his jaw.

"I assume you have a piece of clothing with his scent? I have a tracking dog."

Gage was the one who handed me a shirt. I didn't need to pull it to my nose. The damn thing was ripe with sweat. There were also spots of dried blood.

"This was Fed-exed in this morning," Gage said, already exasperated.

"Just know he's violent, capable of killing with his bare hands," Walker added.

Both Gage and I started to laugh, Gage addressing the man's comment. "Maybe the dossier you have on Maverick doesn't adequately describe the man's skills. He can be a killing machine."

Smirking, I noticed Sheffield paled. I wanted to laugh even harder. I folded the shirt, putting it under my arm.

"What do you want me to do with him if I'm lucky enough to track him down?" I asked. Few people understood how difficult tracking fugitives could be, especially ones who'd planned their escape, which Bruno Escavetti had obviously done. There wasn't a prison system in the world that could compete with most mafia organizations, their network insides just as powerful as in the free world.

"Then you call us," Walker answered.

I had to laugh. "You're assuming he'll cooperate."

"We've heard your methods are… creative in trapping a criminal," Sheffield added.

Creative. I threw another look at Gage.

"I'll get started in the morning."

"No, now," Sheffield barked.

It would seem I had no choice.

I took a minute to pull out my wallet, finding one of my cards inside. It already had my bank account information on it, but only for law enforcement officers. The everyday Joe was required to pay me in cash. "Then you're going to deposit half the funds into my account within one hour. And it's nonrefundable." I dared them to balk at my terms.

They didn't.

They wanted this son of a bitch bad. After Walker took the card from my hand, I grabbed the file. "I need one of your cards so I can give you a call when I'm in range. And don't tread on my turf. I work alone and that's the way it is."

"Alright. But you need to produce."

I moved closer to Sheffield, laughing. "I always produce. I *am* the best in the business."

As I walked out of the building, I could feel all eyes on me. I was certain Gage would make a call later, either berating me or laughing at what I knew would be called 'disturbing' behavior.

As if I gave a shit.

Gage decided to make it sooner, catching me before I made it ten feet.

"You okay with this?" he asked.

I swung around to face him, half laughing. "I wasn't given a real choice in this. You know? There's something they're not telling either one of us."

He squinted as he looked toward the sun. "Yeah, I kinda got that impression too. Be careful with this one, buddy. I have the same bad feeling you do. They're keeping the media quiet on this one so as not to cause hysteria."

"Translation, buddy. They don't know what they're dealing with. That's why it's quiet in the media."

His laugh told me I was right. "You're too good at this game."

"Yeah, but you know how I hate games. By the way, I need a favor while I'd gone."

As he lifted a single eyebrow, he grinned. The last time I'd asked for a favor, it was because I'd stolen a car. That was a lifetime before. "Shoot."

"I'm trying to get Lily into a rental. She needs to get away from that motel. Maybe you could watch out for her. She got a job at Raunchy Ride."

He studied me for a few seconds, his grin widening. "You like this girl."

"Yeah, well, maybe."

"No maybe about it. I didn't find anything about her past that's troubling."

"Maybe I'm wrong and she's just a private person."

"I don't know. Here's the thing. I couldn't find anything on her, period. Unless you want me to fingerprint her, which I take wouldn't go over well, then she's gonna need to be the one to tell you her business."

Fuck. Fuck. I closed my eyes briefly, cursing under my breath. "Just keep an eye on her. She's in danger. I feel it in my bones."

"I'm going to give you a piece of advice. Take it or leave it. Don't let this get too personal. I don't like this tracking job any more than you do. You could get yourself killed."

"That isn't going to happen. The fucker will die before I do."

"Remember what your assignment is. The marshals want him alive."

"Fuck the marshals. I'll do what needs to be done."

I took long strides toward the truck, climbing into the cab then shaking my head as Sam crowded my space. "It looks like we're going on an adventure, buddy." A fucking dangerous one. So much for taking a few weeks off.

Before I could toss the shirt in the back, Sam went nuts, barking and clawing at it.

"Hey. You'll get your chance, my friend."

When he tried to climb over the seat, a strange feeling pooled in the pit of my stomach. I didn't like this scenario at all. There was a chance I was being used, but for what purpose?

"Okay. Calm down, boy. I need to do a few things before we get going."

He finally settled down, his tail thumping hard against the seat.

It was entirely possible Lily had seen the fugitive during her hike. I might as well find out what she knew. As I pulled out of the parking lot, heading toward the Yellowstone Motel, I thought about the gear I'd need to accomplish this feat. It had been a few months since I'd apprehended a criminal, albeit the last guy had been stupid about hiding out in the mountains, allowing me to catch him red-handed breaking into one of the vacant summer cabins. And I'd done it in record time. Somehow, I had a feeling Bruno had formed a plan a long time before his escape. Why Montana? Chicago was a hell of a long way. That meant he had a purpose in being here.

I debated stopping to see Lily. The last thing she needed was to be terrified that someone was after her, but that made catching the asshole imperative. Sam rode shotgun, stoic as he normally was when he knew I was preparing for a trek through the mountains. He'd been a godsend, more so than I'd originally wanted to admit, but after seeing what Snake's dog, Apollo, had managed to accomplish, I'd been sold in getting a tracking dog.

Hopefully, the scent would be easy to hunt down.

Ten minutes later, I pulled into the parking lot of the motel, glad to see Lily's truck still parked in front of the room.

"Stay here, boy. I might be a little while." I still wasn't certain how to ask her what she'd seen, worried how she'd react, but I needed as much information as possible. When I knocked on the door, I took a deep breath, the ache in my loins returning. I liked this girl a little too much.

There was an old-fashioned chain on the inside of the door and Lily opened it tentatively, a look of relief flooding her face.

"Can we talk for a few minutes?" I asked.

There was something about the way she hesitated that cut through me, my protector mode kicking in all over again.

"Sure. Hold on." It took her a couple of minutes to pull the chain, allowing me inside. The ugly space was just as bad as I'd remembered. "What's up?"

She was nervous, more so than the night before, but I noticed the spark in her eyes and there was no discounting the electricity that crackled like dry timber.

"You gonna call Jeff about the rental?"

"You came all the way here to ask me that?"

Shrugging, I quickly scanned the room, noticing she had very little in the way of belongings. "I made a call to him and I think he has a small place, nothing special, but it's a shit load better than this."

When she looked away, I didn't need to be a mind reader to know she wasn't certain she wanted to stay.

"Look, I don't know what you've been through, Lily, but I do know that running isn't going to make things easier. This is a good town with some nice people. When I left for the Marines, I told myself I'd never come back. But as you start to experience things, you realize how much a support system can be helpful. With my parents' deaths, I wasn't given a choice. I had to come back, but it was going to be temporary. Then I fell in love with the city and the mountains all over again. Give yourself a chance to experience a different kind of life."

She gave me a half smile and walked closer. "Does that mean you want me to stay?"

Even her scent was driving me crazy this morning. It was impossible to resist her. As I walked closer, she gave me a mischievous look, no longer the skittish woman I'd first met. I touched her messy curls, my fingers tingling from the touch. "Yeah, I do. Does that bother you so much?"

The way she tilted her head, arching her back was too much to handle. "It doesn't bother me at all."

I had no business taking any extra time with her, satisfying my needs, but a small part of me wanted to make certain she felt wanted. Oh, who the hell was I kidding? I needed to drive my cock so deep inside that she screamed out my name.

The moment I yanked her toward me, the moan she let out was the sweetest reward. "The truth is, Lily, you ain't going anywhere. If you do, I'll hunt you down and lock you away."

The light in her eyes changed, twinkling in the wretched glow of the ugly, ancient lamp. It was exactly what I needed. I fisted the back of her hair, yanking her toward me, crushing my mouth over hers. She tasted like sunshine and cinnamon, the explosive combination driving another round of current into every muscle, deep into my bones. She hadn't just crawled under my skin. She'd ripped it open, exposing the sweltering need that might never be satisfied.

I thrust my tongue inside and she wrapped her arms around my neck, tangling her fingers in my hair. This wasn't about romance but desperate need for both of us. I picked her up, swinging her around and easing her bottom onto the dresser. Every time I dominated her tongue exploring the dark recesses of her mouth, I was reminded how much I'd missed being with someone. But Lily wasn't just someone. She was the light to my darkness.

And that worried me most of all.

This wasn't forever. This was just a moment in time.

Or so I needed to tell myself.

As we drank in each other's lips, I realized how unnerved I'd become. I weaved my fingers through her soft curls, the instinct that had never failed me clawing its way to the surface.

Lily was in extreme danger.

When I broke the kiss, I yanked back her head, raking my teeth across her jaw. She moaned and closed her eyes, pressing her palm against my chest, her fingers clenching around the dense material. The way she wrapped her legs around my thighs, pulling me even closer kept my breathing labored. Suddenly, it was explosively hot in the room, my cock pressing so tightly against my zipper, I could cry out in pain.

I bit down on her lower lip, growling when I did.

She was breathless, yanking at my shirt in her desperate attempt to free me of my clothes. I stepped back a foot, yanking it over my shoulders, cocking my head. "I want you."

"And I want you, cowboy. Fuck me."

The gorgeous woman didn't need to tell me twice.

Her hands weren't shaking this time as she yanked at my belt, pulling it free then immediately going for the button and zipper. I adored the way her shoulders rose and fell from her scattered breathing, but if she didn't hurry, I wasn't going to be gentle in ripping off her clothes.

Laughing, she pushed me back, moving off the dresser, jerking off and tossing her tee shirt. Then she tugged at both sides of my jeans, exposing my throbbing cock seconds later. When she wrapped her hand around the base, immediately squeezing and stroking up and down, I thought for certain I'd lose my load right then.

I cupped her breasts, flicking my thumbs back and forth across her already hardened nipples. They were rosy red, the sight of them making my mouth water. As she was trying to push my jeans down ever further, I lowered my head, lifting her onto her toes so I could swirl my tongue around one nipple then the other. When I took one into my mouth, pulling the tender tissue between my teeth, her soft purrs turned into a series of husky moans. Goddamn, the woman was going to make me crazy.

Panting, she managed to slide her hand between my legs, squeezing my balls. I slid my mouth to her other breast, sucking and biting down.

"Oh, God. You're so bad," she whispered.

I lifted my head, my nostrils flared from the scent of her desire. "Baby, you ain't seen nothing yet."

"Then you better hurry and show me."

Within seconds, we were finally naked, our hunger too intense to wait any longer. I swept her into my arms, slamming her against the wall, lifting her by several inches.

"Oh, God. Oh, my God." She was forced to place her legs around my shoulders, her arms flailing as I buried my head into her sweet pussy, immediately driving my tongue inside. "Jesus. Yes. Yes."

Every sound she made fueled the fire, my heart pounding in my chest as I drove my tongue into her slickened folds. The taste of her was like the ambrosia of gods and I could feast on her for days, weeks. I shifted my head back and forth, growling like the animal I'd become. She bucked hard against me, jutting her hips forward.

As I licked up and down, she continued to pant, tossing her head from side to side. I couldn't seem to get enough, the taste of her like fine wine. When I sensed she was close to coming, I allowed my actions to become rougher, licking her relentlessly, nipping and sucking her clit until I could tell it was extra sensitive.

She clawed at my shoulders and neck, her eyes wild with fire and defiance.

"Oh. Oh. Oh." As she threw her head back, I pulled her pussy lips wide open, plunging my tongue into her tight channel once again.

That was all she could take, an orgasm ripping through her, moans turning into ragged whimpers.

"So… so… bad."

I took her words as a compliment, forcing the single orgasm into a wave. But as her body continued to spasm, I lost the rest of my patience, dragging her down the wall, impaling her with a single brutal plunge.

Her eyes were open wide, her mouth twisted as soft murmurs slipped past her lips. She clung to my shoulders, pinning her legs against me as I fucked her, rolling onto the balls of my feet. Her pussy muscles clamped and released several times, the tightness almost making me lose control.

As my actions became even more savage, she gasped for air.

"Maverick. Yes. Yes. Yes!" Her scream was high pitched, lasting only seconds, but it was exactly what I'd wanted to hear. As I allowed myself to let go, erupting deep inside of her, I was forced to face the fact I wouldn't be able to let her go.

I'd made good on my promise, tracking her down, the predator hunting his prey.

And I'd enjoy every minute of keeping her my prisoner.

When we both stopped shaking, I eased her away from the wall, walking us both toward the bed. She laughed as I dumped her on the comforter, immediately grabbing one of the pillows and pulling it against her chest as she rolled onto her stomach. I flopped on my back, trying to catch my breath.

"That was..." She pressed kisses against my chest, brushing her fingers back and forth.

"Pretty fucking amazing," I finished for her.

She rested her folded arm on my stomach, lifting her eyebrows. "Why are you really here?"

"You know why."

To tease me, she slipped her hand to my still aching cock, rolling the tip of her finger across my sensitive slit. "Tell the truth."

I rubbed my face, taking a couple of deep breaths. "I have a tracking job, one that's dangerous." The way she sucked in her breath allowed another sharp pain in my system. "I don't know how long I'll be gone."

She sat up, looking the other way. "The guy from the mountain."

"Likely."

"You could be killed." As I shifted my arms behind my head, she looked over her shoulder. "Don't do it."

"I wasn't given a choice. He's a bad man from Chicago." As soon as I said the words, her reaction was exactly what I'd hoped wouldn't happen. Her lower lip was quivering and even though she tried to hide it by rubbing her mouth, I'd noticed. "What aren't you telling me about your past, Lily?"

"There's nothing else to tell you."

"You're lying to me."

"Why would I lie to you?" Suddenly, she couldn't look me in the eye.

"Because you're afraid. I'm here to tell you right now that I'll protect you. I don't know how many times you need to hear it before you believe and trust me."

Her laugh was bitter. "You're right. You've told me that before, but you can't be there twenty-four hours a day. You have a life. Besides, you could be dead on the mountain in two days." She climbed off the bed, immediately grabbing her clothes. "And I don't want that to happen."

"You underestimate me, sweetheart, but it's good to see you're worried about me."

"No, you underestimate…" She immediately cut the sentence short. "I don't know what I'm talking about. Just be careful."

"I don't need to be. I have firepower." I wasn't going to get anywhere grilling her about her personal life. "But in all seriousness, I need to ask you a few questions. Can you handle it?"

"I can handle anything," she teased then her smile faded.

"Tell me everything you know about the man you saw."

As she jerked on the tee shirt, I could see her mind going a thousand miles an hour. "I told you what I know. He was in jeans and a dark parka with a ski hat. He had an automatic rifle in his hand. I didn't stop long enough to ask him the time of day. Okay? I was frightened."

"Because you thought you knew him."

She snorted, dragging her jeans from the floor. "I definitely didn't know him."

"If he's the guy I'm tracking, then he escaped from prison."

That seemed to make her take a pause. When she turned her head toward me, she took a few shallow breaths. "Really?"

"Yeah, he'd been there for years." I decided not to tell her the guy's name, at least for now. "Just a run of the mill asshole who found an opportunity to skip out of town."

"Why Montana?"

"He has family here, although the marshals assured me they haven't been contacted by the guy." Yeah, I lied. She'd skip town otherwise.

"Okay."

I got off the bed, watching the flow of emotions rolling through her, my anger increasing. As I pulled her into my arms, she stiffened for a few seconds then molded her body into mine. "I'll be back before you know it. Make the call about the cabin. We'll celebrate your new home when I get back. Can you do that for me?" When she didn't answer, I lifted her chin, forcing her to look into my eyes.

Tears brimmed hers, but she nodded and the haunted look on her face only increased my rage.

One day she'd tell me the name of the asshole who'd hurt her. Then I'd track him down and use my greatest weapon to end his life.

My bare hands.

CHAPTER 10

ily

Foreboding.

The feeling remained in my stomach, keeping it in knots. I'd searched the internet, trying to find any information about an escaped convict to ease my concern. I'd found nothing. Maybe my fears were unfounded, but the nagging remained. But I wasn't going to back down. Not when I'd come this far.

If I could get a little place to call my own even for a few months, that would improve my mood.

As I stepped out of my truck, I eyed the house suspiciously. It wasn't because it was run down, which I'd expected, or because it was in a horrible part of town, because it wasn't. The knot forming in my stomach, shoving the butterflies aside was because the log cabin was utterly gorgeous, the land surrounding it backing up to the snowcapped mountains. While a longer drive to the city than I'd hoped, the stunning location was peaceful.

Jeff stood on the front porch, studying me as I closed the door. He'd been nice enough on the phone, getting the usual details, but he'd very quickly told me he had the perfect place.

That had been the icing on the tilting cake of suspicion. As I walked closer, the entire thing began to smell of a setup.

"You must be Lily. I'm Jeff Jones." When I didn't immediately accept his handshake, he laughed. "We spoke on the phone?"

"Yes, I remember, but there's been some misunderstanding." I accepted his gesture, but my instinct was kicking into overdrive. Maverick had a hand in this. I was certain of it. I didn't need to be beholden to anyone, especially a man.

Hear the man out. Don't be foolish.

"How so?" he asked as he moved toward the door, sticking a key into the lock.

"I gave you a price range. There is no way I can afford something like this, especially since I'd need to purchase furniture." I hated being desperate. At the least the motel from hell was safe and dry.

Or so I believed.

"Well, you might be surprised. This is actually a cabin owned by a couple who is out of the country for a couple years working. They decided on the rent, not me. I tried to talk them out of it, but they were insistent that as long as I found someone who would take care of the place to keep it low. I thought of you immediately." His grin was genuine and as he opened the door, I took a deep breath before walking inside.

When I did, I almost ran away. The cabin was completely furnished, the living room filled with beautiful, comfortable furniture. I pressed my hand across my lips, trying to decide if I could dare believe strangers would be so kind. "This has nothing to do with Maverick?"

He laughed, scratching his head. "I'm not going to lie to you and say he didn't make certain I met with you. He's that kind of guy, forceful as fuck, but I run my business my way."

Yes, Maverick was forceful alright, as he'd told me countless times, refusing to take no for an answer. My body tingled just by thinking his name. The passion we'd shared had been more intense than the time before. I already missed him, worried about the hunt he was on.

I turned in a full circle, the little voice inside my head nagging me to accept. "I don't know."

"Take a look around. I'll be right here."

Giving him a half smile, I moved through the house, my nerves on edge. There was everything I needed. Furniture, linens, plates, and glasses. A working refrigerator. I was stunned, furious with Maverick for interfering, and longing to throw my arms around him. As I walked back into the living room, I took another deep breath. "It's really five hundred a month?"

"Yes, ma'am."

"And the deposit?"

"There is none. I know you're getting on your feet here with your new job and all. Just pay me by the end of the month and we're square."

"I can't take charity."

His laugh put me somewhat at ease. "I don't do charity, Lily. But I do know all about a woman who deserves a break. If you're honest with me, I'll work with you. Fair deal?"

This time I threw out my arm. "Thank you, Mr. Jones. This means a lot to me."

"It's Jeff and if you need anything, let me know. Here are the keys." As he placed them in my hand, he grinned. "There's a nice stream about a hundred yards from here. It's real pretty this time of year."

"Thank you. I look forward to seeing it." I stood in shock after he left, far too many emotions finding their way to the surface. When I finally collapsed on the couch, I allowed a few ugly visions and memories to crowd my mind, a single tear slipping past my lashes. But there would be no more tears after this. I was strong. I was resilient. This was a new life.

And I refused to waste another minute of it.

Laughing, I headed toward my truck, yanking my camera from the duffle bag. As I took a deep breath of the cold, crisp air, I felt free, as if I could do anything I wanted.

Including going back to finish getting my degree. Spending time with Sam had rekindled my desire to work with animals. I'd find a way.

I snapped a few shots, turning in full circle to capture the incredible landscape in a full three hundred sixty degrees. When I lowered the camera, I lifted my head, gazing at the clouds tickling the tops of the mountains. Then I lifted my middle finger.

Watch out, world. There's no stopping me now.

* * *

Maverick

Silence.

One of the many aspects about living so close to several mountain ranges was the quiet that enveloped me as soon as I stepped foot on the terrain. The limited peace I'd enjoyed by hiking through the forests, standing by the raging rivers had been a lifesaver at one point in my life. As I stared up at the peaks of Sapphire Ridge, the ugliness of memories I'd never wanted to resurface hit me in the gut.

Brutally hard.

"Fuck," I hissed, turning in a full circle, forced to yank my shirt over my mouth, the acrid smoke burning my eyes.

"We can't do this," Colt huffed, doubling over in front of me, his knees slamming into the ground.

I was angry, so livid I couldn't see straight. Nothing mattered but saving her. In a moment of insanity, I yanked him up by the collar, smashing him against a tree. A hard crack sounded off within a few feet, the entire top of a tree crashing onto the forest bed.

"What the fuck is wrong with you, man?" Colt snarled, doing his best to shove me aside.

"We're not leaving without her!"

"You're fuckin' nuts. Do you want to die out here?"

Hissing, I reared back, not thinking twice about issuing a savage punch to his jaw.

His head flew to the side, the only sound he made harsh wheezing.

"Stop the shit!" Ricardo bellowed.

Rage was the only thing I could concentrate on, tossing him aside with enough force he was pitched several feet away. Then I headed straight for the flames, refusing to stop.

"You're crazy!" Ricardo roared from behind.

The next thing I knew, I'd been tackled to the ground, two men I'd considered friends jerking my arms behind my back.

"Get off me!" My voice was no longer recognizable, fury and smoke deepening my roar.

"Not a chance, buddy. You're not going to die out here." Colt was panting, forced to put the full weight of his body on mine, pinning me down with one of his fancy wrestling moves. I was bigger than

him, outweighing him by a solid fifty pounds, but even the adrenaline rush did nothing against his trained hold.

I screamed at the top of my lungs, my voice mostly drowned out by the continuous crackling sounds, booms as trees gave up their fight for life, the viciousness of the fire winning.

"Goddamn it. Riggs thinks he's God," Ricardo snarled. "Don't do it."

"We can't save her," Colt said. "We can't. I'm sorry. I'm so sorry."

"Let me go. Just fucking let me go." After a struggling with him, he finally slid off, jerking to his feet. I remained where I was, gasping for air as the pain of losing her tore through me.

"The entire top of the mountain is on fire, Riggs. Listen to me. We did everything we could do," Ricardo implored, the wild look in his eyes exactly the way we all felt.

I scrambled to my feet, glaring at the blue hue of the encroaching flames. As I backed away, I noticed Houston was still mesmerized by the fire. When he slowly turned his head, for the first time since I'd known him there were tears in his eyes.

Riggs turned and stared as the fire consumed everything in its path, flames licking up to the heavens. As I lifted my fist toward the sky, the others did the same. Together in life. Together in death.

Forever.

It was the first and last day I'd shed a tear. Then I'd shut down my emotions, refusing to give a shit about anyone or anything.

If only six kids and one little lady hadn't been so eager to take risks, things might have worked out differently.

At least the Marines kept me from putting a bullet in my brain for a few years. Fuck. There was one reason the nightmares had started all over again.

Lily.

"Christ," I muttered. I'd been out here a full day already. Maybe I was getting too old for this shit, the cold numbing my brain. While there no cell phone reception on the mountain, that didn't prevent me from reading the text Lily had sent. At least we'd been able to exchange numbers. She was using a burner phone, which kept my anxiety high.

Don't die on me, cowboy.

I didn't intend on it.

"Come on, Sam. We got some work to do."

The dog stood stoically, his body rigid and his eyes staring at the same ridge I'd been looking at. He was one of the best tracking dogs I'd ever seen, his natural instincts making my job much easier. He was also protective, which could cost him his life at some point. I refused to allow that to happen. He was my rock, his companionship coming along at a time when I'd reached the end of my rope.

I'd almost pulled the trigger. Not at a suspect. Not at a wild animal. I'd pointed the barrel of my Glock at my temple, ready to end the pain. To this day, I had no idea why I hadn't been able to follow through. Two days later, Sam had come into my life.

Now I had the company of a beautiful, haunted woman who refused to allow whatever horrible past she'd endured to break her spirit.

But the ordeal was weighing on her.

Maybe one day she'd learn to trust me.

As I yanked my gear bag from the Cherokee, slinging it over my shoulder, I snorted under my breath. Why should she trust me? I couldn't save a girl who'd counted on me all those years ago. Shit. There I went again, feeling sorry for myself. What a crock of shit. I'd fought wars, killing enemies without hesitation. I'd been tortured and shot, stabbed, and beaten to within an inch of my life but I'd come out swinging in the end. Why did I have the terrible feeling that protecting Lily was in a whole different league?

I pressed the stinky clothes Bruno had worn under Sam's nose for the fifth time since we'd left, allowing him to take a nice, deep whiff. Then he barked once, leading us both away from what I called the safe zone. The climb could be treacherous, but I'd rely on my instincts and his keen nose.

I trudged through the snow, heading deeper into the forest. I'd combed at least forty miles in the last thirty hours with zero sign of Bruno. No footprints. No torn clothing. At least there hadn't been any sign of violence, but the bad feeling that had grabbed me at Gage's office remained furrowing in my stomach.

Sam and I would find the bastard. One way or another.

As we moved in symphony together, his training with me and vice versa making us a dominating force, I continued to think about Lily. I'd seen more fear in her eyes than I ever had with anyone who'd almost perished on these mountains. It had driven a stake through my heart and a wedge in the back of my mind.

I'd find no issue in killing the bastard who'd put her through hell.

However, she was a strong girl, obviously used to taking care of herself. Something had derailed her. I had to stop thinking with my dick or I'd lose all sense of time as well as direction.

Locating someone was tricky, especially in varying weather conditions. The recent snow had given away to warmer weather, which meant melt. That also meant climbing was dangerous as fuck. If rocks gave away, I could plummet to my death. At least I knew the lay of the land like the back of my hand. I only hoped it'd be helpful.

With little else to go on other than a rancid scent and a sense of why Bruno had arrived in Montana, it had narrowed the search grid. But whatever the marshals hadn't told me was the real reason the asshole was in these mountains. If I had to guess, I'd say it was all about exacting revenge. Maybe they had their reasons for locking me out of pertinent information, but that didn't make my job any easier.

That made him even more dangerous, a wildcard. He'd do anything to keep going, killing anyone who got in his way. I pulled out my compass, double-checking my heading. I'd mapped out a few cabins about two miles ahead. Given their location, one of them would be a perfect hideout. Maybe Bruno thought the heat would pass, the marshals looking elsewhere.

I powered through the deepest snow we'd run into yet, Sam never missing a beat. Two hours later, I was forced to admit I wasn't getting any younger. I leaned against a tree, yanking the travel pet bowl from the bag, pouring my buddy not one but two bowls full before snagging a bottle of water. At this point, I was perspiring from the workout, but my muscles remained tense as they always did when I was on the hunt.

After fetching him some protein-hearty snacks, I remained where I was, allowing my ears to do the work for a little while. As soon as I'd shoved the items back into the bag, I felt the change in Sam's demeanor before hearing the low rumble of his husky growl.

I immediately grabbed my rifle, scanning the woods. He had different cadences for different situations, one for animals and one for humans. The malevolent sound erupting from deep within his throat indicated danger.

And it was closing in.

As I lowered my arm, my palm parallel to the ground, he dropped to his haunches but remained alert. I slowly lowered the bag, creeping forward as silently as the crunch of snow would allow. There was nothing in my line of sight, but I could feel a presence. Whatever it was I sensed was sizing me up for a late morning snack. Seconds later, my belief was confirmed.

Fresh wolf tracks.

And blood.

I bent down, sliding my fingers through the discolored snow. It was fresh.

Sam whined from behind me, his tail sloshing back and forth in the snow. One thing worse than a psychopath determined to satisfy his need for revenge was an injured animal. I gave my boy a few other hand signals, which he recognized immediately, every sound including what his tail had been making ceasing.

I cocked my head, determining the location of the wind. Then I heard tiny cries that curdled my blood.

Wolf pups.

If I had to venture a guess, I'd say the mother wolf was injured and she would do anything, including attacking a human in order to protect her pups. The trail of blood continued, the mother losing too much blood. As I crept through the snow, constantly scanning the area, a single crack of wood forced me to snap my head to the right.

All I saw was a blur as the wolf leapt through the air, the power of her lunge knocking me to the ground. Her canines were exposed, the poor baby frothing at the mouth. She was already losing the battle for her life.

While seconds seemed longer, Sam couldn't ignore the cry of his master, pitching himself into the fight. The three of us pitched and rolled, both dogs and man snarling. I finally broke free, jerking to my feet, doing what I could to protect

Sam. I didn't want to kill the wolf, but even from the look in her eyes, I could tell she was losing the battle already.

The two animals fought, Sam just as powerful as the wolf. When they broke apart, I did what I could to herd her away. "Get out. Go, mama. Protect your babies."

The wolf was having none of it. She jerked toward Sam, flying through the air toward him. I had no other choice.

I fired.

The shot rang out in the air, the horror of the situation weighing heavily on my mind. As the wolf dropped to the snow, Sam let off a horrific howl.

I dropped to my knees, gasping for air.

"Sam. Come."

He immediately headed toward me, his tail once again swishing back and forth. As he started licking my face, I wrapped my arm around his neck. "Jesus, buddy."

A few seconds later, I crawled to my feet, heading toward the location of the whimpers. I found them unharmed, but they wouldn't remain that way for long, another predator discovering them. "Okay, little fellas. Let me see if I can get you some help."

I headed for my bag, grabbing the walkie talkie as I glanced down at the wolf. Her initial injury wasn't caused by an animal. She'd been shot.

"Gage. You there, buddy?"

The hundred-mile range was being stretched. All I heard was static. "Gage. Come in."

More static.

I was about to give up when a clicking noise kept my attention. "You find him?"

"No, but you need to get the rangers up to Crosshair Point. A load of wolf pups."

"Hold on," he said, half laughing. But he knew me. I'd go out of my way to help wild animals where I wouldn't with most humans. "Did you forget what you were doing?"

"Just do it, buddy. I'll mark the spot. Incidentally, did the marshals provide anything else?"

"No. Not a damn thing. But I did some checking."

"Bruno is going after a witness. Isn't he?"

His snort was followed by another short laugh. "Maybe. I don't have clearance, but I know the only living witness is in hiding given his escape. The guy has a sister, but I can't find out where she lives."

"Yeah, well, I'm gonna guess. That's not much to go on. I'll check the cabins at Sapphire Ridge. Like I told the marshals. He'll be a damn needle in a haystack unless I get lucky."

"Just do what you can do."

"Yeah, get the rangers up here," I told him as I turned in a full circle. Someone had been here recently and he or she was armed.

"Will do. Be careful up there, buddy. There's been some reports of vibrations."

Great. I glanced up at the mountains, taking another deep breath. All I needed was for Mother Nature to make her presence known by way of an avalanche. "I'll contact you later."

"Good deal."

I grabbed the gun and my bag and took one last look at the wolf. Maybe I was more like the creature than I knew. "Come on, Sam."

Three hours and four cabins later and exhaustion was setting in, and the light snow falling wasn't helping the situation. There was one more to check. After that, I might call it a night. Sam needed the rest too.

As I moved through another patch of dense forest, I heard Sam's insistent growl for the second time and as I turned my head toward him, the sight of his bared teeth was enough to force me to drop the bag. I checked the ammunition in the rifle, deciding to switch to a handgun. It was cleaner, easier, and would allow me flexibility. After sliding a second magazine into my back pocket, I took a few seconds to hide the rest of the gear. The last thing I needed was for the fugitive to get his hands on more weapons. Then I placed my finger in front of my lips. He knew what to do.

He trailed behind me. I constantly looked from one side to the other. As a hint of smoke filtered into my nostrils, I held the weapon in both hands. As soon as I noticed the corner of a cabin, I hunkered down, listening for any signs that someone was outside.

I gave him the stay sign, moving into the clearing surrounding the house. Then I shifted toward one of the front windows, taking my time peering through it. At first, I saw nothing, then movement a few seconds later. Someone crossed within a few feet. By the description I'd been given, it could be the man I was looking for, but there were no signs of distress.

Remaining low to the ground, I shifted to the second window, taking a few seconds before glancing inside. Bingo. The asshole had two hostages. The fact he hadn't killed them could mean they had nothing to do with the case against Bruno, but their chances at survival were slim no matter how I looked at it. The look of terror on their faces was easy to see. Fuck. He was pacing back and forth in front of them. While he didn't have a weapon in his hands, that meant nothing. This wasn't the best scenario, but I'd need to use the element of surprise. I wasn't about to call the marshals and wait until they arrived. The hostages could be dead by then.

I moved around the house, keeping low to the ground. I had two options, both highly dangerous. But I wasn't getting any younger biding my time. As I returned to the front, I gave Sam the signal to wait. Somehow, I suspected that he'd have a difficult time doing so.

A shudder of the earth beneath me sent a wave of anxiety into my system. I pulled back, moving to the edge of the house, glancing toward the peak. This was the time of year when spring collided with winter. Avalanches weren't unheard of, although it had been a long time since one had occurred. Still, I had a very bad feeling about this entire situation.

Get moving, bud. You need to get this finished.

Very slowly, I returned to the same spot, looking over my shoulder at Sam. He was as agitated as I was, his keen senses better than mine. It was definite. I was getting too old for this shit.

After checking the fugitive's location, I moved to the front door, taking a deep breath then kicking it in.

A sudden wave of vibrations bore into my legs, the energy pitching me forward. Everything in the house was shaking.

This wasn't good.

As he spun around, the weapon in his hand, he didn't hesitate to shoot.

Neither did I.

Pop! Pop! Pop!

CHAPTER 11

Lily

"What the fuck do you mean he's missing?" Scorpion snapped as he passed by the bar. "A fucking avalanche? Not possible."

Avalanche? Was he kidding?

No. No. My mind was screaming but I couldn't utter a word, terror skidding through me like wildfire. I moved closer, straining to hear at least a part of the conversation.

A cold shiver skated down my spine. Then I glanced at the closest television over the bar. There was no report of an avalanche. Was he talking about in the mountains? The news had been all over Maverick's attempt to track down the fugitive, but he hadn't been heard from in over twenty-four hours.

"There damn well better be a search party out for him. If you don't do it, I'll contact the smokejumpers myself," Scorpion snarled, shaking his head. I'd never seen him so angry.

Meanwhile, I was sick inside, barely able to function. At least I had work to keep me occupied or I would have lost my mind.

"You're mighty interested in the news tonight."

I glanced at Missy. She'd been the one to take me by the hand, leading me through every aspect of working the bar. I was grateful for her patience since my mind had been elsewhere for most of the time. "Just worried about the tracker. The weather conditions seem to be worsening."

"We have the craziest weather this time of year, but I wouldn't worry about it down here. We rarely get anything but lovely snow."

"I hate snow. But it sounds bad up there. An avalanche?"

"They rarely happen and usually not too bad. I heard you knew Maverick," she said as she grabbed some cocktail napkins for her tray.

A warm blush swept across my cheeks, and I quickly gave her a glance.

She laughed. "It's not a small town but you wouldn't know it by the gossip. Don't worry. I think it's cool. He's a hot guy but a little rough around the edges," Missy said.

"Do you know him very well?"

"Nobody knows Maverick. He's a loner. And before you ask, no, I don't think I've ever seen him with a woman. Lucky you."

Laughing, I nodded, uncertain I knew anything about him other than I craved his touch, his kisses, and the way he held me when we fucked. Oh, I was such a bad girl.

"Oh, and that table over there in your station," she added, pointing toward a large round top near the door. "They're bad news. A rowdy bunch Scorpion has tossed out before. If you can't handle them, let Scorpion know. He doesn't tolerate bad behavior."

Smirking, I tossed a look in their direction, laughing on the inside. "Don't worry. I can handle myself with misbehaving cowboys."

"I don't know. They're pretty tough," she said in a singsong voice.

"I'm tougher."

"Good for you." As she grabbed a tray of drinks, I returned my attention to the news footage.

"There are reports that well-known tracker, Maverick Dane, has been hired to hunt down a notorious escaped fugitive. Unfortunately, there's been no word from Maverick in over twenty-four hours. Given the conditions on the mountain, a reported avalanche in the area, there's concern regarding his condition."

The reporter was standing at the base of Sapphire Ridge, a location where Maverick had been last reported. The sickening feeling inside refused to leave, my mind an ugly mess.

"Fuck," Scorpion hissed and as he walked by, I got his attention.

"Was your phone call about Maverick?"

He lifted his eyebrows then exhaled. "Yeah, it was. Don't worry about him. He's just out of range for the walkie talkies. He's damn good at what he does."

"That's what I keep hearing. An avalanche?"

As his brow furrowed, I suspected the worst. "Unconfirmed. Plus, that doesn't mean he was in the area. He'd likely left the area before that hit."

"He's been gone almost three days. Isn't that a long time?"

"Not necessarily. There's a lot of mountains to cover and Maverick is meticulous. He's always been that way. He refuses to back down to anything."

"But?" I could tell he had a certain look in his eyes.

He shrugged, still trying to pass it off.

"But he called in the rangers to come and rescue a den of wolf pups. They found his bag. I wouldn't worry."

"Then why hasn't he returned? Why isn't anyone out now looking for him?"

"There's a search party. That was just confirmed."

"Doesn't anyone care about him?" *Like I do?* I heard the demanding tone in my voice and shook my head. "I'm sorry. I'm just worried about him."

"I can tell that. Do you want the rest of the night off?" Scorpion asked, a slight grin on his face.

"No. God, no. I need to work."

"Okay. I'm sure he'll call you as soon as he can. Stop worrying. Maverick is one of the toughest men I know."

I wasn't convinced seeing the worry in his eyes. And even though tough men had bad days, my gut told me something terrible had happened. My thoughts drifted to what little news I had on the man Maverick was hunting for. Why didn't they know his name? Would that make me feel any better?

I pulled out my phone, rubbing my thumb across the screen. Then I pulled up the single text he'd sent.

Keep the fires burning.

I planned on doing so. I'd drive up to that damn mountain myself if I had to. I was still certain he'd pulled a fast one on me regarding the cabin, but I planned on expressing my gratitude privately. At least that gave me a smile.

"Drinks up," the bartender said from behind me. It was time to get lost in my job.

I wasn't the kind of girl who'd said many prayers in her life. The few I had hadn't brought me anything but additional heartache. But I said one anyway.

As I started loading the drinks onto my tray, I heard a ruckus from the table Missy had warned me about. Then the sheriff and a deputy burst in though the entrance, heading toward the bar. What was going on? I almost panicked seeing how quickly they were moving.

Then the men at the table started shouting for service, just as rowdy as Missy had warned me of. They'd made the mistake of sitting in the wrong section.

I was angry, frustrated, and terrified for the man I'd fallen hard for already. A table of assholes wasn't going to get in my way. God help them if they tried.

I'd been here four hours already. My feet hurt, my mind was muddled, and the butterflies in my stomach were increasing every passing hour. Maverick was in trouble. I could feel it. But I tried to keep it together as I walked toward the rowdy group of men.

"Hey, sweetheart? What took you so long?" one of them asked.

"Good things come to boys who behave," I threw back at him. Maybe resorting to my sassy mode would help.

He snorted while the others whistled.

"A tough little honey. You're new here, ain't ya?" the bulkiest of the group of five asked.

I said nothing as I slid a beer in front of him.

"Where's that nasty little mouth of yours now, sweetie pie? Do you need a real man to unlock your heart?" The entire group laughed, and I was anxious enough I had a bad feeling the naughty girl inside of me was going to explode.

As I slowly turned and lowered my head, I kept a practiced smile on my face. "If there were any real men at this table, it might be a possibility."

"What the… I think this little filly needs a lesson in finding a real man," a fourth guy huffed, daring to reach over and tangle his fingers in my hair.

I snapped my hand around his wrist, able to balance the tray in the other. "No touching the merchandise or you won't be using your fingers any time soon."

When one of them placed their hand on my ass, I gave him a hard look.

"If you don't want to lose it, move it," I told him, allowing the anxiety to give me more confidence than I felt. I placed his beer in front of him and gave him a hard sneer.

"Oh, the little lady thinks she's tough, does she?" the cowboy asked, laughing then squeezing my ass cheek.

Sighing, I gave him a pretty little smile then tossed a mug of beer in his face. That made him let me go.

"What the…" he yelped, jerking back. When he made the mistake of lunging toward me, I was ready to throw a punch.

Until a strong hand caught it midair. I could see the asshole's eyes opening wide. Then he jerked up from his seat, shoving the chair back by a few feet.

"Gentlemen, if you continue with those actions, you're gonna be hurtin' for a week. In other words, back the fuck off."

"You ain't man enough to take me," the asshole responded, growling as if he had the brawn to take the man who'd kept me from issuing punishment.

The butterflies exploded, my emotions all over the place.

Maverick.

He was back. He was safe.

He was my hero all over again.

"Step aside, darlin'," Maverick said in a fake growl. When I looked at him, he winked. He was enjoying this.

Meanwhile, I was shaking to my core, tiny little prickles of heat scouring my skin. I moved back, but all I wanted to do was throw my arms around him.

"You think you can handle me, Wolfman?" the asshole asked, his entire group of men laughing as he pushed up his sleeves, acting as if he was going to throw a punch.

Wolfman? Where had that come from?

Maverick shook his head, acting as if this was nothing but a slight bother. "No one touches my woman."

His woman. The possessive tone sent a thrill right through me.

When the asshole was stupid enough to throw a punch, his fist connecting with Maverick's jaw, it seemed the entire bar was ready for a fight, murmurs and shouts coming from every direction.

Then Maverick concentrated his stern look at the man, his eyes colder than I'd seen them before. All he had to do was take two long strides toward him and issue a single, brutal punch to the man's nose. Even over the music, I could hear bones crunching, blood immediately spewing from the guy's nose.

And a smile crossed my face.

My brutal hero had come to save the day again.

The jerk was tossed into a table, knocking over a chair. Even with a crushed nose, it didn't stop him from jerking to his feet, coming at Maverick with murderous intent in his eyes.

Within seconds, a brawl had started, Maverick easily tossing two of the cowboys across their table as patrons chanted for a fight.

"Whoa, boys. This isn't going to happen in my bar," Scorpion snarled, the sheriff and deputy getting in the middle.

Maverick snarled so loudly several of the customers jumped back. "Stay the fuck away from her."

"Okay, buddy. Let the sheriff take it from here," Scorpion told him, giving me an amused glance before pushing Maverick back by a few feet. He acted as if he wasn't finished, howling like a wild animal.

Like a wolf.

The crowd loved it.

I suddenly realized there were lights everywhere, a commotion coming from behind me. But that didn't stop Maverick from uttering a deep growl then turning toward me, yanking me into his arms.

"Did you miss me, sweetheart?" There was a possessive look on his face, the intensity of his eyes as they bore into mine exactly as I'd seen moments before he'd left. He had scratches on his cheek, dried blood on his neck, but he was alive.

I wrapped my arms around his neck, my legs around his thunderous thighs, the entire world around us fading away.

"Yes. You scared me," I told him.

"Aww. You were worried about me. How sweet."

As at least twenty or so people started to clap, whistling and shouting, the wonderful haze remained over us. No one could interfere.

Then they did, the lights from before suddenly in our faces.

"Mr. Dane. Can you tell us about your experience in capturing a notorious criminal?"

"Mr. Dane, how does it feel to save two lives?"

"Mr. Dane. Did you know you're a hero?"

The questions came fast and furious, reporters everywhere and the look in Maverick's eyes shifted to stark coldness, even anger. He swung his head in their direction and I had a feeling he was prepared to launch into them had I not placed my hand on his chest.

"Ignore them," I said just loudly enough he faltered, allowing his heated gaze to drift toward me again.

"Out of my face." His words were little more than a snarl and he kept his arm wrapped around my back, spinning in the other direction then taking long strides through the crowd. Somehow, he managed to shove customers aside, his purposeful steps finally forcing an open path toward the back of the bar.

When he moved down the hallway toward the bathrooms, I sensed the crowd following. Then he smacked his hand on the women's restroom door, taking us inside.

"Get out," he told the three women standing by the sink. "And stay out."

I wanted to laugh, but tears remained in my eyes, the adrenaline rush starting to fade. I couldn't believe he was here or that my reactions were so strong. Only when everyone had left did he lower me to my feet, wrapping his massive hand around the back of my neck.

"Didn't anyone ever tell you not to mess around with raunchy cowboys?" he asked, the same deep husky tone I'd grown to love sending a shower of skitters down to my toes.

"Well, my man wasn't here to keep me in line. You know how naughty I can be."

He rubbed his knuckles across my cheek, shaking his head ever so slowly. "Yeah, I do." When he crushed his mouth over mine, I clamped my fingers around his jacket, pulling him close. He kissed me as if it was our last, sweeping his tongue inside, taking everything he wanted.

And what he believed belonged to him.

There was a newfound level of ferocity, his body remaining tense as he dominated my tongue. The taste of him was like fine cognac and cinnamon, infusing my senses. I was on fire, my nipples aching, my panties already damp. The scent of our combined desire wafted between us, sending spark after spark of electricity.

I was floored at the hunger rolling through me, every touch igniting the embers I'd kept warm just for him.

He was hard as a rock, pressing his throbbing cock into my stomach. I ground my hips back and forth, the sensations jetting through me powerful enough to steal my breath.

When he broke the kiss, he cupped my jaw, digging his fingers into my skin. His chest rose and fell from his labored breathing, a slight growl sizzling my skin.

"You're one bad girl."

"Yes. Like I said, you weren't here to keep me in line."

"I'm here now." He backed away, spinning me around to face the mirror. Without hesitation, he reached around my waist, unfastening my jeans.

"What are you doing?"

"Giving you a reminder to behave," he murmured, his reflection keeping me in awe. I didn't know how it was possible, but he'd gotten more dangerous looking with his scruffy beard and disheveled hair. But he was the most rugged, best-looking man I'd ever laid eyes on.

I didn't fight him as he yanked my jeans and lace thong down to my knees. Every muscle was tense, excitement tearing through me. He had a way of making me feel more alive than I had most of my life.

As I gripped the edge of the counter, he pressed down on the small of my back. I thought for certain he was going to rip off his belt, but when he brought his hand down, smacking my naked bottom four times in rapid succession, I took a deep breath. It wasn't that I craved pain, although when I was with Maverick, I longed to experience everything with him, but his dominating hold on me felt right.

People would think me crazy if they knew my story, the ugliness I'd experienced. But with the rugged cowboy tracker, everything was different. He was caring, loving, and his hunger kept me feeling alive.

I closed my eyes, opening my legs as wide as the tight confines of my jeans would allow, even more excited about the thought of people walking into the bathroom. I should be horrified, ashamed I was being treated like a bad little girl, but my pussy ached more now than ever before.

"You can't confront bad men, sweetheart. One day you'll get yourself into trouble." His words were said with such sincerity, his worry about me evident. He rubbed his fingers from one side of my bottom to the other, taking a deep breath as he rolled the tips down the crack of my ass.

I was so wet, my pussy clenching and releasing.

"Damn, woman. I want to fuck you." When he resumed the spanking, bending me further over the counter, I let myself fall into a sweet surrender.

The pain was invigorating, my mind whirling from the possibilities of what he'd do to me later. I couldn't wait to be in his arms, fulfilling his needs.

And sucking his big, fat cock.

My mouth watered at the thought even as the pain exploded, shifting into blissful anguish. My bottom was on fire, tingling sensations jetting through me. I couldn't breathe, had no way of focusing but I was very much alive. The sound his hand made as it connected with my skin drowned out the honky-tonk music, but it was the rapid beating of my heart that kept me on fire.

As his chest continued to rise and fall, I had a feeling he wouldn't be able to hold back fucking me. The thought was filthy and sinful. Who'd want to be fucked in the bathroom of a raunchy bar?

This bad girl wanted to raise her hand. I'd never wanted anything so much.

He smacked me six more times, one right after the other. Then he slipped his hand between my legs, stroking my clit.

"You're wet," he growled.

"Uh-huh." I licked my lips, panting until I was lightheaded.

"Did you think about me?"

"All the time."

"Did you hunger for my thick cock?"

I shifted my gaze, pursing my lips. "Every. Single. Night."

He took his time rolling his fingers up and down the length of my pussy, using his knee to force my jeans to the floor. His laugh was almost evil as I struggled to yank one foot from the pile, giving him more access.

When he thrust several fingers into my molten pussy, I thought I'd lose it right there.

"Oh, God. I missed you."

"Baby. I ain't going anywhere for a long time," he whispered into my ear then nipped my earlobe, allowing a brief growl to shatter my senses before dragging his tongue down the back of my neck. "But I need to be inside of you. Right here. Right now. I ain't taking no for an answer."

"Who's telling you no?" I gave him a wry smile, opening my legs even wider. As he pumped his fingers inside, curling the tips, I slapped my hand on the glass. Heat was rising between us, the mirror already fogged. I heard noise from behind us but we both ignored it, my amazing cowboy far too busy turning my body into mush to care who might be standing behind us.

Watching.

Hungering.

He was forceful in his actions, driving me to the point of a climax then pulling back. I loved and hated how he teased me, but the electricity was incredible, spiraling us both out of control. We were both panting, our animalistic sounds permeating the space. Nothing and no one could stop us at this point.

Stars floated in front of my eyes and I lolled my head, my legs shaking to the point I was fearful I'd collapse on the floor. He refused to stop, rolling his thumb around my clit as he brought me so close to a moment of rapture. When my body couldn't take it any longer, an orgasm smashed into my system.

"Oh. Oh. Oh. Oh." I slapped my hand on the glass several times, the freestanding piece rattling as if ready to crash to the floor. I didn't care, the rapture too powerful.

"That's it. Yeah, baby. Come like a good little girl."

One climax wasn't enough, a second exploding from deep within. Beads of perspiration trickled down my cheek but nothing in comparison to the sweat rolling down his rugged face. I wiped the glass, desperate to watch everything he did.

With my body still shaking, he took a step away and I almost screamed out. But I should have known what he was doing by the leer on his handsome face.

He wasted no time unfastening his belt and unzipping his jeans, freeing his massive cock. I bit my lower lip from the sight of his swollen, purple tip, his entire shaft throbbing from the desperate hunger and need furrowing into him.

Everything about the moment was naughty and we might go to hell for our blinding sin, but it was well worth it. There was no pretense in his actions, no romance required. He gripped my hip with one hand, digging his nails into my skin the thrust the entire length of his cock inside.

"Oh. My. Yes. Yes!" I knew my scream had to be heard over the roar of music but I wasn't the kind of girl to be quiet about anything I did.

He threw his head back, roaring his moment of pleasure then pulled out, thrusting into me again.

And again.

As he developed a beautiful rhythm, I couldn't stop panting, now clawing at the mirror as our heated breath became even steamier.

He fucked me like it was his last action on earth, his dying wish, the force slamming me into the counter. He was nothing but a wild beast claiming his prey and by God, I thought I'd grabbed a slice of heaven. The moment was amazing, more so than anything I'd experienced in my entire life, and I wanted more.

Much more.

Every sound Maverick made was husky, every growl igniting my senses. My skin was seared, every cell boiling. I couldn't get enough of the man.

"My baby. All mine. All mine." He kept repeating the words as if ensuring I knew better than to talk to another man, let alone touch him. How had this happened so fast?

Panting, I dropped my head, another climax pushing against my system. I was floating on air, consumed with desires and as the vibrations shot up from my toes, I threw my head back, only there was no sound erupting from my mouth.

He breathed against my neck, nipping my earlobe again, and I was certain he was ready to erupt deep inside.

But he had other things in mind.

Maverick had a way of giving me a heated onceover that seared my skin all over again. When he pulled out, I tensed, the inner bad girl telling me exactly what he had planned. As he pressed the tip to my dark hole, I sucked in my breath, my body shaking from anticipation. The same wry smile I'd seen so many times before remained on his face as he breached my opening. A flash of pain was instant, and I dropped my head, gasping for air.

For the rough man to be gentle left me in awe, a series of tickling prickles dancing down the back of my legs. He pressed several inches inside, hitting the tight ring of muscle. Then he couldn't hold back any longer, driving the remaining few inches inside.

A single, short moan slipped past my lips as he yanked me backward, his cock swelling until it stretched my muscles. He wrapped one arm around my waist, lifting me off my feet. There was an entirely different look in his eyes, the deep cerulean blue changing colors, becoming more luminescent. The powerful man had a way of mesmerizing me without him even knowing.

Or trying.

The way he was holding me was possessive, the rough pads of his fingers finding the sensitive skin of my stomach. As he shifted his hips, pulling out then driving back inside, I couldn't stop shuddering.

"What do you want, little girl?" he asked as if I had all the answers in the world.

But there wasn't an easy one that came to mind. What I needed I doubted anyone could provide, but in his arms I believed anything was possible. "Happiness."

"Mmm… Then your wish is granted." Very slowly he allowed my feet to touch the floor, his muscles tensing as he started to fuck me in earnest, his jaw clenched so tightly his reflection was almost scary.

But I had no fear of him, only of myself for falling too hard.

Too fast.

Then he'd realize the woman he held in his arms was far too damaged to be what he needed. As rage built for the past, denying any further joy for the night, I did what I could to hide my fury and sadness.

And within a few minutes, he started to shake, losing control. As he erupted deep inside my ass, all I could think about was when the beautiful time we'd spent together would come to a shattering end.

CHAPTER 12

M*averick*

Bullshit.

The word continued to play in the back of my mind, the ugliness of lies keeping me on edge. Rangers had finally dug out Bruno's body from the several inches of packed snow he'd been caught in, the US Marshals standing by as if they still needed to arrest him. I'd been lucky, maybe using up my last life. Sam had dug me out of the snow, pulling me to safety first, his training keeping him from wasting any time. Then I'd managed to dig the hostages out of the several feet of snow, thankful help had arrived a few hours later. I hadn't thought they'd make it after all they'd been through.

Candy and Mark Wells. If either one of them had anything to do with the Butelli crime syndicate, I was Santa Claus. But they'd been targeted. That much I knew in my gut. The marshals were keeping dark secrets. At some point, I'd force them to tell me.

"The hero returns," Gage said as he clapped me on the back.

I didn't bother shifting on the barstool, knowing he'd slide against the bar, refusing to let me enjoy a night of drinking.

At least until Scorpion allowed Lily to leave for the night. Even now, her eyes watched me as she picked up a tray of drinks, her sly smile keeping my cock at full attention. I was uncomfortable as hell, my balls swollen. She had that kind of effect on me.

I grabbed a handful of peanuts, unable to keep from glaring at the circus that still existed outside Raunchy Ride, reporters taking up temporary residence. At least Gage had forewarned Scorpion about the onslaught of reporters, but not before they'd invaded the interior, shoving their goddamn cameras in my face.

"I was just doing my job," I insisted then yanked the shot of tequila into my hand, powering it back without hesitation. It wasn't my usual drink of choice, but after the unnerving adventure, bourbon didn't cut it.

"You and I know that's not true. It became personal to you." He glanced at the crowd, acting as if he wasn't really interested. I knew better.

"Nothing is personal."

"Bullshit, Maverick. I saw the way you and Lily looked at each other after you walked inside that door. Then you were ready to beat the crap out of that dude for touching her. And if I hadn't threatened them with arrest, you'd be biding your time until you could take them out one at a time."

"Who says I'm not going to do it anyway?" I shoved the shot glass across the bar, getting the bartender's attention.

"You're a loose cannon, buddy. I'm glad you finally found someone to keep you happy, but you can't go off halfcocked every time a man glances in her direction."

"They weren't glancing. They were touching."

"Jesus Christ. She's not Belle."

I slowly turned my head, staring into his eyes. "I told you never to say her name around me."

"Fuck it, man. You need to let that shit go."

"Have you? Are you going to honestly tell me that every time you lift your head, glancing at Sapphire Ridge, you don't think about her? About that night? About…" I couldn't put my feelings into the appropriate words. "When I was buried under the snow, all I could think about was that I'd finally gotten the punishment I deserved for not being able to save Belle. Then I knew I had to protect Lily. That's what kept me alive."

Gage's eyes opened wide. "You're not the one to blame for Belle's death. We all are."

We. The word was being used loosely, the guilt the six of us carried manifesting itself in different ways. When the bartender filled the glass with another hit of tequila, I wrapped my hand around it, using enough force I was surprised the thick crystal didn't shatter in my hand.

I couldn't swallow the new shot fast enough, slamming the thick glass on the bar's surface with a brutal thud. "It's obvious you don't remember shit. Fine."

The tension between us had never been so intense. I was taking out my anger on him for all the rage and remorse that had piled up in my little red wagon over the last few years. The garbage with Bruno had been the last straw. I was itching to break somebody's neck. I couldn't look at Gage, preferring to nurse the beer in front of me.

He moved closer, his voice full of anger. "Really? So that's why I wake up every other night in a cold sweat, Belle's face lingering in the back of my mind. That's why I almost landed in prison when you and the others were off killing people legally. I was the one who spent days on that mountain after you guys left the city, refusing to come down. I don't know what the hell I was searching for but I sure as shit didn't find it. Why the hell do you think I can't have a relationship, Wolfman? It's not because I don't want to commit, to share a home with someone and be able to wake up with her by my side every day. It's because I know better than to try. I'd just destroy her life, killing her spirit if not hurting her given the night terrors I've had for years. Do you want to know why I don't have people over to my house?"

The angst in his voice was dangerously close to erupting in rage. "Why?" I gritted out.

"Because I can't patch up the holes I drive into the wallboard with my fist fast enough." He allowed the statement to dig into the far reaches of my mind before continuing.

"You see that woman over there, the one you were pawing in the goddamn bathroom a few minutes ago?"

The fact he was talking about Lily pushed my irritation to another level and I refused to budge. That's when Gage did something so unexpected that I was momentarily thrown. He yanked my arm, forcing me off the barstool.

"Take a goddamn look, Maverick. See that woman over there? Yeah, you know the one. She cares about you. Granted, she doesn't know shit because you're not the kind of man to open up to anyone. That's why you almost got yourself killed overseas. That's also why you risk your life every chance you get. If you don't want to be honest with her, ain't my business, but do her a favor and walk away. She might not know it, but it'll be the best damn gift you can give her."

He'd never spoken to me this way. Not once in all the years we'd known each other. His words haunted the man inside, enough so my muscles twitched. He was right, my original assessment spot on.

She deserved a better life than I could provide.

"Just stop feeling sorry for yourself," he huffed.

"I'll take that under advisement. Did you get any info on the hostages?"

"Nothing. The marshals are keeping them on lockdown."

"There's something fishy about the entire situation."

He threw up his arms. "Another piece of advice. Let it alone. You did your job. You got paid."

My buddy knew that when something stuck in my craw, I was a bulldog until I figured it out. However, he was right in that I'd get nowhere fast. "Fine."

"Right. I can tell you're not going to listen to me. I'll see you later."

While I watched him taking long strides, disappearing into the crowd, I did what I could to keep the anger from getting the better of me. I shoved the empty glass across the bar for a second time, demanding the bartender's attention.

"What the fuck was that about?" Snake asked as he and Phoenix approached, narrowing his eyes then glancing toward Gage.

"Nothing that matters." I couldn't stand the warm beer and shoved it aside, cursing under my breath. Both knew better than to bug me when I got into this kind of mood. "Are the fucking press gone?"

"Yeah, I think they finally gave up," Phoenix answered. "You're a real hometown hero though. If you hadn't been there, that couple would have died."

"They're not out of danger yet. There's bound to be another mafia enforcer arriving any day now." At least the girl behind the bar didn't shove me aside, bringing the bottle to the bar, her eyes never leaving mine as she poured the glass full. I wasted no time tossing it into my mouth, holding it for a few seconds before swallowing. Maybe I should drink acid instead. That would make the pain disappear faster.

Snake snorted. "You're grumpier than usual. I thought you'd be happy, big paycheck and all."

"Haven't you learned by now money isn't everything?" I yanked out my wallet, pulling out a couple of twenty-dollar bills.

"It's on the house," the bartender said. "Compliments of Scorpion."

Shit. I hated charity under normal circumstances. I left the money anyway.

"You're coming to Houston's big shindig tomorrow night. Right?" Snake pushed.

"You can take a look at how the sanctuary is coming along," Phoenix added. They were relentless, which did little for my fury.

"Riggs. I'm really thrilled that you found yourself in building the sanctuary, but I'm not in any mood for a party." That was the truth. Even though I'd thought about whether it would bring Lily somewhat out of her shell.

"Whatever your problem is, get the stick out of your ass," Phoenix said, ignoring his given name as usual. The fact was he was shoving my self-pity down my throat. "You saved a couple lives. You got the bad guy. And from what I can tell, you found a beautiful woman who somehow can look beyond your surly bullshit. Houston is returning home. You never know, buddy. The gang might all be together for one night only."

His words were harsh, but he couldn't keep the glint out of his eyes. "Let me guess, you conned Colt into handling the music." Colt Rivers lived a dream life as a country music star. At least he'd managed to get out of town unscathed.

"If so, the fucker better watch his step with me," Snake commented. He'd remained angry for Colt for leaving without saying more than a few words. Only Phoenix had maintained any contact whatsoever.

"Jesus Christ, both of you. Just stop by for a few. What it's going to hurt, unless you have big plans," Riggs added.

"Yeah, then we can tease you more since you're on national television." Snake burst into laughter, knowing how much I loathed any and all publicity. When he threw up his hands, acting like he was going to surrender, I lifted my middle finger.

"And you can introduce us to that girl of yours." Phoenix winked as Lily headed toward the bar. "If I weren't hitched."

"Touch her and die. I'm just warning you." At least I could grin, shaking off the events if only for a little while. Unfortunately, I had a bad feeling that refused to leave.

The danger I just went through was nothing in comparison to what was on the horizon. I was certain of it. Maybe Gage was right, and I was a loose cannon.

Somehow, I had a feeling that's exactly the reason I might be able to keep her alive.

"You're coming to the party, Lily. That's final." I folded my arms, remaining in the doorway. She'd turned me down over the phone, so I thought a little personal persuasion was in order.

"I'm working tonight," she said, giving me a mischievous look.

"All I need to do is make a single phone call. You know that. Right?"

Lily grimaced. "I need the money. Somehow, a little fairy must have helped me get a pretty spectacular house. Oh, this one."

When she gave me a stern look, I laughed. "What? I did nothing but make a phone call."

"You're not a good liar."

"You're calling me a liar? I just might need to spank that butt of yours again to remind you who's in charge."

"Nope." She took a step away, laughing. "Seriously, I need to make money to buy groceries so I can eat and have nice things like clothes. Go to the party by yourself, big boy. Or should I call you Wolfman?"

Growling, I gathered her into my arms, swatting her on the bottom. "Who told you?"

"I might have overheard Scorpion use it."

"I'll kill him."

"You're not going to tell me why, are you?"

I gave her a stern look. "Not unless you come to the party. You need to enjoy life."

Her smile faded slowly, a strange look appearing in her eyes. "I do, at least with you. Give me a couple weeks and I'll feel better about taking time off. Okay?" She pressed her hand against my chest, using every bit of her feminine wiles on me.

After bending my index finger, I brushed it back and forth across her jaw. "I love your independence, but I can't ignore the fact you're hiding something from me. Maybe one day you can trust me enough to tell me what that is."

"It's not you, Maverick. The two times I trusted someone I was wrong and paid for it. I'm just… I'm broken."

"You're not broken, baby, just bruised a little. I'm going to write down the address. If you can stop by, that would be great. I'll show you around the sanctuary."

At least her eyes lit up. "I'd love to do it again."

"Again?"

"Be with animals," she answered quickly. Too quickly. "They're my heart too. Aren't you, Sammy boy?"

When he jumped up, standing taller by a few inches, she laughed, the sparkle returning in her eyes.

"Don't spoil him," I teased.

As he started licking her face, I thought she'd fall over from laughter and from his weight. As they continued their love fest, I moved into the kitchen, trying to find a notepad. When I noticed a single photograph on the kitchen counter, my curiosity got the better of me. The girl in the photo looked a lot like Lily. I flipped it over, noticing the date. There was also a city indicated.

"What are you doing?" There was an edge to her voice that surprised me.

"Looking for a piece of paper."

She snatched the photo from my hand quickly, shoving it into her back pocket. Then she tried to smile, but there was no doubt I'd snagged a small piece of her privacy, a detail that could possibly unravel the mystery around who she was. I knew better than to push it.

"I think I saw a notepad around here somewhere." She remained nervous as she looked through drawers, pulling out a pad and pencil a few minutes later. "Here you go." When she walked closer, she refused to look me in the eyes.

I could swear she was worried that I'd put two and two together.

As I scribbled the address, I kept my eyes on her. She was now a nervous wreck. What in God's name was she hiding?

"So, is this a fancy party?" she asked, just as anxious as a few seconds before.

"Hell, no. Phoenix is a real cowboy, even though he became one of the richest men in Montana. My guess is they'll have it in the horse barn."

Her laughter returned but when she lifted her head to look me in the eyes, I noticed hers were clouded with pain.

And fear.

When I found out who'd hurt her, I would become the loose cannon I'd been accused of. Then I'd stand back and be glad that I was. "I like that," she purred. "Maybe I'll stop by for a few minutes anyway. I'll text you if I'm coming. Is that fair?"

"Mmmm… I'm not sure about that but I'll take it."

"That's all you're gonna get, Wolfman."

I laughed but I had a feeling she knew I was faking it for the most part. There was no closing Pandora's Box now that it had been opened.

She was riding on borrowed time. Whoever the monster was out to get her would eventually rear his ugly head.

I'd be there to chop it off.

* * *

Work. She had to work.

I knew it was a damn excuse, but I didn't want to scare her more than I could tell she already had been.

I knew Lily was doing everything to try to get ahead, but she'd taken the extra shift on purpose. So maybe I'd come on a little strong after getting back, but it wasn't as if she'd shoved me away.

Sam whimpered from the seat next to me, his tail constantly thumping against the door.

"I tried, buddy. She just didn't want to come."

Woof!

He didn't buy it either, but there was nothing I could do short of kidnapping her, which hadn't been far from my mind. Huffing, I rubbed my hand across my beard, thinking about her desire to have me shave. Huh. How long had it been? What the hell? Maybe I'd do it later.

I wasn't hanging around at the party for long myself. I had no interest in pretending that everything was hunky dory in life, or whatever people with happy little families would call it. I was happy for Phoenix and Snake that they'd found the loves of their lives, but I wasn't the kind of guy to plan on family get-togethers every couple of weeks, festive celebrations in the summer.

And I didn't have the girl.

Every time either one of us got close, one or the other would pull back. I had to remind myself I'd only known her a few days. As I headed down the road, the amount of ongoing construction continued to surprise me. Phoenix was putting his heart and soul into providing an animal sanctuary that likely didn't exist anywhere else.

All because of the influence and love of a woman.

Fuck me. I was wallowing in the very self-pity both he and Gage had accused me of. It was hard to admit to anyone, let alone myself that I wanted her by my side.

Not just for all the carnal delights.

Chuckling, I noticed Sam was staring at me, his tail no longer thumping. "What? I can think of her that way."

He whined and slumped down in the seat.

"You don't have dibs on her, buddy. You'd never met her if it wasn't for me. Remember that?"

The way he harrumphed meant he was disappointed in my decision not to kidnap her. "I left her with the address. I even commanded she attend. What more do you want?"

His hard gaze was amusing.

Slowing, I allowed the engine to idle as I stared out the windshield.

I should have known the party was going to be a big soiree. Phoenix couldn't do anything without making it over the top.

Still, the number of vehicles lined up on both sides of the street reminded me how much I hated crowds. And people for that matter. I found a spot, taking a few seconds to consider turning around and heading back to the bar to wait for her.

A couple of beers and if she hadn't texted by then, I'd leave. "Okay, buddy. Don't wander off too far." As soon as he was out of the truck he bounded off in search of a playmate. Sighing, I stood where I was for a few minutes, staring at the crowd of people. I'd never been good with parties, but this one bothered me more than it should. If Colt showed up, it would be the first time all six of us were back together since the incident on the mountain.

Maybe the others had moved past the tragedy, but it wasn't easy to ignore the events even if we'd failed to talk about it as a group after being ostracized by almost everyone in town. They'd called us the Bad Boys of Missoula long before Belle had been consumed in the fire. While time had softened memories for some, I could still see the events of the evening as if captured in a movie.

I finally headed in the direction of the noise, immediately catching Snake's eye. He grinned as he lumbered toward me, the limp he'd gotten while serving overseas less pronounced than when he'd risen from the dead. He had the girl on his arm to thank for that, her patience with him surprising almost everyone.

He was as grumpy as I was on the outside, but she'd managed to soften him. Maybe that's what the guys hoped would happen with having Lily in my life. I didn't see it. Not one bit.

"You finally decided to show up," he said as he swaggered closer, proud to have his arm wrapped around his woman. "You remember Chasity."

"How could I forget? I did save her life and all." I was able to laugh as she shook her head.

"I seem to remember I held my own pretty darn well," she purred in her lilting voice.

"Uh-huh. I saved you from eaten by wolves. That's what I remember."

"Very funny." She gave me the same look of chastisement I'd seen multiple times from Lily. The two of them would get along famously.

"Where can a guy get a drink around here?" I asked, eyeing the barn that had almost been torched to the ground only a few months before.

"There's a bar set up in front of the barn. Where's Lily?" Snake asked, his grin remaining.

"Working."

"You mean she couldn't stand being around you any longer."

I punched him playfully and headed toward the corral. Phoenix was holding court as he usually did and as I moved closer, I wasn't surprised he was describing the sanctuary. "We just need another veterinarian, a whole lot of people who love animals in order to handle the other duties and we'll be ready to go in thirty days. I'm not good at hiring people either."

I thought about Lily given her love of animals but shoved it aside. She wasn't ready to settle down anywhere. I had a feeling she wouldn't stay in Missoula for long, the noose around her neck already getting tighter.

Not that I was the kind of man who could handle being tied down under any circumstances. I pulled away, scanning the facility.

The crowd was already lively even at barely seven-thirty in the evening. I felt like a fish out of water standing by myself while everyone else talked in couples or groups. I'd done this to myself, refusing to be a part of the city I'd grown up in. Maybe I still held resentment to the way all six of us had been treated over the years, only Snake considered a true hero after his return from the dead.

At least Houston was getting a warm welcome, already entrenched in the smokejumper life. I knew a few of the guys on the Zullie crew, smokejumpers as tight as teams of Marines. He'd served his country. Now he was going to protect Montana's people. Good for him. He'd found a real purpose in life.

As I headed for the bar, I noticed Sam had already found his buddy, Apollo, the dog Snake had rescued overseas. Sophie wasn't far behind, the pup Wren had rescued months before. At least the furry creatures were already having a good time. I grabbed a cold beer from one of the coolers, popping the top and immediately taking a swig. Then I felt a presence behind me and immediately bristled.

"I wondered if you'd show." Houston's voice was deeper than I remembered, but it still had the same hard edge that had made him appear the ultimate bad boy, the guy who always got the girl.

Including Belle.

Then again, she'd fallen hard for all six of us, refusing to choose just one. A few of us had joked at the time we could deal with sharing her. Everybody knew better. We were possessive alphas, incapable of sharing anything.

I turned slowly and the look we shared didn't need words. I'd been the one to shove everybody away, our tight friendship all but demolished. "I'm here."

"It's good to see you, buddy," he said more in passing as he shifted his angry gaze to the barn. "Phoenix has done a real good job of turning this place around."

"It was doing just fine until his father purposely fucked it up."

"Yeah, well, the man is dead." He chuckled after making the statement. "We're all getting older. You know? We need to bury the past."

"Just like we buried Belle?" Only we didn't. There'd been too much carnage left over from the horrific fire to sift through rubble in an attempt to discover her bones. She had a tombstone but no casket. That would have suited her just fine given she'd been such a free spirit.

He tensed, taking another pull on his beer. "You need to get over it."

"Said the man who ran away."

Houston snapped his head in my direction, crowding my space. When he fisted one hand, I snarled.

"Okay, whoa. None of that shit," Phoenix growled from behind me. "This is a party. If you guys can't behave, then fucking leave."

"It's my party," Houston insisted.

"Things can change, buddy," Phoenix added. "Seriously. We need to celebrate the good times."

Whatever they were.

"Fine," I quipped then started to turn away.

Houston grabbed my arm then held his out for a handshake. "Let's try and remember we were friends once."

I slowly lowered my gaze, taking a deep breath. Then I accepted the gesture. "Yeah, we were. So, smokejumping. That seems like a stretch."

"It's what I gotta do."

I could tell he didn't want to talk about his reasons why. The moment was awkward, a knot forming in my gut.

We both heard a loud voice coming from a microphone then dozens of cheers. "Colt."

"The big star," Houston muttered. "He's with a different woman every photograph. I don't know how he does it cause he's not that good looking."

I snorted beer, almost choking. Colt had been the good-looking one, always singing even then. "Well. Things change. Right?"

We both laughed. Then his expression changed, the same kind of darkness reflected in the mirror every morning crossing his face. "I lost my fiancée in a fire early last year. I was devastated. You don't really appreciate life and the special moments until you don't have them anymore." His words were unexpected, catching me off guard. Huffing, he threw me a look. "Not what you were expecting, huh?"

I had no idea what I'd anticipated with him returning to town, but this wasn't it.

"I'm sorry, man."

"I tried to save her. You know?" he asked, although it wasn't a question that needed an answer. "I did what I could, going back into the house twice, but it was too late. We were going to be married in two months to the day. She had the dress. The location was paid for. Hell, we'd even picked out the cake together." He half laughed but the sound of his pain tore at what was left of the man inside.

"I know you, Houston. You did your best."

"Did I?" He turned to face me once again. "I've played over in my mind how I'd do things differently so many times the images never leave me. Just like with Belle." He lifted his head, searching my eyes. Maybe I'd been wrong. All six of us were damaged goods, incapable of allowing closure.

"Yeah. I have no doubt you tried to be a hero."

Just saying the word seemed foreign, biting. I wasn't good with trying to console anyone.

"Well, you were certainly a hero. You saved two innocent victims. Good for you."

"That's why you became a smokejumper, to try and be a hero?" I asked.

He bristled once again then sighed. "Maybe a little. Maybe to ease my conscience. I don't know. Maybe I'm more like you than I want to admit. We take risks without thinking them through. We act like we're going to live forever, but the clock is ticking, buddy. Take it from me. Accolades and awards mean nothing if you don't have someone to share it with. You know?"

I nodded, as usual my thoughts returning to Lily. "Maybe I do."

"I heard you had a girl. I saw it on television."

"What do you mean you saw it?" I'd purposely ignored the bullshit with the reporters.

"You didn't know?"

"Know what?"

He laughed. "There's some great video of the two of you embracing. She's one beautiful girl. What's her name, Lily? You made the freaking national news. Hometown hero and his girl. The caption is a lot better than that. Impressive. The only bad thing was they had to bring up the shit on Sapphire Ridge again. Assholes. At least they didn't blame us for Belle's death like usual."

There was no reason for my blood to run cold, but it did. "Yeah, it's Lily." Or was it?

He was right in that it was time to let the past die, buried under the same rubble the Belle had been. Now there was another dark moment to deal with, protecting someone I was already falling in love with.

I glanced toward the mountains, ice forming in my veins. If Lily was running from someone, an open invitation had just been sent.

And this time, I'd die in order to keep the woman I loved safe.

CHAPTER 13

ily

"Turn off the news," I said to no one in particular. The bartender glanced in my direction, shrugging her shoulders.

"He's a hometown hero but he wasn't always considered a good guy," she said casually, as if I should just get over it.

Today's breaking news focus had been on some fire almost twenty years before. I'd seen just enough to know both he and some of his friends had been interrogated for a purposely set fire, and the loss of a life. The ugliness weighed on my mind, but I refused to see Maverick as anything but the hero I knew him to be.

"Just turn it the fuck off." I was angry. For him. For me. For life being such a pain in the ass.

"Sure. I'll turn on the basketball game. The regulars prefer that anyway." She gave me a sour look but didn't argue.

Huffing, I turned, not expecting to see Scorpion standing in front of me.

He glanced at the television then back to me, moving closer. "Don't believe everything you hear. People need absolute trash to talk about, nothing more."

"Is it true what they said?" I asked, although I wasn't certain I wanted to hear the answer.

There was something about the way he shook his head defiantly that made me feel better.

"There was an accidental fire on one of the local mountain ranges and a girl couldn't be rescued. Sure, the sheriff's department, the press, and just about everybody in town pointed fingers, but it was a crock of shit. That the piranhas have brought it up now pisses me off."

"The sheriff's department? Isn't the sheriff a friend of his?" I hated to admit I was curious.

Scorpion leaned against the bar. "The incident was almost twenty years ago. At that point in time, Gage was part of the Bad Boys."

"Bad Boys. Wolfman. All these names attached to people. Were these Bad Boys true delinquents?"

He grinned like a kid. "No more than the group I ran with. That's why we know each other. A bunch of stupid guys who thought they were kings way back when. Fortunately, at least for most of us, the military sucked that out of us."

"That's why you're so tight. You served together."

"In the same outfit, the Marines, but we still went our separate ways."

"I'd love to hear what happened on the mountain," I told him, my skills had fishing for information likely obvious.

"No can do, lady. You'll need to hear that from Maverick. If he'll tell you. The difficult time they went through nearly crushed them. They all withdrew from society, their friends. Then they escaped. We all did in a way. Speaking of Maverick. Why aren't you at the big party?"

"Because I had to work."

"Uh-huh. I think you're frightened of getting close to him. I'm taking matters into my own hands. Get out. You're not working another minute. If you don't, I'll fire you."

There was a mischievous glint in his eyes, but I scowled nonetheless. "You're a mean boss."

"It makes me happy to hear you say that. That means I've done my job. I'm serious. Go to the party. I'll be there in an hour or so. You need to get to know the people in this town. Not all of them have bad memories."

"I guess I have no other choice then."

"Nope. You don't. Get moving."

I untied my apron, more excited than I thought I'd be. Maybe I'd just surprise him and show up. I'd brought another shirt with me just in case, humming as I changed. After gathering my things, I headed to my truck, smiling from the thought of seeing Maverick. As soon as I unlocked the door, tossing my things inside, a strange set of vibrations skittered down my spine, fear crawling into every muscle.

Very slowly I turned around, scanning the parking lot. While there were people coming and going, the busy road in front of the bar filled with traffic, there was nothing unusual that caught my eye, including the boogeyman waiting to drag me to hell.

Exhaling, I reminded myself that I was perfectly safe here before climbing inside. But my hands continued to shake as I started the engine. Maybe one day I'd get over the horrible dread that facing a new morning had given me. I'd played out all the possible scenarios so often I could recite them in my sleep.

But nothing had happened to give credence to the terror. I wasn't going to let the monsters win. I had a new life and I planned on enjoying every moment of it.

The location wasn't as far as I'd originally thought and less than twenty minutes later, I was rolling down the last street. Almost instantly several huge buildings came into view. It was easy to see there was significant construction happening on a large ranch. The sanctuary. I couldn't wait to see it.

When I pulled in, I was shocked to find so many vehicles parked along the fence. There had to be two hundred people here at least. I found a parking spot knowing I'd need to walk quite a ways, but the evening was warmer than it had been, the skies perfectly clear. As soon as I stepped onto the gravel, my senses were assaulted by the scent of barbeque, the blaring country music already making me want to tap my boot on the ground.

I couldn't remember the last time I'd been to a party. Years. So many I wasn't certain how to act.

After running my fingers through my hair, I headed for the crowd of people in the distance, the sounds of dogs barking and horses whinnying adding to the festive atmosphere. When I finally came close to one of several groups, I started looking for my man.

My man.

Who was I kidding? I couldn't imagine him being with just one woman. But maybe… A laugh caught me by surprise, the giddiness I felt unexpected. No one paid me any attention as I weaved through the crowd, until I caught someone's eye. The sheriff.

He grinned then pointed to the left, his smile widening as soon as I headed in the direction he'd indicated.

I found Maverick just a few seconds later. His muscular back faced me, the man standing with a group of other men, several of them trying to talk over each other as well as the loud music. Out of the corner of my eye I noticed an attractive cowboy was on a makeshift stage, singing his heart out, people cheering and clapping. Everyone had a drink in their hand and animals were running around free and happy.

I'd never experienced anything like this in all my years. While Carmine had required me to attend a few parties while living at his estate, they'd been forced appearances. Even his guests had been demure, as if required to be in attendance. This was entirely different. Party and chaos were two words that came to mind. As I inched closer to the mountain man extraordinaire, I remained silent, unable to keep a smile off my face.

At least two of the men Maverick was standing with noticed me, having difficulty not drowning in smug looks. When I was within a few inches, I wrapped my arms around him, unable to keep from laughing.

That's when Sam bounded through the crowd, jumping on both of us, the force toppling us to the ground with the hulking mass of a man landing on top of me. The wind knocked out of me, I pushed against him, unable to keep from laughing as Sam tried to lick my face, his entire body wiggling.

"That's a way to make an entrance," one of the guys said.

"That's the kind of girl the big man needs," another snarked.

I pressed my hands against Maverick's chest, trying to catch my breath. "Howdy, cowboy. Were you missing me?"

He didn't react at first, his breathing labored. Then he rubbed his fingers down my cheek, the feel of his throbbing cock pressing against me exciting. "Took you long enough. I'm going to keep you on a leash from now on."

"Oh, is that how you're going to take me?" I purred.

When he lowered his head, his scent became intoxicating, filthy thoughts the driving force in my mind. "That's exactly what I'm going to do."

He remained hovering over me, his lips dangerously close. All I needed to do was lift my head to force a kiss, but I waited for him to react instead. Sam continued to jump and bark, doing his best to get in the middle of us.

"Oh, for the love of God. Kiss her already."

The bold statement forced Maverick to grin, everyone else around us to laugh. Then I noticed my mountain savior had raised his arm, giving the man his middle finger.

"So? Are you going to kiss me?" I teased.

"When I'm good and ready. And baby, I plan on doing a lot more than that."

His words gave me a shiver, my core as hot and wet as it could be. I couldn't resist, lifting my head and grabbing a kiss. Then he fisted my hair, thrusting his tongue inside. As he ground his body back and forth, I became lightheaded. I had a feeling the beautiful moment would have continued had the crowd not started to clap.

He reared back, issuing a growl that could be heard over the music before guiding me to my feet. "You guys are assholes," he said gruffly, but I could tell he was happier than I'd seen him from the beginning of our wicked affair. Maybe the party was good for both of us.

There was something so possessive about the way he was looking at me, his chest still rising and falling. Moonlight shimmered across his face, accentuating the primal look in his eyes. He was already devouring me in his mind.

"You're a very bad man," I said, trying to break the tension.

"You have no idea."

"I think I do," I cooed then noticed his friends were watching us intently. "Aren't you going to introduce me to your friends?"

"They're bad news," he said on purpose then tugged me closer to the group. "This is Lily Sanborn. I don't want to hear a minute of shit from any of you. Lily, that's Houston, the reason for the party. He's single so don't let him touch you or he dies."

I laughed along with everyone else, Houston giving me a slight bow.

"That's Snake, his real name Ricardo but don't call him that. He gets cranky when you do. Gage, the lawman in town. The big guy is Phoenix. He owns the place so be nice to him."

"Yeah, be nice to me," Phoenix teased.

"And Wren could kick your butt for hearing you say that," Maverick laughed. "His wife and much better half."

"Very funny," Phoenix growled.

"The one with the scowl over there is Mustang. And that's Hawk, maybe the gruffest of the bunch of us."

"Speak for yourself, buddy," Hawk snapped.

"He's right," I said to the group.

"Everyone's a comedian," Maverick muttered.

"Wow. Such fascinating names. I'm certain they all have wild stories," I said, noticing how close they all seemed.

"You have no idea," Hawk chortled. "We'll tell you over a drink sometime."

"I just want to know why Maverick is called the Wolfman." I playfully punched Maverick, amused that he rolled his eyes.

As the others started to howl, Maverick pulled me away. "Let's get you a drink."

Sam trailed along behind us, constantly bumping my leg. It was good to see him as always, his happy tail providing a smile.

"You still won't tell me why you're the Wolfman," I pushed, laughing from the way his brow furrowed.

"One day."

"Yeah, I know. If I'm good."

As he wrapped his arm around me in an unexpected move, guiding us through the crowd, I enjoyed the way everyone who was close by congratulated him on being a hero. And every single time the word was used, he cringed, obviously hating the word. I tried to concentrate on the way he walked, the thick denim highlighting his carved butt. No man should look so good in skin-tight jeans. Then there was the scent of his aftershave, although he hadn't shaved in so long I wondered why he bothered. He smelled of freshly cut timber and warm grasses in the spring, with a hint of exotic spice that I couldn't put my finger on.

As we approached the bar, he threw a look toward the stage. When I squealed, he frowned.

"That's Colt Rivers. He's a star. How did you get him to perform?"

"This ain't my party."

"Your friend then. He must have pull with Colt's agent." Granted, the ranch was high dollar, likely worth millions.

"Yup," he said, selecting wine instead of a beer. Then he grabbed a cold one for himself. I could easily tell he knew the singer. "He's an asshole if you ask me."

He should have known me better by now. I wasn't going to let it go. When he walked away in a huff, I caught up with him in a few seconds, yanking his arm. "Oh, no, you don't. How do you know him?"

His glare was surprising. Then his expression softened. "He's from Missoula. He ran with a crowd."

When he pulled away, heading back were we'd come from, even brushing past me, I used my stern voice on him. "You mean the crowd you ran with? The Missoula Bad Boys or something?"

He stopped short, whipping around and taking two long strides in my direction. I was momentarily thrown. "Don't ask about shit you don't know."

"You're right. You keep asking me questions about my life, but you refuse to tell me about yours." I wasn't going to back down. Not to him. Not to anyone.

The darkness couldn't hide his aggravation, but he softened, his smirk turning to a grin, his eyes settling on the way I'd slammed my hand on my hip. "You're not going to let this go, are you?"

"Not a chance, buster."

He flicked his gaze over my head then took my hand. "Come with me."

"Where are we going?"

"Where I say."

"The big he-man."

"Yup. Either come with me or I'll carry you there." There was amusement in his tone but I knew he meant it.

"As long as you tell me the truth."

"What did I tell you before?"

I tromped behind him for a few seconds before purposely moving in front, taking the lead. "I'm always good," I muttered for no other reason that he wasn't going to get the last word in.

For a few seconds, we kept the same stride. Then I realized he'd pulled back. Swiveling, I took a sip of wine on purpose, tapping my boot on the ground.

"Do you know where you're going?" he asked.

"That big building over there." I pointed, assuming that's where he wanted to take me.

"You think you know everything. Don't you, Lily?" He kicked his boot in the gravel and had an ah-shucks look on his face, as if we were kids in high school and I'd teased him.

"What I know is that you're avoiding the past."

Snickering, he shook his head. "You should talk."

"Fine. Let's get this over with." Maybe his bad behavior had rubbed off on me. I headed to the large facility, never once turning to look if he was following. Sam made his way inside first as soon as I threw open the door. Once inside, I was thrown into a moment of shock, enough so I barely registered he'd moved behind me.

Sam went nuts, flying around me and immediately burying his nose in a bucket full of balls.

Woof. Woof!

All I could do was laugh, spinning in circle after circle.

"What do you think?" he asked in a tone that suggested he'd been baiting me in order to get me in here.

"This is amazing." There was no way to describe the setting, the interior reminding me of a resort for humans with children. There was an indoor pool with slides, several playgrounds, and bins full of colorful toys and balls. None of them for humans. I spun around in another circle before racing from one side to the other, touching almost everything at least once.

The glass doors of several rooms highlighted bathing facilities, dogs spas complete with shelves of various shampoos in festive colors.

"I thought you'd like it. They're almost ready to open, although there are at least fifty animals already in the living quarters." His tone was changed entirely, more playful than before.

"Like it? I'd live here. This is incredible. It had to cost a fortune."

"With their state-of-the-art veterinary facility, including for large game animals, in the millions. But Phoenix and his wife aren't the only ones paying for it."

There was an entirely different glitch in his voice. When I shifted my gaze in his direction, I'd be damned if he wasn't blushing. Or maybe it was the LED lighting. Whatever the case, I couldn't help myself, the giddiness I felt releasing several emotions that had been buried deep inside. I raced toward him, tossing myself in his arms. "You invested in this?"

"Maybe a little bit of money. It's for a good cause."

"This is unlike anything I've ever seen before. I would love to see the veterinary facility."

"I thought you might. I know Phoenix and Wren need a lot of help. They're planning on doing some hiring in the next few days."

"Are you trying to get rid of me, cowboy? Make me work all the time?" When Sam threatened to jump into the pool, which was still partially green, I raced after him. "Don't do that, baby. It's not ready yet."

"He's used to swimming in streams and lakes. He can handle it."

"You don't understand what imbalanced pool chemicals can do to a dog's intestines. Not only can they developing gastrointestinal issues, the chemicals can burn the pads on their paws. And if they ingest even a small amount, it can damage their lungs." I spouted off a few other maladies until I realized he was looking at me funny.

Maverick walked closer, a shit-eating grin replacing his sourpuss expression. "Why do I have the feeling you know more about the health of animals than you're letting on?"

"I read a lot."

"Uh-huh. Maybe one day you'll learn to trust me."

"I do trust you," I said then shooed Sam away from the pool, tossing him several balls, one right after the other.

"Then tell me something about yourself that I don't know."

"What do you think you know, cowboy?" I asked playfully as I came closer, not enough for him to grab me, just enough to tease.

He rubbed his fingers across his beard. "You don't like people telling you what to do. You buck against authority. You need constant discipline. How am I doing so far?"

"And you're pigheaded and arrogant, refusing to take no for an answer. A match made in heaven." It was easy to laugh around him, even if we were both skirting around secrets and lies from our past.

Shrugging, he shoved his hands in his pockets. "Guilty as charged."

I wrinkled my nose as I came closer. When he swept me into his arms, the wave of electricity shooting through us was powerful enough to create a heated shiver.

A moment of commotion could be heard from just outside. Then the door was thrown open, Houston racing inside

"Is Snake in here?" Houston demanded, his chest heaving from his ragged breathing.

"What's going on?" Maverick asked with a start.

"Something's wrong with Apollo. He's having a seizure, not anything I've seen before in animals."

"Apollo?" I asked.

"A dog. A special dog who belongs to Snake," Houston said.

"Where is he?" I moved closer.

"A couple hundred yards away."

I gave Maverick a look, handing him my wine. "Take me to him."

The two exchanged glances but Houston led the way, Maverick tossing the drinks in the first trashcan we passed. We ran to the scene, my pulse skyrocketing.

There was a crowd surrounding the dog, who was shaking on the ground, the convulsions violent. As I crouched down, I could tell instantly it wasn't just a typical epileptic seizure. "Is the veterinary facility open, as in fully stocked?" Sam and another dog were clamoring around, trying to provide assistance.

A woman stepped forward, kneeling next to me. "Yes, the clinic is completely ready. Can you do something? Sophie. Come here, baby." The other dog responded, immediately moving toward her.

"Is there a veterinarian at the party?" I was nervous about intervening, but without attention, the dog didn't have long to live.

When a man flew down in front of me, immediately reaching for the pup, I pressed my hand against his arm. "Snake, listen to me. Just be gentle with him. Let him know you're here."

I was surprised when he didn't argue with me, but his eyes reflected absolute terror.

"No," the woman continued. "Neither vet we hired was able to make the party. Can you do something?"

As Maverick squeezed my shoulder, I gritted my teeth. "I'm not licensed, but I was only a couple months away from graduation. I can help him, but I need to get him to the clinic."

The woman glanced at Phoenix then up at Maverick for reassurance. "Come on. Boys. Get the pup. Be careful with him. Follow me. It's better if we drive." The woman wasted no time, heading toward a truck parked close by, jumping into the driver's seat. When I reached the other door, I looked back, watching as Snake eased Apollo onto the truck bed, Maverick and a few of the other guys jumping in afterwards. Seconds later, Sam crowded the space, nuzzling right up to Apollo, Sophie only seconds later. This was bad. Very bad.

I climbed into the passenger seat, my heart racing. It had been long enough I was terrified I'd fuck it up, but I had no other choice.

"I'm Wren Wentworth. Phoenix belongs to me." She threw me a look, a cautionary grin on her face.

"I don't know if I can or should claim Maverick, but I'm Lily Sanborn, a new arrival in town."

"I'm so glad someone finally managed to calm him down." She threw the gear into drive, glancing in the rearview mirror then stepping on the accelerator.

"Hmmm… It sounds like you have stories I need to hear."

"That requires wine. Lots of wine."

"I'll take you up on it." As she headed down another gravel road, I could sense panic. "I love the sanctuary."

"I do too. It's a work in progress, but I'm so happy with it. As long as I can get a few additional good people on board. There are so many animals in need of help. It's crazy." She was breathless, twisting her mouth.

"I know what you mean."

"What do you think is wrong with Apollo? That dog needs to be okay. It would kill Snake."

"I think he's been poisoned." While I hated issuing the statement, it's what I felt in my gut.

"What?" Hissing, she threw a look into the rearview mirror, suddenly nervous.

"I didn't mean it that way. It could be fertilizer. It could be insect repellent. You have a ranch. I'm certain you use chemicals."

"They're kept locked away for that reason," Wren retorted, her breathing rapid. "I'm sorry. We've had some threats. People don't necessary like that hundreds of animals are going to be living close to them."

"That's crazy."

"You don't know this town. There are some good people, but as with any city, there are some real assholes."

She pulled to a stop, barely throwing the gear into park and cutting the engine before jumping out.

I did the same, Wren already calling that she'd unlock the doors. Snake held him close and when I noticed Apollo was barely twitching, the poison working quickly, I knew there was little time before he succumbed to a coma that he might not come out of. "Come on. Get him inside. Hurry."

Snake refused to let anyone help him, but I could tell the man was close to a panic attack. Suddenly, another vehicle roared into the parking area, another girl jumping out. She was close to being hysterical.

"Apollo!"

"It's okay, Chasity," Houston told her but there was no consoling her.

"Get him inside," I encouraged, racing ahead and into the facility. The place was a dream for any veterinarian, but I couldn't take the time to enjoy the view.

"In here," Wren guided, her expression apprehensive.

As Snake carried him into the examination room, I could easily tell I needed to get rid of the audience in order to concentrate.

"Guys. I hate to ask you this, but please stay out here. Wren. I could use your assistance." I gave Maverick an imploring look, silently begging for his help.

"She's right. Let her work," he told everyone in his usual commanding voice, trying to guide Chasity away from the door. She struggled even as he backed her away by several feet.

I walked inside, tension in every muscle. Snake lifted his head, studying me intently. There was so much pain in his eyes.

"Please. Don't let anything happen to him," he said in a haunted voice.

As he walked out the door, Wren closed it behind him.

And I shocked myself, saying a second prayer.

I had to save the baby. Not just for Apollo and his family, but for me as well.

This was my moment of salvation.

CHAPTER 14

Maverick

"Fuck!" Snake yelled as he pounded his fist against one of the walls.

At least ten minutes had passed, maybe more. Time had no meaning at this point.

Chasity rubbed her eyes. "What happened?"

"The pup just collapsed and started seizing," Houston answered after everyone else remained quiet.

I leaned against the wall, closing my eyes. This was the last thing anyone needed. When Sam continued to nudge my leg, I slid down the wall, rubbing him behind the ears. Sophie was pacing the room, her anxiety as high as mine.

"What do you know about this girl?" Hawk demanded. Sergeant Jake Travers had been considered one of the best helicopter pilots in the marines. I'd trained with the man, learning to respect his skills even if I'd never admitted it to him. The two of us were all testosterone at the time.

There was no reason for his question to cause a caustic reaction but it did.

The tone.

The attitude.

The snarky words.

"Enough to know she's better than your sorry ass," I responded, finally snapping my head toward him, narrowing my eyes seeing the grin on his face.

"Hey, buddy. I was just kidding. Is there anything I can do?" he asked.

Exhaling, my stomach was in knots. She had no idea how important saving Apollo was. While I was proud of her for finding courage I didn't know she had, if anything happened to the dog, it would devastate her.

Let alone what it would do to Snake, who was already pacing the front room like a lion prowling a cage.

"No. I don't know what the hell is going on, but it sure seems suspicious that he was poisoned." As soon as I made the statement, half the room seemed shocked, the other nodding.

"He's right." Chasity Garrington had singlehandedly brought Snake out of a deep depression after his return to civilian life. The fact she'd managed to convince him into having physical therapy on a regular basis hadn't only helped his physical state, but his mental state as well. He'd been another guy who was a hair's breadth away from sticking a gun into his mouth.

"He ran off, baby. I thought he was chasing Sam at first so it didn't bother me. Then I heard a yelp. I went to look for him, but he ended up back at the party," Snake snarled, immediately stopping short. The way he glanced at Phoenix was a clear indication they thought something was going on.

"I'm right. Aren't I? He could have been poisoned." I glanced from one to the other, then to Gage, who'd already joined us. Soon, we'd just have the party in here. "What the hell is going on?"

"We've had some issues over the past few weeks, some animals killed." Phoenix obviously didn't want to say anything, the sheepish look on his face a clear indication.

"Some?" This time, I cocked my head as I searched Gage's eyes.

"We have some fanatics who don't like the idea of having a sanctuary in town. Don't ask me why. There's been two incidents before this." Phoenix didn't seem to think it was a big deal. "Both had nothing to do with poisons."

"Then what the hell did the pup get into?" Houston asked.

"The thing is, most poisons take at least a full day to process in a dog's system," I told everyone.

"He's right," Snake added. "But remember, Apollo runs free on the property." With Snake's cabin on the road leading to Phoenix's house, anyone could mistake it as being part of the ranch.

"Why don't we see wait and see what the vet says," Chasity suggested.

"Is she really a veterinarian?" Phoenix asked with no inflection in his voice, but I sensed he was as anxious as the others.

I could lie but I had no clue about anything. "I don't know."

Hawk sighed as he leaned against the wall. "At least she jumped in willing to help. Let's all have a little faith."

The sudden quiet in the expansive room made my skin crawl. I wasn't good at waiting for anything. This was agonizing for all of us.

The clock kept ticking.

Another forty minutes had passed and almost everybody was ready to walk inside the room when the door was opened, Lily walking out first. My muscles tensed seeing the terror in her eyes. Then she smiled.

Sam bounded in her direction, but she put her hand out, palm down, whispering words to him and within seconds, he eased onto his haunches.

"Apollo should be just fine, but Wren made contact with the emergency vet who's making a special house call, so the pup doesn't need to be moved. I don't feel comfortable without having a licensed veterinarian signing off," she told everyone, gently placing her hand on Snake's arm.

"What the hell happened?" he growled.

"It was definitely a poison of some kind. I induced vomiting so his stomach contents will need to be tested. Right now, he's on activated charcoal, but his vitals are a little shaky. Tonight is the real test." She was more authoritative than I'd heard, confident with her diagnosis. "If he continues to improve, we'll be out of the woods in the morning."

"Can we see him, Doc?" Snake asked, his tone full of hope.

"Yes. I know he'd like that. But he does need his rest."

"A large dose?" Phoenix asked as he walked closer.

Lily thought about his question. "Likely, given the violence of his seizures. If you use rat poisoning anywhere on the property, I'd discontinue. I'd also comb the area where you think he went."

"I heard the yelp. Somebody hurt him on purpose," Snake snarled.

"It doesn't happen that fast. It takes at least a full day to manifest any symptoms. Was he lethargic at all before this?"

Snake looked at the other girl before nodding. "Yeah, he didn't eat his breakfast, which wasn't like him."

"Then I don't think it happened when he ran away. Anyway, I did what I could."

"She did fucking great," Wren piped in as she leaned against the doorway of the examination room. "Lily knew exactly what to do. How many classes do you have left before you're licensed?"

"Three but I don't think it's going to happen." The sadness in her voice was filled with regret, which made my blood boil. Someone had kept her from doing what she loved.

"If it's about the money, we'll pay for it if you'll promise to work here." Wren continued to push, which was her personality to a T.

"I can't… I mean I don't…" Lily was flabbergasted, instantly searching for me in the room, all her self-confidence fading.

"She refuses to take any handouts," I answered for her, moving in her direction.

"Who said anything about handouts?" Wren teased. "I'll work you to the bone."

"She will too," Phoenix added. The levity in the room was exactly what my baby needed.

I pulled her into my arms, daring one of them to tease me. She needed support and I planned on giving it to her.

"I'll think about it," she managed.

"Why don't you guys go back to the party?" Phoenix suggested.

"I should stay until the vet gets here," Lily said.

"I'm staying here as well," Snake said. "Thank you, Lily. What you did I'll never forget. If I can repay you in any way, just let me know."

"I'm just happy I could help." Lily's face beamed again.

Chasity headed closer, pulling Lily into her arms. "You're part of the family now. I knew you were good people as soon as Sam jumped all over you."

"Careful. She's really a little witch in disguise," I teased.

"You're incorrigible," Lily huffed. "Remember, he needs rest." She gave me a look before heading back into the room.

Sighing, I glanced at Gage then Phoenix, both heading in my direction. "I don't like this," I told them both.

"I'll have the ranch searched tomorrow. If it was planted, I will find out who. Right now, I'll get a few of the guys to check the barns as well as the living facility where the other animals are. I don't want to shut down the party and scare everyone."

"Do you have any suspects?" I asked Gage specifically.

He shook his head as he rubbed his jaw. "No. The phone calls weren't traceable, but I'll be honest with you, this is typical of fanatic behavior. Don't jump to any conclusions."

"Tell that to Snake," Phoenix snarled.

"I'll continue digging," Gage said, clapping Phoenix on the back. "At this point, that's all I can do. At least Lily was here."

I glanced at the doorway, noticing both Chasity and Wren were keeping Lily company. Yeah, thank God Lily had known what to do. I only hoped she remembered how vital a role she played in the next few days.

My gut told me time was running out.

***

Less than twenty minutes later, another truck pulled in at the clinic, a guy I didn't recognize climbing out. Five minutes later, Lily appeared, taking a deep breath.

"You didn't need to wait for me," she said, although the twinkle in her eyes told me she was glad I had.

"What else do I have to do?"

"Enjoy your friends?"

"Somehow, I'd rather be with you."

She pressed her hand against my chest. "Apollo will be just fine."

"You did a great job."

As she glanced at the perimeter of the area, I sensed she was debating taking the job. Now wasn't the time to push for anything.

"Are you up for walking back?" I asked.

"Absolutely. It's a beautiful night."

She remained quiet as she headed back to the party, but she seemed to be enjoying the quiet time, even if the music could likely be heard in the next county.

"A veterinarian, huh?" I couldn't resist.

"Yes. It's all I ever wanted to be for as long as I can remember."

"An admirable profession."

"For me, it was all about having an excuse to see animals every day. I was never allowed to have a pet, my father refusing to allow one in the house. But when I was fourteen, I was begrudgingly given permission to volunteer in a shelter. Truth be told, it was supposed to be punishment for being a delinquent kid with violent tendencies. For my father, it got me out of his hair."

I almost choked. "You? A delinquent? Eh, I can see it." A father. Even the way she'd issued the single word told me there was an underlying story.

"You're so mean," she purred. "I fell in love with creatures large and small and became determined to become a veterinarian against my father's wishes. He wanted me involved in the family business. But I worked hard, graduated with my bachelor's degree in three years and thought I had the world in the palm of my hand. It took me a long time to get close. Then poof."

"What happened, Lily? Why did the dream die?"

She bristled, her breathing more rapid. "It's not dead. Just on hold. Let's just leave it at that. Okay? You wanted to know more about me. Working with animals is the only thing I've ever truly wanted."

"What about the photographs?"

"I love taking pictures. I feel at peace when I capture that perfect moment. It's like stopping time but it's just a hobby."

"I never thought of it that way. But don't take any pictures of me," I warned her.

Her laugh pushed my cock against my jeans. "You don't know what it means to be around Sam. He's such a good boy." She stopped long enough to pet him, even bending down to wrap her arms around him. "It's time you told me a little secret."

"Uh-oh. I don't know about that."

"You opened up a can of worms," she said with defiance, the lilting sound awakening my primal needs.

"One question. I'll answer one question." I held up my index finger and she acted as if she was going to bite it off, laughing afterwards. It was damn good to see and hear her laugh, a release of demons she held so close.

As she rose to her feet, I could tell she was debating. "Why the nickname Wolfman?" For some reason, I tensed. "Come on. You promised."

"I didn't promise."

"Uh-huh."

"Fine. When I was stationed in Afghanistan, I was initially assigned to a base that wasn't on the front line. I was a bombs expert, our compound top secret. I was out for a smoke one night and noticed something in the dark. To make a long story short, I prevented the compound from being torched. At first, they called me Eagle Eyes. Then because I rarely talked to anyone and walked the camp during the night, they thought Wolfman was better. It stuck."

"The name fits you but for all the wrong reasons."

"Oh, yeah? Then why?"

"Because you're strong and fierce, a true alpha among a sea of betas. You're a natural born leader." For all the teasing we'd done, skirting around the truth for fear of getting too close, to hear her words and more important, to see the look in her eyes, I was floored.

And that never happened to a guy like me.

We walked quietly for a few minutes. Then she did something as unexpected as making her announcement earlier. She intertwined her fingers with mine. It felt right. I felt damn good. Maybe I was no good for her, but it was at that moment I knew I'd never be able to let her get away.

As we neared all the noise, Scorpion was heading toward us.

"Hey. Sorry I'm late. What did I miss?" he asked, glancing from one to the other.

We both laughed. "We'll tell you about it later. Things get busy at the bar?" I asked casually, keeping my grip on her fingers.

"Yeah, but that's not what held me up. The fucking reporters were back again," he said as he groused. "They wanted to interview Lily."

"Why?" she asked. "I'm nobody special. I had nothing to do with saving lives."

"Yeah, why?" I repeated.

"Well, it would seem the reporters found a magic couple to boost ratings. Since you appeared that first night, Lily, people keep asking more about you." Scorpion snorted. "They'll come back, and I'll throw them out again."

"What do you mean I appeared?" she asked, her tone completely devoid of any inflections.

"The entire story went national."

The darkness couldn't hide her paling face.

The scent of barbeque couldn't mask the fragrance of raw terror.

And the noise of the band couldn't drown out her rapidly thudding heart.

"Bastards," I said under my breath.

"That's what I said. I'm grabbing a beer," Scorpion said, totally unaware what was happening. As soon as he walked away, she removed her hand from mine.

"Are you okay?"

She dragged her tongue across her lips, shaking her head several times. "No. Why did they invade my privacy?"

"That's what reporters do. Why does it make you nervous?"

The way she pressed her fingers against her lips was troubling.

"What's going on? Talk to me." She twisted around, backing toward the road. "Where are you going?"

"They found me. I know they did."

"What are you talking about? Who found you?" Now it was plural?

While she was doing her best to hold it together, her body was shaking, her mouth twisting. "I need to go. I'm sorry. I just... I can't stay."

"Baby. You're scaring me. Who's after you? You need to tell me." When I started to walk toward her, she threw out her arm.

"No! Let me go. You don't understand. You'll be killed because of helping me. No. No. I can't let that happen."

Oh, this was bad. "Nobody is going to hurt you or me. Let's talk about this." Her body was swaying back and forth. How the hell was I going to convince her?

"No. No." She was determined, already scanning the darkness as if expecting to be cornered.

I took another step, then another. She stayed where she was.

Boom!

The noise was thunderous, crackling all around. I knew instantly the source of the noise. Firecrackers. I glanced at the sky for a split second. That was all the time she needed, bolting down the road.

"Sam. Come!" I took off after her. I knew without a doubt if I couldn't stop her now, she'd disappear for good.

And I wasn't going to allow that to happen.

* * *

Lily

. . .

Darkness.

I'd never been afraid of it even as a child. I'd reveled in the quiet the darkness offered, the peace that I could wrap myself up in if only for a little while. That had provided me with a level of comfort that no one had been able to take away.

Then the monster had crawled into my life, the metaphorical darkness Giovanni had sequestered me to more oppressive than any absence of light. I'd learned to hate the inside of his house, relishing the warmth and light the sun could offer.

I'd also learned to temper my anxiety, refusing to back down to the bastard, but tonight everything was different. One single weapon had been anonymity. Now even that had been taken. What I feared the most was not knowing which man would retaliate against Maverick, ripping apart his world before taking his life. But I was certain one or both would do so.

I couldn't allow that to happen. Maybe if I left now, the man I'd fallen in love with could be spared. But I had to leave quickly. It was entirely possible Giovanni had sent men to find me, or that he'd come himself to lock me away, taking me back to a life I wouldn't be able to tolerate. All I could think about was getting away. I had to. I'd grab my things, tossing them in the truck. Then I'd leave.

My single dream of learning what had happened to my mother would need to be put on hold.

Anger had started to replace fear as I threw myself inside the cab of the truck, almost flooding the engine in my attempt to get it started. If Maverick caught me, he'd never let me go.

I floored it, noticing he'd made far too much headway toward me. As I smashed my hand on the steering wheel, I continuously looked into the rearview mirror. I'd almost found something special in the beautiful town. I'd been allowed to grasp onto my dream one last time. Now it was being taken just like everything else had been. Oh, God.

I was sick to my stomach, trying to remember how to get away from the ranch. It was so dark. My nerves were shot, the monster's words racing through my mind like a broken record.

"If you run, I'll hunt you down. You will never get away."

The combination of rage and terror continued to ride me, chilling me to the bone.

While I didn't see any headlights directly behind me, I knew it was only a matter of time before I saw them. Maverick wasn't the kind of man who left any stone unturned. He also knew the city and the mountains like the back of his hand. He'd stop at nothing to find me. I wanted him to. I longed to simply collapse in his arms, allowing him to protect me against all the evils of the world, but I continued to remind myself that would get him killed.

My thoughts drifted to Sam, horrified at knowing what the monster would do to him first. God. This was a living nightmare and one I'd caused.

I pushed the truck, skidding around a blind curve, almost losing control.

"Breathe, Lily. Just breathe." I pulled my foot off the gas, slowing to a crawl as I tried to figure out where I was. Seconds later, it hit me hard that I was headed further up the mountains, not toward the cabin. The mistake would cost me more than just time.

I had to find a turnoff, risk returning the way I came. The road remained curvy, completely unfamiliar. At least there wasn't snow on the ground. Fortunately, I noticed a turnoff, but it was little more than a gravel path surrounded by trees. That would make backing out difficult.

After pulling in, I opened the windows, listening for any traffic. There was almost none on this road. I'd passed two cars. That added another layer of fear fucking with my mind. When I was confident no one was coming, I pulled out, only to hear a hard blast of a horn. The massive truck almost rammed into the bed, swerving just in time. When the driver slowed, I thought for certain he was going to come back to finish it off.

He rolled down his window, cursing before gunning the engine. I remained in the middle of the road, gasping for air. I had to get control of myself, or I'd have a wreck. Swallowing, I brushed my hand through my hair before pressing my foot on the pedal. A moment of true loneliness sank in, hitting me hard enough nausea replaced the butterflies I always felt when Maverick was around. Now I'd never see him again.

I'd lost the ability to ugly cry years before because doing so only led to a beating or something worse. I'd found that by holding in my emotions, I'd win a small victory of control, denying the monster what he reveled in the most.

My terror.

Once I'd learned to do that, I'd become less the victim and more the survivor. But now, I was a bitter root of nerves, the anger sweeping through me so intense that I knew I wouldn't hesitate to kill him should he find me.

And he would.

The tears flowed, pent up for so long that I couldn't stop them. After a few seconds, I could no longer see clearly, my chest heaving as every emotion collided. "No. No." I squeezed my hands around the steering wheel, leaning forward, blinking so hard yet I couldn't stop crying. With every muscle tense, I accidentally served to the right, almost running off the road. There was no guardrail to protect me, no strong arms to hold me while I cried.

I was all alone.

When I went to rub my eyes, I started to lose control all over again, hysteria coming dangerously close to taking over. Something crossed the road and I was forced to slam on my brakes. That started a cataclysm as I spun out of control, rotating several times.

Don't panic. Don't panic. Don't panic.

But of course I did, pressing on the brakes in an effort to stop the catastrophe. Just before I jettisoned off the side into the unknown, the truck rolled to a stop. I was shaking all over, still gasping for air. Several knots had formed in my stomach, my throat closing. As I peered out the windshield, I realized just how lucky I was.

Breathe. Just breathe.

All the mantras in the world weren't going to help, but I continued to say it as I righted the truck, slowly heading down the mountain. My luck was in the toilet, headlights just up ahead. As soon as I was close, I sensed the driver was slowing down. I picked up speed once again, but sensed Maverick was the other driver. I was determined to keep the truck under control, constantly scanning the rearview mirror for the next several seconds. I almost breathed a sigh of relief thinking I'd been wrong when it became clear the driver was turning around.

My head was pounding, my heartbeat echoing into my ears. As soon as I rounded another corner, I came to a longer stretch of road. I had to lose him. Still shaking, I slammed my foot on the accelerator, quickly picking up speed and distance between the other vehicle. Then the lights were right there, getting closer with every passing second. I had to find a way to get off this road. I had no clue where I was, the area all residential without any excess lighting.

He was getting closer.

Closer still.

Another round of terror clawed at the surface, and I took my eyes off the road, almost mesmerized by the light blinding me.

Get control. Get fucking control.

When my headlights flashed on a street sign, I prayed it would lead to a busier road. I slowed down by a few miles per hour while the truck behind me sped up. Shit. As soon as I made the hard turn, I thought he was going to blow past me, glancing quickly to find out.

The loud popping noise sounded like a cannon going off and I screamed, the truck immediately swerving back and forth erratically.

A gun. Someone was shooting at me.

The entire truck started to shudder, and I realized a tire had blown. Oh, God. I couldn't help thinking that if I'd known I was going to die today, I would have worn matching underwear. A sick laugh popped from my mouth as I did everything I could to control the truck as it swerved and groaned.

As I pressed on the brakes, inertia pulled the truck the other way, flashes of light from behind me destroying my ability to see anything but vicious shadows threatening to swallow me up. Then one loomed so big that I covered my face with my hands a split second before I felt the horrible thud, the pull toward the windshield and heard the horrific crumple of metal.

Then everything stopped except for a loud hiss.

A strange feeling washed over me as if I was floating, allowing the same moment of peace to silently capture me in warmth. Then I heard another sound, a yell and I finally pulled free of the haze. What… Steam was rising from the hood, my headlights barely projecting any light. But the one behind me was constant. I had to get out.

Disoriented, I fought with the seatbelt, unable to budge it. No. I was trapped. Another round of panic settled in and I jerked at the belt, suddenly noticing a single flame. No. It was a mirage. It had to be. When I smelled gasoline, I let off a high-pitched scream.

The door on the other side was thrown open, someone large jumping into the cab. I couldn't see them. I couldn't think.

"No. No. No!" I threw one punch after another until I heard his voice.

"Stop, baby. It's me. I got you."

"Maverick?"

"I'm here. We need to get you out, okay? Let me get the seatbelt." His voice was calm, comforting, but I sensed something was very wrong.

"It's stuck. You can't be here. You need to leave."

He cupped my chin, forcing me to look into his eyes. "You need to listen to me. We're running out of time. The truck is on fire. Are you hurt?"

"No. I don't think so." I took several deep breaths.

"Good," he murmured as he yanked on the seatbelt. "Shit. It's stuck."

"No." My breathing was to the point of hyperventilating. I did what I could to remain calm as he pulled a switchblade from his pocket. I noticed smoke was billowing into the cab. I didn't want to die. I refused to allow the bastard to win. "Please."

"Hold on. Almost there."

I managed to control my breathing and the second he cut the strap free, I told myself that I would live and I'd keep fighting.

"Okay, come on, baby." He backed out, sliding me with him. When I was cradled in his arms, he took long strides away from the truck. "Goddamn it. Why were you running from me? Why? You almost got yourself killed. Do you know that? Do you have any idea what it would have done to me if you'd died trying to get away from me?"

His words were laced with fury, yet the headlights allowed me to see his concern, the anguish in his eyes.

"I was trying to keep you safe."

"You were keeping me safe? That's my job, lady. I'm getting you out of here."

"What about my truck?"

"Oh, didn't I tell you? I'm a rich man, filthy rich actually. I'll buy you ten trucks, a thousand houses. Money means nothing to me unless I have someone special to share it with. You're not getting away from me that easy."

"Why? Why do you care so much?"

"Because you're mine. Your caustic mouth, your gorgeous body, your rebellious attitude and everything else that comes with it. In case you haven't figured it out. You belong to me."

CHAPTER 15

*M*averick

"Thanks, Gage. I appreciate you taking care of that." I kept my eyes on her as I finished getting the truck towed.

"I'll have a report for you in a couple days for insurance," he told me.

"That won't be necessary. Just have it dumped."

"Okay, buddy. I hope you know what you're doing."

Yeah, so did I.

Lily had remained on edge, still insisting she had to leave town. Once I'd gotten her to my parents' place, she'd remained quiet. At least she wasn't shaking any longer, wrapped up in a blanket by the fire. But she continued to stare at the flames, unblinking for a good portion of the time.

I tossed the phone on the table, finally heading toward the bar for a drink. It had been one hell of a night.

"Any news on Apollo?" she asked a few seconds later.

"I didn't ask. I was too worried about you."

"I told you I'm fine."

"Uh-huh. That's why you ran off and crashed your truck. We need to talk, Lily. Whatever you're going through is eating you alive."

"I know."

I allowed a few seconds to pass. She was still sipping on the same glass of bourbon I'd handed her almost an hour before. Thank God she didn't have any injuries that I could find. And she was damn lucky the truck hadn't exploded. "Lily. Do you trust me?"

She finally turned her head and the sight of tears in her eyes yanked at the protective beast inside of me. "With all that I am and all I know. You've saved my life twice. You're the only person I can trust."

"Then tell me what the fuck is going on. Level with me. I can't help you unless you do."

"Why do you care, Maverick? I'm just a girl you had to rescue."

Exhaling, I closed my eyes. "I'm a hard man, Lily. I've told you that several times. What I haven't told you is that I haven't felt anything other than rage for so long I'd started believing something else wasn't possible. But with you, every emotion has rushed to the surface."

"I'm sorry. I didn't mean to do that to you."

I moved toward the couch, crouching down. I'd never been a romantic man, maybe because my parents had been free spirits or because of what had occurred on Sapphire Ridge. But seeing her turmoil reminded me that life was short. "You're not understanding what I'm saying to you. While it's only been a few days, I can't live without you. Yeah, it's crazy. We don't know each other. But you awakened something deep inside. Whatever you're going through, I won't let anyone hurt you. You need to believe that in your heart."

She remained quiet, but I sensed the closeness building. "I don't want to hurt you."

"That's not possible. I love you, Lily. I'm not an easy man to love. I know that. But I want to try to make a life with you but that's not possible until you place your trust in me."

Her eyes opened wide and as she reached out, brushing her fingers across my cheek, the way I felt about her only intensified. "That means more to me than you know, and you have my trust completely. Will you answer me one question?"

"Okay." I took her hand in mine.

"What was the name of the criminal you were tracking?"

I hesitated before telling her.

"Bruno Escavetti, an enforcer for the Chicago Butelli mafia syndicate." As soon as I mentioned both entities, there was recognition in her eyes. I bristled at the thought. My instinct had been right. "Do you know Candy and Mark Wells?"

"No. Never heard of them."

"They were the hostages. They didn't seem to have any idea why the fugitive broke into their house either."

She nodded a few times, finally returning her gaze to the fire. "Why were you told Bruno was in the state?"

There was something very odd about the look in her eyes. "Eliminating a witness to a crime he committed."

"I doubt that."

"I didn't buy it for one second, but you're going to need to be more specific. You know more than you're willing to admit."

"It's complicated, Maverick. So much so I don't know where to begin."

"Why don't you start with your real name?"

Her laugh sounded bitter, but more in control than I'd heard it recently. "My name is Amelie Rathbone. I'm from Chicago. My mother is dead, and I lived with my father, if you can call him that. He was the man who paid the bills, nothing more." As I'd seen her do many times, she rubbed the locket around her neck, dragging it back and forth across the chain.

As I processed what she'd already told me, she never blinked.

"You have a beautiful name," I told her.

I was rewarded with a slight smile that quickly turned into anxiety.

"Rathbone? Why does that name sound familiar?" I studied her impassive face, doing what I could to keep my anger in check.

She took a swig of her drink before answering. "Carmine Rathbone owns Rathbone Industries, a multimillion-dollar business in Chicago that was funded by my mother's money from her family, grandparents I never knew. She was rich and my father wasn't. Now, he's the toast of the town, rubbing elbows with every powerful person in the city and beyond."

"O-kay." I sat down on the chair in front of her. "Are you suggesting your father has a connection to the crime syndicate?"

"Oh, I know he does. I'm not certain of all the reasons why, but I found several connections that my father initially tried to hide. He has investors who wouldn't look kindly on him being in bed with a monster. I knew something was off and started looking into his business. Our relationship was strained after my mother died in a car crash, more so in the last few months. He never wanted a child. That much was easy to tell. He simply tolerated me."

Jesus Christ. While every kid had issues with their parents, this was ridiculous, but there was more to the story.

"What does this have to do with you?"

As she locked eyes with mine, the smile crossing her face sent ice into my veins. "I think my father knew I was investigating his company and his unscrupulous activities, including trying to pin my mother's death on him. I had plans on coming to Missoula after I graduated veterinary school in order to find the truth. Unfortunately, he was one step ahead of me, delivering a blow I didn't see coming. He sold me to Giovanni Butelli as payment."

I almost choked on my drink.

"Whoa. The fucker sold you? For what? How?" I couldn't believe what I was hearing.

"Marriage."

Hold the fuck on. Was she kidding? I could tell by the look in her eyes the secret she'd been holding was eating her alive. My anger swelled again, my mind already processing methods of revenge.

"So you're married to the pig?" I tried to keep all emotions from my voice, but it was impossible.

"No, which was what continues to confuse me. I lived in the man's house for over two months. It was like he was waiting for something, maybe more control. Maybe he had something on my father. Or he was waiting for my twenty-fifth birthday. That's when my trust fund will be released."

"When is that?"

Lily… Amelie fisted her hand. "I'd lost track of time until this morning. One week from today."

If this was all about her trust fund, the Butelli clan had possibly sent Bruno to retrieve her. Why did I have the feeling there was much more at stake?

"Go on." The entire situation was unfathomable.

"I wasn't privy to much information about being held prisoner in Giovanni's house, but he was careless, likely thinking I wasn't a threat. I paid attention. I played a game. Within a couple weeks, I started overhearing some conversations that led me to believe Giovanni had plans of eliminating my father. I knew something was off. I started trying to find evidence or any scrap of information as to what was really going on, but I was kept on a short leash. Giovanni is a violent man."

"So I've heard."

"See why I told you I was damaged?"

"Baby, you're not damaged. I feel sorry for you about your mother and father, but none of this is your fault."

"Yeah, well, try living with suspicion your entire life. I remember crying when I was little, nightmares plaguing me for years. He told me I needed to grow up, that life was meant to be harsh."

"Fucking bastard." At least I knew where I would be headed for my hunt. I'd squeeze the life out of the son of a bitch with my bare hands.

"I'd tried to achieve his love when I was little. I gave up when I was ten or so." She laughed again, the sound haunting.

"Why Montana? You indicated you were compelled to come here." While a part of me didn't want to believe what she was telling me, there was no doubt it was the truth.

"I was sent a package on the day I turned eighteen. There was no return address, no indication of who'd sent it. but there was a postmark from Missoula. Then I remembered my mother had brought me here, taking me away from the agony and anger. It was funny that I had such few memories of her. Maybe my subconscious was protecting me, but it was so debilitating over the years. I wish I could remember more than just the mountains. I do know we were happy for a little while."

"Did she stay with anyone?"

"No. I remember a hotel room but there are so many gray areas and shadows in my mind I can't be certain of anything. I don't know if she'd left him or just needed space. But I think she was trying to build a new life. So much is an ugly blur and I hate it." Her eyes misted and she clenched the blanket, reaching for Sam who lifted his head.

"You don't need to continue, baby."

"Yeah, I do."

"There were police, and no one was telling me anything. I cried and cried but no one cared. Then my father came to pick me up. That's when he told me my mother had died in an accident."

"But you don't believe it."

She fidgeted, taking another sip. "I never have. I think he killed her. It's my belief she found something or became wise to his schemes. Years later when my memories surfaced, I searched her maiden name, finding out my grandparents were from Missoula. They died before I was born. Now, all I have are scattered memories I can't consider accurate, the picture I showed you with Missoula printed on the back, and this locket."

I allowed my gaze to fall to the necklace she wore, every muscle tense. I couldn't remember when I'd felt this enraged.

"What's special about the locket?"

"I have no idea. Other than there's an inscription inside, a crest of some kind. I've tried to look it up over the years but found nothing."

"Will you let me see it?"

Her smile was thin, but her eyes lit up as she unfastened the chain, handing it to me. The gold on both the locket and chain were worn from her handling the piece. When I opened the clasp, the crest inside immediately looked familiar. There were also two letters and four numbers. Then it dawned on me. "I need to check, but it appears the crest is from a bank and trust, an old one that still has a single branch in town. At least the sign is still there."

Her eyes lit up. "The numbers can't be from a bank account."

I studied them again before rising to my feet. "No, but they might be from a safe deposit box." When I lifted my head, she pressed her hand in front of her mouth again, only I noticed a hint of amusement instead of sadness. "You mentioned photographs. What do you have?"

Amelie unfurled her legs, moving closer to the edge. Sam whined in response. "Somehow, Giovanni managed to get a hold of financial transactions and spreadsheets belonging to the Rathbone Corporation. It would appear my father was extorting money from his own company. If I had to guess, I'd say Giovanni planned on blackmailing my father. But I'm not certain. I quickly snapped a few shots of the paperwork before he could catch me."

She had balls, but if Giovanni knew what she'd taken from him, it was just another reason to have her eliminated.

"Why didn't you go to the police? If you're right about what you photographed, you had a chance to bring down your father."

"First of all, after being sequestered in Giovanni's house, I never went anywhere alone. When I managed to escape in the middle of the night, I had limited time before one or both men would send their soldiers to find me. And I assure you they would have. More important, my father owns half the police department, the police chief included. I couldn't take the chance. That would have been my only one." She glanced away, then smiled. "I need to know what happened to my mother. I don't care about money, but I want to nail my father to the wall if he had anything to do with her death."

"Then that's what we'll do." She seemed surprised by my level of conviction.

"I can't drag you into my fight."

I finished off my drink, placing it with a hard thud on the coffee table. "Baby, in case you haven't figured it out already, I'm already in this fight with you. I ain't backin' down now. I protect my own. That's been my motto for a long time."

The slight smile on her face changed, fire returning to her eyes. "Then what do we do? I left my camera at the house. I don't have a key to get into the safe deposit box if that's what this is. They won't just take my word for it."

"Do you have your real identification?"

After a few seconds she nodded. "My driver's license. I debated tossing it, but I had a feeling I'd need to prove who I was. It's hidden with the camera at the cabin."

"Good. We'll get into the box somehow." Even if I had to convince the owner of the bank the hard way. "There's nothing we can do in the middle of the night. Tomorrow is an entirely different story. We'll find the bank and trust and see if I'm right. We'll also grab your camera. Then we're going to have a long conversation with the sheriff. Finally, we'll make plans to destroy your father after getting the answers you need." At least she wasn't arguing with me.

"You trust the sheriff that much?"

"Implicitly. Gage is a friend first and has been there through some rocky times."

"Okay." A slight look of relief crossed her face. Yet she was searching for my approval or at minimum my words of wisdom regarding the sperm donor who turned out to be her father. What I had to say wouldn't provide her with the comfort she needed.

So I did something else entirely.

I beckoned her with a single finger.

When she acted as if she wasn't going to obey me, I cocked my head. "Come here."

"What if I don't?"

I leaned forward, folding my hands together. "You're already going to get a spanking for scaring the life out of me. If you don't come here, I assure you that your punishment is going to be much worse."

Amelie

Love.

I'd heard him say the word and nothing could have shocked me more. But his eyes reflected more emotions than I thought he was capable of.

Anger. If either one of the men were standing in this room, he'd easily kill them with his bare hands.

Anxiety. I sensed his continued concern as well as his determination to protect me.

Frustration. There was no doubt he was fit to be tied with my behavior, uncertain how to discipline me.

And ultimately love. He was as stunned as I was that he'd admitted something so personal. I wanted so much to ask him what he'd endured in his past that had kept him from falling hard for anyone. Someday I would. Now wasn't the time.

It was crazy, but instead of feeling raw terror, warmth and intense need encapsulated my body. He had a way of pacifying even the worst aspects of life, although he'd never admit he was anything but a brooding, unromantic man. Little did he know I was rubbing off on him.

The real girl was the one with insecurities and chutzpa, not the woman I'd almost turned into because of my father.

With truth came a sense of freedom.

And relief.

Being able to use my real name gave me a feeling of power, as if I could take on the world and easily win. When I was around Maverick, all the anxiety managed to fade away, if only for a little while. The gruff man had a way of making me feel safe, as if nothing and no one would ever be able to hurt me. I don't know what I'd expected when admitting the ugliness of my truths, but he'd kept his gorgeous blue eyes on me, accepting every word I said without admonishment or disbelief.

For that alone I'd be eternally grateful.

I was lucky to be alive, running away and wrecking my truck one of the more ridiculous things I'd done in a long time. How many times would he need to save my life before I realized and accepted that he cared about me?

As I got off the couch, Sam whined in frustration. Even with the few bumps and bruises I'd gotten in the wreck, I couldn't care less about the discomfort or the weight of what the next few days or weeks would bring.

I needed Maverick the same way he hungered for me.

Teasing him, I dragged my tongue across my lips, barely inching closer. By the way his nostrils flared, I sensed he wasn't going to tolerate my mischievous actions but for so long.

He placed his elbows on his knees, folding his hands, studying me without blinking. But as I'd seen several times before, there was only one thing on his mind.

My surrender.

As I inched closer, I tossed my head back and forth, my long strands of hair slapping him in the face.

The growl he issued sent shivers down my spine, my legs tingling. I continued to stay just out of his reach, but I should have known his lack of patience would drive him into action. With a single snap of his hand around my wrist, he yanked me between his legs, his hold more possessive than it had ever been.

"I think I need to remind you again that you're not in charge." His husky tone allowed goosebumps to dance across my arms, my breath skipping.

"Meaning what?" The larger-than-life man managed to pull out the naughty vixen in me, allowing everything else to fade away.

His expression never changed as he moved his hands to my jeans. I found it fascinating that I didn't fight to stop him, even holding my arms out to the sides while he struggled to yank the dense material down my hips. The fact he remained quiet kept butterflies swarming in my stomach.

"When you misbehave, there are consequences." While he was attempting to be authoritative, his stern words and the rugged sound of his voice only managed to keep my panties damp.

When he'd yanked both items of clothing to my knees, I took a deep breath as he dragged me over his lap. I kicked my legs on purpose, forcing him to yank me closer to his chest, his already throbbing cock pressing into my stomach. As he brought his hand down in rapid succession, I gasped from surprise instead of pain. I knew what to expect but there was an added vigor in his actions, refusing to give in to the woman who'd raced away from him.

"Ouch!" I yelped after thirty seconds has passed. The man was relentless, one coming right after the other.

"That's what happens when you try and get yourself killed," he grumbled, adjusting me on his lap a second time.

I wiggled, sensing I was driving him crazy from the friction created. My mind was a blur of desire, my nipples aching as the bounce from his actions allowed the lace from my bra to scratch back and forth. As the sound of his palm cracking against my naked skin filled the room, Sam decided to thump his tail in perfect rhythm.

That's when a warm flush of embarrassment crashed into my system. The pain turned into anguish, jetting down the backs of my legs. It didn't seem he had any intention of stopping soon.

As I continued to shift, moans slipping past my lips, he suddenly stopped altogether. I heard him grumbling under his breath. Then he ripped my jeans and thong to my ankles, fighting to get them off over my shoes. Seconds later he finally did, tossing them aside.

I was so wet and hot I could tell I was staining his jeans. The scent of my hunger mixed with the delicious fragrance of his testosterone. I was lightheaded and in need, panting as he resumed the spanking. Nothing had ever made me so aroused, so much so stars floated in front of my eyes.

"Oh, that really... hurts."

"Yeah? Maybe you'll remember that the next time you even think about doing something so crazy."

"Yes, sir," I said, unable to resist.

"Mmm..." he growled then slipped his hand between my legs. "I like that. I think I'll have you refer to me that way all the time."

As he rolled his thumb around my clit, my breath was immediately stolen. "I don't... think so, buster." The pleasure was intense, enough so I bucked against his hand.

"Oh, you don't, huh?" He ripped his arm free, immediately smacking one side then the other on my bottom repeatedly.

Endless moans rushed up from my throat, my blurry mind unable to think about anything critical. When I laughed nervously, he took exaggerated deep breaths, the primal beast in him breaching the surface.

I slapped my hands on the floor, undulating several times. My bottom was sore, certain to be cherry red in color but all I could think about was having him touch me intimately, allowing me to come.

Perhaps he sensed my near desperate need, sliding a single finger down the crack of my ass. When he dipped his hand between my legs for a second time, I wrapped one arm around his leg.

"Are you going to be a good girl for me?" he asked, his tone more seductive than before.

"Yes, sir."

"No more running away? No more lies?"

I nodded several times, my body shuddering as he pinched my clit. Then as he flicked his finger back and forth across it, another series of moans floated into the air.

"No, sir."

"Good girl." He chuckled darkly then drove several fingers into my tight channel.

"Oh, God!" I jerked up, throwing back my head. "Yes. Please."

He pressed his hand on the small of my back, his breathing as labored as mine. "Relax, princess."

Relax? Who was he kidding?

As he thrust his fingers inside, I did what I could to ride his hand, dozens of deliriously amazing vibrations tumbling through every cell and muscle. He'd kept the fire ignited between us, the crackle of electricity on overload. I allowed myself to fall into a sweet haze, the pleasure multiplying.

I sensed when I was ready to come, the hair standing up on the back of my neck, my breath ripped away.

Then it bolted into me with such ferocity that I couldn't bite back a scream. "Ahhhh… Oh, yes."

"That's it, baby. Slicken my fingers. Come for me like the good little girl you can be."

Why did his words thrill me so much? Why did they also make me feel tingly all over, special, and cared for? I remained tense, the orgasm keeping a rush of adrenaline flowing through my veins.

When I finally started to come down from the high, I was aware he'd reached down, jerking off first one shoe then the other. I heard the thumping sound as he tossed them aside but was incapable of moving from the relaxation floating through my system.

Maverick's breathing remained ragged as he lifted me onto his lap. The look in his eyes was that of a true predator, hungry and possessive.

"Open your mouth," he instructed. The man was completely in charge.

And I loved every second of it, obeying him without hesitation. With a slight smile on his face, he slipped his wet fingers into my mouth.

"Suck me nice and clean, baby."

I wrapped my hand around his wrist, holding his arm in place. As I swished my tongue back and forth, he narrowed his eyes even more. I could tell his jaw was clenched through the mess of his beard and all I could think about was running my fingers through the coarse hair. The man was far too sexy for his own good.

Or mine.

As I wrapped my lips around his fingers, pumping up and down, the subtle yet powerful sound of his low-slung growls kept my heart beating rapidly.

"Mmm… Very good job," he muttered as he removed his hand. "I think you have entirely too many clothes on." He wasn't giving me any room to object, tugging at my shirt, removing it with ease. As he reached around to unsnap my bra, the twinkle in his eyes became more apparent.

He eased one strap down my arm then the other, taking his time to cup my breasts together, rubbing his thumbs across my tender nipples. I wasn't certain if I'd ever been this aroused.

When he'd finally had enough of the hindrance, he pulled it away. There was something kinky about being completely naked while sitting on the lap of a fully dressed man. His eyes pierced mine for a few seconds before allowing his gaze to slowly fall to my breasts. Even the way his chest rose and fell was sexy.

My mouth watered, my hunger increasing. I closed my eyes as he rolled his hand down the back of my head before sliding his fingers under my hair. His hold on my neck was firm, keeping me in place. I was going nowhere until given permission.

As he yanked me into a deep arc, I shuddered to my core. Then I felt his hot breath on first one nipple then the other seconds before he pulled one into his hot mouth. There was no adequate way to describe the raw ecstasy, my mind a complete blank as he nipped and sucked. When he brushed his lips to the other side, I let out another strangled whimper.

I had no idea how long he continued to tease me, but I was shaking from need, ready to beg him to fuck me. When he released his hold on my neck, I took several gasping breaths as I lifted my head, crowding as close to him as possible.

He kept his hand on my back, lightly rubbing the rough pads of his fingers in circles and zigzags. As I lowered my head, he lifted his, our lips almost touching.

"Tell me what you want, baby," he said. "Whatever it is, I'll hunt it down for you. I don't care about the level of darkness the search drags me into or what I'm forced to face during the journey. Your happiness is all that matters to me."

"What do I want?" I repeated, our combined hot breath turning into an inferno. I twisted my body, sliding my knees on either side of him. As I shifted back and forth across his cock, I sensed his animalistic needs ready to explode.

"Uh-huh."

"Everything. As long as it's with you."

CHAPTER 16

*M*averick

Everything.

That's exactly the way I felt, the need for her churning into a frenzy that I'd found difficult to control.

Even more so than at this moment.

I could ravage her without a second thought, but I craved the tenderness of being close as much as she did. I cupped both sides of her face, the ache in my balls forced to wait. As I gazed into her eyes, the rush of emotions shifting from one to the other was more powerful than I cared to admit to anyone.

Including myself.

God, I wanted this woman. All of her. For all eternity.

No one was going to try to take her away from me.

And damn if she didn't look hot with her bottom a beautiful shade of blush.

Oh, I was an evil man.

As Amelie slid her arms around my neck, tangling her fingers in my hair, I rubbed my thumbs back and forth. The feel of her soft skin against my rough fingers gave me a rush, adrenaline and extreme need mixing together. I pressed my forehead against hers, trying to maintain my control.

She tilted her head seconds later, our lips brushing. When she darted out her tongue, it became almost impossible not to devour every inch of her.

"I do love you, Maverick. Right. Wrong. Good. Bad. I don't care. But I'm so afraid this will end."

"It's not ending, baby. Not by a longshot. You're stuck with me whether you like it or not." She chose that moment to capture my mouth, arching her spine as she gripped the back of my neck with both hands. As she shifted against me, the ache turned to sheer pain, my desire off the charts. She had no idea what she did to me, the filthy thoughts that were never far from my mind.

She shifted forward and backward, driving me crazy with the amount of friction she created. As the intimate moment roared into something else altogether, I yanked her even closer, growling into the kiss as she bucked hard against me.

I thrust my tongue inside, exploring every dark inch, basking in her sweetness.

I could kiss her all night long, but I was too wired tonight, my desire a raging bull. She sucked in my tongue, pulling back seconds later to bite my lower lip and the sound of her lilting laughter added fuel to the fire.

I was going to make love to this woman all night long.

The thought of losing her had nearly done me in, the horror of what she told me stored in the back of my mind. Now, nothing would stop me from taking what already belonged to me.

Every. Sweet. Inch.

She laughed again as she pushed her hands against my chest, shifting further down on my lap. Then with her eyes never blinking, she jerked at my belt buckle, her movements full of purpose.

"What do you think you're doing?" I asked in a low voice.

"Taking what I want."

When I started to remind her that I was in charge, she pressed her finger across my lips, shaking her head. I lifted my eyebrows, thrilled she was this comfortable. As she resumed her task, finally freeing my cock, I debated how long I could stand without being inside of her sweet pussy.

She must have read my mind, or her needs were as unbridled as mine, rising onto her knees. "Off," she ordered, yanking on both sides of my jeans.

"Be careful what you ask for, little girl."

"I'm never careful. I need them off." As I lifted my hips, she shifted back and forth until she dragged them down to my knees, reaching behind me to force them to the floor. "You can do the rest. Now."

"Bossy, ain't ya?"

The pouty look she gave me could light a thousand fires. "You have no idea, grumpy cowboy."

"I'll show you grumpy." I dipped her low as I reached down, fighting to get my boots off, breathing hard from the angle as I dragged the jeans to the floor, kicking out of them.

"I think you need more exercise," she purred. "Some cardiovascular activities are in order."

The flirty girl had a way of making me laugh but this time I narrowed my eyes. "As I said. Be careful what you ask for."

"I'm in a daring mood." She rose onto her knees a second time, giving me a mischievous look.

When she placed my cockhead against her pussy lips, I couldn't resist sucking on one of her perfect rosy nipples.

"Such a bad boy."

"Mmm…"

She sat down on my cock, driving the entire length inside. I let out a heavy breath, my muscles shaking from the way she shifted her body. She kept her arms slung over my shoulders, biting her lower lip as she stared into my eyes.

There was a connection that I'd never felt. No words were needed, no directions necessary. And there was no one that could tear us apart. As she continued bucking against me, my longing to feel her heated skin against mine only continued to increase.

"Hang on, princess." As soon I rose to my feet, she wrapped her legs around my waist, digging her knees into my hips. After easing one arm under her heated bottom, I couldn't resist, pumping her up and down on my cock several times.

She never blinked as I headed toward the bedroom, fighting to turn on the light. As soon as I did, my arm hit a lamp on the dresser, tossing it to the floor.

Amelie laughed, shaking her head. "A little clumsy of you."

"You're sportin' for another spanking."

Using her thigh muscles, she moved up and down, squeezing her pussy muscles at the same time. "I don't think you want to do that."

"You're such a tease." I took long strides to the bed, easing her down, remaining on my knees.

She yanked at my shirt, fighting with me to get it over my head. I never broke the connection as I tossed it aside, leaning down onto my forearms. I remained hovering over her, brushing my fingers back and forth across her cheek.

"What are you looking at?" she asked, her hand moving up and down aimlessly on my back.

"The most beautiful girl in the world."

"You're blind."

"Oh, no, I'm not. I have perfect vision." I pulled my cock almost all the way out, thrusting into her again. When I repeated the action, she lifted her head, closing her eyes.

The feel of her tight pussy kept me locked in the moment, driving deep and hard into her. As her muscles pulsed around my cock, I took several ragged breaths. I wanted this to last for a long time.

"Look at me, baby."

She slowly opened her eyes, biting her lower lip. The way her long eyelashes skimmed across the shimmer of her cheeks was captivating. I'd memorized every inch of her lovely face, the way her mouth turned up when she was nervous about something. The light crinkle of her nose when she was furious at something I'd said. And the cute faces she made when talking to Sam.

I hadn't lied to her.

She was perfect in every way.

"What do you see?" I asked, pulling out and teasing her all over again.

"The most amazing man on the face of this earth." She raked her nails down my back with one hand, rubbing the fingers of the other through my beard. "My rugged mountain man."

She was so wet, the heat shifting between us combustible. I wasn't going to be able to hold back for long.

But the night was early.

We never took our eyes off each other as my rhythm changed. She kept her legs wrapped around me, pressing one hand against my chest. As the electricity soared, I did what I could to keep the magic, the beauty of our togetherness. But my needs outweighed everything else. My body tensing, a smile crossed her face as she squeezed her muscles, clamping around the thick invasion.

I threw back my head, pumping into her like the true beast I'd become. And as I erupted deep inside of her, I couldn't stop from roaring.

"Mine, baby. All mine."

* * *

Amelie

I couldn't help myself, tracing every line on his face, sliding the tip from one side of his jaw to the other. He'd been so quiet since we'd made love, holding me close as if fearful someone would break into the house. He'd called Sam into the room, making certain the pup stood guard as well. The man was more protective than I'd realized.

He had his arms wrapped around me, aimlessly rubbing his fingers along my back. He kept dancing vibrations in my system, the longing for him ebbing and flowing. I couldn't seem to get enough of the man.

There were so many questions I sensed he had on his mind, but I also could tell he didn't want any additional ugly details. That would fuel too much anger and would send him into a rage. He was right. We needed to make a plan and follow through with it. A part of me was excited. The other was terrified at what I'd find.

As I leaned on his chest, he slowly lowered his gaze.

"What's on your mind?" he asked.

"You."

He chuckled, rubbing his jaw then easing his arm behind his head so he could gaze into my eyes. "What about me?"

I took a leap of faith, one I knew would open up a can of worms. "What happened on Sapphire Ridge all those years ago?" As expected, he tensed but instead of pulling away, he took a few seconds to think about the question.

"Not much to tell. When I was in high school, I ran with five other guys. We were pretty tight, all from different backgrounds. My parents were always working at that point, and I was an only kid who liked to get into trouble. So we did it together."

"The Missoula Bad Boys."

"It wasn't official or anything. We were called delinquent by school officials, kids destined to head to prison by the sheriff's office and unintelligent by our teachers. While we never did anything too extreme, we were damn lucky we hadn't gotten into more trouble than we had. This girl who had nobody in her life refused to take our crap. She had a little mouth on her, smart as a whip but had been tossed around in the system for years. All six of us took her under our wings."

"Ah. All six of you fell in love with her. Right?" I could sense him tensing.

Exhaling, he nodded. "I think so, some of us talking about how special she was. There wasn't a one of us who didn't have darkness inside of him, the reason for acting out. Belle was able to pull us into the light and keep us there."

"She sounds wonderful."

"Yeah. We all felt responsible for her, and it was good for us. We started taking her with us everywhere, including to the mountains. One day we decided to stay all night. It was beautiful and we planned on making a fire and sitting around telling ghost stories or some shit. If you want to know the truth, I think every single one of us planned on making a move on her that night." He took a deep breath, a portion of the memory allowing him to smile. "Anyway, Phoenix started a fire, but it kept going out. Snake was trying to help, but he got distracted. With the sun hidden behind the trees, after a couple hours it was freezing up there. The wind was blowing like a son of a bitch. Houston wanted to leave but it was already starting to get dark so most of us didn't want to make the trek. Big bad boys afraid of the dark."

I continued stroking his chest as his breathing changed. "You didn't huddle up for warmth?"

"Hell, no. We were arguing back and forth, and I think Belle got sick of our pettiness, so she took a walk into the woods. I can't remember who followed her first. She loved nature, birds, and small creatures."

"A little bit like me."

He shifted his gaze. "Yes, but the way I feel about you isn't because of the way I cared about Belle. You need to know that."

"It's okay, Maverick. I already feel honored. Go on."

"Some of us started arguing, Snake and Colt ready to start a fight, and I got fed up, tossing some liquor onto the fire. It flared and none of us were paying attention. I headed into the woods to try and get her back so she could warm up. The next thing I knew, the woods were on fire." His breath caught and he fisted the hand behind his head.

"You went to look for her," I encouraged.

"Yup. I think all of us did, which left the fire unattended. Within a few minutes, it was too late. The weather had been so dry that year that the underbrush went up like a matchstick. The fire raged and we tried to find her. We were still arguing, getting into a screaming match. No one wanted to leave but it got to the point we knew we'd perish. And we left. We left her there."

As he looked into my eyes, I sucked in my breath, sliding further up on the bed. "It wasn't your fault, baby."

"Like hell it wasn't. If I hadn't thrown the goddamn bourbon on the fire, it wouldn't have gotten out of hand."

"Baby. You said it was windy, right? And it had been dry?"

"Yeah, but it's my fault, Amelie. My fault. Don't you get that?"

"What I get is that you're blaming yourself for an accident. If I had to guess, I'd say the other five Bad Boys have felt the same way for all these years. The fact the townsfolk blamed all of you for the death of that girl didn't help."

"They showed the shit on television?"

I nodded and he shook his head, grumbling under his breath.

"There was also a clear shot of my face."

He took a deep breath, snarling. "I could kill the reporters for putting your life in jeopardy."

"I don't know if it mattered. With that killer in town, that means he already knew you were here."

Sighing, he thought about what I was saying and nodded. "Perhaps your father figured you'd return to Montana."

"I never told him about the necklace. He saw me wear it but never asked where I'd gotten it. I was so young that I doubt he thought I remembered. He certainly tried to push her out of my mind, removing every picture. Her clothes and every personal effect vanished from the house before we made it back to Montana. He told me later it was because he didn't want me to suffer, but I knew better. He damaged me so much."

He pulled me tightly against him, lifting my chin. "You're special, Amelie. Don't forget that."

His eyes were momentarily filled with sadness. "I know you were in love with her, but you need to let Belle go. She'd want you to move on with your life. Wouldn't she?"

"Yeah, she would."

"The guilt is eating you alive. Do you ever talk about what happened with the others?"

"Not all of us. We've avoided it like the plague, everyone but Gage leaving town for as long as possible."

"You need to talk about it. If you're feeling this way, don't you think every man is feeling the same way you are?"

"Not all of us."

"That's why you hate Colt?"

"I hate him because he didn't react at all after the tragedy, as if it was no big deal."

Sighing, I tried to find the right words.

"My mother was the world to me, Maverick. She was the light to my darkness. My father never paid us any attention, but she was the one who read me stories and played with me in my room. She took me shopping and made the holidays special. I felt like a real princess. When I lost her, I was so empty inside that I didn't cry. I didn't say anything. I was numb and went through the drudgery of life."

"With a cold asshole as a father."

"Yes. I was sent away to school for a few years. Honestly, that helped. It wasn't until the necklace arrived that I shed a tear. On that afternoon, I shed thousands, sobbing until I fell asleep from exhaustion. Why I'm telling you this is that everyone grieves differently. Just try and remember that."

When he managed to smile, I slowly lowered my hand to his cock, stroking the tip. "You're a very naughty woman."

"Uh-huh."

"You're also one of the smartest I've ever known."

"Don't you forget it either."

"Come here," he instructed, beckoning me with a single finger.

"Who, me?" I moved onto all fours, straddling his body.

"No more teasing. If you do, I'm certain I can think of some very creative methods of punishment."

I crawled further up, remaining on my knees. When I leaned down, he took the opportunity to roll me over, quickly dumping me onto all fours. Without any hesitation, he drove his cock into my pussy with enough force I was thrown forward.

"Oh, my God. You're so mean. So mean," I murmured as waves of pleasure jetted through me.

"Something else for you never to forget." As he fisted my hair, all I could do was smile. He thrust hard and fast, the sound of his skin slapping against mine in perfect rhythm. Sam lifted his head, his tail thumping twice. Then he fell back asleep. The entire scene made me smile.

Maybe this was what normal was all about.

When he pulled out, I held my breath, knowing exactly what he was going to do. The second he pressed the tip of his cock against my asshole, I tensed. Then with tenderness, he slipped it inside, taking his time while my muscles stretched to accommodate his wide girth. I closed my eyes, slipping into a beautiful fantasy as he drove another couple of inches inside.

The pain was glorious and fleeting, but I couldn't stop shaking. As the wetness grew between my legs, my inner thighs slickened, he thrust the entire rest of his shaft inside. Every animalistic sound he made fueled the fire between us, yanking us out of the sadness and guilt, worry and frustration.

In those few precious seconds, being lost in another human being was the sweetest feeling in the world. He pulled out, every sound he made creating another wave of tingles. Then he plunged again.

And again.

I kept my eyes closed, the various senses awakened from his touch, the heat of his breath on my skin. As he fucked me long and hard, growling like a beast, I couldn't be happier or more sated. I bucked hard against him, meeting every savage thrust, breathless as my pulse raced. Beads of sweat trickled down onto my back, slowly falling to the comforter. There was something cathartic about it.

Maybe we were both damaged in some ways, but together we were on fire.

Within seconds, I could tell he was close to coming. He wrapped his body around mine, holding me around the waist. Every muscle tensing, his breath skipping, he finally released deep inside. He would always be a man who took what he wanted, but only I could provide exactly what he needed.

Love that could withstand every adversity, every difficulty, and bring endless moments of joy.

My hero was right. No one would be able to take that away from us.

CHAPTER 17

*M*averick

"Wait right here," I told Amelie, giving her a stern look. "I'm going inside first."

"It doesn't look like anything has been disturbed."

"Looks can be deceiving."

She nodded, a slight look of apprehension on her face. "I hid the camera in the closet in the bedroom under a pile of my clothes."

"Okay. If there's no sign of disturbance, you can come in and grab some things."

"Maverick. I'm not going to be pushed out of my life. I'm finished with that." She unfastened her seatbelt, and I grabbed her chin, pinching it between my thumb and forefinger. "Listen to me. Whether Bruno Escavetti was here because of you or for an entirely different reason, it's entirely possible he learned of your existence anyway. We're not going to take unnecessary risks. Do you hear me?"

While she gave me the same mischievous smile I'd seen so many times before, I knew she'd participate in risky behavior before all this was over. I'd put a call in to Gage early in the morning, warning him that we were coming to see him. Then I'd given him the information she'd provided for me in order to discover all he could about the two men involved.

The story as well as the ramifications was complicated, unbelievable, and dangerous. The combination could prove to be deadly.

"Yes, sir," she mused. At least her rebellious nature remained.

I lifted a single eyebrow. "Remember what I said."

She pulled away, folding her arms and easing against the seat.

"Sam. Don't let her out."

Woof!

I grabbed my weapon before opening the door. Her eyes remained on me as I slipped it behind my back under the waistband of my jeans. While she said nothing, I could swear I heard her heart beating a thousand times a minute. She should be nervous. Desperate men did desperate things, especially for money.

With her keys in my hand, I headed for the door, glancing in the window before stepping onto the porch. After unlocking it, I carefully opened the door, moving inside. There were no sounds and upon initial inspection, I could see no signs of visible disturbance. I moved through the small cabin, searching every closet. From what I could tell, no one had been inside. When I returned to the living room, I expected to see her standing in the doorway. At least she'd followed my orders this time.

I motioned for her to come in then headed into the bedroom. Sam bounded in first, immediately jumping on the bed.

"Everything looks fine," she said as she moved toward the closet. After a few seconds, she pulled the camera into her hand, checking it. "The pictures are here."

"Do you mind if I take a look?"

She handed it to me then picked up a duffle bag, immediately grabbing a few clothes. I pulled up the photographs, flipping from one to the other. Seeing how many she'd taken of the mountains was incredible. "These are fantastic."

Half laughing, she shook her head. "Maybe I'll become a photographer instead."

"You certainly could make some money, but I think you have your heart set on finishing your education."

"Why does that sound like if I stay then you're going to require me to finish veterinary school?"

"First of all, you're staying. Period. Second, I saw how you were at the sanctuary. You belong working in a facility like that. You'd be happy there."

Exhaling, she nodded then took the camera from me, flipping through several pictures. "Maybe so."

"Uh-huh. You're a terrible liar."

She gave me an evil eye then handed me the camera again. "There are your pictures."

She'd gotten several financial documents, but they would need to be printed to make them readable. How had Giovanni gotten his hands on the documents? From what I could tell, they would normally go to a board of directors, and I doubted her father would hand them over readily.

Unless another deal had been made or unless she was right that Giovanni had more unscrupulous plans in mind for Mr. Rathbone. I wouldn't care if they killed each other off.

"That should be all I need. We can go," she said with tenseness in her tone.

"Remember, we'll get through this."

"I know. I just have a lot on my mind." She tossed the bag onto the bed, heading toward the nightstand. After pulling the drawer, she peeled away something she'd taped on the underside.

Clever girl.

She stared down at the license, running her finger across the surface. "This is the real me. Now you know I'm not lying."

"I already knew that, babe." I glanced at the photograph and sighed. What a freaking mess.

As we left the cabin, my gut told me that whoever was after her would wait until the heat from capturing Bruno died down. That would give us a couple of days maximum. Then one or both would strike. We needed to act quickly.

I jumped inside, squeezing her leg. Whatever we'd find in the safety deposit box could change her life. Or it could ruin it. I didn't like the odds but there was no other choice.

I'd looked up the location online, happy that I'd been right. A single branch still existed, the original one opened in the early eighties. They'd maintained an entity while so many other banks had been bought or merged.

Amelie remained quiet the entire time, still fondling the locket. "I wonder where the key is?"

"Maybe we won't need one."

"You know better. And after all this time, who says they even have security boxes?"

"Let's not jump to conclusions at this point. Okay?"

"Always the voice of reason," she half whispered. "I've used this necklace to give me peace so many times I think I'm wearing the finish off."

"I'll polish it for you."

I threw her a look, shaking my head. When she narrowed her eyes, a startled look on her face, I instantly bristled. "What's wrong?"

"There's something strange about the locket." She struggled to remove it from around her neck, holding it into the light. "Wait a minute. I never noticed this before. There's a little catch on the back."

"Can you get it open?"

"I don't think so. Do you have a tool or anything in your truck?"

"Check the glove compartment."

She did, shoving everything around then finding an old Swiss Army knife. "This should do it."

I continued driving as she fiddled with the knife. We both felt extreme pressure to find answers, my instinct working overtime. When she gasped, my grip on the steering wheel tightened.

"It's a key."

Snorting, I glanced at the GPS, making the next turn. "Then I guess we're destined to find out."

"What if the news is horrible?"

"You wanted the truth. Right?"

"More than anything."

"Then it is what it is. Maybe whatever we find will provide you with peace."

"My voice of reason," she purred. "Or maybe it will give me the evidence I need."

"Are you really prepared to destroy your father?"

She thought about the question before answering. "When I was little, I tried to be the best girl possible. I needed his attention and his love. As I grew older, I no longer needed his praise or his fatherly ways. I was forced to rely on myself. I was a lonely kid, jealous of families who spent time together. But I learned early on that if I wanted to have that perfect Hallmark experience, I'd need to create it myself." When she turned her head toward me, I felt the heat of her stare.

The electricity shooting through me doubled, my mind attempting to process whether we could be a family. Maybe two would turn into three or four. Was I cut out to be a father? The answer was easier than I'd anticipated. Without a doubt.

I noticed the sign, saying a silent prayer that the bank was still in business. When I turned into the parking lot, I was able to breathe a sigh of relief seeing the number of cars. She had her hand clenched around the locket, her face pinched when I pulled in and parked, cutting the engine.

"I couldn't do this if you weren't here."

"I don't believe that for a second, lady. You're a hell of a lot stronger than you know."

"But you give me courage. You've allowed me to believe in the impossible."

Before I opened the door, I squeezed her hand. "Sometimes the truth isn't the easiest to accept."

"I know that. But this is something I need to do." After giving me a smile, she pulled her hand away, opening the door. "We'll be right back, Sam."

The pup wagged his entire body then sat back on his haunches. He knew something was wrong.

So did I.

I kept my hand on the small of her back as we walked inside, forced to wait for almost five minutes before we were acknowledged.

"Can I help you?" the man behind the desk asked.

"I'm here to get into a safety deposit box," Amelie said with no hesitation, no fear in her voice. She was the strongest woman I knew.

"Of course. What's the number?"

She handed over the locket and he glanced from her eyes into mine. "I have identification." As she pulled out her driver's license, the man scrutinized it for a very long time. "And I have a key."

He said nothing as he pulled up a computer file, checking and double-checking her ID. "You are authorized on the account. Follow me."

Amelie's only moment of faltering was to reach for my hand, locking her fingers with mine. I couldn't imagine what was going through her mind, the trepidation that she'd risked her life in order to discover the truth.

He led us through a set of double doors, using a keypad to unlock the area where the boxes were located. "You're just in time. We'd already sent out notices that this branch is closing, all items are required to be removed within fifteen days or they'd be destroyed."

She tipped her head, glancing into my eyes. The room reminded me of a tomb, no sound getting in or out. When he used a key to open another set of small doors, I heard her breath catch. Without another word, he pulled the box onto the large table, giving us both a nod then leaving.

The box itself was no larger than one designed for shoes or boots. She hovered over it, clenching the necklace with enough force her knuckles were white. "It's now or never."

I stood back, allowing her whatever privacy she needed. Her hands shaking, she slipped the small key into the lock, exhaling before lifting the lid. From my vantage point, I could see several envelopes, including some that indicated personal letters. While I wanted nothing more than to find out what the hell was really going on, I used every ounce of patience to wait.

This was a defining moment.

She took her time, opening every envelope carefully, reading over the contents at least twice. One had to be a contract of some kind, or perhaps financial statements. It was difficult to tell. However, I'd been correct in my assumptions. There were three handwritten letters. As I studied the woman I'd fallen head over heels in love with, tears slipped past her long eyelashes. All I wanted to do was drag her into my arms, holding her as she fell apart.

But she surprised me again, wiping away the tears with the kind of fury I'd witnessed time and time again. Then she lifted her head, her expression one of sheer defiance.

"My mother outwitted the bastard." She pulled several pieces of paper from the largest envelope, shifting them in my direction. All I had to do was pull one into my hand to know she was now in the possession of paper gold in the form of stock certificates from over twenty years before. I was shocked to see them. However, they were listed in a corporation's name.

"A dummy corporation your mother set up."

"Yep. One of the letters confirms it," she said, her eyes now twinkling.

"As the majority stockholder. They didn't transfer to your father after her death."

"Nope. Before she was killed, and I believe more than ever that she was murdered, she changed her will and the trust fund, buying a significant number of stocks."

I had to laugh. "He thinks you'll just have the trust fund, making you a small owner like other carefully controlled investors, but when you inherit your mother's share, you'll have controlling interest."

"Exactly. If what I'm reading is correct, when I was sent the locket, she thought I'd find the box then."

As soon as she pointed to the change in the will, I gritted my teeth. "You never needed to go through the bullshit you did. As of right now, you own that company."

"Yes, as well as the money she protected in another account, and the smaller trust fund that Daddy dearest knows about. She purposely made it small so it wouldn't draw his attention or place me in any additional harm. But in the event of my death, all of it went to charity."

It was impossible not to grin. "Your mother was highly intelligent."

"She was also intuitive. My father still believes he has majority interest in the stocks and will even when I turn twenty-five."

"Well, from what I noticed of the pictures, your father could have manipulated the stocks, which is another criminal act."

Her laugh was bitter but almost joyful. "I know he did. He convinced all his buddies to join in, likely partying with a portion of my mother's money. If Giovanni knew any of this, he's poised himself to be king of the city after betraying my father."

"Jesus fucking Christ. Your mother anticipated something terrible was going to happen."

"My father killed her."

"Baby. That was over twenty years ago. We might not be able to find the truth."

She shook her head several times. "She wrote in the letters that he threatened her. She tried to keep us safe, but he found her."

"I know, but that doesn't mean he went through with the deed."

"You don't know him. He's a monster."

What little I knew kept me enraged. A few minutes were all I needed with the man. I'd break his neck with a single snap of my hand.

I moved closer, darting my eyes toward the paperwork. "What else?"

"She had help, friends in Missoula. Take a look. Escavetti was here with one purpose in mind. Me." After she handed me another one of the letters, I quickly scanned the six paragraphs obviously penned by her mother.

Then I lifted my head. The couple who'd obviously taken Amelie and her mother in, providing them with a secure place to hide was Candy and Mark Wells, the two people Bruno had been sent to murder.

What other surprises lurked in the pages her mother had died in order to protect?

* * *

Amelie

The truth will set you free.

The words sounded harsh in my mind, not comforting, but they played out over and over again, becoming a mantra that had already left scars in my mind. Otherwise, I was numb inside, uncertain I was capable of anything but using the anger inside, the need for revenge. The coming days and weeks would bring additional truths to light.

That terrified me more than the heartfelt letters of a mother written to the daughter she knew she'd never see into adulthood.

"Like I mentioned before, you can trust Gage."

Maverick's words were heartfelt, the anguish in his voice still evident. I believed him of course, but no one knew what my father was capable of. I was no longer certain if I knew either. What I'd accepted a long time ago was that money and power meant everything to him. "I know. I just hope he believes me."

"He already does. Your mother knew what would happen. She did what she could to protect you. It's time to end the charade."

Leaning forward, I gazed out the windshield at the sheriff's office, a lump remaining in my throat. "I know you're right. I'm just afraid it will change everything."

"Yeah, it will, but that's what needs to happen. What it won't do is change the way I feel about you."

He had no idea that his support meant the world to me. "I want my father and Giovanni taken down. I won't stop until that happens. I don't care what needs to be done. I also need to meet with Mark and Candy." While it seemed everything was coming together, there were still too many unanswered questions, and the reason Giovanni had waited to enforce the contract he and my father had entered into was tops on the list. And how had he found the couple? Who had tipped him off?

Maverick's presence was powerful, every room he entered into absorbed by his aura. But on this day, he acted as if he'd storm a castle wrestling a dragon. His need for revenge was evident, but as one man, he couldn't take on an army.

But it seemed he didn't care.

He was determined to protect me at all costs.

I'd told myself I'd never fall in love, but it was impossible not to around the hulking mass of a man.

He remained close, a formidable mass that no one dared mess with. I took comfort in his protective stance.

While a deputy tried to escort us to Gage's office, Maverick was having none of it, taking long strides down a corridor, not bothering to knock before entering the room. Gage's expression was unreadable but if he was perturbed at the forceful entrance, he certainly didn't let on.

"Close the door behind you," the sheriff stated, his tone gruffer than before.

Maverick took the letters and legal documents from my hand as well as the photographs that he'd printed from my camera, placing them on his desk. Gage didn't bother looking down. The sheriff stared at me for a few seconds then looked away, rubbing his jaw. He glanced down only once without touching the items, which both annoyed and confused me.

"You better say something," Maverick barked, his irritation worse than mine.

Gage continued to take his time before planting his hands on the desk, leaning over with his eyes pinned on me. "Amelie Rathbone. Well, it's good to meet the real woman."

"Do you think I wanted to hide behind a lie?" Was he accusing me of wrongdoing?

Maverick puffed up immediately, fisting both hands. They were friends, not enemies, yet the man who'd sworn to protect me wasn't going to allow anyone to challenge my story. For that and so many other things I loved him, but adoration wouldn't matter in the end if no one believed my story.

"Whoa," Gage said as he threw out his hand. "Maybe I should start over."

"Yeah, you better," Maverick warned.

Gage gave him a harsh look then shook his head. "You have a true champion in this man, Amelie. I hope you know that."

"I do." I wasn't certain what I was supposed to say at this point.

The sheriff took the time to glance at the documentation provided, his eyebrows lifting when he scanned the photographs. Then he sat down on his chair with a hard thud, shifting it back and forth. "I don't know where to begin with this. I've been on the phone since you called."

I sensed Maverick was ready to explode. He slammed his hands on Gage's desk, leaning over and hissing. His thick beard was unable to hide his fury. "Don't you dare give us any shit, Gage. This woman is in danger. One or both of those pigs are coming after her."

"Take a breath, Maverick. This isn't the type of situation I deal with every day," Gage retorted.

"No. You just handle drunks in bars."

I was shocked how they treated each other, more so when Gage grinned. "That's included you a couple of times." He lost his smile when he noticed Maverick wasn't interested in playing along.

"The hostages from the mountain were mentioned in one of her mother's letters," Maverick told him.

Gage whistled.

"That adds another missing piece to this puzzle and also that you were right in that the marshals wanted to track Bruno down for several reasons."

"The Wellses knew about the safe deposit box," I half whispered.

"Maybe. Maybe not, but Giovanni managed to track them down." Gage shook his head. "Here's the deal, folks. I have a couple buddies who joined the FBI. One owed me a favor. I used it up on this one. I know sorry isn't what helps you at this point but I really am. What you've been forced to deal with is horrific, Amelie. Your father is a very dangerous man but not nearly as much as Giovanni Butelli. Whether anyone wants to believe or admit it, the Cosa Nostra has ruled Chicago for decades. But the squeeze has recently been put on them during the last few years."

"The squeeze?" I asked, hating the way my hands continued to shake.

"Pick a law enforcement agency and whatever acronyms you want. FBI. CIA. DEA. Hell, even Interpol wants a piece of them. With their international arms deals from Europe to South America, Giovanni and his father have been on the most wanted list for years. However, they've been too savvy to get themselves caught in a mess. But they're hurting for cash. Between deals gone bad, betrayal within their ranks, and other crime syndicates gaining power, their organization has shown signs of fracture. Even the pandemic cut their resort and casino profits."

"Where do my father and his company come into all of this?"

Maverick leaned back, folding his arms, his glare just as harsh as before.

"Your father has spent almost twenty years exploiting weaknesses and blackmailing some very influential people, and not just in Chicago. That's just a theory, but widely known in certain circles. As you know, he also had some pretty powerful friends, men and a few women who influence more than just the bottom line in their businesses." Gage laughed. "If Carmine Rathbone had kept his nose clean, at some point he would have become one of the most powerful people in the world."

"Get to the point," Maverick huffed.

Gage narrowed his eyes. "Patience, my friend. This shit needs to be made into a movie. I have it under good authority that your father has one vice."

When he held up his index finger, locking eyes with mine, I could tell he was curious if I knew. I played out scenarios in my mind and what I knew about Giovanni's organization. They owned several legal businesses including profitable resorts and casinos. "Gambling."

"Very good." Gage nodded. "The problem with your father is that he has no luck. I doubt we'll ever learn the actual number, but he was in the red to the Butellis to the tune of millions of dollars. If you ask me, I'd say Giovanni lured him into the world of high dollar gambling. That's just a good old sheriff's intuition."

I grabbed the copies of the photographs, glancing at the numbers. Now they started to make sense. "He was using investor money to fund his gambling, fucking with the very men who helped make him so powerful." When I looked up, Gage was grinning.

Maverick was still fuming.

"Yup. Like I said, we won't know how much and while it might be chump change to the Butellis, Giovanni saw it as an opportunity to infuse more than capital into the syndicate."

"He leveraged Carmine's entire business against him," Maverick added. "Then he could put pressure on those who were squeezing his family."

I was still confused, my mind fuzzy in trying to put the pieces together. "Why was I part of the bargain?"

Maverick snorted, picking up the codicil my mother had added. "Because he figured out that Carmine didn't have the controlling shares. That left you as the only possible candidate." He handed it to Gage who couldn't keep from widening his grin. "Notice the corporation name."

"Let me guess. If I look this up, eventually the trail will lead to your mother."

Nodding, I couldn't believe the lengths my father had gone to.

"Maybe I should be a betting man," Gage said in passing as he picked through the information we'd found.

"The company's value has already dropped. I'd discovered that a few months ago. I'm certain the investors had a feeling something was going on behind their backs. With the exchange of the shares, the stocks would jump at least at first after I had control." I'd paid enough attention to my father's company to know how volatile the situation had been through the years. He used friends as investors, promising and delivering tremendous success. With his failure, their businesses could crumble as well. "And with me taking control, the men who invested in his company would take a huge fall."

"Only if you were twenty-five and had the power could Giovanni control what you did with them. That's what he wanted. That's what he was led to believe or somehow discovered." Maverick growled under his breath. "The man was playing your father for control of an empire."

"Well, then Butelli is a brilliant businessman," Gage said. "But everyone underestimated your mother. Congratulations, Amelie. You're a wealthy woman."

"I couldn't care less about money. I just want my father destroyed."

He glanced at the pictures again. "What you have is enough to incriminate your father for several crimes but up to this point Giovanni hasn't been officially tied to any crime. The contract is unscrupulous, but from what you've told me, it could be perfectly legal."

"What about Bruno's escape?" Maverick asked.

Gage shrugging. "I've going to venture a guess since I haven't heard dick about anyone from the Butelli organization being arrested for aiding a fugitive, that Giovanni dangled a huge carrot to Bruno without offering much support."

"He expected the man to be hunted down."

"What about my mother's murder?" I demanded, inching closer to Gage's desk. When he shared another look with Maverick, I lost my temper. "You don't seem to understand what I've lived through over the years, the worry and certainty that the man whose sperm allowed me to be born was responsible for murdering my mother in cold blood over greed and lust for power. I was treated like a piece of trash, while he was forced to deal with me because of his desire to find the shares of stock my mother had hidden away."

They shared another look and I wanted to scream.

"Your mother died in a car accident. Before you jump, I managed to find the accident report. She was in a vehicular incident with another car. There was no investigation to see if it was anything but accidental. There's no way after all these years we'll be able to find anything."

Goddamn it. I closed my eyes, trying to keep from becoming emotional. "How did Giovanni know about Missoula? How did he have any idea Candy and Mark existed?"

Maverick yanked the documentation in his hands. "This is a legal document executed by a local attorney. With a deep dive search, he could have found it. Your father obviously mentioned you and your trust, dangling a much larger carrot."

"Yeah, more like a priceless diamond carat," Gage teased. "There's one more piece that makes sense now. Giovanni invested in your father's company a few months ago, Small potatoes but it's another connection."

Now I was able to laugh. "My shares would make the corporation more profitable, and he'd get control of them with our marriage. With some careful finagling, he'd control the empire without breaking a sweat."

"Yes," Gage nodded. "Very astute. However much he knew, neither your father nor Giovanni had any clue you already owned the majority or things might have turned out a lot differently."

Yes. I'd be dead by now.

"That means Giovanni is even more dangerous, especially if he hears the news about her ownership." Maverick cocked his head, waiting until Gage nodded in affirmation.

"At this point, I'm going to have a long chat with the attorney listed on this codicil. If he's alive, he's going to answer to some questions. He was the only one who could have known about the Wells family. Maybe we'll find something there."

"I want to be at that meeting," Maverick snarled.

"Not gonna happen, buddy. You'll beat the crap out of him."

"Yep. If he doesn't talk."

"Thank you for finding out what you did," I intervened, wrapping my fingers around Maverick's arm.

Gage glanced at Maverick, both sharing another knowing look. "Amelie. You do realize I'm going to need to provide the documentation to the FBI. Depending on how they handle the situation, the funds could be frozen until the investigation is concluded."

"I know and as I said, I couldn't care less about money." A huge knot had formed in my stomach. "What about Giovanni? Is there anything we can do?"

"There damn well better be," Maverick said in his usual demanding tone.

"While I haven't seen the contract for your upcoming marriage, I'll venture a strong guess that your father made certain it was an ironclad document. Carmine lost money in a legitimate casino. Unless he turns on Giovanni or there's evidence found that the Butellis planned and initiated Bruno's escape, I don't see what can be done."

I shrank back, nodding several times.

Maverick was incensed, his chest rising and falling. "Amelie is still at risk."

"Butelli might now know she's here. Whether or not your feel-good story on the news was noticed remains to be seen," Gage told him.

"That's bullshit and you know it, Gage."

"Once the heat is on her father, Butelli won't be stupid enough to try and take her. Contract or no contract."

That's where I knew he was wrong. Giovanni was lying in wait in the shadows. He'd find the perfect time and when he did, I'd be chained in a room until my birthday. Then I'd be tossed aside.

"At minimum she needs security," Maverick insisted.

The reality of everything that had transpired in my life, the ugliness of what my mother had endured should become crippling, but I refused to allow it.

As they bickered, I thought about what needed to happen.

There was only one way to draw a predator into the open.

Setting a trap.

"I know what we need to do, but you're both going to need to trust me," I told them both. As they looked from one to the other, I felt more confident than I had in a long time.

Soon, Giovanni would have no choice but to hunt me down.

And I'd be waiting…

CHAPTER 18

melie

Maybe the old adage was right after all that truth would set me free. It had certainly given me courage.

While the FBI had taken the information, they'd promised me that they wouldn't move in until I was there to see my father's demise.

I only hoped they'd keep that promise.

"I don't like leaving you right now."

"Right now, you don't like anything. I think you'd keep me locked in the house if you could. You haven't let me out of your sight for five minutes. I thought you were going to rip the bathroom door off, so I had no privacy."

"That's not a bad idea. Consider it done," he teased.

"Oh, no, you don't."

"I am in charge."

"You just think you are." I moved closer, rising on my tiptoes so I could kiss his lips. "You need to trust me."

"It's not you I'm worried about," he growled then wrapped his arm around me, pulling me closer.

"Yeah, you need to start relaxing. I'm perfectly safe." He captured my mouth, immediately sweeping his tongue inside. The taste and feel of him so close had me melting almost instantly. All I wanted was time to grieve then enjoy spending days and nights with him, but not until every aspect of my nightmare was finished.

I wrapped my arms around his neck, tangling my fingers in his hair as he dominated my tongue. Always the protector. Always the big mountain man who'd saved me from death.

I knew he'd be there again.

When I pulled away, I pressed my hand on his chest. "Don't worry. Sam will be here with me while you're gone."

Hearing his name, Sam barked then moved closer from the open invitation. I lowered my hand to the pup's head, rubbing gently.

"Don't do anything foolish. You have the weapon I gave you."

"Yes, I'll keep it close. Just relax."

"Right. Not until the fucker is dead."

"I know Giovanni. He won't let anyone do this but himself. I fooled him and he needs to save face."

"Yeah, yeah. Trust you." He backed away, a scowl on his face. "You can always back out."

"No. This needs to be done. I can't live my life looking over my shoulder."

"Sam. You protect her. Hear me?"

Woof. Woof!

Maverick moved toward the door, stopping long enough to glance over his shoulder. "I'll only be gone a couple hours. There is a deputy outside if anything happens."

The man was taking this to the extreme. But that made me love him even more.

"I'm going to be fine. Giovanni is still in Chicago. Remember?" The FBI had at least kept a close eye on the man while they tried to build a case against both men. That gave us both some feeling of comfort. But would change given the bone I'd tossed in his direction. At least we'd have advance knowledge of his arrival.

"Don't leave the house."

"Yes, sir. I'll be right here. Just go do your thing and we'll have dinner when you get back. If you're lucky, maybe I'll plan a special dessert."

"Uh-huh. You can't tell me what to do and you better be right here. If I call you, pick up the phone."

When he walked out the door, a heavy feeling fell into the pit of my stomach. I knew what I'd suggested was insane, but there was no other logical way of ending this.

"And lock the door."

"Yes, sir." I did as he asked, heading to engage the lock. Then I moved to the window, looking out as he walked to his truck, which was parked next to the new one he'd insisted on purchasing for me. I'd tried to tell him that I had money, or at least I would soon enough, but being the he-man that he was, he merely gave me a controlling look and paid the salesman in cash.

At least I had an option if necessary.

I noticed the deputy's car and took a deep breath. Everything was going to be okay.

When I backed against the door, Sam remained where he was, his tail swishing back and forth on the floor.

"What do you want to do, buddy?"

He barked once then headed for the kitchen. It would seem my little companion was hungry. After grabbing his bowl and filling it with food, I leaned against the counter. My nerves were raw but that wasn't going to stop me. Maybe a glass of wine would help.

There was something so comforting about having Sam with me, but I was a live wire. Giovanni was cagey, a man on a mission, yet knowing his world was about to come crashing down just like my father's took a portion of the anxiety away.

As I poured a glass of wine, I tried not to let hatred flush everything else out of my system, but the vengeful thoughts racing through my mind had clawed their way into every molecule. I continued to remind myself that this would be over soon enough. But would it?

Ugh. I hated the way I was feeling, the anxiety coursing through me.

I sat town at the kitchen table, glaring at the letters and information from the box. Most had been taken from me by the representative of the local FBI field office. But I had my letters.

As I pulled one into my hand, I felt another swell of emotion as I read the words.

"My dear daughter,

If you're reading this, then I'm probably dead. You'll have so many questions in the future, some that will never be answered. By now you know your father isn't a good man, but it wasn't always that way. He loved me once as I did him. I only hope in time you can forgive him. Enjoy your life. Fall in love. Have children. Family is the only thing that matters. You were my world and I'll always be with you.

I love you.

Mommy"

I played the words in my mind as I pushed it aside. Then as I closed my eyes, I suddenly felt Sam's head resting on my legs. I wrapped my arms around him and for the last time, I allowed myself to cry.

The monsters wouldn't win. I was in love with a wonderful man. I had a new home and soon, I'd have the job of my dreams.

Soon…

* * *

Maverick

"I can't believe I let you talk me into taking you with me to this meeting," Gage snarled as soon as I was out of my truck.

"You should have talked to him yesterday."

"I couldn't track him down yesterday."

"Aren't you the sheriff?" I threw out at him.

Huffing, he grumbled under his breath. "Like I said, I can't believe I allowed you to tag along."

"You knew I'd force my way in. That's why. I can't believe I let the two of you talk me into this shit. Since when do you use a victim as bait?" The attorney's office was on the other side of Missoula, the area of town not the best. Ken Taylor was a small-time attorney with a limited clientele, well past the age of retiring. I'd spent time finding out everything I could, which had led me to believe the man was on the up and up.

"Remember was we talked about. Giovanni needs her alive. He has no idea about the new will. Only the FBI know at this point. And he's still in Chicago. I had that confirmed an hour ago."

"I don't trust the fuckers either."

"You don't trust anyone, Maverick."

He was right about that. I refused to trust the system or most humans. "What do you hope to get out of Mr. Taylor?"

"Confirmation he was coerced into sharing information about the Wells family or about Amelie's mother. Let me do the talking."

"You're sure he'd going to talk?" I barked.

"You haven't seen me interrogating a prisoner. He'll talk."

"He will if I'm given a few minutes with him. Let's get this over with. I need to get back."

He started to head for the three-story building, the man's office on the third floor. An appointment hadn't been made. "You can't keep Amelie under lock and key."

"I can do anything I want."

"I have one of my best deputies on her because we're buddies. Just relax. But I can't afford to do that for long."

As we headed into the building, my throat tightened. I'd almost called her several times. Maybe I was being overprotective, but she meant everything to me. I would not lose her. Not now.

We headed up the stairs, taking them two at a time. The man's office was all the way down at the end of the hallway.

"He's a one-man show. No assistant or paralegal. He has an excellent reputation, so I'm still thinking Butelli found out some other way." Gage was telling me what I already knew.

"How?"

"I haven't worked that out yet," he said, throwing me a look.

As we closed the distance, I noticed his office door was cracked. "What the fuck?"

Gage stopped short. "Stay right here." He pulled out his weapon.

I did as well.

"Oh, for Christ's sake." At least he didn't try to stop me as I advanced. As soon as he pushed open the door, I knew something was wrong.

I pushed past him into the second room. "Fuck." The attorney was lying dead from a single bullet to the brain.

Assassination style.

Gage stormed closer, crouching down. There were bruises everywhere, the man's face worked over prior to his death. "He's been dead a couple hours. Obviously, he was tortured before he was killed."

"That means he talked."

"Not necessarily. But what good is it now?" Gage asked as he stood.

"Maybe he got a call when the box was accessed."

He took a deep breath. "Then he knows she's in town."

"Fuck. This can't be happening." What had he told Giovanni? No. No. No. I yanked out my phone, realizing the reception was shit. "I need to get to her. She's in danger. He's going for her next."

"I'm calling my deputy." He immediately pulled his phone into his hand, but my gut told me it was already too late.

"Fuck that, Gage. He's here. The fuckers lied." I raced out the door and down the hallway, not wasting any time. As soon as I was outside, I yanked out my phone, dialing Amelie's number.

It rang. And rang.

Then the call went to voicemail.

As I bounded outside, I heard a noise and I reacted, twisting to the side.

Pop! Pop!

***

Ten minutes earlier

Amelie

The first glass of wine had gone down too easily, the second as well. As I poured a third, I pulled out the chicken breasts that had been purchased the night before to defrost. It seemed like forever since I'd done any cooking.

"What do you think, Sam? Should we have rice or potatoes?"

He cocked his head, giving me the cutest look. "I know. Men and their potatoes. Right?" Laughing, I grabbed my wine, returning to the living room and to the window. As I flicked open the blind, the late afternoon sun created a blind spot, but the deputy's car was still parked where it had been all along. The day was surprisingly warm, enough so I knew the poor guy had to be getting hot inside the vehicle.

I scanned the surrounding area. "What do you think? Should I get the deputy a bottle of water or a Coke?"

Sam wagged his tail. I returned to the kitchen, putting the wine on the table then grabbing the water from the fridge. "Come on, buddy. We'll say hi for a few seconds. Okay?"

He trailed behind me. After glancing through the blinds once again, I unlocked the door, opening it cautiously. Sam was quiet, happy as could be.

Until I stepped out on the porch.

Then he issued the kind of growl that made hair on the back of my neck stand up on end. Terror swept through me as I scanned the perimeter, my gut telling me something was terribly wrong. "Let's go back inside, buddy." Before I had a chance to grab his collar he took off, heading to the deputy's car. "Sam. Come back here. Come on."

Sam jumped up on the driver's door and I expected to see it open. When I didn't, my throat started to close. I walked two steps closer then froze.

There was a single bullet hole in the windshield, the deputy shot dead.

I backed away, trying to control my breathing. "Sam. Come, baby. Come now."

Fortunately, he reacted to my sense of urgency, turning his head and immediately baring his teeth. Then he reacted without hesitation, flying toward me, lunging in the air as I started to turn around.

Pop!

The horrible whimper dragged a scream from my throat. As Sam went down, I lifted my head. The nightmare would never end.

"Well, well, my beautiful Amelie. I didn't know you were such an animal lover." Giovanni stood with a grin on his face, lowering his weapon as if knowing he'd won the game.

I gasped for air, the horror of seeing Sam covered in blood yanking on every emotion I'd experienced.

Rage.

Sadness.

Despair.

And love.

"You bastard!" I reacted without thinking, flying toward him and pummeling my fists against his face.

He shoved me aside, but I refused to back down, smashing the water bottle against his head. Without little effort, he backhanded me. I started to tumble to the ground but caught myself, backing away.

"Did you really think you could hide from me, you little bitch? I told you that I'd hunt you down. You're such a fool."

"You're too late. The company already belongs to me. You can't get your hands on it." I glanced at Sam, my heart aching, tears forming in my eyes. He'd killed the baby. He'd killed the most beautiful creature in the world.

"You think I don't know? Do you really think that the attorney your mother hired wasn't going to break?" He laughed as he walked closer, taking his time to torment me.

"You can't change anything. You just want money."

"No, I want more than that. I want it all. And I'm going to take it all, including you. I can't wait to enjoy my time with you before you aren't needed any longer. It's best you come with me without causing any issues. I will hurt you otherwise."

"You won't be able to take me. I'm with someone now. He'll stop you."

"Maverick Dane? I don't think he's coming to your rescue," he said, laughing.

"That's bullshit." I had to get to the house. I shifted slightly, trying to keep him engaged. If I could get close, I could lock the door and grab the weapon Maverick had left.

"He's dead, my beautiful bride to be."

"You're lying."

"I'm afraid not, my princess. You see, my associate put two bullets in his brain. He was meeting with the attorney your mother hired. Oh, but he was already dead too." He laughed and I sucked in my breath.

There was no way. A wave of nausea mixed with fear, my mind fuzzy as ugly visions popped into my mind.

He couldn't be gone. Not a chance. I'd know it. I'd feel it.

"No. He's not dead. He'll come to save me."

"Tsk. Tsk. There are no heroes in this world, Amelie. Only monsters and madmen. Now, come with me. You don't want to piss me off."

When he took a long stride in my direction, I continued backing away. Then I turned, bolting for the door. He was too quick, wrapping his hand around my hair and yanking me to the ground. As I scrambled to try to crawl away, a deep rumbling growl permeated the light breeze.

"Aahh!" My scream was stilted, cut off.

As Giovanni reached for me again, twisting my body, a flash caught my eye as Sam threw himself on top of the monster, his snarls and yelps floating toward the sky. I crawled away then struggled to get to my feet.

Everything shifted into slow motion, Giovanni dropping his gun as he fought with Sam, the pup snarling and slobbering, biting Giovanni's face and neck. Another rumble occurred as a vehicle roared up the driveway.

Giovanni rammed his fist into Sam's muzzle, knocking the dog away and grabbing the gun. As he lifted the weapon toward me, I heard another roar.

This time from a hulking mountain man who'd accepted the role of my hero.

The sounds of gunfire seemed muffled in slow motion, but it allowed me to capture the moment that the light left Giovanni's eyes a split second before he slumped to the ground.

As I slowly dropped to the earth, crawling toward Sam, I heard sirens, tires crunching the gravel.

The moment I covered Sam's furry body with mine, I felt Maverick's weight as he wrapped his arms around me. I gasped for air, unable to stop the tears. I pushed hard against the ground, listening for any breath sounds. Then I threw my head back.

"He's gone. He saved me. No. No. No!"

* * *

Maverick

Numb. That was the only word to describe the way I felt.

"What's the word on Sam?" Phoenix asked as soon as he entered the clinic, Sophie trailing behind him.

I rubbed my eyes, glancing toward the door. "He's alive. That's all I know."

"How long have they been in there?"

"Too long," Snake answered from across the room.

As I glanced down at Apollo, I thought about the fact it had only been a few days since she'd saved Apollo's life. But it seemed like a lifetime. "A couple hours."

He patted me on the shoulder then leaned against the wall. "I heard what happened. You saved her life."

"Technically, I think Sam did."

"That's because you trained your boy."

I closed my eyes, tapping the back of my head against the wall. "I almost lost her."

"But you didn't. You killed two bad guys instead. Giovanni and one of his henchmen. It's all over the news. Is Gage handling the situation?"

"Yeah, the Feds are on their way."

"Don't worry about that. Just concentrate on taking care of your family, my friend. That's most important."

"Yeah, I think you're right."

"I'm always right."

"Same shit, different year," Snake snarled but I could see a grin on his face.

"Incidentally," I said, half laughing. "And just out of curiosity. Why do you have a guy tied up outside?"

Phoenix grinned like a kid. "I found the asshole who planted the poison red-handed. I hogtied him to give him a small taste of my kind of revenge. Just going to let him stew until Gage can free up a deputy. If that takes a few hours, a couple days, I don't care."

"That might be a while. One of his was gunned down."

"Shit," Snake snarled. "You were lucky you didn't get killed in the process."

"Nothing was going to stop me from saving Amelie's life. Not one damn thing." I stared at the door to the examination room, my chest tightening.

"She's a special and very tough lady," Phoenix murmured.

"Yeah, and she suggested the damn thing. She even went on camera for an interview hoping the jerk would roll into town. It was already in motion."

Snake whistled. "That's the kind of lady who can handle a brute like you."

The two men laughed, and I knew in my heart they were right. But her mindset was different. I could feel it in my bones.

Another few minutes of tension passed, my blood still boiling.

"I'm going to ask her to marry me," I said out of the blue.

Phoenix seemed startled at first. "That's fantastic, buddy. You are inviting us to the wedding. Right?"

"Hell, no," I said, the heaviness on my heart causing everything in my body to ache. The exhilaration when I'd pulled the trigger, killing the bastard had given me a temporary high. I wanted to do the same thing to her fucking father.

"Yeah, he will," Snake said and walked closer, holding out his hand. The man had changed so much since he'd returned. I only hoped my life could be as happy as his. If Sam was lost, it would kill her. There was no doubt.

I shook his hand then stiffened as I heard the door. All three of us tensed and I held my breath.

Both Amelie and Wren returned to the main room, the look of anguish on my baby's face too much to bear. As she walked closer, there wasn't one of the three of us who wasn't holding his breath.

She took me by the hand, pulling me toward the room.

It was to say my last goodbyes. I sensed it.

Anger rushed through me, violent and demanding. As soon as we were near the doorway, she squeezed my hand, rising onto her tiptoes and kissing my cheek.

"He's going to be just fine." Her words didn't register at first until she pushed me through the door.

A single tail thump was all I needed. I yanked her closer, kissing the top of her head. "I love you, baby. God, I love you."

"She's a natural," Wren said from behind us. "But she still won't accept the job. You need to convince her otherwise, Maverick."

I glanced into Amelie's eyes and knew why.

She wasn't staying.

"Shhh… He needs his rest. Go give him a kiss, daddy dog." She followed behind me, keeping her hand pressed on the small of my back just like I'd done for her.

As I gazed down at my boy, I realized I was a lucky man. Even though I knew what she planned on doing, in my mind I had a family, and I would do everything in my power to keep them safe.

From monsters and men.

CHAPTER 19

*A*melie

Chicago.

Chi-town.

The windy city.

No matter the name, the place where I'd grown up meant nothing to me. Absolutely nothing. I hated the cold, the winters, the extreme wind.

And most of all, I hated my father.

I'd been taught the difference between right and wrong, my mother instilling it at an early age. I remember a few things she'd said, including about forgiveness.

Maybe I wasn't that kind of girl. I couldn't imagine ever being able to forgive my father for what he'd done. It was funny how memories were triggered, the last few days bringing dozens of them, most involving my mother. The happy times. The laughter. Her voice when she read to me and the look on her face when I colored a picture or picked a flower from the garden.

There were also the kind that nightmares were made of, vile acts I'd witnessed my father do, the anger that had always been his method of handling anything. I was willing to bet the man was eaten up inside with rage, but I had serious doubts he had any guilt whatsoever. He thought he was God.

I knew him to be the devil.

And I was here to drive a stake through his heart.

I'd known the minute Giovanni was killed I would need to return. I couldn't pretend that the horrible events hadn't occurred or that I didn't have a responsibility to the people who worked for Rathbone. However, I wanted no part of the corporation and its ugly world.

But I was getting ahead of myself.

First things first.

I adjusted my new suit, smoothing down my skirt before walking into the lobby of my father's building. He had a spectacular view of the river and the glistening lights of the city. He'd positioned himself in the most expensive, posh building right on the top floor. I held my head high as I walked past the receptionist. She didn't try to stop me. She'd been berated by my father for years. I often wondered why she'd stayed with the firm.

Maybe out of fear.

No more.

I walked down the long corridor, catching the eye of several employees. They didn't know me. I'd made only a few appearances to his office over the years, none by my design. But today was entirely different. I felt like I had the world captured in the palm of my hand.

Sadness would come.

Tears would flow.

Hatred would abate.

But not today.

This was the first day of the rest of my life. Cliché or not, that's exactly the way I felt, and it had offered courage.

There was no need to knock. This was my office now.

When I walked in, I was happy to see he was alone. He didn't hear me at first, frantically searching for something on his computer. I walked closer, folding my arms and plastering on a smile.

The bastard finally lifted his head, his eyes narrowing. Then he glanced down at my two-thousand-dollar suit, a gift to myself. Borrowed credit until my funds were released but well worth the ridiculous expense. I was certain he'd learned just this morning he had no access to his money.

"Hello, Daddy dearest. Happy to see me? If you're looking for access to your funds, I'm sorry to tell you it's been denied."

Snarling, he jerked up, his chest rising and falling as his face puffed out. He'd aged in the couple of weeks. What a shame. He'd soon learn what hardship was all about.

"You little bitch. Did you really think running away was going to accomplish anything?"

"Oh, it accomplished several significant goals." When he reached for his phone, I laughed. "Calling your buddy Giovanni? The one who was planning on betraying the sweet deal you made together?"

That caught him by surprise, and he hesitated, uncertain where I was going.

"Don't bother. He's dead. Someone I care about very much killed him before he had a chance to do any additional harm. Now, just so you know, while you still own several shares of stock, you're no longer the owner." I allowed the words to sink in.

He dropped his phone, planting his hands on his desk as he leaned over. "Do you think I'm a fool? I know what you're trying to do, rallying the investors against me."

Stock had plummeted overnight, rumors spread of the company's freefall. I hadn't been able to help myself, finding the perfect method of beginning the destruction of his company. It was amazing what a few phone calls, promises of exclusive interviews had done in less than twenty-four hours. It was just the beginning.

"They'd already started catching on that you were using their money for all that nasty gambling you were doing. I'm certain the Security Exchange Commission is working very closely with the FBI to ensure the criminal charges brought against you for espionage, extortion, blackmail, stock manipulation, and several other additional charges will mean your loss of ownership of every single stock. That goes for your buddies on the board as well."

I took a deep breath, enjoying the various shades of coloration on his face. They were vibrant, beautiful in my mind.

"You've lost your mind. You have no proof."

"That's where you're wrong. You see, you made the mistake of opening your mouth, trusting Giovanni. In turn, he took your trust and twisted it around. I managed to capture some pretty interesting photographs that I shared with the authorities. You were using investor funds to try and get out of your gambling debts. You should have known better than to trust a mafia monster. Selling me off wasn't good enough. Any regrets for destroying my mother?"

He was suddenly expressionless but there was a slight twitch in the corner of his mouth.

"Sadly, I can't prove you killed her, but wouldn't it be better to clear your conscience?"

"You have no idea what you're talking about."

"Don't I?" I slammed my hands on his desk, causing an instant reaction. He snarled, his anger increasing. "You had her brake lines cut. You knew where she'd gone. You made certain that she wouldn't return home. Did you know I was in the car with her? Did you know I almost died? Do you even care? Tell me, you fucking son of a bitch. I deserve to have some peace."

His hesitation pushed me harder.

"Tell. Me. Now!"

My father swung a look toward the door then grinned. "Yes, I had her killed. You have no idea what she had planned. She was going to destroy me. I couldn't allow that to happen."

I took a deep breath, easing back then nodding. Grief threatened to derail everything, tearing me apart, but at least I knew. When I turned around, walking to the door, his laugh fueled the anger. Just before I opened the door, I shifted so I could look at his face one last time.

"Enjoy your time in prison, Father. You're going to be there for the rest of your life." Satisfied, I opened the door, moving aside as several police officers walked inside. I'd gotten his confession on tape. It had been a gamble, goading him by guessing about the brakes. Would his ruin bring peace? No. But I knew what would.

Maverick

Why the fuck was I here?

The crowd was thick inside the bar, Raunchy Ride lively, the music blaring. I'd been talked into coming out, which I now regretted.

"Hey. There he is," Scorpion greeted me as I headed toward one of the tables. It seemed we were having a party, something else to piss me off. Houston, Colt, Snake and Chasity, along with Phoenix and Wren were crowded around the table. Gage stood off to the side. At least his expression wasn't one of happiness like everyone else. How could anyone enjoy a night out when life was shit?

Or maybe that was just my life.

I noticed Hawk and some of the other guys, a few of the smokejumpers as well. I knew they were trying to cheer me up, but I was in a surly mood, eager to beat the crap out of someone. Maybe I'd get my chance.

"Didn't think you were coming," Gage said as he pushed an open bottle of beer in my direction.

What I needed was something more potent. Maybe a few shots of tequila would settle my mood.

"I almost didn't. I'm not in the mood to see people."

"Tell us something we don't already know," Phoenix teased.

I took a long pull of the brew, gazing around the place. Nothing felt right without Amelie. Not a damn thing.

"How's Sam doing?" Colt asked from across the table.

"Better. He's acting like his old self. Just moping." I was grateful he was doing okay, owing his life to Amelie. Even that left a bitter taste in my mouth.

"Like you are," Snake dared to say, his grin more evil than normal.

"How long has she been gone?" Chasity asked.

"Too long. Four days. She's not coming back." I heard the angst in my voice and sighed. I'd called her once, but she'd been different on the phone, abrupt. I'd known then she wasn't coming back even if she hadn't told me the words.

I could sense most of my friends had no idea what to say to me. What could be said? I fucked it up. I didn't tell her enough how important she'd become to me. As soon as Colt walked closer, I bristled, even though I remembered what Amelie had told me about forgiving and healing.

Yeah, I just didn't have it in me.

"Why are you still here?" I asked.

"Maybe I missed being home."

I snorted my reply and we stood silently for a full minute, the others glaring at us.

"I'm sorry about everything," he said.

"What are you sorry about? You have a great life."

Colt laughed. "Don't believe everything you read. About Sapphire Ridge. I know you still don't think I gave a damn. You're wrong."

"Sure. Whatever."

"Have you ever listened to one of my songs?" He turned his head in my direction.

"Can't say I have."

"Well, maybe you should. Almost every song was written about regret and my love for Belle. She was special to all of us. I just couldn't bear the loss so I ran as fast I could. All the cars and money, women and awards, they mean nothing to me."

"Why the hell are you telling me this?"

He took a swallow of his beer, the tension between us remaining. "Because I think you need to hear it. We all need to come to terms with what happened and move on. That includes you. If you love this woman, don't let her out of your life. That's my best piece of advice. Hell, it's my only piece of advice." He laughed, but I heard the sadness and anger. It was the same as I'd felt almost my entire life.

"Yeah, well. She has a life, one she was forced to run from. She doesn't need to run any longer."

Gage nodded in agreement. "I heard the Feds picked up several of Butelli's men. They made a huge sweep. They won't be bothering her. And I don't know what she did, but Amelie managed to get a confession out of Rathbone for the murder of her mother."

"That's incredible," Snake exclaimed.

"And sad," Wren said, her sigh an indication of the way I felt.

"That's something anyway." I'd been grilled by the Feds for my part in Giovanni's death, but in the end, I hadn't been charged. Even if I had been, I wouldn't have changed a thing.

"I heard you asked her to marry you," Wren said, her smile another attempt at cheering me up.

"I didn't have a chance." Would it have changed the outcome? I doubted it.

"Did you buy a ring?" Chasity piped in.

Huffing, I looked away before nodding.

"You have it with you, don't you?" Phoenix pressed. "We want to see it."

"Why? So all of you can have a good laugh at my expense?" The bitterness I felt was shining through like a beacon of the disgruntled man I'd turned into.

"Come on. One look," Snake chided.

I gave him an evil glare. Why the fuck were they pushing this? They kept their eyes pinned on me and I had a feeling they wouldn't let it go. I yanked the box from my pocket. I'd been carrying the damn thing around with me for some crazy reason. As if I honestly expected she'd suddenly drop back into my life. I'd lost my mind if I really believed that tall tale.

After fingering the stupid black velvet, I opened the box and set it on the table.

The oohs and aahs were about ready to push me into overdrive. They didn't want to see me explode tonight. I was ready to snatch it when some asshole decided to put their hands over my eyes.

I froze, ready to react. I'd get my chance to beat the shit out of someone.

Then I heard her voice and shuddered.

"I wasn't gone that long and you're asking another woman to marry you?"

Amelie.

What. The. Fuck?

When she eased her hands away, the first thing I saw was all the shit-eating grins on my friends' faces. They'd been in on this.

I turned around, issuing a husky growl, shaking my head as my woman laughed. Then I wrapped my arms around her, sweeping her off her feet.

And wouldn't you know it, every person at the table and others close by started clapping.

Within seconds, all sound was drowned out. There was no one else in the room but the two of us. I cupped her face as she wrapped her leg around mine, barely able to breathe or think clearly.

"You're here. You came back. I thought I'd never see you again."

"You're not so smart then, my sexy mountain man. This is my home. You and Sam are my family. I'm never leaving again."

As I captured her mouth, I lost every ounce of rage and remorse, guilt and hatred. There was nothing more important than the woman who was in my arms.

Right where she belonged.

The taste of her was even sweeter, the feel of having her in my arms the best in the world. When she pressed her hand against my chest, breaking the kiss, the mischievous glint in her eyes was exactly the same as before.

"You're right," I told her. "You're never going to get out of my sight again."

"That's just fine with me. Do you think you can handle me, cowboy?"

"Oh, I'll handle you just fine, baby. Including keeping you in line. That might be my full-time job."

"I have other things for you to do in mind." Her purr almost drove me crazy. "So, are you going to ask me?"

"Ask you what?" I eased her down and she cocked her sweet little head, giving me a pouting look.

"To marry you."

"Do it. Do it. Do it," they all chanted.

I'd never felt so awkward in my life. When I turned around, grabbing the box, I narrowed my eyes. "Bastards," I whispered, but I couldn't keep a grin off my face. When I turned around, she had a demure look on her face. The entire bar was suddenly crowded around me. Shit. For all the years I'd hated grandstanding, I knew this had to be right.

So I did what any brute of a man should do. I dropped down on one knee. "My sweet Amelie, my resident bad girl, will you do the honor of becoming my wife?"

She scrunched her nose, tapping her index finger across her lips as if debating. I could swear you could hear a pin drop in the entire expansive bar.

Five seconds passed.

Ten.

Fifteen.

"Yes!" As soon as the word erupted from her mouth, the entire bar cheered.

As I pulled her into my arms again, I couldn't resist whispering in her ear, "You're getting a spanking tonight."

"For what?"

"For you being you, my beautiful yet naughty woman."

* * *

Maverick

"There's the place," Amelie said as she pointed toward a diner. I pulled into the parking lot, eyeing the location suspiciously as I'd done almost everything in the last few days. While the danger had passed, I remained concerned, even with Gage's assurances that none of Giovanni's men had even had the opportunity to leave Chicago.

"Are you sure about this?" She'd told me this was the last thing on her agenda, a necessity to ease her mind. I understood, but I was worried she'd succumb to another wave of anger or sadness.

"Yes. I just need to meet them. My mother thought highly enough of the Welles that she mentioned they were good people. There was a reason. It's the last piece of the horrible story to put into place. Then I plan on putting the past behind me."

I cut the engine and an awkward tension shifted between us, the unknown about what could happen eating at both of us. "I get it, baby. I just don't want you hurt."

She unfastened her seatbelt, shifting until she could face me. Then she took my hand into hers, bringing it to her face. "I'm safe with you. I'm happy. I love you. That's all that matters."

Exhaling, I leaned over, giving her a quick kiss. "You kicked butt."

She laughed. "I did what was necessary."

"We have plans to make."

"I need to enroll in the university, and finish my degree. And I have a job."

"Your job is pleasing me." Her brow furrowed when I laughed.

"We shall see. I have ideas that I think you're going to enjoy."

As I shot her a look, she gave me a heated one. "Just remember who's boss of the family."

"I like the term."

"Just out of curiosity, what do you hope to learn from the Wellses?"

"Honestly? Nothing of importance. Maybe I just need to end the final chapter. They were the last people to see her alive."

Nodding, I thought about all she'd endured over her lifetime, the anger just below the surface. I wanted nothing more than to champion her, ensuring her life was filled with joy. The woman had changed my entire perspective and I refused to take that lightly.

We both climbed out at the same time and I shifted my gaze toward the mountains. Maybe a man like me deserved the peace she'd given me.

"Be gentle with them, Maverick." She placed her hand on my arm, giving me a heated look.

"You're awful bossy now that you're a rich woman."

She laughed. "You haven't seen anything yet, my mountain man." As we walked inside, she tensed. I recognized the couple and guided her toward the table in the back, both of us sliding into the booth.

Candy blinked then smiled. "You must be Amelie. You look just like your mother."

"Thank you. I'm glad you're safe," she told them.

"We wouldn't be if it wasn't for this man right here," Mark said as he nodded toward me, respect in his eyes. "We didn't get a chance to thank you for what you did."

"I was doing my job, Mr. Wells. I'm sorry for what you had to go through."

"We're happy to be here and meet you." Candy squeezed her hand.

"My mother mentioned the two of you were her friends." Amelie glanced from one to the other, my baby so full of hope.

Mark seemed reflective, turning his head toward his wife. "We were friends of your grandparents. We knew your mom when she was a little girl."

"I didn't know that," Amelie said.

I clamped my hand around her leg under the table, the possessive man inside of me kicking in.

"Your mom moved away to go to school. She only came back when her mom and dad died. Your grandparents were devoted to each other. They died within a couple days of each other."

"I remember going to their graves, but I have very few other memories of being here."

"You were only here for a couple weeks," Candy said. "Elizabeth, your mother, needed support and a friendly face or two. I think she was trying to find a way to get out of Chicago. We wanted her to stay at the house, but she refused. She was afraid that her husband would find out where she'd gone."

"She also wanted our advice on an attorney. She mentioned a little about what she was trying to do, to make certain you were protected. We gave her a name of a man we trusted," Mark added. "She went to see him two days before she died."

Amelie swallowed hard and I could see her pulse increasing. "A car accident?"

"Yes," Candy said quickly. "The roads were icy. We didn't hear about it for a couple of days after expecting to see you both for dinner."

"I heard I was in the car," Amelie said softly.

"Yes. You weren't hurt, or at least that's what we were told. By the point we found out, your father had already taken you with him."

"That fast?" Amelie pushed.

Mark nodded. "That fast."

"What about a funeral?"

"We were told he had your mother cremated." Candy was obviously still distraught. "She didn't have any other family and Carmine didn't know we existed. Or so we thought." She looked at her husband.

"We tried to find out if what your mother had told us was true, even mentioning something to the sheriff, but without any evidence, there was nothing anyone could do," Mark added.

"At least my father is going to prison." Amelie's voice was more detached than before.

Candy leaned forward, wrapping her hand around Amelie's. "I can tell you that your mother loved you very much. You were her special princess. Her eyes lit up every time you were in the room. She left something for you. At first, I couldn't understand why. Then I realized it was because it belonged to her mother, my friend. It was something she wore every day. She said she'd come back to claim it one day. I kept it all these years. I'd hoped you'd return to Missoula one day."

She handed Amelie a small white box. Amelie hesitated before opening it, taking shallow breaths when she did.

The locket was almost identical to the one holding the key. Elizabeth Rathbone had made certain the locket would reach her daughter, even after her death.

As Amelie held it in the light, she smiled then pulled the two sides apart. Inside was a picture of Amelie as a young girl with her mother holding her.

A single tear slipped down her cheek. "Thank you so much. This means the world to me. I don't have anything else, including many memories."

"I'm glad we had a chance to see you," Candy said quietly.

"We should get going," I told her.

Amelie nodded. "Thank you for meeting with us. I heard you're in the process of leaving town."

"We had our eye on a little house in Oregon near the coast. This is the perfect opportunity to make our dreams come true."

"Thank you for taking the time to meet with us." Amelie squeezed my hand under the table.

"Your mother was a very special woman. She wanted the world for you, honey," Candy said. "Live your life how you want. I have a feeling Maverick isn't going to let anything happen to you. It's nice to see how much in love the two of you are."

Amelie's face turned red but she smiled. "He tries to keep me in line. We're getting married."

Candy clapped her hands together. "Your mother would be so happy." As she narrowed her eyes, I almost laughed seeing the way she was scrutinizing my beard. "This beautiful girl needs to see your face on the day you take your vows."

"I'll take that under advisement," I told her.

As Amelie gave both of them a hug, I stood back watching, admiring the strong woman who'd soon become my life.

I'd considered myself a bad man, so rough that no woman could handle the beast dwelling inside of me. But I'd learned several things over the last few weeks.

One: That love came when you least expected it.

Two: That living in the past meant darkness, the future the only way to find the light I'd been seeking for years.

And three: That even a man like me deserved salvation. As puffy clouds drifted across Sapphire Ridge, I knew in my heart that Belle had forgiven me, that she'd forgiven all of us.

Now it was time to forge a future with the woman I loved.

* * *

Amelie

I'd never been the girl who had dreams of her future husband or the perfect wedding. When I turned eighteen, I realized that marriage wasn't in the cards for me. The thought of being in a stark white dress, a veil covering my face as I walked down an aisle in a church full of people who I didn't really know repulsed me.

This day, this moment, and the man I'd pledged forever to love had dissolved the ugliness of my thoughts.

And my nightmares.

The dress was white, but not traditional by any means. My shoes were tennis shoes, bright red in color and our guests were dressed casually.

"You look beautiful," Wren told me. She continued to fuss with the crown of flowers on my head like she would a long, gauzy veil, but I hadn't attempted to stop her actions. She'd become the sister I'd never had.

Working at the clinic was incredible as well as exhausting. My last semester of school was looming in the horizon, but there'd be time to enjoy my new life with my husband and the furry buddle of joy who was never far from my side. Sam had licked away my tears, giving comfort when I needed it.

He was also the cuddliest creature I'd ever known.

"The day is perfect," Chasity added as she pulled the bouquet of flowers from the holder. I'd chosen white roses instead of red, my mother's favorite color. Around my neck was the necklace she'd saved for me, asking the Welles to keep safe. I would cherish it always, as well as my few memories.

I glanced at the sky, the trees almost to the point of hiding the gorgeous view. This was Sapphire Ridge, the exact location of where Belle had been lost. It had been Maverick's idea, his attempt at allowing her ghost to rest, his conscience as well. The forest had recovered, although not to the same majesty I imagined it'd had twenty years before. Chasity was right. There were fluffy clouds in the cerulean blue sky, the light breeze tickling my skin as I moved. And the sun was high in the sky, the golden glow providing warmth as well as hope.

My attorney was still in the process of selling my father's business, a corporation I wanted nothing to do with. Several men on the board of directors had been arrested for stock manipulation, the scandal in Chicago all anyone in the city could talk about.

They'd made their bed. I felt no remorse in what I'd done.

I'd pledged a significant portion of my newfound wealth to the very charity my mother had noted in her will. I'd never known how much she cared about animals, but it gave me a sense of peace in choosing to work for the sanctuary.

My life was exactly where I wanted it to be, and I had a sense my mother was smiling from heaven.

Since I had no father to walk me down the aisle, straws had been selected from the men who'd been on the mountain with Maverick. Five men who'd sworn their friendship to each other, struggling yet maintaining their pledge. They'd suffered a significant loss, forced to endure countless years of guilt, but they remained strong and caring.

I was honored to now call them my friends as well.

As the music of the harp player began, all five men crowded around me. They would be walking me down the aisle together.

A path of flower petals guided my way as I took careful steps through the green pasture toward the man I loved. As he turned, I was forced to take a deep breath from the sight of him.

He'd shaved his beard, allowing me to see his gorgeous, chiseled face for the first time. As the sunlight twinkled in his eyes, his adoration clearly seen on his face, I realized I was the luckiest woman alive.

And when he took my hands into his, tingles scattered across my skin, I knew in my heart I'd found my forever.

My love.

My home.

My life.

We said our vows in reverence, words chosen that meant something to both of us.

Then the crowd cheered as Sam sauntered down the aisle. In his mouth was a small basket with the rings. He was so proud of himself, even if he couldn't keep his eyes off Sophie and Apollo.

When Maverick placed the ring on my finger, I could see tears in his eyes.

As the minister announced we were married and that Maverick should kiss his bride, doves were released, soaring high in the sky.

"I love you, my perfect princess," he whispered.

"I love you, my gorgeous mountain man."

As the crowd watched the birds seeking freedom, the words he'd told me slipped into my mind, a mantra that he'd never forgotten said together as the Missoula Bad Boys.

Brothers in arms.

Bad boys, cowboys, soldiers, sailors, airmen, and Marines.

They'd been labeled delinquents, incapable of redemption.

And they'd gone our separate ways.

Heroes. Monsters. Sinners and saints.

Above all they'd been men honoring our country even while a terrible secret loomed just below the surface.

There were those who would never forget, praying they'd never return.

Others would stop at nothing to prevent them from doing so.

They were intent on finding salvation by protecting those they loved.

But demons from a single act would never allow them to forget.

Six men determined to right the wrongs from their past.

Six men prepared to do what it took.

No matter the cost.

Together in life.

Together in death.

And now, together in love and salvation…

The End

AFTERWORD

Stormy Night Publications would like to thank you for your interest in our books.

If you liked this book (or even if you didn't), we would really appreciate you leaving a review on the site where you purchased it. Reviews provide useful feedback for us and our authors, and this feedback (both positive comments and constructive criticism) allows us to work even harder to make sure we provide the content our customers want to read.

If you would like to check out more books from Stormy Night Publications, if you want to learn more about our company, or if you would like to join our mailing list, please visit our website at:

http://www.stormynightpublications.com

BOOKS OF THE MISSOULA BAD BOYS SERIES

Phoenix

As a single dad, a battle-scarred Marine, and a smokejumper, my life was complicated enough. Then Wren Tillman showed up in town, full of sass and all but begging for my belt, and what began as a passionate night after I rescued her from a snowstorm quickly became much more.

Her father plans to marry her off for his own gain, but I've claimed her, and I plan to keep her.

She can fight it if she wants, but in her heart she knows she's already mine.

Snake

I left Missoula to serve my country and came back a bitter, broken man. But when Chastity Garrington made my recovery her personal crusade, I decided I had a mission of my own.

Mastering her.

Her task won't be easy, and the fire in her eyes tells me mine won't either. Yet the spark between us is instant, and we both know she'll be wet, sore, and screaming my name soon enough.

But I want more than that.

By the time my body has healed, I plan to have claimed her heart.

BOOKS OF THE MONTANA BAD BOYS SERIES

Hawk

He's a big, angry Marine, and I'm going to be sore when he's done with me.

Hawk Travers is not a man to be trifled with. I learned that lesson in the hardest way possible, first with a painful, humiliating public spanking and then much more shamefully in private.

She came looking for trouble. She got a taste of my belt instead.

Bryce Myers pushed me too far and she ended up with her bottom welted. But as satisfying as it is to hear this feisty little reporter scream my name as I put her in her place, I get the feeling she isn't going to stop snooping around no matter how well-used and sore I leave her cute backside.

She's gotten herself in way over her head, but she's mine now, and I protect what's mine.

Scorpion

He didn't ask if I like it rough. It wasn't up to me.

I thought I could get away with pissing off a big, tough Marine. I ended up with my face planted in the sheets, my burning bottom raised high, and my hair held tightly in his fist as he took me long and hard and taught me the kind of shameful lesson only a man like Scorpion could teach.

She was begging for a taste of my belt. She got much more than that.

Getting so tipsy she thought she could be sassy with me in my own bar earned Caroline a spanking, but it was trying to make off with my truck that sealed the deal. She'll feel my belt across her bare backside, then she'll scream my name as she takes every single inch of me.

This naughty girl needs to be put in her place, and I'm going to enjoy every moment of it.

Mustang

I tried to tell him how to run his ranch. Then he took off his belt.

When I heard a rumor about his ranch, I confronted Mustang about it. I thought I could go toe to toe with the big, tough former Marine, but I ended up blushing, sore, and very thoroughly used.

I told her it was going to hurt. I meant it.

Danni Brexton is a hot little number with a sharp tongue and a chip on her shoulder. She's the kind of trouble that needs to be ridden hard and put away wet, but only after a taste of my belt.

It will take more than just a firm hand and a burning bottom to tame this sassy spitfire, but I plan to keep her safe, sound, and screaming my name in bed whether she likes it or not. By the time I'm through with her, there won't be a shadow of a doubt in her mind that she belongs to me.

Nash

When he caught me on his property, he didn't call the police. He just took off his belt.

Nash caught me breaking into his shed while on the run from the mob, and when he demanded answers and obedience I gave him neither. Then he took off his belt and taught me in the most shameful way possible what happens to naughty girls who play games with a big, rough Marine.

She's mine to protect. That doesn't mean I'm going to be gentle with her.

Michelle doesn't just need a place to hide out. She needs a man who will bare her bottom and spank her until she is sore and sobbing whenever she puts herself at risk with reckless defiance, then shove her face into the sheets and make her scream his name with every savage climax.

She'll get all of that from me, and much, much more.

Austin

I offered this brute a ride. I ended up the one being ridden.

The first time I saw Austin, he was hitchhiking. I stopped to give him a lift, but I didn't end up taking this big, rough former Marine wherever he was heading. He was far too busy taking me.

She thought she was in charge. Then I took off my belt.

When Francesca Montgomery pulled up beside me, I didn't know who she was, but I knew what she needed and I gave it to her. Long, hard, and thoroughly, until she was screaming my name as she climaxed over and over with her quivering bare bottom still sporting the marks from my belt.

But someone wants to hurt her, and when someone tries to hurt what's mine, I take it personally.

BOOKS OF THE EAGLE FORCE SERIES

Debt of Honor

Isabella Adams is a brilliant scientist, but her latest discovery has made her a target of Russian assassins. I've been assigned to protect her, and when her reckless behavior puts her in danger she'll learn in the most shameful of ways what it means to be under the command of a Marine.

She can beg and plead as my belt lashes her bare backside, but the only mercy she'll receive is the chance to scream as she climaxes over and over with her well-spanked bottom still burning.

As my past returns to haunt me, it'll take every skill I've mastered to keep her alive.

She may be a national treasure, but she belongs to me now.

Debt of Loyalty

After she was kidnapped in broad daylight, I was hired to bring Willow Cavanaugh home, but as the daughter of a wealthy family she's used to getting what she wants rather than taking orders.

Too bad.

She'll do as she's told or she'll earn herself a stern, shameful reminder of who is in charge, but it will take more than just a well-spanked bare bottom to truly tame this feisty little rich girl.

She'll learn her place over my knee, but it's in my bed that I'll make her mine.

Debt of Sacrifice

When she witnessed a murder, it put Greer McDuff on a brutal cartel's radar… and on mine.

As a former Navy SEAL now serving with the elite Eagle Force, my assignment is to protect her by any means necessary. If that requires a stern reminder of who is in charge with her bottom bare over my knee and then an even more shameful lesson in my bed, then that's what she'll get.

There's just one problem.

The only place I know I can keep her safe is the ranch I left behind and vowed never to return.

BOOKS OF THE DANGEROUS BUSINESS SERIES

Persuasion

Her father stole something from the mob and they hired me to get it back, but that's not the real reason Giliana Worthington is locked naked in a cage with her bottom well-used and sore.

I brought her here so I could take my time punishing her, mastering her, and ravaging her helpless, quivering body over and over again as she screams and moans and begs for more.

I didn't take her as a hostage. I took her because she is mine.

Bad Men

I thought I could run away from the marriage the mafia arranged for me, but I ended up held prisoner in a foreign country by someone far more dangerous than the man I tried to escape.

Then Jack and Diego came for me.

They didn't ask if I wanted to be theirs. They just took me.

I ran, but they caught me, stripped me bare, and punished me in the most shameful way possible.

Now they're going to share me, and they're not going to be gentle about it.

BOOKS OF THE KINGS OF CORRUPTION SERIES

King of Wrath

After a car wreck on an icy winter morning, I had no idea the man who saved my life would turn out to be the heir to a powerful mafia family… let alone that I'd be forced into marrying him.

When this mysterious stranger sought to seduce me, I should have ignored the dark passion he ignited. Instead, I begged him to claim me as he stripped me bare and whipped me with his belt.

He was as savage as I was innocent, but it was only after he made me his that I learned the truth.

He's the head of the New York Cosa Nostra, and I belong to him now…

King of Cruelty

Constantine Thorn has been after me since I saw him kill a man nine years ago, and when he finally caught me he made me an offer I couldn't refuse. Marry him and he will protect me.

Only then did I learn that the man who made me his bride was the same monster I'd feared.

He's a brutal, heartless mafia boss and I wanted to hate the bastard, but with every stinging lash of his belt and every moment of helplessly intense passion, I fell deeper into the dark abyss.

He's the king of cruelty, and now I'm his queen.

King of Pain

Diego Santos may be wealthy, powerful, and sinfully gorgeous, but his slick veneer doesn't fool me. I know his true nature, and I had planned to end this arranged marriage before it even began.

But it wasn't Diego waiting for me at the altar.

By all appearances the man who laid claim to me was the mafia heir to whom I'd been promised, but I sensed an entirely different personality, one so electrifying I was swept up by his passion.

A part of me still wanted to escape, but then he took me in his arms and over his knee, laying my deepest, darkest needs bare and then fulfilling them in the most shameful ways imaginable.

Now I'm not just his bride. I'm his completely.

King of Depravity

When Brogan Callahan swept me off my feet, I didn't know he was heir to a powerful Irish mafia family. I didn't find that out until after he'd taken me in his arms… and over his knee.

By the time I learned the truth, I was already his.

I went on the run to escape my father's plans to marry me off, but it turns out the ruthless mob boss he had in mind is the same sinfully sexy bastard who just stripped me bare and claimed me savagely.

He demands my absolute obedience, and yet with each brutal kiss and stinging lash of his belt I feel myself falling ever deeper into the dark abyss of shameful need he's created within me.

At first I wondered if there were bounds to his depravity. Now I hope there aren't…

King of Savagery

I knew Maxim Nikitin was a man to be reckoned with when I went undercover to help the FBI bring him down, but nothing could have prepared me for his raw power… or his icy blue eyes.

He caught me, and now he's determined not just to punish me, but to tame me completely.

Every kiss is brutal, every touch possessive, every fiery lash of his belt more intense than the last, yet with every cry of pain and every scream of climax the truth becomes more obvious.

He doesn't need to break me. I belong to him already.

BOOKS OF THE SINNERS AND SAINTS SERIES

Beautiful Villain

When I knocked on Kirill Sabatin's door, I didn't know he was the Kozlov Bratva's most feared enforcer. I didn't expect him to be the most terrifyingly sexy man I've ever laid eyes on either...

I told him off for making so much noise in the middle of the night, but if the crack of his palm against my bare bottom didn't wake everyone in the building my screams of climax certainly did.

I shouldn't have let him spank me, let alone seduce me. He's a dangerous man and I could easily end up in way over my head. But the moment I set eyes on those rippling, sweat-slicked muscles I knew I needed that beautiful villain to take me long and hard and savagely right then and there.

And he did.

Now I just have to hope him claiming me doesn't start a mob war...

Beautiful Sinner

When I first screamed his name in shameful surrender, Sevastian Kozlov was the enemy, the heir of a rival family who had just finished spanking me into submission after I dared to defy him.

Though he'd already claimed my body by the time he claimed me as his bride, no matter how desperately I long for his touch I vowed this beautiful sinner would never conquer my heart.

But it wasn't up to me...

Beautiful Seduction

In my late-night hunt for the perfect pastry, I never expected to be the victim of a brutal attack... or for a brooding, blue-eyed stranger to become my savior, tending to my wounds while easing my fears. The electricity exploded between us, turning into a night of incredible passion.

Only later did I learn that Valentin Vincheti is the heir to the New York Italian mafia empire.

Then he came to take me, and this time he wasn't gentle. I shouldn't have surrendered, but with each savage kiss and stinging stroke of his belt his beautiful seduction became more difficult to resist. But when one of his enemies sets his sights on me, will my secrets put our lives at risk?

Beautiful Obsession

After I was left at the altar, I turned what was meant to be the reception into an epic party. But when a handsome stranger asked me to dance, I wasn't prepared for the passion he ignited.

He told me he was a very bad man, but that only made my heart race faster as I lay bare and bound, my dress discarded and my bottom sore from a spanking, waiting for him to ravage me.

It was supposed to be just one night. No strings. Nothing to entangle me in his dangerous world.

But that was before I became his beautiful obsession...

Beautiful Devil

Kostya Baranov is an infamous assassin, a man capable of incredible savagery, but when I witnessed a mafia hit he didn't silence me with a bullet. He decided to make me his instead.

Taken prisoner and forced to obey or feel the sting of his belt, shameful lust for my captor soon wars with fury at what he has done to me... and what he keeps doing to me with every touch.

But though he may be a beautiful devil, it is my own family's secret which may damn us both.

BOOKS OF THE BENEDETTI EMPIRE SERIES

Cruel Prince

Catherine's father conspired to have my father killed, and that debt to the Benedetti family must be settled. Just as he took something from me, I will take something from him.

His daughter.

She will be mine to punish and ravage, but when she suffers it will not be for his sins.

It will be for my pleasure.

She will beg, but it will be for me to claim her in the most shameful ways imaginable.

She will scream, but it will be because she doesn't think she can bear another climax.

But when she surrenders at last, it will not be to her captor.

It will be to her husband.

Ruthless Prince

Alexandra is a senator's daughter, used to mingling in the company of the rich and powerful, but tonight she will learn that there are men who play by different rules.

Men like me.

I could romance her. I could seduce her and then carry her gently to my bed.

But that can wait. Tonight I'm going to wring one ruthless climax after another from her quivering body with her bottom burning from my belt and her throat sore from screaming.

She will know she is mine before she even knows she is my bride.

Savage Prince

Gillian's father may be a powerful Irish mob boss, but he owes a blood debt to my family, and when I came to collect I didn't ask permission before taking his daughter as payment.

It was not up to him… or to her.

I will make her my bride, but I am not the kind of man who will wait until our wedding night to bare her and claim what belongs to me. She will walk down the aisle wet, well-used, and sore.

Her dress will hide the marks from my belt that taught her the consequences of disobeying her husband, but nothing will hide her blushes as her arousal drips down her thighs with each step.

By the time she says her vows she will already be mine.

BOOKS OF THE MERCILESS KINGS SERIES

King's Captive

Emily Porter saw me kill a man who betrayed my family and she helped put me behind bars. But someone with my connections doesn't stay in prison long, and she is about to learn the hard way that there is a price to pay for crossing the boss of the King dynasty. A very, very painful price…

She's going to cry for me as I blister that beautiful bottom, then she's going to scream for me as I ravage her over and over again, taking her in the most shameful ways she can imagine. But leaving her well-punished and well-used is just the beginning of what I have in store for Emily.

I'm going to make her my bride, and then I'm going to make her mine completely.

King's Hostage

When my life was threatened, Michael King didn't just take matters into his own hands.

He took me.

When he carried me off it was partly to protect me, but mostly it was because he wanted me.

I didn't choose to go with him, but it wasn't up to me. That's why I'm naked, wet, and sore in an opulent Swiss chalet with my bottom still burning from the belt of the infuriatingly sexy mafia boss who brought me here, punished me when I fought him, and then savagely made me his.

We'll return when things are safe in New Orleans, but I won't be going back to my old home.

I belong to him now, and he plans to keep me.

King's Possession

Her father had to be taught what happens when you cross a King, but that isn't why Genevieve Rossi is sore, well-used, and waiting for me to claim her in the only way I haven't already.

She's sore because she thought she could embarrass me in public without being punished.

She's well-used because after I spanked her I wanted more, and I take what I want.

She's waiting for me in my bed because she's my bride, and tonight is our wedding night.

I'm not going to be gentle with her, but when she wakes up tomorrow morning wet and blushing her cheeks won't be crimson because of the shameful things I did to her naked, quivering body.

It will be because she begged for all of them.

King's Toy

Vincenzo King thought I knew something about a man who betrayed him, but that isn't why I'm on my way to New Orleans well-used and sore with my backside still burning from his belt.

When he bared and punished me maybe it was just business, but what came after was not.

It was savage, it was shameful, and it was very, very personal.

I'm his toy now, and not the kind you keep in its box on the shelf.

He's going to play rough with me.

He's going to get me all wet and dirty.

Then he's going to do it all again tomorrow.

King's Demands

Julieta Morales hoped to escape an unwanted marriage, but the moment she got into my car her fate was sealed. She will have a husband, but it won't be the cartel boss her father chose for her.

It will be me.

But I'm not the kind of man who takes his bride gently amid rose petals on her wedding night. She'll learn to satisfy her King's demands with her bottom burning and her hair held in my fist.

She'll promise obedience when she speaks her vows, but she'll be mastered long before then.

King's Temptation

I didn't think I needed Dimitri Kristoff's protection, but it wasn't up to me. With a kingpin from a rival family coming after me, he took charge, took off his belt, and then took what he wanted.

He knows I'm not used to doing as I'm told. He just doesn't care.

The stripes seared across my bare bottom left me sore and sorry, but it was what came after that truly left me shaken. The princess of the King family shouldn't be on her knees for anyone, let alone this Bratva brute who has decided to claim for himself what he was meant to safeguard.

Nobody gave me to him, but I'm his anyway.

Now he's going to make sure I know it.

BOOKS OF THE MAFIA MASTERS SERIES

His as Payment

Caroline Hargrove thinks she is mine because her father owed me a debt, but that isn't why she is sitting in my car beside me with her bottom sore inside and out. She's wet, well-used, and coming with me whether she likes it or not because I decided I want her, and I take what I want.

As a senator's daughter, she probably thought no man would dare lay a hand on her, let alone spank her thoroughly and then claim her beautiful body in the most shameful ways possible.

She was wrong. Very, very wrong. She's going to be mastered, and I won't be gentle about it.

Taken as Collateral

Francesca Alessandro was just meant to be collateral, held captive as a warning to her father, but then she tried to fight me. She ended up sore and soaked as I taught her a lesson with my belt and then screaming with every savage climax as I taught her to obey in a much more shameful way.

She's mine now. Mine to keep. Mine to protect. Mine to use as hard and as often as I please.

Forced to Cooperate

Willow Church is not the first person who tried to put a bullet in me. She's just the first I let live. Now she will pay the price in the most shameful way imaginable. The stripes from my belt will teach her to obey, but what happens to her sore, red bottom after that will teach the real lesson.

She will be used mercilessly, over and over, and every brutal climax will remind her of the humiliating truth: she never even had a chance against me. Her body always knew its master.

Claimed as Revenge

Valencia Rivera became mine the moment her father broke the agreement he made with me. She thought she had a say in the matter, but my belt across her beautiful bottom taught her otherwise and a night spent screaming her surrender into the sheets left her in no doubt she belongs to me.

Using her hard and often will not be all it takes to tame her properly, but it will be a good start…

Made to Beg

Sierra Fox showed up at my door to ask for my protection, and I gave it to her… for a price. She belongs to me now, and I'm going to use her beautiful body as thoroughly as I please. The only thing for her to decide is how sore her cute little bottom will be when I'm through claiming her.

She came to me begging for help, but as her moans and screams grow louder with every brutal climax, we both know it won't be long before she begs me for something far more shameful.

BOOKS OF THE EDGE OF DARKNESS SERIES

Dark Stranger

On a dark, rainy night, I received a phone call. I shouldn't have answered it... but I did.

The things he says he'll do to me are far from sweet, this man I know only by his voice.

They're so filthy I blush crimson just hearing them... and yet still I answer, my panties always soaked the moment the phone rings. But this isn't going to end when I decide it's gone too far...

I can tell him to leave me alone, but I know it won't keep him away. He's coming for me, and when he does he's going to make me his in all the rough, shameful ways he promised he would.

And I'll be wet and ready for him... whether I want to be or not.

Dark Predator

She thinks I'm seducing her, but this isn't romance. It's something much more shameful.

Eden tried to leave the mafia behind, but someone far more dangerous has set his sights on her.

Me.

She was meant to be my revenge against an old enemy, but I decided to make her mine instead.

She'll moan as my belt lashes her quivering bottom and writhe as I claim her in the filthiest of ways, but that's just the beginning. When I'm done, it won't be just her body that belongs to me.

I'll own her heart and soul too.

BOOKS OF THE DARK OVERTURE SERIES

Indecent Invitation

I shouldn't be here.

My clothes shouldn't be scattered around the room, my bottom shouldn't be sore, and I certainly shouldn't be screaming into the sheets as a ruthless tycoon takes everything he wants from me.

I shouldn't even know Houston Powers at all, but I was in a bad spot and I was made an offer.

A shameful, indecent offer I couldn't refuse.

I was desperate, I needed the money, and I didn't have a choice. Not a real one, anyway.

I'm here because I signed a contract, but I'm his because he made me his.

Illicit Proposition

I should have known better.

His proposition was shameful. So shameful I threw my drink in his face when I heard it.

Then I saw the look in his eyes, and I knew I'd made a mistake.

I fought as he bared me and begged as he spanked me, but it didn't matter. All I could do was moan, scream, and climax helplessly for him as he took everything he wanted from me.

By the time I signed the contract, I was already his.

Unseemly Entanglement

I was warned about Frederick Duvall. I was told he was dangerous. But I never suspected that meeting the billionaire advertising mogul to discuss a business proposition would end with me bent over a table with my dress up and my panties down for a shameful lesson in obedience.

That should have been it. I should have told him what he could do with his offer and his money.

But I didn't.

I could say it was because two million dollars is a lot of cash, but as I stand before him naked, bound, and awaiting the sting of his cane for daring to displease him, I know that's not the truth.

I'm not here because he pays me. I'm here because he owns me.

BOOKS OF THE CLUB DARKNESS SERIES

Bent to His Will

Even the most powerful men in the world know better than to cross me, but Autumn Sutherland thought she could spy on me in my own club and get away with it. Now she must be punished.

She tried to expose me, so she will be exposed. Bare, bound, and helplessly on display, she'll beg for mercy as my strap lashes her quivering bottom and my crop leaves its burning welts on her most intimate spots. Then she'll scream my name as she takes every inch of me, long and hard.

When I am done with her, she won't just be sore and shamefully broken. She will be mine.

Broken by His Hand

Sophia Russo tried to keep away from me, but just thinking about what I would do to her left her panties drenched. She tried to hide it, but I didn't let her. I tore those soaked panties off, spanked her bare little bottom until she had no doubt who owns her, and then took her long and hard.

She begged and screamed as she came for me over and over, but she didn't learn her lesson...

She didn't just come back for more. She thought she could disobey me and get away with it.

This time I'm not just going to punish her. I'm going to break her.

Bound by His Command

Willow danced for the rich and powerful at the world's most exclusive club... until tonight.

Tonight I told her she belongs to me now, and no other man will touch her again.

Tonight I ripped her soaked panties from her beautiful body and taught her to obey with my belt.

Tonight I took her as mine, and I won't be giving her up.

MORE MAFIA AND BILLIONAIRE ROMANCES BY PIPER STONE

Caught

If you're forced to come to an arrangement with someone as dangerous as Jagger Calduchi, it means he's about to take what he wants, and you'll give it to him… even if it's your body.

I got caught snooping where I didn't belong, and Jagger made me an offer I couldn't refuse. A week with him where his rules are the only rules, or his bought and paid for cops take me to jail.

He's going to punish me, train me, and master me completely. When he's used me so shamefully I blush just to think about it, maybe he'll let me go home… or maybe he'll decide to keep me.

Ruthless

Treating a mobster shot by a rival's goons isn't really my forte, but when a man is powerful enough to have a whole wing of a hospital cleared out for his protection, you do as you're told.

To make matters worse, this isn't first time I've met Giovanni Calduchi. It turns out my newest patient is the stern, sexy brute who all but dragged me back to his hotel room a couple of nights ago so he could use my body as he pleased, then showed up at my house the next day, stripped me bare, and spanked me until I was begging him to take me even more roughly and shamefully.

Now, with his enemies likely to be coming after me in order to get to him, all I can do is hope he's as good at keeping me safe as he is at keeping me blushing, sore, and thoroughly satisfied.

Dangerous

I knew Erik Chenault was dangerous the moment I saw him. Everything about him should have warned me away, from the scar on his face to the fact that mobsters call him Blade. But I was drawn like a moth to a flame, and I ended up burnt... and blushing, sore, and thoroughly used.

Now he's taken it upon himself to protect me from men like the ones we both tried to leave in our past. He's going to make me his whether I like it or not... but I think I'm going to like it.

Prey

Within moments of setting eyes on Sophia Waters, I was certain of two things. She was going to learn what happens to bad girls who cheat at cards, and I was going to be the one to teach her.

But there was one thing I didn't know as I reddened that cute little bottom and then took her long and hard and oh so shamefully: I wasn't the only one who didn't come here for a game of cards.

I came to kill a man. It turns out she came to protect him.

Nobody keeps me from my target, but I'm in no rush. Not when I'm enjoying this game of cat and mouse so much. I'll even let her catch me one day, and as she screams my name with each brutal climax she'll finally realize the truth. She was never the hunter. She was always the prey.

Given

Stephanie Michaelson was given to me, and she is mine. The sooner she learns that, the less often her cute little bottom will end up well-punished and sore as she is reminded of her place.

But even as she promises obedience with tears running down her cheeks, I know it isn't the sting of my belt that will truly tame her. It is what comes next that will leave her in no doubt she belongs to me. That part will be long, hard, and shameful... and I will make her beg for all of it.

Dangerous Stranger

I came to Spain hoping to start a new life away from dangerous men, but then I met Rafael Santiago. Now I'm not just caught up in the affairs of a mafia boss, I'm being forced into his car.

When I saw something I shouldn't have, Rafael took me captive, stripped me bare, and punished me until he felt certain I'd told him everything I knew about his organization… which was nothing at all. Then he offered me his protection in return for the right to use me as he pleases.

Now that I belong to him, his plans for me are more shameful than I could have ever imagined.

Indebted

After her father stole from me, I could have left Alessandra Toro in jail for a crime she didn't commit. But I have plans for her. A deal with the judge—the kind only a man like me can arrange—made her my captive, and she will pay her father's debt with her beautiful body.

She will try to run, of course, but it won't be the law that comes after her. It will be me.

The sting of my belt across her quivering bare bottom will teach Alessandra the price of defiance, but it is the far more shameful penance that follows which will truly tame her.

Taken

When Winter O'Brien was given to me, she thought she had a say in the matter. She was wrong.

She is my bride. Mine to claim, mine to punish, and mine to use as shamefully as I please. The sting of my belt on her bare bottom will teach her to obey, but obedience is just the beginning.

I will demand so much more.

Bratva's Captive

I told Chloe Kingstrom that getting close to me would be dangerous, and she should keep her distance. The moment she disobeyed and followed me into that bar, she became mine.

Now my enemies are after her, but it's not what they would do to her she should worry about.

It's what I'm going to do to her.

My belt across her bare backside will teach her obedience, but what comes after will be different.

She's going to blush, beg, and scream with every climax as she's ravaged more thoroughly than she can imagine. Then I'm going to flip her over and claim her in an even more shameful way.

If she's a good girl, I might even let her enjoy it.

Hunted

Hope Gracen was just another target to be tracked down… until I caught her.

When I discovered I'd been lied to, I carried her off.

She'll tell me the truth with her bottom still burning from my belt, but that isn't why she's here.

I took her to protect her. I'm keeping her because she's mine.

Theirs as Payment

Until mere moments ago, I was a doctor heading home after my shift at the hospital. But that was before I was forced into the back seat of an SUV, then bared and spanked for trying to escape.

Now I'm just leverage for the Cabello brothers to use against my father, but it isn't the thought of being held hostage by these brutes that has my heart racing and my whole body quivering.

It is the way they're looking at me…

Like they're about to tear my clothes off and take turns mounting me like wild beasts.

Like they're going to share me, using me in ways more shameful than I can even imagine.

Like they own me.

Ruthless Acquisition

I knew the shameful stakes when I bet against these bastards. I just didn't expect to lose.

Now they've come to collect their winnings.

But they aren't just planning to take a belt to my bare bottom for trying to run and then claim everything they're owed from my naked, helpless body as I blush, beg, and scream for them.

They've acquired me, and they plan to keep me.

Bound by Contract

I knew I was in trouble the moment Gregory Steele called me into his office, but I wasn't expecting to end up stripped bare and bent over his desk for a painful lesson from his belt.

Taking a little bit of money here and there might have gone unnoticed in another organization, but stealing from one of the most powerful mafia bosses on the West Coast has consequences.

It doesn't matter why I did it. The only thing that matters now is what he's going to do to me.

I have no doubt he will use me shamefully, but he didn't make me sign that contract just to show me off with my cheeks blushing and my bottom sore under the scandalous outfit he chose for me.

Now that I'm his, he plans to keep me.

Dangerous Addiction

I went looking for a man working with my enemies. When I found only her instead, I should have just left her alone… or maybe taken what I wanted from her and then left… but I didn't.

I couldn't.

So I carried her off to keep for myself.

She didn't make it easy for me, and that earned her a lesson in obedience. A shameful one.

But as her bare bottom reddens under my punishing hand I can see her arousal dripping down her quivering thighs, and no matter how much she squirms and sobs and begs we both know exactly what she needs, and we both know as soon as this spanking is over I'm going to give it to her.

Hard.

Auction House

When I went undercover to investigate a series of murders with links to Steele Franklin's auction house operation, I expected to be sold for the humiliating use of one of his fellow billionaires.

But he wanted me for himself.

No contract. No agreed upon terms. No say in the matter at all except whether to surrender to his shameful demands without a fight or make him strip me bare and spank me into submission first.

I chose the second option, but as one devastating climax after another is forced from my naked, quivering body, what scares me isn't the thought of him keeping me locked up in a cage forever.

It's knowing he won't need to.

Interrogated

As Liam McGinty's belt lashes my bare backside, it isn't the burning sting or the humiliating awareness that my body's surrender is on full display for this ruthless mobster that shocks me.

It's the fact that this isn't a scene from one of my books.

I almost can't process the fact that I'm really riding in the back of a luxury SUV belonging to the most powerful Irish mafia boss in New York—the man I've written so much about—with my cheeks blushing, my bottom sore inside and out, and my arousal soaking the seat beneath me.

But whether I can process it or not, I'm his captive now.

Maybe he'll let me go when he's gotten the answers he needs and he's used me as he pleases.

Or maybe he'll keep me...

Vow of Seduction

Alexander Durante, Brogan Lancaster, and Daniel Norwood are powerful, dangerous men, but that won't keep them safe from me. Not after they let my brother take the fall for their crimes.

I spent years preparing for my chance at revenge. But things didn't go as planned...

Now I'm naked, bound, and helpless, waiting to be used and punished as these brutes see fit, and yet what's on my mind isn't how to escape all of the shameful things they're going to do to me.

It's whether I even want to...

Brutal Heir

When I went to an author convention, I didn't expect to find myself enjoying a rooftop meal with the sexiest cover model in the business, let alone screaming his name in bed later that night.

I didn't plan to be targeted by assassins, rushed to a helicopter under cover of armed men, and then spirited away to his home country with my bottom still burning from a spanking either, but it turns out there are some really important things I didn't know about Diavolo Montoya...

Like the fact that he's the heir to a notorious crime syndicate.

I should hate him, but even as his prisoner our connection is too intense to ignore, and I'm beginning to realize that what began as a moment of passion is going to end with me as his.

Forever.

Bed of Thorns

Hardened by years spent in prison for a crime he didn't commit, Edmond Montego is no longer the gentle man I remember. When he came for me, he didn't just take me for the very first time.

He claimed my virgin body with a savagery that left me screaming… and he made me beg for it.

I should have run when I had the chance, but with every lash of his belt, every passionate kiss, and every brutal climax, I fell more and more under his spell.

But he has a dark secret, and if we're not careful, we'll lose everything… including our lives.

The Don

Maxwell Powers swept into my life after my father was gunned down, but the moment those piercing blue eyes caught mine I knew he would be doing more than just avenging his old friend.

I haven't seen him since I was a little girl, but that won't keep him from bending me over and belting my bare backside… or from making me scream his name as he claims my virgin body.

He's twice my age, and he's my godfather.

But I know I'll be soaking wet and ready for him tonight…

BOOKS OF THE ALPHA DYNASTY SERIES

Unchained Beast

As the firstborn of the Dupree family, I have spent my life building the wealth and power of our mafia empire while keeping our dark secret hidden and my savage hunger at bay. But the beast within me cannot be chained forever, and I must claim a mate before I lose control completely…

That is why Coraline LeBlanc is mine.

When I mount and ravage her, it won't be because I want her. It will be because I need her.

But that doesn't mean I won't enjoy stripping her bare and spanking her until she surrenders, then making her beg and scream with every desperate climax as I take what belongs to me.

The beast will claim her, but I will keep her.

Savage Brute

It wasn't his mafia birthright that made Dax Dupree a monster. Years behind bars and a brutal war with a rival organization made him hard as steel, but the beast he can barely control was always there, and without a mate to mark and claim it would soon take hold of him completely.

I didn't know that when he showed up at my bar after closing and spanked me until I was wet and shamefully ready for him to mount and ravage me, or even when I woke the next morning with my throat sore from screaming and his seed still drying on my thighs. But I know it now.

Because I'm his mate.

Ruthless Monster

When Esme Rawlings looks at me, she sees many things. A ruthless mob boss. A key witness to the latest murder in an ongoing turf war. A guardian angel who saved her from a hitman's bullet.

But when I look at her, I see just one thing.

My mate.

She can investigate me as thoroughly as she feels necessary, prying into every aspect of my family's vast mafia empire, but the only truth she really needs to know about me she will learn tonight with her bare bottom burning and her protests drowned out by her screams of climax.

I take what belongs to me.

Ravenous Predator

Suzette Barker thought she could steal from the most powerful mafia boss in Philadelphia. My belt across her naked backside taught her otherwise, but as tears run down her cheeks and her arousal glistens on her bare thighs, there is something more important she will understand soon.

Kneeling at my feet and demonstrating her remorseful surrender in the most shameful way possible won't bring an end to this, nor will her screams of climax as I take her long and hard. She'll be coming with me and I'll be mounting and savagely rutting her as often as I please.

Not just because she owes me.

Because she's my mate.

Merciless Savage

Christoff Dupree doesn't strike me as the kind of man who woos a woman gently, so when I saw the flowers on my kitchen table I knew it wasn't just a gesture of appreciation for saving his life.

This ruthless mafia boss wasn't seducing me. Those roses mean that I belong to him now.

That I'm his to spank into shameful submission before he mounts me and claims me savagely.

That I'm his mate.

BOOKS OF THE ALPHA BEASTS SERIES

King's Mate

Her scent drew me to her, but something deeper and more powerful told me she was mine. Something that would not be denied. Something that demanded I claim her then and there.

I took her the way a beast takes his mate. Roughly. Savagely. Without mercy or remorse.

She will run, and when she does she will be punished, but it is not me that she fears. Every quivering, desperate climax reminds her that her body knows its master, and that terrifies her.

She knows I am not a gentle king, and she will scream for me as she learns her place.

Beast's Claim

Raven is not one of my kind, but the moment I caught her scent I knew she belonged to me.

She is my mate, and when I claim her it will not be gentle. She can fight me, but her pleas for mercy as she is punished will soon give way to screams of climax as she is mounted and rutted.

By the time I am finished with her, the evidence of her body's surrender will be mingled with my seed as it drips down her bare thighs. But she will be more than just sore and utterly spent.

She will be mine.

Alpha's Mate

I didn't ask Nicolina to be my mate. It was not up to her. An alpha takes what belongs to him.

She will plead for mercy as she is bared and punished for daring to run from me, but her screams as she is claimed and rutted will be those of helpless climax as her body surrenders to its master.

She is mine, and I'm going to make sure she knows it.

MORE STORMY NIGHT BOOKS BY PIPER STONE

Claimed by the Beasts

Though she has done her best to run from it, Scarlet Dumane cannot escape what is in store for her. She has known for years that she is destined to belong not just to one savage beast, but to three, and now the time has come for her to be claimed. Soon her mates will own every inch of her beautiful body, and she will be shared and used as roughly and as often as they please.

Scarlet hid from the disturbing truth about herself, her family, and her town for as long as she could, but now her grandmother's death has finally brought her back home to the bayous of Louisiana and at last she must face her fate, no matter how shameful and terrifying.

She will be a queen, but her mates will be her masters, and defiance will be thoroughly punished. Yet even when she is stripped bare and spanked until she is sobbing, her need for them only grows, and every blush, moan, and quivering climax binds her to them more tightly. But with enemies lurking in the shadows, can she trust her mates to protect her from both man and beast?

Millionaire Daddy

Dominick Asbury is not just a handsome millionaire whose deep voice makes Jenna's tummy flutter whenever they are together, nor is he merely the first man bold enough to strip her bare and spank her hard and thoroughly whenever she has been naughty. He is much more than that.

He is her daddy.

He is the one who punishes her when she's been a bad girl, and he is the one who takes her in his arms afterwards and brings her to one climax after another until she is utterly spent and satisfied.

But something shady is going on behind the scenes at Dominick's company, and when Jenna draws the wrong conclusion from a poorly written article about him and creates an embarrassing public scene, will she end up not only costing them both their jobs but losing her daddy as well?

Conquering Their Mate

For years the Cenzans have cast a menacing eye on Earth, but it still came as a shock to be captured, stripped bare, and claimed as a mate by their leader and his most trusted warriors.

It infuriates me to be punished for the slightest defiance and forced to submit to these alien brutes, but as I'm led naked through the corridors of their ship, my well-punished bare bottom and my helpless arousal both fully on display, I cannot help wondering how long it will be until I'm kneeling at the feet of my mates and begging them take me as shamefully as they please.

Captured and Kept

Since her career was knocked off track in retaliation for her efforts to expose a sinister plot by high-ranking government officials, reporter Danielle Carver has been stuck writing puff pieces in a small town in Oregon. Desperate for a serious story, she sets out to investigate the rumors she's been hearing about mysterious men living in the mountains nearby. But when she secretly follows them back to their remote cabin, the ruggedly handsome beasts don't take kindly to her snooping around, and Dani soon finds herself stripped bare for a painful, humiliating spanking.

Their rough dominance arouses her deeply, and before long she is blushing crimson as they take turns using her beautiful body as thoroughly and shamefully as they please. But when Dani uncovers the true reason for their presence in the area, will more than just her career be at risk?

Taming His Brat

It's been years since Cooper Dawson left her small Texas hometown, but after her stubborn defiance gets her fired from two jobs in a row, she knows something definitely needs to change. What she doesn't expect, however, is for her sharp tongue and arrogant attitude to land her over the knee of a stern, ruggedly sexy cowboy for a painful, embarrassing, and very public spanking.

Rex Sullivan cannot deny being smitten by Cooper, and the fact that she is in desperate need of his belt across her bare backside only makes the war-hardened ex-Marine more determined to tame the beautiful, fiery redhead. It isn't long before she's screaming his name as he shows her just how hard and roughly a cowboy can ride a headstrong filly. But Rex and Cooper both have secrets, and when the demons of their past rear their ugly heads, will their romance be torn apart?

Capturing Their Mate

I thought the Cenzan invaders could never find me here, but I was wrong. Three of the alien brutes came to take me, and before I ever set foot aboard their ship I had already been stripped bare, spanked thoroughly, and claimed more shamefully then I would have ever thought possible.

They have decided that a public example must be made of me, and I will be punished and used in the most humiliating ways imaginable as a warning to anyone who might dare to defy them. But I am no ordinary breeder, and the secrets hidden in my past could change their world… or end it.

Rogue

Tracking down cyborgs is my job, but this time I'm the one being hunted. This rogue machine has spent most of his life locked up, and now that he's on the loose he has plans for me…

He isn't just going to strip me, punish me, and use me. He will take me longer and harder than any human ever could, claiming me so thoroughly that I will be left in no doubt who owns me.

No matter how shamefully I beg and plead, my body will be ravaged again and again with pleasure so intense it terrifies me to even imagine, because that is what he was built to do.

Roughneck

When I took a job on an oil rig to escape my scheming stepfather's efforts to set me up with one of his business cronies, I knew I'd be working with rugged men. What I didn't expect is to find myself bent over a desk, my cheeks soaked with tears and my bare thighs wet for a very different reason, as my well-punished bottom is thoroughly used by a stern, infuriatingly sexy roughneck.

Even though I should have known better than to get sassy with a firm-handed cowboy, let alone a tough-as-nails former Marine, there's no denying that learning the hard way was every bit as hot as it was shameful. But a sore, welted backside is just the start of his plans for me, and no matter how much I blush to admit it, I know I'm going to take everything he gives me and beg for more.

Hunting Their Mate

As far as I'm concerned, the Cenzans will always be the enemy, and there can be no peace while they remain on our planet. I planned to make them pay for invading our world, but I was hunted down and captured by two of their warriors with the help of a battle-hardened former Marine. Now I'm the one who is going to pay, as the three of them punish me, shame me, and share me.

Though the thought of a fellow human taking the side of these alien brutes enrages me, that is far from the worst of it. With every searing stroke of the strap that lands across my bare bottom, with every savage thrust as I am claimed over and over, and with every screaming climax, it is made more clear that it is my own quivering, thoroughly used body which has truly betrayed me.

Primitive

I was sent to this world to help build a new Earth, but I was shocked by what I found here. The men of this planet are not just primitive savages. They are predators, and I am now their prey…

The government lied to all of us. Not all of the creatures who hunted and captured me are aliens. Some of them were human once, specimens transformed in labs into little more than feral beasts.

I fought, but I was thrown over a shoulder and carried off. I ran, but I was caught and punished. Now they are going to claim me, share me, and use me so roughly that when the last screaming climax has been wrung from my naked, helpless body, I wonder if I'll still know my own name.

Harvest

The Centurions conquered Earth long before I was born, but they did not come for our land or our resources. They came for mates, women deemed suitable for breeding. Women like me.

Three of the alien brutes decided to claim me, and when I defied them, they made a public example of me, punishing me so thoroughly and shamefully I might never stop blushing.

But now, as my virgin body is used in every way possible, I'm not sure I want them to stop…

Torched

I work alongside firefighters, so I know how to handle musclebound roughnecks, but Blaise Tompkins is in a league of his own. The night we met, I threw a glass of wine in his face, then ended up shoved against the wall with my panties on the floor and my arousal dripping down my thighs, screaming out climax after shameful climax with my well-punished bottom still burning.

I've got a series of arsons to get to the bottom of, and finding out that the infuriatingly sexy brute who spanked me like a naughty little girl will be helping me with the investigation seemed like the last thing I needed, until somebody hurled a rock through my window in an effort to scare me away from the case. Now having a big, strong man around doesn't seem like such a bad idea…

Fertile

The men who hunt me were always brutes, but now lust makes them barely more than beasts.

When they catch me, I know what comes next.

I will fight, but my need to be bred is just as strong as theirs is to breed. When they strip me, punish me, and use me the way I'm meant to be used, my screams will be the screams of climax.

Hostage

I knew going after one of the most powerful mafia bosses in the world would be dangerous, but I didn't anticipate being dragged from my apartment already sore, sorry, and shamefully used.

My captors don't just plan to teach me a lesson and then let me go. They plan to share me, punish me, and claim me so ruthlessly I'll be screaming my submission into the sheets long before they're through with me. They took me as a hostage, but they'll keep me as theirs.

Defiled

I was born to rule, but for her sake I am banished, forced to wander the Earth among mortals. Her virgin body will pay the price for my protection, and it will be a shameful price indeed.

Stripped, punished, and ravaged over and over, she will scream with every savage climax.

She will be defiled, but before I am done with her she will beg to be mine.

Kept

On the run from corrupt men determined to silence me, I sought refuge in his cabin. I ate his food, drank his whiskey, and slept in his bed. But then the big bad bear came home and I learned the hard way that sometimes Goldilocks ends up with her cute little bottom well-used and sore.

He stripped me, spanked me, and ravaged me in the most shameful way possible, but then this rugged brute did something no one else ever has before. He made it clear he plans to keep me…

Auctioned

Twenty years ago the Malzeons saved us when we were at the brink of self-annihilation, but there was a price for their intervention. They demanded humans as servants… and as pets.

Only criminals were supposed to be offered to the aliens for their use, but when I defied Earth's government, asking questions that no one else would dare to ask, I was sold to them at auction.

I was bought by two of their most powerful commanders, rivals who nonetheless plan to share me. I am their property now, and they intend to tame me, train me, and enjoy me thoroughly.

But I have information they need, a secret guarded so zealously that discovering it cost me my freedom, and if they do not act quickly enough both of our worlds will soon be in grave danger.

Hard Ride

When I snuck into Montana Cobalt's house, I was looking for help learning to ride like him, but what I got was his belt across my bare backside. Then with tears still running down my cheeks and arousal dripping onto my thighs, the big brute taught me a much more shameful lesson.

Montana has agreed to train me, but not just for the rodeo. He's going to break me in and put me through my paces, and then he's going to show me what it means to be ridden rough and dirty.

Carnal

For centuries my kind have hidden our feral nature, our brute strength, and our carnal instincts. But this human female is my mate, and nothing will keep me from claiming and ravaging her.

She is mine to tame and protect, and if my belt doesn't teach her to obey then she'll learn in a much more shameful fashion. Either way, her surrender will be as complete as it is inevitable.

Bounty

After I went undercover to take down a mob boss and ended up betrayed, framed, and on the run, Harper Rollins tried to bring me in. But instead of collecting a bounty, she earned herself a hard spanking and then an even rougher lesson that left her cute bottom sore in a very different way.

She's not one to give up without a fight, but that's fine by me. It just means I'll have plenty more chances to welt her beautiful backside and then make her scream her surrender into the sheets.

Beast

Primitive, irresistible need compelled him to claim me, but it was more than mere instinct that drove this alien beast to punish me for my defiance and then ravage me thoroughly and savagely. Every screaming climax was a brand marking me as his, ensuring I never forget who I belong to.

He's strong enough to take what he wants from me, but that's not why I surrendered so easily as he stripped me bare, pushed me up against the wall, and made me his so roughly and shamefully.

It wasn't fear that forced me to submit. It was need.

Gladiator

Xander didn't just win me in the arena. The alien brute claimed me there too, with my punished bottom still burning and my screams of climax almost drowned out by the roar of the crowd.

Almost…

Victory earned him freedom and the right to take me as his mate, but making me truly his will mean more than just spanking me into shameful surrender and then rutting me like a wild beast. Before he carries me off as his prize, the dark truth that brought me here must be exposed at last.

Big Rig

Alexis Harding is used to telling men exactly what she thinks, but she's never had a roughneck like me as a boss before. On my rig, I make the rules and sassy little girls get stripped bare, bent over my desk, and taught their place, first with my belt and then in a much more shameful way.

She'll be sore and sorry long before I'm done with her, but the arousal glistening on her thighs reveals the truth she would rather keep hidden. She needs it rough, and that's how she'll get it.

Warriors

I knew this was a primitive planet when I landed, but nothing could have prepared me for the rough beasts who inhabit it. The sting of their prince's firm hand on my bare bottom taught me my place in his world, but it was what came after that truly demonstrated his mastery over me.

This alien brute has granted me his protection and his help with my mission, but the price was my total submission to both his shameful demands and those of his second in command as well.

But it isn't the savage way they make use of my quivering body that terrifies me the most. What leaves me trembling is the thought that I may never leave this place… because I won't want to.

Owned

With a ruthless, corrupt billionaire after me, Crockett, Dylan, and Wade are just the men I need. Rough men who know how to keep a woman safe… and how to make her scream their names.

But the Hell's Fury MC doesn't do charity work, and their help will come at a price.

A shameful price…

They aren't just going to bare me, punish me, and then do whatever they want with me.

They're going to make me beg for it.

Seized

Delaney Archer got herself mixed up with someone who crossed us, and now she's going to find out just how roughly and shamefully three bad men like us can make use of her beautiful body.

She can plead for mercy, but it won't stop us from stripping her bare and spanking her until she's sore, sobbing, and soaking wet. Our feisty little captive is going to take everything we give her, and she'll be screaming our names with every savage climax long before we're done with her.

Cruel Masters

I thought I understood the risks of going undercover to report on billionaires flaunting their power, but these men didn't send lawyers after me. They're going to deal with me themselves.

Now I'm naked aboard their private plane, my backside already burning from one of their belts, and these three infuriatingly sexy bastards have only just gotten started teaching me my place.

I'm not just going to be punished, shamed, and shared. I'm going to be mastered.

Hard Men

My father's will left his company to me, but the three roughnecks who ran it for him have other ideas. They're owed a debt and they mean to collect on it, but it's not money these brutes want.

It's me.

In return for protection from my father's enemies, I will be theirs to share. But these are hard men, and they don't just intend to punish my defiance and use me as shamefully as they please.

They plan to master me completely.

Rough Ride

As I hear the leather slide through the loops of his pants, I know what comes next. Jake Travers is going to blister my backside. Then he's going to ride me the way only a rodeo champion can.

Plenty of men who thought they could put me in my place have learned the hard way that I was more than they could handle, and when Jake showed up I was sure he would be no different.

I was wrong.

When I pushed him, he bared and spanked me in front of a bar full of people.

I should have let it go at that, but I couldn't.

That's why he's taking off his belt…

Primal Instinct

Ruger Jameson can buy anything he wants, but that's not the reason I'm his to use as he pleases.

He's a former Army Ranger accustomed to having his orders followed, but that's not why I obey him.

He saved my life after our plane crashed, but I'm not on my knees just to thank him properly.

I'm his because my body knows its master.

I do as I'm told because he blisters my bare backside every time I dare to do otherwise.

I'm at his feet because I belong to him and I plan to show it in the most shameful way possible.

Captor

I was supposed to be safe from the lottery. Set apart for a man who would treat me with dignity.

But as I'm probed and examined in the most intimate, shameful ways imaginable while the hulking alien king who just spanked me looks on approvingly, I know one thing for certain.

This brute didn't end up with me by chance. He wanted me, so he found a way to take me.

He'll savor every blush as I stand bare and on display for him, every plea for mercy as he punishes my defiance, and every quivering climax as he slowly masters my virgin body.

I'll be his before he even claims me.

Rough and Dirty

Wrecking my cheating ex's truck with a bat might have made me feel better… if the one I went after had actually belonged to him, instead of to the burly roughneck currently taking off his belt.

Now I'm bent over in a parking lot with my bottom burning as this ruggedly sexy bastard and his two equally brutish friends take turns reddening my ass, and I can tell they're just getting started.

That thought shouldn't excite me, and I certainly shouldn't be imagining all the shameful things these men might do to me. But what I should or shouldn't be thinking doesn't matter anyway.

They can see the arousal glistening on my thighs, and they know I need it rough and dirty…

His to Take

When Zadok Vakan caught me trying to escape his planet with priceless stolen technology, he didn't have me sent to the mines. He made sure I was stripped bare and sold at auction instead.

Then he bought me for himself.

Even as he punishes me for the slightest hint of defiance and then claims me like a beast, indulging every filthy desire his savage nature can conceive, I swear I'll never surrender.

But it doesn't matter.

I'm already his, and we both know it.

Tyrant

When I accepted a lucrative marketing position at his vineyard, Montgomery Wolfe made the terms of my employment clear right from the start. Follow his rules or face the consequences.

That's why I'm bent over his desk, doing my best to hate him as his belt lashes my bare bottom.

I shouldn't give in to this tyrant. I shouldn't yield to his shameful demands.

Yet I can't resist the passion he sets ablaze with every word, every touch, and every brutally possessive kiss, and I know before long my body will surrender to even his darkest needs…

Filthy Rogue

Losing my job to a woman who slept her way to the top was bad enough, and that was before my car broke down as I drove cross country to start over. Having to be rescued by an infuriatingly sexy biker who promptly bared and spanked me for sassing him was just icing on the cake.

After sharing a passionate night, I might have made a teensy mistake in taking cash from his wallet in order to pay the auto mechanic, but I hadn't thought I'd ever see him again…

Then on the first day at my new job, guess who swaggered in with payback on his mind?

He's living proof that the universe really is out to get me… and he's my new boss.

ABOUT PIPER STONE

Amazon Top 150 Internationally Best-Selling Author, Kindle Unlimited All Star Piper Stone writes in several genres. From her worlds of dark mafia, cowboys, and marines to contemporary reverse harem, shifter romance, and science fiction, she attempts to delight readers with a foray into darkness, sensuality, suspense, and always a romantic HEA. When she's not writing, you can find her sipping merlot while she enjoys spending time with her three Golden Retrievers (Indiana Jones, Magnum PI, and Remington Steele) and a husband who relishes creating fabulous food.

Dangerous is Delicious.

* * *

You can find her at:

Website: https://piperstonebooks.com/

Newsletter: https://piperstonebooks.com/newsletter/

Facebook: https://www.facebook.com/authorpiperstone/

Twitter: http://twitter.com/piperstone01

Instagram: http://www.instagram.com/authorpiperstone/

Amazon: http://amazon.com/author/piperstone

BookBub: http://bookbub.com/authors/piper-stone

TikTok: https://www.tiktok.com/@piperstoneauthor

Email: piperstonecreations@gmail.com

Manufactured by Amazon.ca
Bolton, ON